Sis Svangurd
and the
Not Quite Dead

Every man has his price. Mine, as he'd correctly deduced, was a chance to attend the fifteenth ecumenical council, even if I had to murder some perfect stranger in order to get in.

I'm not actually a believer – a lifetime studying the scriptures is a straight-line route to atheism, in my experience – but I'm one of those people who can't resist a good old-fashioned intellectual slugfest over the minutiae of dogma. And since this council, convened by the patriarch in faraway Choris Anthropou, was intended to sort out once and for all the eternally vexed question of the dual procession of the Holy Spirit – well, there you go. Be there or be square.

Besides, I told myself as I finished up the copy I was making of Momius' Analects, it's not like I had a choice. I did, after all, swear a solemn vow when I became a monk, twenty years ago. It would be good for me to obey a direct order which I found distasteful and morally repugnant. Especially if it meant I got to go to the party.

K. J. PARKER

SISTER SVANGERD AND THE NOT QUITE DEAD

orbit-books.co.uk

ORBIT

First published in Great Britain in 2026 by Orbit

1 3 5 7 9 10 8 6 4 2

A CIP catalogue record for this book
is available from the British Library.

ISBN 978-0-356-52092-6

Typeset in Horley by M Rules
Printed and bound in Great Britain by Clays Ltd, Elcograf, S.p.A.

Papers used by Orbit are from well-managed forests
and other responsible sources.

MIX
Paper | Supporting
responsible forestry
FSC® C104740

Orbit
An imprint of
Little, Brown Book Group
Carmelite House
50 Victoria Embankment
London EC4Y 0DZ

The authorised representative
in the EEA is
Hachette Ireland
8 Castlecourt Centre
Dublin 15, D15 XTP3, Ireland
(email: info@hbgi.ie)

An Hachette UK Company
www.hachette.co.uk

orbit-books.co.uk

For Constantia
Who illuminates manuscripts
Especially this one

1

"Murdering princesses," I said, "isn't what I signed up for. I'm a priest, for crying out loud. Get someone else to do it."

He gave me that look, which I guess I deserved. I know I'm obnoxious when I'm being pompous. "First," he said, "you'll do as you're damn well told. Second, you're a monk, not a priest." He picked up my dainty little ivory-handled penknife and used it to clean under the nail of his left index finger. "Third," he went on, "not all princesses are the same. Fourth," he added, peering down at the manuscript I was copying, "there's only one C in *necessary*."

He's about twenty-two, so a good ten years younger than me, and he looks like what he is, a rich and powerful bureaucrat's sister's son. He's short and slight, with a squint, a receding hairline, a nose that looks like it was squashed in by his maker's thumb while the clay was still wet, and an Adam's apple the size of my fist. He's also my head of department, and as sharp as a razor.

"Look," I said, trying my dying-spaniel expression, "there's got to be someone better qualified for this job than me. I'm a scriptorium clerk. I copy out books. I don't know the first thing about court etiquette and diplomatic protocol."

"Yes, you do," he said. "And besides, you won't need any of that stuff. This princess is also a nun. You know about nuns and convents and ecclesiastical councils." He smiled at me. "Your partner's up for it. I get the impression she can't wait to get started."

That I could believe. "Ecclesiastical council," I repeated. "You don't mean the—"

"Yes." The smile broadened into a grin. "Thought that'd change your mind."

The trouble is, he knows me too well. "I suppose if you order me to do it, I have no choice."

I'd made him happy. "Yes, Brother Desiderius, you shall go to the ball," he said, and left the room.

Every man has his price. Mine, as he'd correctly deduced, was a chance to attend the fifteenth ecumenical council, even if I had to murder some perfect stranger in order to get in.

Ecumenical councils are when all the heads of the worldwide church of the Invincible Sun, all the patriarchs and archbishops and abbots and archimandrites and all their many, many chaplains and advisers, get together in one place to hammer out some burning issue of doctrine. It's a once-in-a-lifetime thing, and if you're the slightest bit into heavy theology, you'd cheerfully strangle your grandmother, or a nun, for a chance to sit in on one of the big debates. I'm not actually a believer – a lifetime studying the scriptures is a straight-line route to atheism, in my experience – but I'm one of those people who can't resist a good old-fashioned intellectual slugfest over the minutiae of dogma. And since this council, convened by the patriarch in far-away

Choris Anthropou, was intended to sort out once and for all the eternally vexed question of the dual procession of the Holy Spirit – well, there you go. Be there or be square.

Besides, I told myself as I finished up the copy I was making of Momius' *Analects*, it's not like I had a choice. I did, after all, swear a solemn vow when I became a monk, twenty years ago. Of the three heads of that vow, circumstances and my physical appearance have dictated that two were never going to be a problem. The third head, obedience, has always been my weakness. But weaknesses, I told myself firmly, are just opportunities for self-improvement in disguise. It would be good for me to obey a direct order which I found distasteful and morally repugnant. Especially if it meant I got to go to the party.

"Oh, come on," my partner said. "Lighten up a little. How often do you get a chance to guzzle a real live princess?"

Sister Svangerd and I have been a team for a while now. We came together back in the old country, when we did special ecclesiastical operations for the archduke: the previous one, not the present incumbent, who dissolved all the monasteries in the duchy and had us driven out of the jurisdiction. Luckily we'd already had a run-in with the young smart-arse we now work for, and in spite of the fact that he'd caught us red-handed trying to steal a politically sensitive book from the abbot's library, he thought enough of us as operatives to take us on after the dissolution, doing basically the same sort of thing we'd done for the duke, only (he insisted) rather better. Unlike me, Svangerd came to the cloister relatively late in life, after seven years in the hospitality and entertainment sector in Auxentia City. One of those sudden epiphanies of faith turned her into a passionately sincere believer and she takes her vows desperately seriously, but you'd never think she was a nun in a million years. Among the baggage carried over from her previous life is a fanatical hatred of the upper classes, with a particular emphasis on hereditary royalty.

"I don't want to," I said. "Besides, I seem to remember reading something somewhere about Thou Shalt Not Kill."

"Thou shalt do no murder," she corrected me, "which is very different. You ought to know that, being a scholar."

"Yes, but—"

"Murder," she went on, plainly not having heard me, "is when you guzzle someone and it's against the law. So if the people who make the law tell you it's fine, it can't be murder, can it?"

Svangerd's attitude to questions of doctrine can best be described as refreshingly straightforward. With her past, she had to fight like a wildcat before they'd let her be a nun. But fighting is what she's best at, so naturally they assigned her to the Mission Militant, which suited her just fine. I got seconded to the mission because I'm six foot five of mostly muscle and can do majuscule cursive – which, if you're not familiar with the term, is a type of lettering suited to copying manuscripts legibly and very fast. Svangerd and I work well together. I like her a lot. She thinks I'm an idiot.

"Anyway," she went on, wiping a spot of honing oil off her cheek, "it's a direct order from a superior officer, so it's not up to you. And you'll have a chance to drool over a roomful of bishops. You'll like that."

The oil came from the whetstone, on which she was sharpening one of her many knives. I wouldn't go so far as to say she's got a thing about weapons, or at least not in any unhealthy sense, because there's a remote chance she may read this one day. Let's just say she takes a proper interest in the tools of her trade, and leave it at that.

"I'd quite like to attend the debates," I said, "But maybe slaughtering the delegates is too high a price to pay."

"Just one delegate," she pointed out. "Tell you what. You can listen to her droning on about the essential unity of the Trinity and then scrag her. Can't say fairer than that."

"I'm surprised at you," I said, passing her a rag to wipe the blade on. "She's the nominal head of your order."

"Nominal," she said. "Actually, she didn't want them to let me in. Said I was indelibly tainted. But I don't hate her because of that. After all, she had a point."

"No," I said. "You hate her because she's a princess."

"I don't hate anybody," she said. "It says in the Book, thou shalt not hate. But if doing my job and obeying a legitimate order delivered through the proper chain of command means there's one less blue-blood in the world, then hooray for obedience." She shrugged, nearly cutting herself. "I wish you'd sharpen your conscience on somebody else for a change," she said. "You can be really boring when you're conflicted."

Which more or less settled that. "We'd better get started, then," I said. "There's a lot of homework to do."

She smiled at me. She does, sometimes. "We can have a rummage through the Stack," she said. "Oh go on, it'll be fun."

Oh, for crying out loud, I thought. "If you insist. Only this time—"

"What?"

"Nothing."

The Stack is her term for the restricted artefact store, which lives in a converted charcoal cellar under the old refectory, which is now guest quarters for visiting dignitaries. To get there, you go down a long and horrible spiral staircase, tight as a screw thread with no handrail, so you need both hands for clutching at the wall to keep from falling and therefore can't hold a lamp or a candle to see your way in the pitch dark. "Don't be such a girl," came her cheerful voice from a long way below me, as I edged my terrified way from step to step. She can see in the dark like a cat, it goes without saying.

My questing toe identified the bottom step, and I groped my way along the corridor until my head connected with the edge of an open door, which meant I'd arrived. A moment later, I heard the scrape of a tinder-box, and she lit a lamp.

She likes the restricted artefact store. I find it depressing. Every time I go there and see all the many and various gadgets stacked on the shelves, I can't help but picture myself in a guardroom somewhere, trying to explain to a sceptical watch captain precisely why I was caught with something like that hidden up the sleeve of my habit. Mind you, I'm prejudiced. Thanks to my size and bulk, I can generally subdue the opposition simply by thumping them. Small and delicately built operatives like Svangerd need a bit of help from human ingenuity.

"This is new," she said, lifting a complicated-looking brass thing off a shelf. "I wonder what it does."

"That's an astrolabe," I said. "You use it for navigating at sea. No, don't press—"

Something whirred past my ear and went *chink!* against the wall. "Neat," she said, and put it back where she'd found it. "Oh look, they've still got this. I think it's my favourite."

This was a miniature crossbow, not much bigger than a handspan, all steel, with a screw mechanism to span it. She's been dying to play with it ever since she first saw it. I keep telling her, the effective range could only be about ten feet (less if the target's wearing anything more substantial than linen), it'd take ten minutes to reload and she'd be much better off with a heavy stone in a sock, but she refuses to listen. "You could hollow out a book," she said, "and hide it in that."

"You'd stand a much better chance of hurting someone if you just hit him with the book," I said. "Admit it, you do have a tendency to overcomplicate things, just because you enjoy playing with the kit."

"Piss off," she replied cheerfully. "They never had stuff like this when I was growing up."

Svangerd has saved my life seventeen times, usually with a weapon. When she's in the Stack, she acts like she's twelve years old. I suppose I shouldn't begrudge her a few simple pleasures. "Let's think about what we're actually likely to need," I said.

"All right." She'd found one of her favourites, a garotte made to look like a rosary. She explained to me once how the additional surface area of the beads increases the mechanical advantage. "It'd help if we knew what we were supposed to be doing."

"We know," I told her. "We murder the princess."

She made an impatient noise. "Yes, but when? Is it supposed to look natural, or are we making a statement? Are we making it look like someone in particular did it? All that stuff makes a difference to what we're going to need."

"What we need," I said, "is probably a cushion. Or a flight of stairs."

"Why do you always insist on spoiling everything?"

At which point we heard footsteps on the staircase, and Brother Artaphernes came bustling in, asking what we thought we were doing there and did we have a docket from Supply? We did (I'd forged it myself), so he pulled an evil face and told us to take the stuff we'd been issued and get out. She stuck her tongue out at him, but only when his back was turned.

Forging documents is dead easy, and I'm good at it. It's all about honesty. In order to create a successful forgery, you need to tell the truth, the whole truth, and practically nothing but the truth.

The *practically* is the thing you want to achieve. Thus, in order to fake a restricted articles docket, I'd sneaked into Supply when the clerks were all at matins and helped myself to a sheet of their parchment, one of their pens, a bottle of their ink, and a genuine docket to use as a template. Therefore, when I'd finished, everything about it was genuine apart from the choice of words. I crept back there during nones and sealed it with the departmental seal, than which nothing on this earth is more authentic. Result: a perfect forgery, though I do say so myself.

I needn't have gone to all that trouble, of course. If Brother Artaphernes had caught us in the Stack without a docket, all he'd have done was moan at us, and Svangerd would have called him a rude name, and that would've been that. But I'd forged the perfect docket because that's how I do things. The way I see it, life should be smooth, organised, predictable and not marred by unpleasantness, such as conflict and displays of emotion. Also, the more I practise, the better I get.

She comes at life from a different angle. When she wants something from the Stack she waits till the wee small hours, when everybody's in the chapel singing lauds, and creeps down the stairs dressed all in black with burnt cork smeared on her face and hands. Why? I ask her. Because I don't want the whole world knowing every bloody thing I do, she says.

Now I come to think of it, I don't think either of us has ever been down there with a genuine docket, obtained by going to our operations controller and asking. Other members of the Mission Militant do that, all the time, but not Svangerd and me. My boss – the young man we met earlier – reckons that's what makes us different – not better, he hastens to add, but different, definitely. He calls us his knights. I used to think that was a compliment until he explained it. A knight in chess, he pointed out, doesn't zoom along a straight line, like normal pieces. Oh no. If it wants to get somewhere, it insists on going three steps straight and then one sideways, and if it gets to jump over someone's head during the process, so much the better. That's Svangerd and me, he said. Right, I said, thank you so much. Don't mention it, he said.

I unrolled the mission briefing. "The princess," I said.

She yawned. She accepts briefings as a necessary evil, stuff you need to know before you can wade in and start slaughtering guards, but a bit tedious and old-womanish. "I know about the princess," she said. "Everybody does."

"Good for you," I said. "Now pay attention. Here's what we know. She was born Hildigund daughter of Ingvar, fifty-two years ago, in her father's castle at Hrafnsvik. Earl Ingvar was the high king's second cousin, nobody special; he had about ten thousand acres of rock and puffin guano, and forty-odd ships—"

"A pirate."

I nodded. "But a very well-connected one," I said. "Hildigund was the younger of two daughters. The elder, Irmengard, married the Count Palatine, which was a hell of a match for a pirate's daughter, but by all accounts she was pretty. Hildigund hung around at home until her father couldn't stand the sight of her any more, then he packed her off to a convent, where she stayed for twenty years."

"Packed off," she repeated resentfully. "I wish someone had packed me off to a convent when I was seventeen. You know what I was doing when I was seventeen?"

"Yes," I said. "Anyway, then the Social Wars came along, and eventually Gratian became high king, but not before his entire family had slit each other's throats, all except for Earl Ingvar, Sister Hildigund, and Countess Irmengard and her son. That made Hildigund a princess. By this time, she was prioress of the Flawless Diamond in Segwald—"

"Was she? I didn't know that."

I smiled. "Fancy," I said. "Anyhow, Gratian's only kid died in a riding accident, so Earl Ingvar was suddenly the heir to the throne. He died—"

"Gratian had him killed."

"There's no proof of that," I said. "And it doesn't matter if he did or not. What matters is, the current heir is Sighvat, son of the Count and Hildigund's sister Irmengard, who's delicate—"

"Wrong in the head," she said. "Has to be kept in a darkened room, with guards on the door round the clock."

"Delicate," I repeated. "If anything happens to him, the count and the countess, Hildigund is it. That would be very bad news, obviously, because she's well past child-bearing, so there'd be no succession and we'd be looking at civil war."

"I don't know why people make such a fuss about civil wars," she said. "Really they're no different from any other sort of war, and everyone seems to be dead keen on those."

"War is an abomination," I told her, "it says so in the scriptures. You ought to know that, being a true believer."

"Piss off," she said equably. "So we guzzle Hildigund to make sure she can't ever be high queen, which is fair enough. Sort of begs the question, though: Why now?"

I shrugged. "That's not in the memo."

"Don't suppose it is. I'm guessing someone's planning on taking out the nutcase and the count and countess directly afterwards, but that's just speculation." She stretched out in her chair and put her hands behind her head. "None of our business, right?"

"Right," I said. "Anyway, Hildigund isn't called that any more, she's Mother Eugenia and she's the abbess of the Teardrop. That means she's got more land in her own right than the Ischian Confederacy and more money than anyone north of the Bitter Sea." I paused for a moment. "Talking of which," I went on, "how come you never chose a name in religion?"

She shrugged. "Never really felt I deserved one, since you ask."

Sometimes she can surprise me. "Really?"

"Yup. Choosing a name is supposed to be like a baptism; you're getting rid of all the junk and shit from your previous life. Truth is, I don't think I'm ready."

That shut me up for a few seconds. "I suppose you can look at it that way," I said. "I got given mine when I was a novice, so it just sort of happened. And I always hated my real name, so—"

"What is your real name?"

"None of your business. Anyway, if that's your reason I suppose it does you credit."

"Glad you approve," she said, "not that I give a damn. Is the lecture over now?"

"No," I said. "We need to go over what we know about her principal actions as abbess, known views and opinions, connections and antecedents—"

"Later," she said. "Right now I've got pins and needles in

my foot and I need a pee. You can go away or you can stay and watch, entirely up to you."

I left.

The briefing document I'd just gone through with Svangerd was written by my pal Egil. These days he's the abbot's acting deputy head of Research, but we go way back. I went to see him in his office just off the south cloister.

"You again," he said. "Go away."

I sat down on the window seat. That was, of course, tactical. Egil worked like mad to get an office with a window, which in a nominally egalitarian order is a recognised mark of status. When he's not working, which is a lot of the time, his greatest joy is to sit on his stool and look out of his window, seeing with his mind's eye the vast distance between where he started and where he is now. "Why me?" I said.

"Why you what?"

"Why did I get put on this murdering princesses thing?" I made myself comfortable, filling the whole window. "I don't naturally spring to mind when they're handing out wet jobs."

"Your pal does," he replied. "And for some reason best known to herself, she likes working with you."

"No," I said, "There was a memo about eighteen months back, keep her away from sharp objects because she has a tendency to get carried away. As far as I know, that's still in effect, so—"

"You oughtn't to have seen that."

"I can read upside down. So there's a memo specifically saying, no more killing people for Svangerd until she's learned to curb her enthusiasm. Therefore, we can deduce, that wasn't the reason. Therefore if that wasn't the reason, what was?"

He yawned. "Gives you a chance to go to the funfair."

"Appreciated," I said. "But that's not the reason."

"What's the matter with you? Squeamish? Chicken? Suddenly got religion?"

"Yes," I said. "Look, this isn't the sort of thing I should be doing. There are other officers better qualified, and it's a sensitive job that needs to be done properly. Also, when anyone gives me something nice, I get suspicious."

He picked up his ruler and started scribing lines on a sheet of parchment with a small piece of soapstone. "You always were an ungrateful bastard."

I took the ruler away from him. "Yes," I said. "When I was a kid, we always saved the last of the apples so that, when it was time to slaughter the pig, we'd have something to lure her out of the pen with. What's going on, Egil? Why is everything suddenly coming up apples?"

He looked at me. "Since you insist on asking," he said, "I wrote in my report, this is obviously a job for Lauzeric and Anthemius. I even checked to make sure they were available, which they were. Then I filed my report, he read it and made a decision. That's what he does. I don't argue with him, and in return I get a room with a window. If you don't like it, go and pester him."

"Right," I said, giving him his ruler back. "I see. Thank you."

Properly speaking, Egil gets a window because he needs the light, for reading and writing by. Lesser mortals, assigned to less important functions, have to go out into the cloister garden. There's always a dozen or so readers and writers there during daylight hours, so it was perfectly natural for me to join them. I sat on a bench under the chestnut tree and removed from my sleeve the half-sheet of coarse recycled parchment I'd picked up off Egil's desk, while his attention was on the ruler I'd just taken from him with my other hand. I can read upside down like it was my mother tongue, but I can't read through a folded sheet.

Another thing I can't read is Old High Permian. That's because it's a dead language. Even here, where learning is concentrated like crows round a dead fox, there can only be half a dozen scholars who understand it. Nobody's written anything in it for seven hundred years, or so I'd been led to believe. I can recognise the letters, because basically it's a series of straight vertical lines with squiggles poking out of them (the Permians only ever used them for scratching on metal) but that's as far as I go. Egil, who I've known for a very long time, is no linguist, and I doubted very much that he was whiling away his leisure hours by compiling the definitive edition of the surviving Old Permian texts. I'd stolen the folded sheet because it had my name written, in Robur capitals, on the bit I could see – mine and half a dozen others, which I didn't recognise.

Nuts, I thought. As I believe I already mentioned, I relish the quiet life.

Brother Lauzeric and Brother Anthemius are two canons from our daughter house in Laxardal. From time to time you hear weird rumours about them, and they have an uncanny knack of being in interesting places at interesting times. Like me, they specialise in making copies of rare old books, usually ones of which only one copy is known to exist. They're also renowned editors, which means they travel a lot, comparing texts, hunting out variant readings so they can amend, annotate and restore. Things go missing and people die in places they visit. I've never met them, as it happens. They're who I'd have chosen for the job, if anybody had asked me.

It occurred to me, on my way back to the east wing, that Egil is a careful man, to whom confidential material is routinely entrusted. He doesn't leave things lying around where dishonest people can steal them. He's also, though he would probably dispute it if challenged, my friend. More nuts.

Properly speaking, Svangerd and I work for Simocatta, abbot of the Golden Star in Leerstad. Neither of us have ever met him. I saw him once, when he preached a very fine Ascension Day homily on predestination in the chapel royal. She reckons she met him a long time ago, before she left the world, but she says a lot of things. For years, the ruling passion of his life was his rivalry with our previous boss, the duke. Both of them were book collectors. Not in the usual way, which is all about heart-breakingly lovely illuminations and gem-encrusted bindings of unspeakable vulgarity; what they both obsessed over was rarities.

There are only so many books in the world – ten thousand have been written, according to Dimo of Schanz, ever since the world began, down to the present day (his present day – he died three hundred years ago), of which four thousand are written in Echmen and haven't been translated, and three thousand have been lost for ever. Four and three make seven, so that leaves three thousand. Four hundred of those are scripture, the standard texts that everybody's read or heard and some of us know by heart; there are hundreds of copies of them, in some cases thousands. Four hundred from three thousand leaves two thousand, six hundred, in different degrees of rarity. Pretty well any decent monastic library will have Jotapians's *Confessions* and Theuderic's *Meditations.* I know of, and have seen with my own eyes, fifteen copies of Saloninus' *Principia Mathematica*, and thirteen *Ideal Republics*. But, staying with Saloninus for the moment, there are only six known copies of the *Genealogy of Morals*, only four of *Daybreak* and just two copies of his *Collected Plays*. As for his *Downfall of the Gods*, there used to be one copy, in Abbot Simocatta's collection, until it was destroyed by fire. Luckily for the human race, a couple of murderous individuals working for the duke inveigled their way into his library, secretly copied the book and smuggled it out of the country. The copy was subsequently published, causing an ideological earthquake that led to the disestablishment of the church in the duchy, the dissolution of all the monasteries, and the two murderous individuals I mentioned just now being forced to flee for their lives and ending up working for Abbot Simocatta. That's what you get for doing the right thing, apparently.

Dimo of Schanz reckoned that it was high time (three centuries ago) that someone started writing some new books, to replace the ones that were lost and top up the pool, so to speak. That, of course, is just plain silly. It's a knack we seem to have lost as a species, along with clockwork and stained glass and underfloor heating, back when the old empire fell. In Dimo's time, there were still men and women around whose great-grandparents could remember the empire, so I guess Dimo was one of the last few for whom the things they did back then made any sort of sense. There was still a tiny ember of living memory, a few names and place names, making it possible for him to believe that the people who built the cities and made the things and wrote the books were ordinary real people, not gods and giants. From our perspective, that's impossible to believe or even imagine. We see the ruined walls and tumbledown towers, we dig up their filigree and cloisonné and their rusted-solid clocks, we conserve and steal their books, and we know deep down in our hearts that there are some things – a lot of things – that human beings used to be able to do once upon a time but can do no longer: that as a species we've shrunk and diminished, and we'll never be smart like that ever again.

It's like dog-breeding, according to my old boss the duke. You start off with a big dog, first cousin to a wolf, and you fiddle about with it for dozens of dog generations until you end up with something not much bigger than a rat, with floppy spinach-leaf ears and a little stub of a tail – and that, according to my old boss, is what the Invincible Sun has been doing to us, ever since the old empire fell. Presumably we couldn't be trusted with the strength and the speed of the wolf, because look at what we did to the empire. Therefore it was necessary to diminish us into something small, cute and stupid. If I believed in the Invincible Sun, that theory would make a lot of sense. As it is, in order to accept the theory, I'd have to believe that we did it to ourselves, either deliberately or because we were too reckless and ignorant to realise what the consequences of our actions would be. And that makes a certain degree of sense too, now I come to think of it.

Moral: don't let me get started about books, or I guarantee I'll bore you to death. Suffice it to say, I rather like the things – some more than others, I have to admit, but nobody's perfect. She reckons that if I was walking along a riverbank and I saw a drowning man clutching a book and I could only save one of them, I'd save the book. That's a trifle unfair. It would depend on what the book was. But I guess that by the time I'd dived in, grabbed the book from the drowning man and turned to the flyleaf to see the title, it'd be too late anyhow.

One thing my superiors never seem to realise when they send me on inconvenient junkets to foreign parts is that I actually have work to do here, at home. Presumably they reckon I spend my life sunning myself in the cloister garden or idly browsing through unsuitable books in the Old Library. If only.

"Go away," I accordingly said, when she came breezing in the next morning. "I'm working. Also, you shouldn't be here. This is the men's side."

She grinned. Nobody would have seen her, of course. She'd have gone round the back of the stables, shinned up the drainpipe, crawled in through the skylight, crept down the disused back stairs and flitted like a ghost through the corridors. She likes doing stuff like that. "Call that work?" she said, peering over my shoulder. "Drawing pictures in the margins of books?"

She had dust and cobwebs all down the left side of her habit, and a cut on the back of her right hand. "This," I said, "is a special illuminated missal, to be presented to the elector's youngest son on his name-day, which is in three weeks' time. If it's not ready by then—"

She yawned. "I think all the pictures are silly," she said. "Actually, they're more than that; they're blasphemous. I mean, why do rich people have pictures in their prayer books? It's so they've got something nice to look at during the boring old prayers. Which means they aren't listening to the prayers, which means their being at divine service is a mockery and a vanity. So, by painting your pretty pictures, you're actually encouraging them. That's really bad."

I was drawing the outline of a leopard crouched in a bed of lilies. I had no idea what it thought it was doing there. "The images," I said, "are aids to meditation. Taken in conjunction with the text, they make the subconscious mind receptive to the multiple levels of meaning implicit in the words of the scriptures.

Any fool knows that. Would you mind moving to your left? You're in my light."

"What's a leopard got to do with the seventy-third psalm?"

I took a deep breath, which didn't help. "I don't know," I said. "But He does, which is why He put that particular image in my mind. I do this job not just because I have exceptional graphic skills but because I have a proven track record of divine inspiration. Satisfied customers reckon that my illuminations increase the spiritual value of their devotions by up to twenty-six per cent—"

"Bullshit. You don't even believe."

"Beside the point. If He chooses to make me the vehicle of His light, what have my personal opinions concerning His existence got to do with anything? Look, I've got to concentrate on this or it'll all come out cock-eyed. Please go away."

"Fine," she said. "In that case, I'll just take your agreement as read and carry on, shall I?"

I put my pen down on the desk. It rolled off onto the floor and disappeared under the edge of the lectern. "No you bloody well will not," I said. Her shadow was across my page, which meant she was standing by the door. "At least tell me what I just agreed to," I said. "That way, it won't come as a complete shock."

The shadow moved. "While you've been in here doodling," she said, "I've been working out a plan of operations. Basically, we need to keep it simple. In, do the job, out again, no messing."

"You always say that," I said. "And it always ends the same way. Please let's not go through all that again."

If she'd hit me for saying that, it wouldn't have been the first time. "Fine," she said. "You do all the planning. You think of a way of getting us into the state apartments, past all the guards—"

"Already done that," I said.

Credit where it's due, she's always prepared to listen. "Go on, then," she said.

I opened the lid of the desk and took out a scrap of parchment. "This," I said, "is the floor plan of the old imperial palace in Choris Anthropou." I held up my hand to forestall her objections. "I know, there isn't one. No plan of the building is known to exist. But there is, because the palace is very old, and six hundred years ago it was described in detail in Psammetichus' *Principles of Architectural Theory.* I looked out the abbot's copy, read it carefully and made this plan."

"Smart," she said.

"Thank you. Right then, this is the entrance hall, which leads out into the square, on the opposite side of which is the temple, which is where the council will meet. With me so far?"

"I think you've got it upside down," she said.

"Well spotted." I turned it the right way up. "*This* is the entrance hall. This here is the grand staircase, which Psammetichus reckoned was the eighth wonder of the world. It leads to the first floor, with state apartments for all the most important delegates. The princess will be on the east side, because she reckons she can't sleep in a room that faces out onto the street."

"How do you know——?"

"Because she made a hell of a fuss about it when she paid a state visit to Earl Rothgar in Schanz about four years ago," I said. "It was noted in dispatches by our man in Schanz because they had to turf the Mezentine ambassador out of his room and give it to her, and he threatened to stalk out in a huff, which would've scuppered the trade negotiations, which were important to us because back then we were getting a lot of our salt from Beal

Auzida. I remember things," I pointed out, "and years later, they come in handy."

"So she'll be in a room in the east wing. Go on."

"On the east side," I corrected her. "Now, Psammetichus devotes a chapter and a half of book six of *Principles* to ventilation. He points out that in a building with more than one floor anywhere north of the Olbian Caucasus, you need tubes for smoke to go up, otherwise people on the ground floor are apt to suffocate or freeze to death. Now, there's a grand fireplace in the middle of the entrance hall, here. I know that, because Bakkehard wrote an ode to celebrate the wedding of Gunthamund and Ortriz, four hundred and thirty years ago, and he specifically mentions the fireplace hung with garlands of ivy and mistletoe, extending from one corner of the room to the other. From which we can deduce that the fireplace is in the exact dead centre of the hall."

She looked at me. "Who the hell is—?"

"Bakkehard of Odestat. Very minor court poet, wrote very long, bad poems, one of the last authors in the imperial tradition before the extinction of learning in the West. None of his work survives apart from snippets quoted in Kievegund's textbook on Classical Robur grammar, to illustrate the use of the pluperfect subjunctive."

She gave me a sort of shocked look, as if she found it hard to believe that people like me really exist. "Cool," she said. "So there's a fireplace. Or there was a fireplace, four hundred years ago."

"And where there's a fireplace," I said, "in a building of that period, there's bound to be a chimney. And it gets hellish cold in Choris in winter, so the principal guest rooms are bound to have fireplaces too, which will connect to the main chimney by way of flues. Do you know what a flue is?"

"No."

I told her about flues. "Chances are," I went on, "that the flue leading from the fireplace in the princess's room to the chimney will be wide enough for someone to crawl along, if they don't mind getting their hair all sooty. So in order to get into her room without being seen, all you need to do is get up on the roof and climb down the chimney and find the right flue, and there you are."

"You got all that out of some stupid old book?"

"There are no stupid books," I said, "only stupid—"

"How long did that take you?"

I smiled. "Not nearly as long as you'd think," I said. "Like I said, I tend to remember things. And I made a copy of Kievegund's grammar for the duke's daughter about eight years ago, so that bit of Bakkehard stuck in my mind. It was such a dreadfully bad poem, it was hard to forget."

She nodded. "Clever you," she said. "But my way's better."

I like her a lot, but sometimes she just makes me feel tired. "Go on."

"It's simple," she said. "We waylay her personal chaplain, knock him on the head, steal his clothes, go straight up to her room and do her. No mucking about. No crawling around in confined spaces."

"It's crude. It's violent. It won't work."

"Says you." She gave me a long look, part contempt, part analysis. "You're a selfish bastard," she said. "And a coward. But mostly selfish."

I'm a lot of things, I freely concede, but those two qualities wouldn't have sprung immediately to mind. "What makes you say—?"

"Oh, come on." Her fists were clenched; bad sign. "You come

up with a plan that depends on someone crawling along a narrow shaft. Obviously you can't do that: you'd get stuck. So the poor sucker doing the crawling will be me. Right?"

"Now you come to mention it—"

"Why's that, I wonder? Is it just because you're chicken, or is it because you really don't fancy killing a woman?"

She was so pleased with herself for figuring that out that she let me have three seconds or so in which to marshal my thoughts and arguments. "To be honest with you," I said, "I don't fancy killing anyone. Is that so bad?"

"Chicken," she said. "And selfish."

"Not really," I said. "I'd say it was more having at least a tiny degree of respect for the sanctity of human—"

"Shut up," she said. "Your precious conscience kicks up about guzzling a woman, or a nun, or a princess, but you haven't got the guts to tell *him* to stuff his job, because you like your nice soft number in the scriptorium. So you figure, if I make her do it, that means the blood's on her hands. Chicken, selfish and it doesn't even *work*. You'd still be as guilty as me. You're pathetic, you know that? Only a complete moron lies to himself."

There are times when I don't like the truth very much. "Fine," I said. "Guilty as charged. But so what? You don't mind killing women, or nuns, or princesses. In fact, you positively enjoy it. No, don't do all that emoting, it's true. You love killing aristocrats. It'll be your birthday and All Saints all rolled into one."

"We'll do it my way," she said. "Agreed?"

"Absolutely not. It's crude. It's too risky. We'll get caught. We'll start a war."

"Glad we've got that sorted out," she said. "I'll go and make the arrangements."

*

Money: a bit of a sore subject, between you and me. When I was a kid, before I left the world, I had an uncle. Through no fault of his own he got into debt; he owed his landlord forty deniers rent and six deniers for seed corn, and then it rained all spring and he got washed out and nothing grew. My uncle tried borrowing the money but all his family and friends were in the same boat, and he came up thirty deniers short. So the landlord took him to the hiring fair at Jokulsness and sold him. He fetched forty-two deniers, and the landlord scrupulously paid over the balance to my father as his next-of-kin. Hard but fair, our landlord.

Thirty years later, I breeze into the abbot's exchequer with a bit of parchment in my hand, a bored clerk glances at it, waddles over to one of the big iron-bound oak chests, jangles a few keys and hands me a linen purse containing a hundred deniers. I sign a receipt and that's that. Nobody will ask me what I spend it on, and if I try and give some of it back after the mission's over, the clerk will give me a horrible scowl and curse me under his breath, because paying expenses out is dead easy but paying them back in again once they've been issued is an administrative nightmare. It can only be resolved by cutting a page out of the ledger, copying everything out again in slightly smaller lettering (to fit in a new entry) and pasting the new page in, with affidavits annexed to authorise the removal and substitution of a page . . . So if I have anything left over at the end of a job, which I usually do, I have to run the gauntlet of the beggars on the priory steps, handing out ludicrous amounts of silver without getting my arms ripped out of their sockets in the process. I don't know what she does with her leftover expenses, but I have a shrewd suspicion she's endowing an order of poor friars back in her hometown, wherever that is. Anyway, money makes absolutely no sense, like everything else in this business.

I got my money from the exchequer, a new travelling gown and boots from the wardrobe, various specialist tools from the scriptorium, the Stack and the dispensary, and a set of impeccable credentials from the abbot's chaplain, authorising me as a delegate to the council. While I was in the chaplaincy office, I scarfed up half a dozen quarter-sheets of his parchment and leaned on his seal with a lump of soft wax in the palm of my hand while his attention was on other things.

I do my own wax casting. It's a bit of a rigmarole. You use the wax impression you've furtively obtained to make a plaster matrix, which you use to make a wax matrix, which you encase in clay. You melt the wax out of the clay, which leaves you with a mould into which you pour molten bronze. That gives you a more-or-less perfect copy of the original, and the rest of the day's your own.

I collect seals; it's a hobby of mine, like some people collect old books or icons by the great masters or weapons of historic significance. I've got half a dozen chaplaincy seals – they keep changing the pattern, which is a nuisance; depending on the purported age of the document you're faking, you have to know which pattern was current when. People in my line of work have come to grief over details like that, but not me.

"What the hell are you doing in here?" Brother Artifex wanted to know, when he caught me in his workshop using his furnace and crucible.

"Classified," I said.

"Piss off. How many times do I have to tell you, don't screw around with my stuff without asking. When you ask, I say yes. When you don't ask—"

"Sorry." I gave him my charming smile. It's not very good and I really need to get another one. "I needed some bits and pieces for a job."

He scowled at me. "When people want bits and pieces they come to me," he said. "They tell me what they want and I make them. They don't just wade in and overheat my crucibles."

"Can you overheat a crucible? I thought—"

"You were wrong. Give it here."

Oh dear. My fault. I'd figured that I'd be safe, because the third Monday in Advent is when Brother Artifex goes to the woods to collect his winter supply of charcoal. What I hadn't taken into account was the heavy rain three days earlier, which by now would have drained down off the hills and swollen the river to flood, making the ford at Spitz impassable. That's the trouble with high precision and dead reckoning. You need to allow for all the variables, not just the ones you happen to remember.

It was his workshop, so he took over. The casting went off just fine, and he broke open the mould. "What's that?"

"Classified."

"It's a seal." He picked it up in the tongs and peered at it. "Are you supposed to have this?"

"Of course," I said. "Ask Father Prior if you don't believe me."

He gave me that look of his, which always reminds me of a screw thread. "Nothing to do with me," he said. I think it was slowly dawning on him that by not asking him to make me a hooky seal, I'd actually done him a favour, in a left-handed sort of a way. "Anything else you want, while you're here?"

Yes, I didn't tell him: some keys, to be cast from the wax impressions in the little box in the sleeve of my gown, and a thin, sharp blade, capable of being concealed in the spine of a pocket-size missal or psalter. "So," I said, "you weren't able to go and fetch the charcoal."

"No."

"Nuisance, that."

"Guess I'll just have to go tomorrow," he said warily, "when the river's had a chance to settle down."

I nodded. "Mind how you go," I said.

I looked in the index – six calf-bound volumes the size of paving-slabs – and saw that the abbot's copy of Hvittinga's Old High Permian grammar and lexicon was in the New Building, second floor, room six, east wall, sixth shelf, location 47. Only it wasn't.

That was a nuisance. There are eight known copies of Hvittinga, spread across the known world with annoyingly large gaps between them. The closest one was, in fact, in Choris Anthropou, which was where I was headed. Of course, it was possible that someone had wanted to look something up and had neglected to fill out a docket and file it with the librarian. People can be so careless.

So I tried asking around, but nobody I knew had heard of any of the other names on the list, the one with my name at the top of it. I didn't ask Egil, of course.

Life, I've always firmly believed, was supposed to be simple. The purpose of a living thing is to reproduce. Ancillary to that purpose, it needs to stay alive long enough to find a mate and do the job, which means it has to find and eat food. If it's a mammal, it also needs to survive until its offspring is old enough to look after itself. That's basically it. Anything else is just over-complication and self-indulgence.

Holy Mother Church, of course, begs to differ. Holy Mother Church holds that the purpose of human life is to glorify the name of the Invincible Sun, and nothing else. Ancillary to that purpose is staying alive and procreating further generations of worshippers – but strictly ancillary. Back in the old empire, of course, there were philosophers who had all sorts of crazy notions – liberty, the pursuit of happiness – which they set out in detail in books which are now mostly lost. A few tantalising quotations remain, preserved in books on grammar, rhetoric and bee-keeping, but mostly they're gone for ever and, guess what, life goes on. When I was a kid, everything really was pretty simple, on a farm in the Mesoge, the armpit of the known world. The Mesoge was the anvil on which my worldview was forged, and I see no reason to revise my opinions.

Life was supposed to be simple, and human beings were designed to live the simple life. Coping with the complicated shit is an unnatural skill. I have many unnatural skills, of which I'm not proud, but not nearly enough.

2

"Cheer up, for crying out loud," Svangerd said, as I lifted our trunks onto the cart. "It's an adventure. Out of the office. It'll be *fun*."

A cold, crisp morning; travelling clothes; new boots still gleaming with sheep's wool grease; a stack of books tied together with string to read on the journey. Two of them I'd copied myself, privately, when I was supposed to be somewhere else doing something else: Saloninus' *Human, All Too Human* and Inguiomar's *Progression of the Holy Spirit*. Both of them were technically illegal in three of the jurisdictions we'd be crossing on our way to Choris, but we were delegates to the council so we had both diplomatic immunity and benefit of clergy; basically, we could burn down an orphanage and sell the charred bones of the orphans for bonemeal, and the worst we could expect would be a leisurely deportation. Not that I'd ever dream of doing such a thing, and Svangerd wouldn't either, unless the orphans happened to be aristocrats.

"This is not fun," I said firmly. "This is work. We're putting ourselves in harm's way to do a difficult, morally dubious—"

"Bullshit," she said, settling herself in the back of the cart and securing three-quarters of the rug we were supposed to be sharing. "How much money have we got?"

I told her. She smiled. "We'll need to do ourselves pretty well along the way," she said. "Roast dinner at all the inns, with wine. That's what delegates to these things do. We need to maintain our cover."

I gave her the bent eye. "Chastity, obedience and what was the third one?"

"Men," she said, "have this habit of mixing up piety and being miserable. It's a man thing and it's stupid. The Invincible Sun gave us fun because he intended us to use it. I'm going to have fun on this trip whether you like it or not. You can do what you like."

Her definition of fun doesn't entirely square with the one you'll find in Eumeric's *General Lexicon*. "Just don't get us arrested," I said. "I hate that."

"They can't arrest us; we're delegates. I think I'm going to like being a diplomat."

As well as the six books tied up with string, I had my pocket-sized copy of Brihtmer's *Confessions*. I pulled it out and opened it at random. "We may need the money for bribing officials or buying information," I said. "It'd be really stupid if we jeopardised the mission just so you can stuff your face with roast beef in oyster sauce."

"Haven't had that for years," she said. "Actually, you're probably right. We'll go easy on the way out, then blow everything we've got left on the way back. How does that sound?"

Sister Svangerd always has the last word: that's as inevitable as winter. The trick is to manoeuvre her to the point where the last word is something you can bear to live with. "Fine," I said.

"Good. Read your book."

Most of the first day we were in territory we both know only too well. We changed horses at Dui Chirra and again at Ancola, and we rolled into the Constancy & Grace at Tin Chirra just as it was starting to get dark. Svangerd had stayed at the Constancy before; however, I waved our diplomatic passes under the innkeeper's nose and told him he'd be breaking the law if he refused to let us in, and he believed me. "Just keep her under control, for crying out loud," he muttered, as I unloaded our trunks. "I'm trying to run a business here."

Svangerd was as good as gold, mostly because I got her into a cut-throat game of checkers, which kept her occupied and away from the other guests. She's a world-class checkers player and there's only one man in the known world who can beat her on a regular basis. That's me. She, of course, hates to lose at anything, which is why we only play checkers in an emergency. At some point in the early hours of the morning I contrived to forfeit the tournament by falling asleep. By that stage there wasn't much point in going to bed, so I stayed where I was until dawn, and then we got back on the cart for the long trundle down the hill to Metousa Bay.

An hour or so before noon, she nudged me in the ribs. "We're being followed," she said.

I stuck my finger in my book to mark the place and closed it. "No," I said. "There's a covered chaise behind us, and it's been there for over an hour, but that's because the people in it want to go to Metousa, same as we do. It's a seaport. That's not following."

She was looking ahead. "In a mile or so we'll be down into the Ceun valley," she said, "where it's always misty at this time of year, because of the river. My guess is, they're waiting for that, and then they'll make their move. We need to be ready for them. Which trunk are the weapons in?"

"What weapons?"

She gave me that look. "Two riding swords, type fifteen, two three-pound poleaxes with takedown shafts. Oh, come on. Don't tell me you—"

"I needed the space for our diplomatic robes," I said. "Also, there are legal problems about carrying weapons in diplomatic luggage. The last thing we need is hassle with customs."

The same look, only treble strength. "Positively the last time I let you pack," she said. "Stuff it, we'll have to make do with what we've got."

"We haven't got anything." Doubt flared in my mind. "Have we?"

She was lifting the hem of her habit to get at her boot. "No thanks to you," she said. "Here. Don't lose it; it's one of a pair."

Here turned out to be a long, thin dagger. "Put it away, before you poke somebody's eye out," I said. "You're being ridiculous. There is no danger. We are not being followed."

The road from Berd to Metousa crosses the river at a ford. When we got there, we found it blocked by an abandoned lumber cart. The chaise closed up behind us, in the mist. I hate it when she's right.

The carter turned round and gazed at us. "What's going on?"

"The gentlemen in the chaise behind are going to try and kill us," I said. "If I were you, I'd run."

So he did. Svangerd handed me the dagger I'd refused earlier. I gave it back. "That's no bloody good," I told her. "What I wouldn't give right now for a type-fifteen riding sword. Or a poleaxe."

There were six men in the chaise. They fanned out as they approached us, and I felt that wave of utter helplessness that always washes over me when I'm faced with the prospect of violence. It makes me think I'm six years old again, and about to be beaten up by my older brothers.

I glanced round at her but she wasn't there. She likes to move, whereas I prefer to fight from a fortified position. Well now, I thought.

The key to this violence business is concentration. I considered the man walking towards me. I could see that he had a short axe in his left hand and a spear in his right. The axe was something he'd brought from home; the spear was military issue, from the war before the war before last. Something about the way he looked, I'm not sure what, told me plain as anything that in real life he worked at the docks. Fair enough; not much going on in his line at this time of year, before the trade winds start to blow. I waited till he was about eight feet from me, then I threw a trunk at him.

The sharp corner of the trunk caught him in the middle of the forehead, which was sheer luck. I'd aimed to miss left, since he was probably left-handed and would therefore flinch left (my right), but a trunk is hardly a missile of precision. Luckily for me he didn't flinch at all. I launched myself off the cart and landed on his ribcage.

That earned me a spear and a hand-axe. I chucked the spear at the man on my right – that close, I couldn't miss – and converted the twist of the throw into a demi-volte to avoid the haymaking slash from the billhook of the man on my left. He didn't miss by much, but by then I'd stepped in behind him. The axe was nice and sharp, so I dropped my hand to waist level and drew-cut him on his right side, just under the ribcage. The pain clouded his thinking long enough for me to sink the beard of the axe in the back of his head. As I did so, I was uncomfortably aware that I had no idea what was going on behind me, a level of negligence that should have proved fatal if there was any justice in this world, which fortunately there isn't. I swung round, but there was nobody there.

"Svangerd?" I yelled.

She stepped out from behind the cart. She was breathing heavily and grinning. There was blood on her left sleeve, but I didn't think it was hers. "Are you all right?" I said.

"Fine," she said. "How about you?"

She was looking at me. I glanced down and saw a slash in my habit just above the right hip. Through it I could see a cut, about a forefinger long, which was bleeding. I could have sworn the billhook had missed me clean, but apparently not.

"Trust you to get yourself cut up the first day out," she said. "I take my eye off you for two minutes and look what happens."

"It's nothing."

"There's my brave soldier. Right, let's find someone to talk to."

Her three were long past talking, needless to say. The man I'd hit with the trunk was still breathing, but I wouldn't have paid money for him at market, as my father used to say. That left the man I'd thrown the spear at. He was sitting on the ground, gazing at the wooden pole sticking out of his gut with a comical expression on his face. Under other circumstances he'd have broken my heart.

Svangerd reached for the spear-shaft and gave it a brisk twist. The man screamed.

"Who sent you?" she asked.

He opened his mouth to speak, and blood came spilling out, down from the corners of his lips and in a stream over his chin. That did it for me. I ran round behind the cart and threw up.

"No good," Svangerd said, joining me a few moments later. "I suppose we could hang around and see if the one you brained wakes up, but I don't think he will." She looked at me, and I made a vague effort to wipe my face clean. "This really isn't your sort of thing, is it?"

"No," I said.

"Pity. You're not bad at it. But where I grew up you wouldn't have lasted five minutes."

I stood up. My habit was drenched in blood on one side and sick on the other. "I'll have to wear my dress robes," I said.

"Just as well you brought them. Go and sit in the cart. I'll see if there's any plantain."

Where Svangerd learned to sew up wounds I don't know and have never liked to ask, but she's neat and quick, which is all you can really ask for. She also knows about washing the dirt out and sweetening cuts with plantain juice, which I've read about but never actually seen anyone else do in practice. "It'll stiffen up and hurt like buggery in an hour or so," she said cheerfully, "so you'd better shift those bodies now, while you feel like doing it. Don't strain too much or you'll burst the stitches."

I dumped the bodies back in the chaise, and that was all my strength used up for the day. She turned the horses loose, then scrabbled together some twigs and dead brambles to kindle a fire under it. Clearing up after yourself is good manners.

"I don't think we'll be seeing the carter again," she said, climbing up onto the box of the cart. "I'll drive."

"No."

"You're in no fit state," she said firmly. "Also we need to make up time if we're going to catch the boat."

I groaned, but no use. Svangerd doesn't know how to drive a cart, but she thinks she does. She also likes to go fast. On previous occasions the nightmare hadn't lasted very long, because she'd either hit a tree or ride over a pothole and crack an axle. This time, though, it seemed to go on for ever.

"We need to talk," she yelled over the thunder of the wheels, "about who those men were. I've been racking my brains and I can't think."

I couldn't think either, because of the fear.

"For one thing," she went on, "this junket of ours is supposed to be a secret. For another, why guzzle us so close to home? It leaves plenty of time for the abbot to send somebody else. Also, I don't suppose you noticed, but those men weren't exactly at the top of their profession. We saw them a mile off and they couldn't fight for honeycomb. The sort of people who'd want to stop us going to the shindig would have better men at their disposal, don't you think?"

"Would you mind slowing down just a little bit?"

"On reflection, we should've taken the chaise," she said. "But to get back to what I was saying," she went on, as the offside back wheel grazed a large rock and my teeth came together like hammer and anvil, "I've been turning over in my mind who it could've been and none of them rings true. There's the princess's lot, obviously, but how in God's name would they know about us? There's the Sashan, because Sashan intelligence knows everything about everything everywhere, only we'll be doing the Sashan a favour, so why stop us? Of course it could be someone inside the Order, which would explain how they knew, but I don't remember pissing anybody off enough to want to kill us. How about you?"

"I don't know. Maybe someone you gave a lift to once."

"Funny man. This is serious. If the object of our mission is common knowledge, we're going to be in shit up to the armpit."

"Maybe we should go back."

"Wash your mouth out with ashes and water."

"You said it yourself," I said. "There's still time for them to send another team. If you're right and our cover's blown before we start, there's no point us going on. Also, we're liable to get killed, which I object to."

"Don't be such a girl. All I'm saying is, it'd be nice if we had some idea what's going on, so we don't go making stupid mistakes which we could avoid with a little common sense and forward planning. How's the leg?"

"Painful," I said. "Hurts like hell every time we go over a rut."

"The plantain will take the heat out of it," she said blithely. "No offence, but you need to be more careful. Like I said, those boys were hardly the brightest and the best, and you let them get to you. I'm not criticising; I'm just saying, that's all."

I like Svangerd a lot. Some times, though, more than others.

Metousa Bay isn't what it was. Three hundred years ago it was one of the Nine Ports, back when they had the monopoly on the herring and salt cod business, and they actually extended the old imperial harbour and built a new jetty, to shelter the east side of the bay. Then the Aram Chantat and the Auzida appeared out of nowhere and turned the whole of the east coast of the Bitter Sea into a wasteland. There was nobody left to eat herrings, so Metousa dwindled away into what it is now: a small town that happens to be on the edge of the sea. Once a month the stone barges put in, to load granite and basalt blocks from the quarries at Stachel – in the old days a fleet of barges arrived every week, and they say that there are palaces in Iden Astea and Moy Ennep built exclusively out of chunks of the Stachel downs, which is hard to imagine – and if you're lucky and you have a chit from the right abbot, you can hitch a lift on one of them as far as Mavais, where you can take your pick of ships bound for Choris.

Svangerd hates sea travel. I don't mind it one bit. I feel just the same standing on a deck as I do in the street or the cloister. She suffers the torments supposedly reserved for perjurers and men who kill their mothers, though she does her level best not to let it show.

"You'll be fine," I promised her. "These things aren't like other ships. I've been on them loads of times. They're big and heavy and flat-bottomed, so they don't roll and wallow about, and there's never any bad weather this time of year. Give it a day or so and you'll have forgotten you're on a ship, trust me."

There's a curious irony in the fact that every time I utter the words *trust me*, something screws up. Even more curious is the fact that she continues to listen to me, even when I use the dreaded formula. "I don't know what you're making such a fuss about," I said, as she clung to the rail with bits of half-digested food sticking to her chin. "It's a bit frisky, but no big deal."

A wave smashed into the side of the barge, drenching us

both with spray. I didn't mind all that much. I was washing my soiled habit by wearing it, and the spray had done a pretty good job of rasping the ingrained blood and vomit out of the fibres. She'd borrowed an old oilskin from one of the barge hands. "I hate you," she said. "I hope we both drown."

"About what you were saying the other day," I said. "I've been giving it some thought, and I agree with you. It doesn't make sense. Who'd want to kill us before we get to Choris?"

I think she sincerely intended to answer my question, but what came out was a horrible retching noise.

"It's a real shame you insisted on killing that man," I went on, "before he could tell us anything. That's the trouble with you, though, you do tend to get carried away. Yes, fair enough, first things first, neutralise the threat and then think about the good of the mission. But I should point out that I managed to defend myself perfectly adequately and still leave two out of three of the bad guys still alive and capable of imparting valuable information, whereas you—" At which point I had to move quickly. I got it wrong, but only because the wind changed suddenly and I ducked into the projectile vomit instead of out of its way. "Not to worry," I said. "The rain'll clear it off in two shakes."

She turned her head and glared pitifully at me. "Why don't you go below," she said, "where it's dry?"

"A bit of rain never hurt anybody," I said. "Besides, we need to talk about this. As I see it, the only logical conclusion is that there's a security breach at our end. Someone back at the abbey told those idiots exactly where to find us and what we're doing. That's really rather serious, don't you think?"

She'd got her elbows under the rail and her fingers clenched tight, like a blacksmith's vice. "It doesn't have to be that," she whispered, her throat raw from vomit burns. "Been thinking about it. Maybe just robbers."

I'd thought about that too. A cart from the abbey in the middle of nowhere; carts coming in to the abbey tend to be carrying bulk goods of little intrinsic value, but carts coming out could well be carrying books, or icons; nearly everything we make is small, portable and extremely valuable to the right buyer. In fact, when you come to think of it, it's amazing how rarely we get robbed. But we usually don't, and that surely was the point.

"Robbers don't drive about in chaises," I pointed out.

"Professional assassins don't use billhooks," she managed to reply before another billow rendered her speechless. Good point, which had already occurred to me. I'd dismissed it from my mind, but only because I couldn't find a way to account for it.

"I still think we should've turned back when we had the chance," I said. "Still, too late for that now, so we'll just have to soldier on and make the best of it. But it means we're going to have to rethink our strategy from the ground up. If they know who we are and why we're really going to the council—"

"Who's *they*?"

Another good point. "I don't fancy the idea of being arrested the moment I step off the ship," I said. "Yes, we've got diplomatic credentials and benefit of clergy, but that assumes they're playing by the rules, which is probably an unwarranted assumption. Even so. Killing us in a muddy riverbed's a bit extreme when all they have to do is put us back on the boat and not let us into Choris. On the other hand, doing that would probably be a diplomatic incident, whereas if we got ourselves killed by generic bandits, that'd be unfortunate but nobody's fault. Hence, I suggest, the steps they went to in order to make the attackers *look* like robbers. Am I making any sense here?"

"No."

"Just thinking aloud, really."

"Go and do it somewhere else."

It did occur to me to wonder whether I should have told her about the list, with my name on it, written in an obscure dialect of a dead language nobody knows how to read. The problem with that was that I could easily anticipate her proposed course of action, which would be to back my friend Egil up against a wall and break his fingers one by one until he told her what she wanted to hear. The moment might well come when I'd be glad to let her do that, but it hadn't come yet, and I don't have so many friends that I can afford to fritter them away on idle speculation. I told myself that Egil had a lot of papers in his room, that it was highly unlikely that he could read or write Old High Permian, and people came and went into his place every minute of the day, so planting something like that on him would be easy as pie. I didn't actually say *trust me* to myself, but it was sort of implied.

"My leg," I told her, on the eighth day of our sea voyage, "is feeling ever so much better."

Eight days on a stone barge had reduced her to a wilted flower. What little she'd managed to eat had come straight back out again, and her voice had dwindled down to a tiny whisper. The sea, however, was being flat and still and butter-wouldn't-melt, like a dog that's just killed a chicken, so I'd managed to prise her away from the rail and build her a little nest of blankets in the hold. We were due to arrive in Mavais early the next morning, a day late because of the bad weather but still with plenty of time in hand.

"I'm really looking forward to the council," I said. "I particularly want to hear Anthemius and Eudo of Schanz debating the doctrine of unified purpose. I read Carrhasio's defence of Anthemius, but—"

"You're full of shit," she croaked irritably. "You don't even believe."

"No, but it's still fascinating. If you regard it all as an intellectual exercise, it's really very rewarding. Take Orosius' deconstruction of predestination, for example. If you go along with it, you're implicitly signing up for an entirely mechanistic view of the creation process, whereas if you go to the opposite extreme and side with Aviduus and Lutomer of Gratz—"

"Piss off and stop tormenting me."

Someone who didn't know her as well as I do could take offence at that, but I grinned and told her to drink plenty of fluids. Then I went up on deck to see if we were in sight of land yet.

Most people don't care much for Mavais, but I rather like it. I'm not sure why. It's a run-down, dog-poor sort of a place, what's left of it. When the empire fell, and refugees escaping from the Aram Chantat crowded into the peninsula and dug a broad channel across it to make themselves into an island, they built a regular imperial city to live in, the last of its kind. The idea was that they'd exist entirely on sea trade and never go anywhere near the Aram-infested mainland, and for sixty years or so that was a good working proposition. But then the few surviving imperial outposts fell to the Aram or the Auzida and there was nobody left to trade with. The Aram never did get the hang of ships, so the only vessels on the sea were Sherden pirates; they had several goes at Mavais, but the first thing the Mavasines did when they got there was build massive walls on the approved imperial pattern, so the Sherden never stood a chance.

Mavais never fell. It just sort of faded away. Long after the Aram and the Auzida went back to wherever they came from, the Mavasines refused to risk setting foot on the mainland. Instead, they demolished two-thirds of the city, starting at the walls and working inwards, and ploughed it up for farmland. The houses were mostly empty anyway, since well over half the population died in three waves of plague over forty years, and these days the Mavasines are just dog-and-stick farmers living on a small island. They'll still tell you they're the last true blue-blood remnant of the old empire, unconquered and unsullied, but point to one of the inscriptions on the walls behind them and ask them what it says, and either they know it by heart or they guess. Still, a surprising number of good things have managed to survive in Mavais, mostly by benign neglect, and it's still a useful seaport, because of where it is.

The first things you see, therefore, are the old walls, rising up out of the sea like an outstretched hand, palm facing – thus far, but no further. They're the last ever made out of the legendary imperial powdered stone, the secret of which has been lost for six hundred years. Apparently there was a mountain in Antecyrene made out of a special kind of rock you could grind into dust; then, if you mixed the dust with sand and water, you could cast it, like bronze, into any shape you liked. The walls of Mavais are built out of hundreds of thousands of absolutely identical, perfectly straight and square one-ton blocks, mortared together and faced with more of the magic dust paste so that it looks like the whole wall is one solid piece of stone. The neighbours, and most of the Mavasines themselves, say that the wall was built for the gods by the giants, who demanded the goddess of love as payment for their work, and that was how the first war in heaven started. An easy mistake to make, if you don't happen to know the true story. Walls like that would be worth the price, if you ask me.

Ships from Choris call at Mavais to pick up linen from north Blemmya and salt from Olbia, so finding a ride wasn't a problem. I left her at the convent, to recover from her ordeal and catch up on her confessions, and strolled up into the old town to refresh my memories of the sights before going down to the docks and finding us a boat.

By some strange chance I'd put some of our money in the pocket of my habit, presumably for safekeeping, and it was still there when I happened to pass the door of a shop I remembered from my previous visit. If you ask the man who runs it what his business is, he'll tell you, scrap metal and general salvage – by which he means things that turn up, in the ground or at the back of old sheds, and which nobody in his right mind could possibly want for anything; things like books and icons and statues, along with rusty cart springs, broken lamps and old furniture so wormy it falls to bits when you try and lift it. The last time I was there I paid a denier for the collected comedies of Notker, complete apart from the last volume; as far as I know, it's the only surviving copy of *The Gentleman in Black* and *Creatures of Impulse*, and the version of *Pollio's Thumb* is very different from the one in the abbot's manuscript. Like I said, things like that occasionally still come to light in Mavais, if you can be bothered to look for them down among the cracked trivets and two-legged chairs. Old sources talk about there having once been an imperial library at Mavais. If it didn't burn down (as most libraries eventually do) then all the books from it must have gone somewhere.

So I went in and poked around, and I'd found a nice old Mezentine stiletto, which I knew she'd like, and an almost pristine copy of Anectho's *Commentaries* (not particularly rare, but a steal at half a denier and useful as a swap for something else if I happened to meet a book freak at the council) when the shopkeeper came up behind me and made a sort of choking noise, presumably to get my attention.

"You like old stuff, then," he said.

"Yes."

"I've got something really old," he said. "Out back."

I didn't hold my breath. Anything that isn't still hot from the forge or wet from the mason's trowel would be really old as far as he was concerned, and since he charged the same for a pitchfork head with one tine missing as he did for a late Mannerist icon of the Transfiguration, I assume he attributed equal value to both. "Sure," I said. "Oh, and what do you really want for this icon? You've got it down for a denier, but I imagine that's just rustic humour."

"Half a denier," he said without looking, and I paid him before he could change his mind. "This way."

The front of his shop was a timber-frame shack, thatched with barley straw. Out back was through a breathtakingly lovely late imperial arch, leading into what must once have been the private chapel of a substantial merchant's house. There was just enough flaking stucco left to show that the back wall had been a floor-to-ceiling Annunciation (if I knew more about it, I could probably have identified the artist), and the floor was paved with slabs of the same miraculous cast stone as the city walls were made of. The room was full of junk and stank of mildew and rot, and in the middle of it, sitting on a rusted-out farrier's forge with the bellows-leather hanging in rags, was a box.

"Three deniers," he said.

I looked at the box. The box seemed to look at me. "No, seriously," I said. "How much?"

"Two."

I hardly dared get close to it. At some point, some lunatic had painted it with lime whitewash, which had turned a sort of orange-grey under the influence of our common enemy, Time. Ignore the whitewash and consider the proportions. I'd seen them before, and I never forget a ratio.

"Two deniers for an old box."

"There's stuff in it."

"Probably just old papers," I said.

"I thought you liked old papers."

I steeled myself, took a long stride forward and lifted the lid just enough to see inside. Old papers. "I might be able to shift it in Choris as a spice-box," I said. "Half a denier."

He shrugged. "I'm sick of the sight of the bloody thing," he said. "Three farthings."

Just a box, painted white, measuring maybe seven inches by five by four. The one I'd seen just like it sat on the desk of the late duke, my previous employer. It was Echmen burr rosewood – the trees are extinct now; five hundred years ago the reigning Echmen emperor had the last few of them cleared and burned, so that his suite of rosewood furniture would for ever be unique – and it was made in Mezentia by a craftsman whose name has been lost, but who was without doubt the finest cabinetmaker there's ever been. The duke wasn't really fussed about the box. What he cared about was what was inside it. The unknown craftsman made boxes like the duke's to house very special books.

I walked out of the shop and fifty yards down the street, then ducked in under an arch and lifted the lid, a bit wider this time. Inside I saw four rolls of cream-white parchment, about as long as my index finger. Rolls, mark you, not bound books, codices. I had to lean against the wall to steady myself, and anybody passing would quite reasonably have assumed that I was drunk. Which, in a sense, was true. Exhilaration and intoxication.

The Mezentine cabinetmaker who made the boxes worked for just one customer. We know him as the general secretary, which is short for general secretary pro tem of the Loyal Opposition.

What I needed to do was think, but that wasn't easy with my brain churning like Svangerd's stomach in a gale. Talking of Svangerd, there was a chance, slim but real, that she might recognise the box for what it was, in which case nothing would keep her from smashing it to bits, burning the fragments and dumping the ashes in running water. That complicated things. Also, I was going to Choris, and in Choris, at an ecumenical council, there was a good chance I'd be able to find someone who'd be able to read what was written on the four scrolls. But once he'd done that he'd be in on the secret . . .

Suppose you lived in a big city and someone gave you a rat in a jar and told you, this is a plague rat. Also inside the jar is a gold ten-bezant piece, and you and your family are starving. So long as the rat stays in the jar, nobody's going to get sick, but you and your wife and your six kids are going to starve to death, sure as apples; and who knows, you or one of your kids might be the one in fifty people who are immune to the plague. A bit like that.

Needless to say, I don't believe in the general secretary or the Loyal Opposition. If I believed in them, I'd have to believe in a lot of other stuff, such as the Invincible Sun, Good and Evil, life after death and all manner of other superstitious nonsense. What was inside the box, therefore, couldn't possibly be *real* – But a great many people, ninety-nine per cent of all living humans, would beg to differ with me on that point, and half of them would want to know what the writing on the rolls said, and the other half would cheer Svangerd on and hold her coat for her while she got rid of them for ever and ever.

The true gospels; being an accurate and authentic account of the Invincible Sun's ministry on earth as incarnate Man. As opposed to the Gospels, which purport to be an accurate and authentic account but probably aren't; what they are is, of course, scripture, and the bedrock and foundation of the faith and Holy Mother Church.

Here's the thing. The Gospels contradict each other. There are large chunks in the First Gospel that are plainly interpolations, added at a later date by someone who wanted to steer the infant Church in a direction it ultimately didn't take. There are also a lot of improbable stories, wacky miracles, angels and demons, the sort of things even bishops can't quite bring themselves to believe in, but they don't actually say so out loud. The official line is that the Gospels are the Word of the Invincible Sun filtered through the minds and perceptions of the fallible humans who heard the Word and wrote it down, hence all the garbage. As to provenance, the Gospels seem to have been written somewhere between seventy-five and a hundred years after the events they describe, so presumably by second-generation believers recording an oral tradition that was starting to get a bit frayed at the edges. But for all their faults they're scripture, the most precious scripture of all, and there are half a dozen prayers you're supposed to say to cleanse your spirit before you so much as open the book.

And then there are the true gospels. They're written in Volusian, an extremely rare and obscure dead language hardly anybody can read these days, which happens to be the language that everybody was speaking and writing in the place and time when the Ministry took place; they've never been translated, for obvious reasons. Very little is known about them, but one thing we do know is that they were written much earlier, say about fifteen to twenty years after the Ministry, and about eighty per cent of the content is identical; the same incidents described, the same speeches and parables and sermons. But an awful lot of things (the improbable stories, wacky miracles, angels and demons) are left out, and in their place there's other stuff: other incidents, other speeches, parables and sermons, that make perfect sense in context, but which leave you with a rather different message than the one you get from proper orthodox scripture.

Holy Mother Church has known about the true gospels for a very long time, ever since she was a bunch of wild-eyed fanatics meeting in rooms over stables and hiding in drains from the police. She takes the view that the true gospels are heresy: forgeries concocted by the Evil One to lead the faithful astray. Look, she says, at the subtlety of the deception – eighty per cent true, twenty per cent poison; unless you happened to know (because you'd been told) that these abominable texts were evil lies, you could very easily believe them and be seduced into blasphemous error, because they're so horribly plausible. Furthermore, Holy Mother Church added at a later date, they don't actually exist. What people call the true gospels are actually forgeries, concocted centuries later by enemies of the faith who also went back and altered the manuscripts of the Early Fathers, inserting references to the true gospels to give them a spurious provenance. Fortunately (says Holy Mother Church) the original manuscripts of the true gospels were long ago hunted out and destroyed, so if anyone shows you a set of four old books and tells you that's them, they're lying or deluded. Furthermore, anybody claiming to own or have read them is undoubtedly an agent of the Loyal Opposition, and it's your duty to hand them over to the nearest canons juridical for immediate execution. In particular, be on your guard for small rosewood Mezentine boxes, exquisitely made, containing four small rolls of cream-white parchment written in Volusian.

Served me right for fooling about in shops when I ought to have been finding us a boat to Choris. I pulled myself together with a snap and made a decision.

Nobody knew what I'd got. The man in the shop knew I now had a box, but nobody knew what that box was, or it wouldn't have been in the shop. For now, unless I told someone or I took the box somewhere it could be recognised by an expert, the rat was still in the jar and no danger to anybody. There are a great many disused wells in Mavais. I could lift the lid and drop it down, and chances were that nobody would ever find it. Or I could put it on the fire, or wait till we were on the boat to Choris and drop it over the side. If I did that, it wouldn't be a problem any more, not to me, not to anyone.

On the other hand, it was – well, what it was. Indescribably important, a slice of human knowledge and experience that couldn't be allowed to perish, not if I planned on ever sleeping again. I had a duty –

I have lots of duties. That's fine so long as they don't conflict, but all too often they do, and that's why my life is not, on balance, a happy one. Naturally I couldn't just keep the bloody thing, as my very own, as a *possession*. In theory at least, my vow means that I have no possessions, merely the use of certain artefacts owned by the order. That meant that my choice was properly between killing the box and giving it to someone. The right someone.

The abbot. Oh boy, yes. Abbot Simocatta would love to have it. Having got it, he'd be embarrassingly grateful to me for the rest of his life and quite possibly make me his successor. Was he the right person to have the box? Decidedly not. It would sit on his desk in pride of place, and the four rolls of parchment would stay inside it, unread, since none of us at the abbey could read them, and he wouldn't dare tell anyone else what he'd got for fear they'd turn up under his castle walls with an army and try and take it away from him. And then he'd die and I'd take his place, and the problem would come back to me, like a homing pigeon.

But I was going to Choris, to an ecumenical council. And I wouldn't have to come right out with it and say, I have this box with me, in this very building. I could say I knew where it was, or I had an idea where it might be, and gauge the reaction. If it turned out that the man I was talking to belonged to the burn-the-abomination school, then I'd go away and look for it

and not find it, and that would be that. If, however, he promised me faithfully that it would be kept safe and transcribed
and studied by serious scholars – assuming, of course, that he
was telling the truth. Not always a safe assumption, I've found,
when dealing with people.

Or I could look for a safe place, right here in Mavais, and
leave it there, so at least I wouldn't have the wretched thing on
me, a responsibility and a threat to my life. Echmen rosewood
is amazing stuff. It doesn't warp or crack like other woods
do, and things kept in it stay good for ever, and the nameless
Mezentine craftsman could make a box that was genuinely airtight – somewhere like the gap between the top of the wall and
the rafters in an old shed somewhere, the sort of place nobody
would ever think to look, just long enough for me to go away,
get my head together, then come back and fetch it. We'd be
passing through Mavais on our way home from Choris after
the council.

But there was a good chance we wouldn't be coming back,
bearing in mind what we were going to Choris to do . . . It
shows what an effect the box was having on me that it had
driven all that out of my mind, until I suddenly remembered it.

You need to tell Svangerd, nagged a little voice in the back
of my head. Bullshit, I told it. She only needed to know if the
rat managed to find its way out of the jar. In the meantime, I
was doing her a favour by not telling her, since she tends to
fret when she thinks that instruments of pure evil are loose in
the vicinity. In fact, the only responsible thing I could possibly
do, at least until I'd reached an informed decision, was not tell
anyone. In my shoes, Svangerd would've taken responsibility
one step further, gone back to the shop and killed the owner;
bearing in mind what was at stake, for once she wouldn't be

overreacting. But I guess I'm basically childish and frivolous by nature, because as far as I was concerned, that would be one step too far.

If only I had a friend in Mavais I knew I could trust – but I didn't. Which meant the box was coming with us to Choris. Nuts.

3

"Where the hell did you get to?" she said. "And did you find us a boat?"

"The *Squirrel*," I told her: "ketch, a hundred and seventy-five tons, leaving here for Choris on the dawn tide, arriving Choris in three days. Two deniers each and we bring our own food. All right?"

"Three days on a poxy little ketch. Swell."

If I'd got us on a bigger, slower ship, she'd have moaned about the extra day. "Cheer up," I said. "It'll be fine. The only really tricky bit will be getting round Dagger Point, and after that it'll be plain sailing all the way. Trust me."

I'd already been round Dagger Point twice, though on both occasions it had been summer, and I suffered no more than a thorough drenching and a very mild concussion. It's not quite as easy in the spring. I don't know anything about sailing and navigation, but apparently there's a different sort of tide and a change in the direction of the wind, and you're liable to get caught between the pestle and the mortar, which

we were. The crew of the *Squirrel* were used to making the
run at that time of year and I don't suppose we were really in
any significant danger, except maybe once or twice, when the
foremast snapped and when a stupidly big wave nearly flipped
us over like a pancake. And, just as I'd promised her, after
Dagger Point it was all calm and nice, comparatively speaking.
Anyway, she was too busy dying to bother going through my
luggage (a habit of hers when she's bored), and so I didn't have
to worry about her finding the box.

"I've made up my mind," she said, as the white towers of
Choris Anthropou appeared on the skyline. "We're walking
back."

"No we—"

"Yes, we *are*," she said firmly. "I'm perfectly serious. If we go
north up to Olbia, then follow the coast round and then head
north-east up through Permia, it shouldn't take more than
eight months, and we'll stand a much better chance of getting
home alive. I mean it."

"All that fuss and nonsense over a bit of weather," I said.
"You need to get a grip if you want to stay in this line of work."

Everyone goes on about the beauty and grandeur of Choris
Anthropou, but I have to admit, I can take it or leave it alone.
You've got the core of the old imperial city, which is really
rather fine but not a patch on Mavais or Iden, if you ask me;
the rest of it is just narrow, cluttered streets of thatched wooden
houses, the only difference being that there's an awful lot more
of them than you'll find anywhere else. The Auzida smashed
up the old imperial aqueduct, so water is always a problem in
Choris. They've got more than a hundred wells, but over half
of them run dry in the summer, and nobody's ever figured out
a way of patching up the old imperial cisterns so they'll hold

water worth a damn. Consequently they fill up in the spring rains, then leak for a month or so, turning the streets under West Hill into a muddy nightmare, and by the time water's most needed, in the summer heat, they're bone dry. This means there's never any water available to put out fires, so if you've been away from Choris for more than a year or so, don't expect to be able to find your way round the maze of streets in Lower Town from memory, because large parts of it will have burned down and been rebuilt since you were last there. Stay away from Riverside unless you enjoy cholera, and don't go east of the Foundry under any circumstances. North Hill is where all the rich people live, merchants and goldsmiths and the men who own the factories and tanneries in South Port. They've colonised the ruins of the imperial suburb and done their best to rebuild them, which accounts for the rather weird blend of architectural styles – marble, granite and adobe in the same frontage, and late Principate town houses roofed with reed thatch – but the result is rather sad, if you ask me. Probably the most depressing sight in Choris is what used to be the Gardens of Florian, which is now the pen where the bear-baiters keep their stock in trade. They've built a massive wooden stockade, rather more defensible and much better maintained than the city wall, with fortified gatehouses every hundred yards and a regular patrol along the perimeter, to stop people breaking in and stealing the bears. The Hippodrome, where the emperors used to watch the chariot races, is now a sort of communal market garden, with the south end mostly used for rearing and training fighting cocks. Nobody's ever tried to rebuild the Golden Star or the Hope, so the only big temple still in regular use is the Pearl, which sprawls like a beached whale among the watercress sellers in Towngate. The dome is still intact, but at some point someone stripped all the gilded copper off the roof of the nave and replaced it with salvaged slates, which blew off because nobody understands slate roofing any more. These days it's reed thatch, with storks nesting in it and making a hell of a racket during the Eucharist.

Choris people don't mind any of that, of course, because it's what they've always known and they can't imagine anything different. For someone like me, though, who knows Choris from the descriptions in thousand-year-old books, it's all a bit depressing. You feel like you've come home, but home is a desolate ruin; the trees have been cut down, the damp's got in behind the plaster, and nobody could be bothered to do anything about it. But Choris natives think it's the most glorious place in the world, and the giants who built it roofed the Pearl with thatch because that's what you make roofs out of; and besides, Choris thatch is by definition better than any thatch anywhere else in the world, and if you don't agree you know what you can do.

The other thing about Choris is the smell. It takes eighteen months to get used to it, apparently, and then you don't notice it at all.

"This place stinks," she said. "It's like one big shitheap."

"Yes," I said, "but maybe you shouldn't say so quite so loud, or people might think you're being unkind about their city. That over there," I said, pointing, "is the Theatre of Athanaric. Or at least, that's where it used to be."

"I don't like this town," she said. "I came here when I was nineteen. I didn't like it much then."

She never talks about her life before she joined the order – understandably, I guess. That, therefore, constituted an almost unprecedented confidence and outpouring of her inner soul, suggesting she was in a good mood, in spite of the smell. "I'm not crazy about it myself," I said. "Right, if that's the theatre, we need to head up the hill as far as Coppermarket, at which point we should be able to see Old Town above us on our left."

"If you say so," she said. "What've you got in that sack?"

"Nothing. Just a few old books I bought in Mavais."

Which was, of course, strictly speaking true. After a couple of false starts, we emerged from the thatch-and-timber thickets into the broad, paved streets of the old city. North of Horsefair and inside the old inner wall you're quite high up and the smell isn't nearly so bad. There are fewer people in the streets, and they tend to be better dressed and not quite so liable to murder you for the nails in your boots. Also, you can see where you're going. "That big white thing over there," I said, pointing. "That's the watchtower of the citadel, which backs onto the university, which is where we're going."

The university was founded fifteen hundred years ago by Basiliscus II, to be a meeting place and centre of excellence for scholars from all across the empire. A century before the Fall, Bauderic gave it to Holy Mother Church, and these days it's a beehive of busy clerics, mostly accountants and their clerks, recording the receipts from the outer dioceses and paying it over to the various stipendiary prelates who live in Choris full time and do whatever it is they do, to the greater glory of the Invincible Sun. The university houses the biggest and most comprehensive collection of nephews, brothers-in-law and off-relations of noble houses to be found anywhere on earth, and accounts for two-thirds of the revenues of our Holy Mother. There's also a library, which you can't get into without a special pass signed by a bishop, a hall of records and the Chapter House, formerly the summer palace of Genseric the Wise. That's where all the ecumenical councils have been held. It's the only building still standing this side of Echmen big enough to hold that many delegates, and it's always been my life's ambition to get inside it.

"This isn't what I was expecting," she said, as we took our place in a line outside the Chapter House gate. "We may need to think of another plan."

The same thought had occurred to me. My plan was founded on the descriptions in old books which I told you about earlier, but I could see at a glance that it wasn't going to work. The Chapter House, according to the books, boasts a dome, built by the legendary Pauscinna, sheathed in gold and visible for miles around because of its unique height. I looked at the Chapter House. There was no dome.

"Oh, that," said the man next to us in the queue, when I asked him if he knew what had become of it. "It collapsed about forty years ago. They've got what's left of the roof shored up with timbers and covered over with oilskins, and I think there's a committee working on how to fix it permanently. I gather that when it fell in, it took out the whole of the upper storeys. A great pity, but what can you do?"

"A nuisance," I agreed. "So what are they doing about accommodation for the delegates?"

"I gather we're supposed to make shift for ourselves," he replied. "I'm all right because I've got a guest room at the consulate. How about you?"

After we'd presented our credentials to the clerks and been accepted as bona fide delegates, we went looking for somewhere to stay. Since I'd been to Choris before and knew the ropes, it didn't take me very long.

"It's a hayloft," she said.

"Nothing wrong with a nice hayloft," I said. "It's warm and dry and there's plenty of soft, sweet-smelling hay, and we can afford it and there's absolutely nothing else. We're lucky to have found it. You heard the man. There's bishops sleeping in doorways all over town. Well, archdeacons, at any rate."

Because I'd solved the problem, by finding us a nice hayloft, everything to do with accommodations automatically became my fault. I've noticed this tendency before, and it explains a great deal about the world and human life. Why would anyone want to fix anything when you get punished so severely just for trying? "We're going to look like idiots," she said the next morning, doing her best to get the wisps of hay off her habit. "And you know what that means? We'll be conspicuous. And the one thing in the world we can't afford to be—"

"There'll be loads of others in the same boat," I said. "I take it you haven't come up with a plan yet."

"Don't be stupid. How can I plan anything when we haven't even set foot inside the place?"

I'd been hoping she'd say that, because it meant we'd spend the first session of the council sitting peacefully on a bench listening to the speeches, rather than sneaking around throttling guards and getting arrested. The first item was the keynote address, given by our target, the princess. After that, there was to be an open debate between Hrabanus and Luitbrand of Nissenbracht on the essential unity of the Word, which I was determined not to miss. Hrabanus, as you know as well as I do, maintains that because the Word was with the Invincible Sun and the Word was the Invincible Sun, it naturally follows that they are indivisible in essence and substance. Luitbrand, however, contends that once uttered, the Word was both united with and separated from the speaker, and must therefore represent two substances sharing one essence. Since Caradacus would be speaking in support of the motion, and Beppa of Stachel was bound to weigh in against it, we were in for a real treat, and I didn't want to miss a single word, nuance or impassioned gesture.

So we filed in to the Chapter House, which was hot and smelled the way you'd expect a building to smell when crammed with a thousand men and women in thick wool robes. We wanted to see without being seen, so we stayed at the back and stood up so we could look over people's heads.

The Chapter House was built under the empire and I imagine that it was once a miracle of applied acoustics. The collapse of the dome spoiled all that, of course, so from where we were, we could barely make out anything the princess said in her opening address. No big deal – a positive, in fact, as far as I was concerned, since it wouldn't have made it any easier for me to kill her if I'd been thrilled to the marrow by her eloquence and wisdom. Instead, we got a reasonably clear view of her at a distance of maybe a hundred yards; enough to be sure we'd recognise her and not go killing the wrong woman out of ignorance, as has been known to happen. What I saw was a shortish, stoutish woman with short grey hair, who stood up perfectly straight and talked to a thousand very important people like an officer addressing troops. There was no hint of hesitation or nerves, nor did she make any effort to show off or play to the gallery. The impression she gave was of a woman who wasn't afraid of anybody and didn't need anything from anyone because she had it all already. Not somebody you could ever bring yourself to like, but if she told you to do something, you'd do it, not because she was scary or gorgeous but because you'd naturally assume it was the right thing to do.

After her speech there was a recess, to give everybody a chance to flood out into the cloisters and breathe. "Well," Svangerd asked me, "what do you reckon?"

"You first," I said.

"She walks with a slight limp, so she's probably not too fast on her feet," she said, "but did you see the way she lifted that heavy book on and off the lectern? I'd say she has better than average upper body strength for a woman her age. Good hearing, too. Someone dropped something and made a noise right at the back, and she heard it and stopped for a moment. She's short-sighted, because I saw her peering at the book, but that may mean she's got good eyesight at longer distances. I don't think she scares easily, but she notices things. She was constantly looking about her while she was speaking. And she's got a loud voice, good lung-power, because she wasn't shouting but I could hear every word."

"Could you? What did she say?"

"What? Oh, the usual stuff."

Svangerd has ears like a bat. "What usual stuff?"

"Oh, I don't know. I wasn't paying attention."

I'd been paying attention, but all that useful information about our target had gone over my head like a flock of geese. I was about to ask her for more details when someone tapped me on the shoulder, and I heard my name being muttered in my ear. Not my name in religion. The one I was born with.

I glanced over my shoulder and saw a short, bald man in a plain brown habit. "I'd like to talk to you," he said. "About a box."

The delegates were starting to move back into the main hall. "You go on," I said to Svangerd. "I'll catch you up."

She looked at me. "But you particularly wanted to hear—"

"Won't be a minute," I said.

She looked at me again, and whatever she saw in my face was enough to persuade her. Terror, probably, tinged by the sort of desperation that could easily turn to violence if she did anything to hinder me. "Don't be long," she said. "I'll take notes."

Everyone had gone back inside. Just me and the short man, in the empty cloister.

"What box?" I said.

"You know what box," he replied. He had a mild, soft face, the sort you instinctively feel sure you can get the better of, a fairly nondescript city accent and very small hands with short, stubby fingers. "Why don't we sit down? I rather like this cloister. It reminds me of the old days."

Something told me that this man and I were not destined to be great friends. I don't know what. One of those pesky instincts, probably. "I don't know anything about any box."

"Right now," he said, "it's wedged into a little space where the rafters meet the floorboards in a hayloft over a stable behind the More Joy in Heaven in Cat Street. You piled up some loose hay round it so she won't see it. You're afraid that if she does, she'll insist on it being destroyed. You don't want that, but you have very mixed feelings about the box." He smiled at me. "If you want to carry on denying it, please feel free. But we both know the truth."

"All right," I said. "Who are you?"

"I think you can probably figure that out for yourself."

"You're overestimating my intelligence. Tell me."

"In so many words?" Something was amusing him. "It's all right," he went on. "I'm not going to take your precious box away from you. If I'd wanted it, I'd have gone round to the

More Joy and helped myself. But it's still there. You can run back and make sure if you like. In a minute, after we've had our talk."

"You're not who you say you are," I said.

"I never said anything."

"You can't be," I said, "because they don't exist. They're a myth. Legend, superstition and old wives' tales. The opiate of the masses."

He was enjoying talking to me, I could tell. There was a tiny smirk on his face that meant pure harmless entertainment. "I exist," he said, and before I could move, he lifted one hand off his knee and slapped me across the face with it. "See? Pretty solid, for an illusion."

I have fast, trained reflexes. They hadn't been nearly fast enough. Any harder and he'd have drawn blood, but they're not allowed to do that, so people say. "All right," I said. "You're real. Proves nothing. *I'm* real, for crying out loud, but that doesn't make me an angel. Why are you pretending to be an entirely legendary, mythical monster?"

"Monster." His eyes twinkled. "If you don't believe in us, why call us names? You can't hate and fear something that doesn't exist. Well, you can, but it's silly. Maybe that lovingly crafted scepticism of yours needs repointing where it's starting to crumble." The smirk widened into a grin. "Now you're going to bluster and act all tough and ask me how I know about the box. But you know perfectly well how I know. Don't you?"

He was making my skin crawl. Not much does that. "I don't believe," I said, "in the Invincible Sun. Therefore it follows that I don't believe in the Loyal Opposition. The same goes for dragons, unicorns, elves, angels, revenants, little men in Ostar who hop around on one foot with their faces in the middle of their chests, or goblins or the Tooth Fairy. Accordingly, any explanation of perceived events that relies on elements of the supernatural must, by definition, be false. Got that?"

He nodded. "Blessed are those who have seen and yet have not believed," he said. "It takes a special kind of idiot, and you know what, I rather like special people. So much so that I'm prepared to overlook the word *monster*, which is denigratory and probably counts as hate speech. I shall try not to let it sour what I hope will be a long and fruitful working relationship."

I jumped up, then sat down again. "Quite," he said. "There's no call to get all worked up, because of course I can't be what I say I am. Though, for the record, I haven't said anything. Have I?"

"What," I said, "do you want?"

"Ah." Broad smile. "That's better. So much more business-like than all that silly posturing. What do I want? Well, let's see. This is mostly just a chance for me to introduce myself, getting to know you, that sort of thing."

"Why would you want to do that?"

"It's the natural thing to do. I've been assigned as your new case worker, and I believe in being absolutely upfront and honest about who I am and what I do, whenever that's possible. I don't sneak about watching people through keyholes and cracks in shutters. I walk up to them, shake hands and say hello."

He stuck out his hand. I'm not in the least bothered by spiders. Svangerd is, and maybe you are; in which case, imagine you're lying on your back with your head clamped in a vice so it can't move, and there's a spider walking about on your face. A bit like that. "You can do what you damned well like," I said. "I have no idea how you found out about the box, and I don't care. Just stay out of my way or so help me I'll smash your face in. Understood?"

He turned his head ninety degrees to the left, then back again, then ninety degrees to the right. "The other cheek," he explained. "It means, go ahead and hit me if it'll make you feel any better. Go on, there's nobody looking. You look like thumping somebody would do you good. I won't make a fuss or report you to the magistrate."

I noticed that my right fist was clenched. I opened it slowly. "Fine," I said. "You don't want anything, except to play games and risk a broken jaw. You know about the box but you don't want it. What do you want? My soul?"

He rolled his eyes. "That's a stupid misconception," he said, "which we really don't like to see encouraged. We don't go around stealing people's souls, like pickpockets at a fair. We're in it for the long game, as you perfectly well know." He paused, then smiled again. "Sorry," he said, "it's a bit of a sore topic. Feel free to needle me about it if you wish, but we both know the score."

I looked at him. I felt like I wanted to strip off all my flesh with a bit of broken glass and wash my bones in lye. "Have you finished?" I said. "Can I go now?"

"Your friend."

"What about her?"

He beamed. "It's really rather cute," he said. "You – let's say, you admire her tremendously. But you're a virgin; you joined the order when you were twelve years old; the lusts of the flesh intrigue you and terrify you in roughly equal measure and if a woman were to put her hand up your habit you'd run a mile. She, on the other hand—"

"Stop it."

"She, on the other hand, got sold to a whorehouse at more or less the same age as you joined the order, so her perspective on the act of love is rather different from yours, and considerably better informed. If you ever lay a finger on her she'll snap it off like a carrot, but because you're a man, not specifically because you're you. Actually, she's amazingly healthy and well-adjusted considering what she's been through, which can only be attributed to her faith, which is pure and clear and absolutely indestructible. Oh, sorry, did you want to hit me? I'll try and keep still."

I wanted to hit him, very much. "Is there any point to this?" I said. "Or are you just enjoying yourself?"

"Guilty as charged." He shrugged. "I'm sorry, but you asked for it. In future, let's make it easy for each other and try and do without all the posturing. In a posturing match I'm bound to win, and it gives me no pleasure. How does that sound?"

"Tell me what you want," I said, "and then for God's sake leave me alone."

"For God's sake," he repeated. "Just a common expression or formula, so I won't hold you to it, this time. I think I told you what I wanted. I'm just saying hello, making myself known to you. After all, we're supposed to be diplomats, aren't we?"

I'd been too busy feeling disgusted to think. The way he said *supposed*.

"You're here to murder somebody," he went on. "Which is absolutely fine by us, by the way. Not because it's murder, but because it'll advance the medium-term strategy and bring us one step closer to a number of objectives. We could reach those objectives by a whole heap of other methods, of course, so we don't really care one way or another. So you can set your mind at rest, we won't be interfering. You carry on, and best of luck to you. I'd go a step further and say, if there's anything we can do to help, feel free to ask. But I don't suppose you'd like that. No, thought not. Ah well. The offer stands, in case you change your mind." He gave me a wicked look. "Out of interest," he said, "are you going to tell her about this conversation?"

"No. Of course not."

"Really? I'd have thought she's got a right to know. Still, that's between you and your conscience. I imagine she'd hit the roof if she ever found out you'd kept it from her. Lucky for you, you're the designated point of contact, so I only get to talk to you, not her."

"I'd stay clear of her if I were you," I said. "If you told her all that stuff, she'd cut your head off."

"Which is probably why you're the designated point of contact," he said. "Well, that explains that, then. Actually, I'd sort of figured that out for myself." He stood up. "Will you just look at the time," he said. "I've been nattering away, and you've missed the debate you particularly wanted to hear. Sorry about that. It was thoughtless of me. Tell you what, I'll have a transcript made and sent to you. Not quite the same thing as seeing it live, but better than nothing."

"No, thank you."

"Suit yourself. It was actually really rather good. Beppa made a point about the dual procession of the unified essence that left Caradacus without a leg to stand on. Still, spilled milk and all that. Be seeing you."

"I do not believe," I said, "in the Loyal Opposition."

"Bless you, my child. And stay well clear of the fermented cabbage. You know it doesn't agree with you."

I tried to grab him, but he slipped past my hand as though it wasn't there and walked sedately to the door that leads into the Mercy Chapel. I ran after him but I couldn't see him anywhere.

"It was a lot of theological stuff," she told me. "Boring, and a bit blasphemous, if you ask me. People shouldn't talk about that sort of thing; it's not respectful."

"Did Beppa disprove Caradacus' position on the dual procession of the unified essence? Come on, it's important."

She yawned. "Well, he said something that made everybody start clapping, and the man he'd been arguing with looked daggers at him. Why's it important? And who was that short man you were talking to?"

I wanted to tell her so much. But if I did, I knew what the result would be. Sister Svangerd isn't afraid of anything, but the agencies of Evil terrify her. Which isn't a contradiction. The agencies of Evil don't exist, therefore they're not a thing, therefore she's not afraid of any thing. Even so, I needed her sharp and at the top of her game if we were to get out of Choris alive, not cowering in front of an altar with her rosary gripped between her fingers. "I don't know," I said. "He was making out he's on to us, but I don't think he really knows anything."

I had her attention. "You clown," she said. "If he knows what we're here for, we've got to get rid of him. Who's he working for?"

I shrugged. "He wasn't easy to get information out of," I said.

"Bet I could."

"Probably not a good idea," I said. "We really don't want to draw attention to ourselves unless we absolutely have to. He didn't know anything, trust me. He was just fishing."

"You've gone and made a mess of everything," she said. "What did you tell him?"

"Absolutely nothing."

"All right, let me think." She sat down on the same stone bench he'd sat on, closed her eyes and put her head in her hands. For Svangerd, thinking is a physical activity. "All right," she said. "He's on to us, but he doesn't know what we're going to do or when we're going to do it, because we haven't decided that for ourselves yet. He's not security or he'd have had us arrested. That means he belongs to somebody else. Someone who wants the princess kept alive, but isn't security. So why not just go to the guard captain and tell him who we are and have us locked up?" She looked at me, inviting input. I kept my mouth shut. "Because he's in the game too, presumably, and he's up to something and doesn't want to break cover." She scowled. "This is useless. You should've guzzled him while you had the chance."

"In the cloister," I said. "With a thousand delegates a few yards away."

"Perfect opportunity, actually," she said. "I'd have sworn blind you were sitting next to me during the debate, only you fell asleep, which is why you can't tell anyone what was said. It wouldn't stand up to a proper investigation, but it doesn't have to. You should've done him and dropped the body in that cistern over there. That'd have been the sensible thing."

"Yes, well, I didn't do it, so there we go." The delegates were starting to flow back to the main hall. "If I see him again, I'll point him out to you. Meanwhile, we really need to figure out how we're going to do this thing. My idea is clearly a washout, so we'd better think of something else."

"I'll think of something else," she said firmly. "You've made enough messes for one day."

The next item was a debate on the proposed amendments to the Ordinary Creed, with Megabazus proposing the motion and Gudmund the Weasel opposing it with every fibre of his considerable being. As a display of intellectual and rhetorical athletics, it was like watching a prize fight between two arch-angels, but I have to confess my attention wandered. I had a bad feeling about pretty much everything, and I tried to escape from it by focusing on practicalities. Where would the princess go between sessions, where was she sleeping at night, how many guards were there, did she eat alone or in company, could we maybe get to her while she was on the toilet, that sort of bread-and-butter stuff that usually responds so well to me-thodical analysis. Try as I might, however, I couldn't focus. I caught myself framing the same questions over and over again, and then drifting away into half-formed uneasy speculation. Was I wrong, about the Invincible Sun and ghosts and spooks and goblins and all that stuff? I knew I wasn't, but sometimes knowing isn't enough.

Here's a case in point. I grew up in the Mesoge; enough said. Actually, we were a cut above the neighbours; we were head tenants rather than serfs, we lived in a proper house with an upper room which you reached by a ladder, my father had ten men working for him as well as his sons and nobody ever went hungry at our place, not even at midwinter. But I'm from the Mesoge, a fact I've never tried to conceal, and I lived there till I was twelve years old. In the Mesoge you're all grown up at that age, and eighteen years later you're probably dead. The Mesoge uses people up the way a carthorse gets through shoes;

it doesn't matter, because there's always plenty more where they came from.

Nothing comes easily in the Mesoge, and there are two kinds of special pest, which can make all the difference between pulling through and going under. Both of these pests do more or less the same things. They're both eight feet tall and horrendously strong. They roam about in the wilderness, and God help you if you happen to run into one. If you're lucky, they'll rip your arm off or crunch your leg into splinters. During the day they tend to avoid human settlements unless they're hungry or desperate, but at night they like to snoop around farmyards and cattle-pens, and get up on the roofs of houses. Their principal weapons are their claws, and they can run faster than any man.

One of these pests, the bear, is fairly widely spread across the rest of the known world. Our bears are black. They have brown bears in Olbia, grey bears in Sashan and Echmen, and I gather there's a sort of golden-yellow bear in Blemmya, though it's comparatively small and inoffensive and tastes quite like pork.

The other sort of pest (we call them walkers) is strictly a Mesoge phenomenon. Walkers are human, or at least they were while they were alive. In the Mesoge we have a saying: too mean to die. If you're thoroughly disagreeable and antisocial during your life, chances are you'll be back, and the Great Change won't have improved you very much. It's next thing to impossible to kill you since you're dead already, so you don't really give a damn. The tendency runs in families, and all the families in the Old Country are hopelessly interrelated and interbred. My great-uncle on my mother's side was a walker. For all I know, he still is.

Holy Mother Church categorises bears as natural and walkers as an abomination, meaning supernatural in origin and deliberately created by Evil for a malign purpose. This means that if your landlord is an abbey or a bishopric and you get attacked by walkers, they're obliged to send somebody, but if you've got bears, you have to cope with them yourself.

I think the distinction is fatuous. As far as I'm concerned, they're both just wildlife, a commodity in which the Mesoge is deplorably rich. I'm also absolutely convinced that a thousand years ago, under the old empire, they knew of a perfectly rational scientific reason why certain families in the Mesoge don't stay dead when they die, and almost certainly explained the reason quite clearly and conclusively in a book, which has since been lost. The walker phenomenon certainly raises some interesting points about the nature of life and death, which I'm sure the imperial philosophers explored and sorted out with their usual thoroughness, but does it prove anything about Good and Evil, God and the devil? I don't think so. I have no patience with superstition, the supernatural or anything else that begins with super-, as I think I may already have hinted, and I see no need to drag Evil into it, particularly since I don't think it exists.

Svangerd could probably kill a bear, if she had the right kit handy. She'd certainly give it her very best shot. But a walker would paralyse her with fear, assuming she'd been told in advance what it was, and that it was somehow supernatural in origin. Back home, we don't give a damn. You're just as dead if you get scrunched up by a bear, and bears are almost as difficult to deal with, though mostly they stay dead after you've done with them. Actually, the contingency never arises, since bear is good eating. I don't recall anyone ever trying to eat a walker, not even during a famine year.

The point being, I believe in walkers, as a natural but unexplained phenomenon. I have to believe, since I grew up with them. They're a fact of life, like thunderstorms – which some people regard as indisputable proof of the existence of God, and which I treat as bad weather. Or the Sun. It's God or a bright thing in the sky, depending on your level of ignorance and credulity.

These days we write, those few of us who can, all our letters the same size. Under the empire, they went through a phase of writing the first letters of sentences and people's names a bit bigger, though it didn't last very long. Accordingly, you could turn a word into a name by sticking a Big Letter in front of it. For instance, you could write sun as Sun. Doing that made the bright thing in the sky into a name, then a person, then God. You'll have noticed that I've adopted this mannerism myself, partly out of antiquarian interest, partly to show what tricks you can play with people's heads just by altering the height of a letter. It's still just a trick, though, same as religion, and if I can do it, so can any bloody fool.

"I've decided," she said. "We do it tomorrow morning, early. We sneak in, we guzzle the princess, we're out of here and on our way before anyone has a chance to put two and two together." She paused and looked at me. "You're not making difficulties. Why?"

"Because you haven't told me the details yet."

"Fine. All right, how about this? In our order, the first office of the day is lauds. She'll be there, naturally, in the Lady Chapel. I've had a scout around, and to get to the chapel from anywhere outside the building, you've got to go through a fairly narrow cloister. Now there's a window, looking out onto the cloister garden. We wait in the garden, then when she and her goons process down the corridor and get to the narrow point, all we've got to do is hop in through the window, do the guzzle, then run away like fuck the way we came in. We may have to waste a few guards, I don't know, but in a confined space it's nothing we can't handle. You can beat up on the guards while I do the actual guzzling, or the other way round if you like, doesn't make any odds to me. What do you think?"

"Fine," I said.

She stared at me. "You what?"

"It sounds like a good idea. A basic blind canyon manoeuvre, like Calojan at the Laban Forks. And you've got an escape route, which is always nice, and the early hours of the morning is a good time. We might be able to get a couple of berths on a boat leaving on the dawn tide, and then we'd be out of town before anyone comes looking for us. Definitely one of your better plans."

"What's the matter with you?" she said.

She knows me quite well. "Nothing," I said.

"Bullshit. What's the matter?"

"Nothing. On balance, I think you're right. You do the killing while I hold off the guards. You know what I'm like, I might make a mess of it."

She had that worried look. "Fine," she said. "That's what we'll do, then. Meanwhile, you go and find us a boat. I'll have another look round, see what I can find out about her morning routine. Won't be easy, because I don't want to rattle any cages, but I should be able to get something out of the chapel novices. And I'll plan us a route from the gardens to the street. There may be a wall to climb, or perhaps we can duck out through the stable yard."

"I'll leave all that to you," I said.

As I think I mentioned before, she isn't scared of anything, but she worries. "You sure you're feeling all right?"

"Never better."

I walked down to the docks, pausing in a deserted alley to make a few changes to my costume. The monastic habit is a wonderfully versatile thing. Just by swapping the leather belt for a piece of old rope and turning in the facings of the cowl, you can go from being a distinguished scholar to a street-corner mendicant friar in a matter of seconds. I made a point of kneeling in some mud and getting dirt on my sleeve, and then I was ready to go.

I try and keep my ears open wherever I am, so I'd already picked up the useful fact that the herring boats put out to sea just before first light. I found the skipper of one such boat in a dockside bar and asked him if he'd mind giving me and a poor sister a lift as far as the crab-fishing station on Long Spit, which is six miles off the coast. He looked at me and said no. I showed him two deniers. He said yes. See you in the morning, I said, and left the bar.

So far so good. That was the boat we wouldn't be taking. I'd made a point of talking quite loudly, and the poor-friar character I'd assumed wouldn't have been nearly so free with clinking money; when the watch came looking for suspicious characters boarding boats in the early hours of next morning, I was pretty sure they'd remember me.

Leaving a little later was a wine cog, shipping bulk Olbian white to Scona. From Scona, we could easily get a boat to Mavais, or somewhere else, depending on how hot we'd made things for ourselves by that point. The cog's master was sorry but he couldn't spare deck space for a couple of freeloaders. I whined and said that he'd get his reward in heaven. We haggled, and ended up agreeing on his reward in heaven plus three farthings, which is exactly the sort of deal you'd expect a genuine friar to make. Fleeing assassins don't bicker over halfpence. That was the boat we'd be on.

I stopped on my way back to Old Town to dust off my knees and sleeve, turn out my hood and change my belt, then I was just in time to catch the tail end of the debate between Melboin and Gundarius on the physics of transubstantiation. It was vintage stuff from two theological giants I've always idolised, and I didn't follow a word of it. My mind was on other things.

As we were filing out of the Chapter House, I caught sight of the short man. He saw me and smiled, and then I lost sight of him behind someone's shoulder.

4

"A job for Aliz, I think," she said.

Aliz is her name for a seven-inch artilleryman's stiletto, one of her most treasured possessions. It's a narrow, square section length of best Olbian steel, tapering to a needlepoint; the blade is marked at one-inch intervals, the idea being that catapult crews use them for measuring the diameter of stone balls. She likes it because she can tell at a glance how far she's stuck it into some poor devil's neck. I think the idea of giving a name to a weapon is morbid bordering on grotesque. It's one of those points on which we long ago agreed to differ.

"Good choice," I said.

That disconcerted her more than ever. "Fine," she said. "What are you taking?"

"Me? Nothing. I don't know what we're likely to face, so whatever I choose will probably be wrong, and I don't want to lumber myself with unnecessary kit if I've got to climb walls in the dark. If needs be I can thump somebody and take what they've got. Talking of which, have you got any rope?"

"Of course."

"Of course you have. I was only making conversation."

I was working on a couple of passes. In order to be on the spot bright and early, we needed to stay in the chantry after vespers and wait there till the bell went for lauds. But if something went wrong with that, we'd need to be able to get back into the main basilica between midnight and third watch, and all I could think of on that score was a couple of diplomatic tickets which a guard wouldn't think to question. All I could come up with was a pair of letters of identity, from Abbot Simocatta (because I happened to have a fake copy of his seal matrix in the toe of my left boot; no idea how it got there) to the princess's personal chaplain. I knew for a fact that the abbot and the chaplain didn't know each other and had never had occasion to correspond, but a junior guard captain on the night shift wouldn't know that. He'd see the big seal and the strained expressions on our faces, and think of the trouble he'd be in if he screwed up some important diplomatic deal, and that would be enough to get us past the door and out through the vestry window.

The seal was right, because I'd faked it myself. The parchment was right, because I'd helped myself to a full sheet from Simocatta's clerk's desk while he was away taking a pee: likewise the ink and the wax. That just left the handwriting. I was taking exceptional care over that, even though my putative guard captain would never have seen an example of Simocatta's clerk's fist, because a convincing forgery must always be perfect. Otherwise, you can guarantee that the most unlikely people will sense there's something wrong, and then you're in real trouble.

Exceptional care in this instance meant writing fast, because that's what Simocatta's clerk would have done. Writing fast and with extreme care is a neat trick, which it's taken me years to master. Svangerd isn't the only obsessive craftsman in our little outfit.

"You'll need to crease those up a bit, make them look like they've been carried around in a pocket."

I gave her my sour look. "What you do, Grandma," I said, "is you make a hole in the pointed end with a sharp instrument, taking care not to fracture the shell—"

"What are you talking about?"

"Grandmothers and sucking eggs. Go and sharpen something, I'm trying to concentrate."

Fact is, I'd been trying to concentrate ever since I talked to the short man, but with a deplorable lack of success. I'd reached the stage where I was shouting down the little voice at the back of my head; the next step would be to send in the troops and have it arrested. I had this mental image of Svangerd smiling at me in a patronising fashion, and encouraging me to have faith, like she did. I hate faith. It's the antithesis of reason and everything the old empire stood for. I would be bitterly ashamed if I thought I was guilty of it, especially faith in atheism.

Once the passes were dry I made a point of creasing them up real good, leaving them looking as though they'd been run over by a cart loaded with masonry blocks. I gave her one and tucked the other in my sleeve. "How do I look?" she said.

"Convincing," I told her, the highest compliment you can pay in our line of work.

"I decided against the rope," she said. "If we get caught and searched, we couldn't explain it away."

Under other circumstances I'd have kicked up a fuss, but

I couldn't be bothered. "Have it your way," I said. "Are you ready?"

"Yup."

"Right, then." I realised I wasn't even scared, which disturbed me considerably. "We'd better go."

She didn't move. "What's the matter with you? Come on, I need to know. What's got into you lately?"

"Nothing, really. Toothache."

She peered at me. "Why didn't you say? Well, that's not a problem. Ten seconds and a pair of tongs. If you'd said earlier, I could've fixed it for you, easy as pie."

The basilica was crowded for vespers. We sat at the back, behind a pillar. Waltharius of Schanz gave the sermon, on a text from Symmachus' *Patristics*, but we were in the dead spot and I couldn't make out a word he said. When the service was over, we flattened ourselves against the back of the pillar and stayed in the shadows until the vergers killed the lamps and locked the main and side doors. Piece of cake.

"We'd better go and make sure the door to the cloisters is still open," she hissed in my ear. "I didn't hear the bolt get shot, but I don't want any awkward surprises."

She's much better than me at finding her way silently in the dark. I followed, holding the end of her belt. "The door's open," she assured me. "We're fine. Now we just sit here till we hear the matins bell."

Simple as that. "Don't fall asleep," I told her.

"Piss off."

No chance of me falling asleep, at any rate. To keep from thinking about what I didn't want to think about, I thought about various things: Marduin's commentaries on Procopius, the height of the cloister garden wall, digging a drain with my brothers across the back meadow when I was ten, the small scar on the side of Svangerd's neck, the melody of the plainsong in the melismatic Gloria, how I'd set about making an undetectable copy of the White Book of Uisbach. All that got me was an intense feeling of unease and a mild but persistent headache; also, one of my back teeth started to throb, which if nothing else proves that teeth have a sense of humour.

At some point I realised she was muttering under her breath. I made a special effort and listened. She was praying, fast and intense: the general confession and the pleas for intercession, over and over again. And why not, I thought. It was something to listen to, so I listened.

What with one thing and another, I'd forgotten that there's a genuine Mezentine clockwork clock in the basilica at Choris, probably the last working example in the world, unless there's one in Echmen somewhere. The chime is broken, of course, but every hour on the hour it makes a dull thunking noise, where the hammer hits the spot of empty air where the bell used to be, and the base of the hammer arm slams into the receiver. The first time it did it, we both jumped out of our skins. The second time, we didn't mind. Then we sat waiting for the next one, like slaves or kids waiting to be hit.

We never got to hear it. Instead, we heard yelling, people running about, someone in a high, scared voice shouting orders we couldn't quite make out. We both recognised that kind of row. It's what you usually get when someone like us has done something, and the proper authorities discover the body.

"Oh, for crying out loud," she said. "Now what?"

I tried to think, but the noise got in the way. "Abort," I said. "This is no bloody good."

She thought for maybe three seconds, then said, "Agreed. Let's get out of here."

"No. We don't know where anyone is or what's going on. We sit tight until the yelling's stopped, then we head for the cloister."

"Right."

It was a bad place for us to be in the circumstances, but I felt a wave of relief that made me feel light-headed. I'd been let off murdering a princess, if only for a few hours. That's a good feeling.

The noise went on for a long time, and I started to worry. I really didn't fancy the idea of soldiers making a thorough search of the basilica. "Changed my mind," I said. "Let's go."

She swore at me quietly, and I carefully opened the cloister door. It had one of those tongue-and-bar latches that make a noise like a cavalry battle if you drop them too quickly. My hands were shaking, but I managed it. Out into the air – it was too dark to see any difference, but there was a fresh draught coming up the cloister, which I felt on my face, and the stale-incense-and-musty-old-soft-furnishings smell was gone, so we were outside. Then it was a simple matter of feeling for and locating the garden side of the cloister wall, and following that until we found our window. Through that, and we were in pale moonlight. That made me wince and her swear; it was light enough to show us up when we moved, if anyone was watching. But the shouting and running about was further away than it had been when we were in the basilica; meaningless, of course, because there could be patrols anywhere, if they were looking for someone.

Under such circumstances, I tend to abdicate responsibility and follow where Svangerd leads. She makes some really bad decisions in such cases, but she can see in the dark much better than I can, so she knows when someone's coming. She darted off like a cat; I followed her.

Amazingly, we got across the cloister garden without any trouble and reached the base of the wall. It was much higher than it had looked from a distance, when I checked it out earlier. Rope would've been really useful. I didn't say anything.

Some people have the charming habit of setting splinters of broken pottery in mortar on the tops of walls. The trouble is, with a high wall, you don't know till you get there. The idea is, you take a heavy blanket with you, to lay over the sharp edges. We didn't have a heavy blanket. But we did have my habit.

It was almost dark enough for me not to mind stripping down to bare skin with Svangerd tutting impatiently next to me, but not quite. It's all right, I told myself, and total humiliation is the least of your potential problems, but I wasn't convinced. So sue me. I'm not used to being naked.

She looped my habit round her neck, then shinned up the wall like a squirrel. I followed, slowly and with enormous difficulty; there were cracks in the pointing, big enough for her slim fingers and tiny feet, largely inadequate for mine. She pulled me up the last couple of feet. There were no potsherds on top of the wall, but I guess you can't be too careful.

I lowered her as far as my habit-sleeves would go and she dropped the rest. I threw the habit down after her, then swung myself over and scrabbled with my toes for a foothold. There wasn't one. I was still looking when my fingertips gave way. I slid down the wall, with the bricks rasping the skin off my kneecaps and stomach. How I didn't break a bone or two when I landed I have no idea.

I insisted on taking a moment to put my clothes back on,

even though she hissed at me. Then we were off, her running and me hobbling painfully on an excruciating twisted ankle, following the wall until we came to the stable block. At which point I tripped over something, went sprawling and felt my head crack into something very solid.

I assume I must have taken a nap at that point, because I remember waking up. There were men standing around looking down at me. Svangerd and a man were kneeling beside me, and the hem of my habit was up under my chin.

"Look what they did to him," Svangerd was sobbing. "There was nothing I could do; they just kept hitting him."

"How many of them were there?" someone asked.

"Three, no, I think it was four. It was so dark, and it happened so quickly."

The man kneeling beside me looked horribly military; a guard lieutenant, at a guess, in a padded gambeson with rust stains – I could see them quite clearly, so someone must've had a lantern – and one of those round flowerpot felt hats they wear under helmets. I couldn't see the other men so well, but I was pretty sure they were the lieutenant's patrol. Joy unbounded.

"I'm guessing," the officer said, over his shoulder, presumably to his sergeant, "that they came from the cloister garden, shinned over the wall and came down hereabouts. Spread out and take a look. They're probably long gone, but you never know."

The soldiers disappeared from the circle of light, leaving me, Svangerd and the lieutenant. A great deal now depended on how bright the lieutenant was. If he was smart, the kind of young man destined to go far in the service, he'd figure out that my injuries weren't the sort of thing you get from being beaten up, but were entirely consistent with sliding down a brick wall – in which case, he probably had just under a minute to live. If he was a bit dumb and rattled by all the fuss and still half asleep, he stood a fair chance of staying alive. Which only goes to show that Saloninus' famous theory of the survival of the fittest sounds very fine but doesn't actually work in practice.

Time for me to do something, though I really didn't feel like it. I stood up, dragging my habit down as I did so. "What happened?" I said. "Who were those men?"

The officer looked at me doubtfully, then made up his mind. "Get him to a doctor," he told her. "I think he's all right, but that bang on the head might need looking at. I'm sorry, I'd better go."

"Of course," she said. "Thank you."

He gave me one more look, then darted off into the darkness. I could see which direction he went in, because he had the lantern.

"What the hell's going on?" I said. "Did he say?"

She shook her head, then stopped and pulled something out of the ground: Aliz, her pet stiletto, which she'd planted in case she was searched. She slid it back into her boot and dropped her hem. "I told him we were on our way to matins," she said. "Let's get out of here. We can't do anything tonight."

By the time we got back to the More Joy in Heaven, my skinned knees had stiffened up and I could barely hobble. I just about managed to climb the ladder to the hayloft. "Don't be such a girl," she told me. "It's only a few scratches."

"That's easy for you to say. What in God's name led you to think that that wall was a viable escape route?"

"I didn't have any trouble," she said. "Nor did you, till you tripped over that trough. You should learn to look where you're going. Still," she conceded, "it turned out all right. It was much easier to explain us away with you lying there all covered in blood than if we'd just been walking along with our hands in our sleeves." She yawned. "Complete fucking waste of time," she said. "And now presumably there's been some sort of thing, and security will be tight as a drum till the end of the council. We should've guzzled the bitch as soon as we got here, like I said we should."

"I'm not going to be fit to do anything for at least a couple of days," I said. "Maybe by then things'll have calmed down a bit, I don't know. What the hell could all that flap have been about? We need to find out."

"You really think so?" she said, but her heart wasn't in it, I could tell. "I'd better go and do that, then. Stay here and try not to fall over anything. You always were a bloody liability."

She wasn't gone long. When she came back, she had the oddest look on her face.

"We needn't worry about guzzling the princess," she said. "Someone's done it for us."

And done it in style. They found her when it was time to go to matins. She was on the floor of her room. Every bone in her body was broken, and her head had been crushed flat.

I've seen injuries like that. Once I was there when they dug a man out from under a collapsed stack of bricks. Another time I was in a war zone; I arrived with the army that relieved a siege, and a few hours earlier, the city had been bombarded with heavy catapults. They were rolling heavy shot and collapsed masonry off people who'd been out in the street when the bombardment started. It's not something you easily forget, even if you're from the Mesoge.

But there were no brick-stacks in the princess's room, and nobody had been loosing off artillery. And the relevance of the Mesoge reference will become clear shortly, when I tell you that the first time I saw a body smashed up like that, I was seven years old.

The dead woman was my aunt. It was one night in winter, and she must've heard the chickens squawking and reckoned it was a fox, because they found her beside what was left of the chicken coop. My father told me it was a bear, because he reckoned I was too young to know the truth. But I knew about all that stuff already, thanks to my brothers, and the flat head gave the game away. Bears rip you up and crush you till all your bones snap, but they don't stamp on your head. Something else does that.

Crisis of conscience time. While Svangerd was chattering away about the technicalities – no sign of a forced entry, apparently; the guards saw nothing; as far as she could tell it had been the perfect hit – I was thinking about a short, annoying man I'd spoken to recently, and who'd told me a lot of lies.

I knew they were lies, because the organisation he referred to doesn't exist. I knew that. How did I know that? Because I had faith –

Yes, but walkers aren't the supernatural, I told myself. An afterlife of sorts and malevolent revenants are a well-documented phenomenon in the Mesoge; that's science, not superstition, and there's most definitely a sound scientific explanation for it, which Saloninus or one of those guys wrote down in a book a thousand years ago, and which has since been misplaced. You knew all about walkers long before you met the short man. Nothing has changed. It's all right.

Yes, I thought. But this isn't the Mesoge.

If the killing had happened in Hrafnsvik, where the princess was born, or Segwald, where she lived and worked, I might just have been able to accept it. Hrafnsvik is roughly six hundred miles from the Mesoge border. Segwald, maybe seven-fifty. But Choris – halfway across the known world, two and a half thousand miles if it's a step, with both the Bitter Sea and the Friendly Sea in the way; besides, it wasn't just about distance. Choris is another world. The sun shines most of the year. You don't get bears in Haymarket or Temple Row.

You don't get bears, because a very long time ago, under the empire, the last bear was killed by the emperor's huntsmen, making Choris a safe place to live. The Mesoge was never part of the empire; too cold, too miserable, not worth the effort of invading. At which point I paused in my train of thought, uncertain whether that point was for or against the motion. Whereupon I realised I wasn't entirely sure what the motion was.

Nothing, I repeated to myself, has changed. Walkers were real yesterday, and the day before that, and when you were a kid in Einarsness. Therefore if they're real today, so what? The relevant fact is that someone had found a way to weaponise one of our quaint old Mesoge traditions, and had turned the result loose on the woman we'd have had to murder. I couldn't begin to imagine how he'd done it, but that was because I'm ignorant, not because it's impossible. Do try not to get those two mixed up.

And the short man? Just some wanker who thought he could scare me by making the results of intense surveillance sound like goblins-and-spooks stuff. Nothing to see here. Move on.

*

"This is wonderful," I said, interrupting her in mid-sentence. "You know what this means? Someone's done our job for us. We can go home."

She looked at me. "Have you been listening to a word I said?"

"No."

At times I wonder why she puts up with me. "I was saying," she said, "that whoever did this, they were making a statement."

"Probably. What about it?"

"Not just killing her: crunching her to bits. That's sending a message loud and clear."

"Agreed," I said, agreeing with her more than she realised. "What message?"

She grinned. "No idea," she said. "That's why I think we should stick around and find out."

"Absolutely not." As I said the words, it occurred to me to wonder how many other delegates to the council had been born in the Mesoge, to a family with a proven record of producing walkers. "For a start, they're bound to call the council off after what's happened, so we'd have no reason for hanging about here. Also, we don't have orders to investigate anything. We can't just go making up our own orders."

"Fine. We'll write home and ask for instructions."

"That'd take the best part of a month. We can't do that. We haven't got enough money, for a start."

She smiled. She has ways of raising money in hostile territory. "Not a problem," she said. "Look, be sensible. Whatever's going on here, Simocatta's going to want to know about it. If we go back now with nothing to tell him, he'll be livid. Well? He will be, you know that."

She was right, of course. In which case we had to stay. In which case, I needed to tell her what I knew. Some of it, anyway.

So I told her about growing up in the Mesoge, about bears and other vermin. I'd like to say she took it well, but she didn't.

"No," I said, when I finally managed to get a word in. "You were right: we've got to stay. This needs to be investigated. More to the point, it needs to be investigated by us. I know about these critters, from personal experience."

She gave me a dreadful look, as though she'd just caught sight of cloven hooves under the hem of my habit. "You, maybe," she said. "Not me. I'm going home. You can do what you damn well like."

"No," I said. "I need to be here because of what I know. You need to be here to look after me."

"Piss off."

"Listen," I said. "Right now, I'm a valuable asset. I know stuff about walkers that nobody else knows, unless they're from the old country too. It's not stuff you can read in books, or intelligence reports, for that matter. For a start, I know how to deal with them."

Her eyes widened.

"Exactly," I said. "I don't suppose there's anyone else south of Butter Cross who knows that. Therefore it makes sense that I should be here. And to quote a certain person whose opinion I deeply respect and believe, I'm not fit to be let out on my own without a nursemaid." I smiled. "That'd be you."

She shuddered, as though she was freezing cold or she'd just swallowed a worm. "I was just being nasty," she said. "You can handle it. I'd just be in the way."

"I need you here," I said; at which point it occurred to me

that I'd just signed myself up for considerably more than I'd intended. Where had this idea of fighting and killing walkers come from? Me and my big, eloquent mouth. "Think about it," I said. "We need to know who sent it, who's controlling it. Who's likely to know that?"

She shrugged.

"Walkers," I said, "aren't animals you can tame and train to perform simple tasks. If someone managed to catch one and bring it here and turn it loose on a specific target, that's completely unprecedented and amazing. It's still a long way from taming the bloody thing."

"So?"

"So," I said, "it'll want to carry on behaving the way walkers behave. Which means, now it knows there's easy pickings in these parts, it'll be back."

She looked at me. "If that's a reason for sticking around, it's not a very good one."

"Yes, it is," I heard myself say, though a riot was breaking out in the back of my mind, where I keep my common sense and survival instinct. "Walkers can talk. Therefore, they can answer questions."

"You want to catch this thing and talk to it?"

No, I thought. "Yes," I said. Then, with a merry grin, "For all I know, it could be my uncle."

She gave me her best that's-not-funny look. "That's horrible," she said. "You should be down on your knees praying for absolution, not making stupid jokes."

I realised I'd handled it very badly. The last thing I needed was a stake through my heart while I was sleeping. Explaining that it wasn't like that, it was just a hereditary condition, like a weak heart or the Teufelstein nose, would only make things worse. "It's all right," I said, "I'm still me, the same person I was ten minutes ago. I'm not suddenly going to sprout horns and a tail."

That didn't help. She gave me a cold, wary look, as though she'd just caught me peering into a baby's cot and licking my lips. "So what do you reckon you need me for?" she said.

To fight the monster, I didn't say. "Backup," I said. "Come on, you don't need me to spell it out. This isn't something I can do on my own. You'd be the first one to say it."

Suddenly it occurred to me that I was asking too much; in which case, I was going to have to do this incredibly stupid thing on my own. How had I got myself into this mess? Answer: the pig and the cart. In case you've never kept pigs, I'd better explain. If you want to load a pig into a cart, don't try and shoo him in or whack him with a stick, because that'll just make him resolve to die before he cooperates. What you need to do is shoo or drag him by the ears away from the cart, in which case he'll back into it, because that's the opposite of what he thinks you want; and then you slam the tailgate real quick and congratulate yourself on belonging to a higher species.

Quite. I'd just backed myself into the cart, the tailgate was down and latched, and I had a pretty shrewd idea of where the cart was going. I've known myself for thirty years, and even now I surprise myself with my own stupidity.

No, not really. I was kidding myself. I'd far rather have believed that I was stupid rather than suicidal, or (even worse) having doubts about my faith. Hence the wishful thinking and the excuses.

I realised, thinking it over during the course of a long day spent not listening to the debates I'd have sold my grandmother for a chance of hearing a few hours earlier, that I wanted to talk to this walker. I wanted it very much. In particular, I wanted to ask it one question. Do you happen to know, I wanted to ask, a short man?

It was practically inevitable that the walker would crush my ribs and stamp my head flat long before I got to ask my question – and that would be just fine, because that would mean that the question never got asked, so if the answer was yes, I'd never get to hear it.

Something the short man had said – blessed are those who have seen and yet have not believed. I've never minded being alive – I can't really put it any more strongly than that. I don't love my life. I can put up with it just fine, but does the thought of a day breaking which I won't be there to see fill me with terror? No, not really. You're terrified of death because of other people: wives, husbands, children, parents – the ones you love who'll be devastated and heartbroken when you're gone, because they love you. It took me a while to figure it out, but I count it as a blessed revelation. The enemy isn't Evil or death or the Loyal Opposition. The thing that makes human life a misery is love, because love plus loss equals pain, and loss is inevitable.

So I'm lucky, because nobody's going to be heartbroken and inconsolable when I go. I'm one of the few members of my species who can truly say that his life is his own. You have no idea how liberating that is. Everybody else spends his life holding a knife to the throats of those he loves most, but not me.

Therefore, if the walker killed me, big deal. But I know myself reasonably well, and I knew that I had no choice but to ask him the question, or die trying.

Or I could ask the short man. Of course, he might lie to me. But it was worth a shot.

Assuming I could find him. Instead of listening to Donatus of Litharend on the ambivalence of grace, therefore, I spent the afternoon session scanning the hall for a short man, but I couldn't see him there. Asking around was pointless but I did it anyway. Have you seen a short man? Most of those I asked gave me the benefit of the doubt and reckoned I was drunk or trying to be funny.

I went back to the More Joy when it was starting to get dark. Svangerd wasn't there. Drat, I thought, or words to that effect.

Never mind. There's a lock on her trunk, but it's one of those barrel-and-pin jobs run up by a blacksmith; I can pick those any day of the year in less time than it takes to recite the Lesser Confession. She'd be bound to have something I could use, unless she was trotting round out there with her entire travelling armoury concealed about her person – in which case she was in grave danger of toppling over and not being able to get up again.

No dice. I found six or seven knives in among her underwear, but they were all slim, elegant things, designed to make small, deep holes, or slice effortlessly into soft-skinned game. What I wanted was an axe, or better still a beanhook. What I did find among the small clothes and cutlery was an icon, crudely painted on a piece of wood; I'm guessing it was a chunk from an old shutter, using home-ground pigments and laughably poor draughtsmanship, the Absolution. There was something about it, don't ask me what, that told me she'd painted it herself. It's an exercise they make you do in the Reformatory, so I gather. The idea is, you take your faith and externalise it, so that when the doubts and horrors come back, you've got a reserve, like the pots of money people bury during an invasion. She'd wrapped it in half a yard of genuine Echmen silk, worth thirty deniers.

In my line of work you need to be able to paint, to do the illuminations in the margins and the decorated initial capitals. I'm quite good at it, though I say so myself. In my time I've done Absolutions and Ascensions and Transfigurations and Raisings of the Dead that have brought tears to the eyes of the most miserable priors and precentors this side of the Hog's Back. Meaningless to me; it's just art, a skill, a trade. It never occurred to me that it could be good for anything, until then. I wound the silk carefully around it and put it back where I'd got it from, and closed the lid and reset the lock. Then I nipped out to the stables, poked around for a while, and stole a hatchet.

Now then; it's all very well fighting and winning the internal battle that allows you to permit yourself to do a very stupid thing. That still leaves the practicalities. How was I going to get myself and my little hatchet inside the basilica, and from there to the guest lodge, where my fellow-countryman was most likely to turn up?

Security – a term which encompasses everybody from the Lord Chamberlain down to the expendables with the padded jacks and the halberds – isn't much good at anticipating, but very good indeed at reacting. I imagine that their credo is: lightning always strikes twice in the same place. Therefore, since Svangerd had been at pains to suggest to the officer we met that the bad guys had at some point been inside the cloister garden, I was prepared to bet my liver and kidneys that the cloister garden would be crawling with armed men; likewise the basilica and the cloisters. If my homeboy ran into them, he'd go through them like a wolf in a hen coop, but that didn't help me particularly. I wanted to be alone with him, for as long as it took to ask one quick, civil question.

Walkers seem to enjoy fighting by all accounts, but it's ancillary to their main objective, which is killing. They're also smart. On balance, therefore, I decide to work on the assumption that he'd prefer to sneak in round the back to smashing and crushing his way through a company of the household guards. Accordingly it followed that I needed to get inside the guest wing of the lodge: precisely the task that Svangerd had addressed and given up on as too difficult, hence our attempt to waylay her in the cloister on the way to matins. Nuts, I thought.

Because my weaknesses are so very weak, I tend to play to my strengths. Or rather strength: penmanship. Stick a sharpened goose feather in my fist and I'm ready to take on the world.

While I was around and about looking for the short man, I'd happened to pass an open door in a cloister. Through the door I'd caught sight of a desk and a high stool, carefully situated to catch the light through a tall, narrow window. That told me a clerk lived there; better still, as it turned out, the clerk was away from his desk. I nipped in and secured a sheet of parchment, a bottle of ink and a pen.

Examining my haul in my hayloft at the More Joy, I discovered how lucky I'd been. The parchment wasn't new; it was hard, rough and thin, the result of being sanded down with brick dust to get rid of what had been previously written on it – second- or third-grade stuff, the kind of material used for internal memos, requisitions, dockets, chits and passes. Likewise the ink: thin and greyish, watered down. Every office and scriptorium has its own recipes for adulterating ink to make it go further, when used for ephemeral purposes. Practical upshot: if you try and fake a routine internal document like a pass using parchment and ink bought from a stall in the market, the result will look all wrong. What you need is the stuff the real clerks use, which you can't buy. You have to steal it. Which, it turned out, I'd done.

Next stage in the process was using my imagination, a tool I despise and distrust. I imagined that I was an overworked, underappreciated member of the clerical staff, hauled out of bed in the middle of the night to carry a message to some nob in the nobs' lodgings. Now then; who am I, what am I doing and what does the writing on my scrap of parchment say?

One side of the page was easy enough. It said: *Allow access for the bearer to all parts of the inner lodge, signed X*. Who X was, I left till later. Now then, the other side. A happy thought struck me, like heavy rain falling on a man dying of thirst. The other side would be written in code.

That just left the identity of X. Now the problem with X is that if you forge his signature and they catch you and take you to him, and he says, I never wrote that, you're screwed. In which case, let X be dead. To be precise, let X be lying in state in the Mercy Chapel of the basilica with her head roughly the shape and thickness of the Book of Common Prayer.

Ask not what you can do for your princess, but what your princess can do for you. In my case, she could have written a secret message, in code, and arranged for it to be delivered by some clerk. The fact that death had intervened wouldn't necessarily vitiate or frustrate his errand. It wasn't perfect by any means but it would probably do; always assuming I could get sight of a copy of the princess's signature.

I nearly gave up at that point. But then I remembered that early on the first day of the council, she and a dozen or so other ecclesiastical swells had signed an Act of Anathema, condemning Nauseric's *Nine Propositions* as heresy, and that Acts of Anathema are published by being nailed up on the door of the basilica for thirty days. The outside door, please note, not the inside. Anybody, any member of the public, can stroll up Hill Street to the main door and stand there gawping till the guards move him on, and I, though you may not think it to look at me, am a fully qualified member of the public.

It wasn't really light enough to see by at that point, but there were a couple of guards on the door, helpfully holding lanterns. I stood there for as long as it would take a slow reader to mumble his way through the Act, concentrating on the signature, then walked away.

"Excuse me," I said to the guard sergeant, "I'm wondering if you could help me. I'm lost."

He gazed at me, as if wondering how creatures like me could be permitted to exist. "Restricted area," he said.

"So I should hope, with all these dreadful things going on. I've got a message for His Grace the Precentor of Neidhol. They gave me directions but I seem to have got turned around. I've been wandering about in these corridors for ages, so I was hoping—"

He held out his hand. I gave him my beautiful forgery. Guard sergeants can't read, of course. "Wait here," he said.

"All right. But please don't be too long. I understand it's quite important."

Two troopers in padded jacks and kettle hats moved into place in front of me, like chess pieces. They looked worried, as well they might. I'm not sure I'd have wanted sentry duty the night after someone got their head flattened.

The sergeant came back with a boy lieutenant, who was plainly terrified. He had my forgery in his hand. For a moment I thought he'd seen through it, and I was going to have to do something stupid.

"Who did you say you wanted to see?" he said.

"Sigbrand, Precentor of Neidhol," I said. "You wouldn't happen to know—"

"I'll take you to him."

Nuts. All I wanted to do was get past this checkpoint. I knew Sigbrand was at the council, because I'd heard him speak, but I didn't know him and he didn't know me from a hole in the ground. "Thank you," I said, "but if you tell me where he is, that'll be fine. I don't want to waste your time or give you any trouble."

"No unescorted civilians beyond the inner gate," he said. "Come on, this way."

I followed. Hard to know what to do for the best. I could slip away, run and hide, but then they'd come looking for me and that would spoil everything. I could put the boy lieutenant to sleep and hide him in a dark corner, but at some point he'd wake up and start yelling bloody murder – same outcome. Whatever I was going to do, I needed to do it before we woke up the precentor, and I had no idea, obviously, when that would be. I'd more or less decided to bash the lieutenant and abort the mission when we turned a corner and I found myself face to face with a short man.

"Hello," he sang out, "what the devil are you doing here?"

It was a cheerful, sing-song voice, suggesting an old friendship forged in beer. "Hello," I said.

"It's great to see you. Why the hell didn't you tell me you were coming to this bash?" He turned his head and beamed at the lieutenant. "Old pal of mine," he said. "Haven't seen in him God knows how long."

The lieutenant did a little nod, such as you'd use to acknowledge superfluous information from a superior officer. "Look," the short man went on, "are you in a hurry? Only I've got half a bottle of some really good stuff, and you look like you could use a couple of belts." Before I could think of an answer, he turned back to the lieutenant and said, "It's all right, you can leave him with me. You get on."

"Yes, sir," the lieutenant said, and stalked off, leaving me alone in a lantern-lit corridor with the short man. "You," I said.

"Correct. Don't look at me like that. The wind might change and you'll stick like it."

"Why do the guards take orders from you?"

"Oh, everybody around here knows me." He grinned. "Lucky for you I happened to turn up," he said. "That fake pass of yours wouldn't fool a blind man."

"Who are you? Really?"

"You know perfectly well," he replied. "Since when did you get to be so very brave?"

"I don't know what you—"

"Single-handedly seeking out an afterwalker, armed only with a little hatchet. Very Mesoge. Isn't that what Slipnir the Strong does in Gamling and the dragon?"

I took a deep breath. "I won't need to, if you'll give me a straight answer."

He nodded. "No. No, I didn't send the afterwalker, I didn't scoop it up off the fells in Einarsness and bring it here, I didn't train it or anything like that."

"It's nothing to do with you."

"I didn't say that exactly."

"Then you're—"

"That's why they call it the long game," he said. "Sooner or later it finds its way into everything, like bindweed. I wouldn't worry about it if I were you. Forget about the heroics. Go to bed. Enjoy the rest of the debates and go home."

"Or?"

"Or risk the frustration of trying to find something out and failing. That's a bitch, believe me."

"Just that?"

"Well." He beamed at me. "Right now, you're also in danger of getting your head turned into a roof-tile. But don't let me stop you if your heart's set on it, because strictly speaking that side of it's none of my business. I'd hate to see anything happen to you, but you're not my responsibility."

For a moment I reckoned I knew how the Aram Chantat felt when they stood underneath the walls of Choris Anthropou. What they wanted was inside there, but because they didn't have siege artillery they knew they couldn't get at it. Of course, the Aram Chantat had more sense than me. They gave up and went home.

"I don't believe you," I said.

He grinned. "Your privilege," he said. "As a matter of fact, I never tell lies. But I guess you'll have to find that out for yourself. All right," he went on, "since you insist, your best bet would be to go up this corridor, turn right, brings you out onto a sort of landing. There's a stairwell – duck under that and sit tight, he should be along at some point between now and the matins bell. Properly speaking it's not in the interests of the long game for me to give you any hints, but you might like to bear in mind that the staircase leads to a bell tower."

He slapped me on the shoulder, so hard it hurt. "Take care of yourself. Enjoy the speeches."

He lifted the lantern off the hook in the wall and walked away, leaving me in darkness.

5

The long game. You can think of it as a myth, like I do, or a moral paradox, or a precept in orthodox theology. Probably better not to think of it at all, but I had no choice.

The idea is that Evil exists and has a plan, enormously detailed and intricate, like the works of a Mezentine clock. Compressed springs power shafts that drive trains of gears, operating cams and sears and escapements: a hundred different processes working independently at the same time, to bring about one culminating outcome, which will not be pleasant. But Evil can never win, because Good is stronger, backed by the omnipotent power of the Invincible Sun.

Evil, therefore, puts off the inevitable day of its defeat by extending the scope of the exercise. The game can't be lost, because it's everlasting; games and sets can be lost, but not the match, not until the end of time itself; world without end, amen. Good can frustrate Evil, nothing easier, but Evil plans ahead, anticipating each reverse and defeat, allowing for it, making the defeat an essential building-block of the greater design. Thus Evil infects rats in Echmen with plague fleas and puts them on a ship to Aelia. Good sees to it that the ship never arrives. Therefore there is no plague, and half a million people don't die. And one of the people who doesn't die is Carnufex the Irrigator, slaughterer of a million innocents, who should've died of the plague when he was three years old.

Actually that's an incredibly crude example. The long game is infinitely subtler and more complex than that. In the classic long game, Carnufex would've been stopped by other means when he was twelve, but that interference would itself have been anticipated and used as the foundation for something even bigger and worse, which would in turn have been prevented, which would in turn have served to bring about an even more disastrous possibility. That's assuming you believe in all this shit, which of course I don't.

The beauty of the long game, of course, lies in the way Evil protects its plans from interference by using Good as a sort of human shield. Another hopelessly crude example: Good King Rothgar frees the serfs, abolishes slavery and stops the hundred-year war against the Permians. As part of his reforms he dispossesses the hereditary aristocracy and divides their land between the oppressed peasants. Consequently, a hundred and fifty years later, when the Permians invade, there are no competent generals to lead the army, because they always came from the old nobility; the Permians win and slaughter every living thing west of the Bitter Sea.

That's a particularly bad example because it's so large-scale and monolithic. The details of the long game are much smaller, more intricate, more deeply embedded in the fabric of all our lives. More to the point, the scope of the plan is inconceivably huge, with every possible contingency anticipated and allowed for. Think of it as a huge volume of water, testing every surface it touches for a way out, a crack, a fissure, a weakness. Stop it up at one point and it immediately finds another, or another dozen, or another million. It flows, it builds up pressure and it only needs one chance; above all, it thrives and flourishes on its own ambiguity, because who can possibly hope to know whether any given event is Good, or simply collateral Good in the interests of Evil?

Sensible people like me take a long step backwards and point out that all this nonsense is a pretty good argument for saying that neither Good nor Evil actually exist; if they're so closely bound up with each other that they're practically interchangeable, is there really a difference between them? Then apply Saloninus' razor – the simplest explanation is bound to be the right one – and you're left with the obvious conclusion: there is no Good and Evil, and morality is just fashions in belief and behaviour.

Sensible people like me, however, are few and far between. Most people believe in the Invincible Sun and the eternal battle between light and dark. I could point out that truth doesn't operate on democratic principles, and if a million people unanimously vote for a cow to be a horse, the cow is still a cow; a fat lot of good it would do me, so I rarely bother.

Long story short: I don't believe in the long game; everybody else does. On that point, therefore, we agree to differ. You can see why theologians love it and moralists find it a wonderful excuse for condemning everything as being wrong; I confess I find it irresistibly entertaining, like an ongoing game of chess, or a story with no ending. But the idea that a short man could be lurking in the shadows orchestrating my actions and those of everybody around me? Bullshit.

I believe that; honestly I do. Blessed are those who have seen and yet have believed.

So, if I refused to believe the short man, I had no choice but to ask the walker. Guess who my own worst enemy is. Go on, guess.

The truth is, I'm not the most patient man who ever lived. When I'm working with Svangerd I find it easier to be patient, because she's about as tranquil as a thunderstorm, and I can score points off her by showing off my ability to sit still and wait. When I'm on my own, however, after a few minutes I start to seethe and fidget, like a man sitting on a beehive.

Immobility, furthermore, breeds doubt. After an hour sitting in the stairwell, with pins and needles in both feet and a crick in my neck, I found myself wondering if there really was a walker at all. It was so massively unlikely, here in Choris, where the sun shone and there were always people everywhere, the absolute antithesis of the Mesoge. Maybe – intriguing thought, which hadn't occurred to me before – maybe the princess was killed by someone who wanted to make it look like the work of a walker. Why would anyone want to do that? No idea, but surely that was more likely than the alternative. I gave it some thought. You wouldn't do that unless you expected the walker's MO to be recognised. Was there anyone else at the council apart from me who came from the Mesoge, or who was likely to be familiar with our cherished cultural traditions? Unlikely, but not impossible. Was this a message aimed at that putative individual; and if so, what was the point?

I was letting myself get quite excited by this possibility when I heard something. It had been dead quiet up till then.

People who live in civilised places don't know what real quiet is like.

The noise I heard was fingers tapping. It's an annoying habit, one that I'm often guilty of when I'm bored. In fact, when I heard it I assumed it was me, doing it without realising. Then I found that it wasn't.

The tapping stopped. It was pitch dark. My eyes were open, but they might as well have been tight shut. Listen for it breathing, I told myself, until I remembered that walkers don't breathe.

Maybe they can smell fear; I don't know. Something must have prompted it to attack, at that particular moment. A hand grabbed my shoulder. The fingers reached nearly to my spine and the thumb dug into the muscle two inches below my collarbone.

The hatchet was shoved down inside my habit, to keep it from being seen. I couldn't get to it, not without loosening my belt. Steel doesn't cut walkers anyway, so that was beside the point.

He'd got me pinned down with one hand. The other hand would be groping for my head, to squash it. I squirmed, like a rabbit when you take it out of the snare. Small, weak things can be devilish slippery to keep hold of. I found myself loose from his grip. I jumped up, bashed my head against the underside of the stairwell, ignored it, scrambled to get out of the way. He grabbed my foot, but all he got was my boot.

I heard something clatter on the stone floor. That would be the hatchet, shaken loose. I groped for it and my fingers closed around the shaft. A hiding to nothing, but I couldn't think of anything else, so I swung the hatchet as hard as I possibly could, and felt it connect.

I don't know if you've ever done any forge work, but if you have, think of when you go to hit the hot steel really hard, miss and hit the anvil instead. It rings like a bell and the hammer bounces, sending a shock up your arm to your shoulder. I felt the hatchet bounce. No matter. Like I said, I didn't know what else to do, so I hit him again.

Same outcome. But, I realised, I wasn't being squashed flat or torn to pieces; maybe that was cause and effect. I hit him four or five times more, putting everything I'd got into it. Then one more blow, which met empty air and made me stagger forward. My knee hit something as hard as stone, but not where the floor or the stairs ought to be. I felt the hatchet fly from my hand and heard it clatter on the floor. *Nuts*, I thought, or words to that effect.

Still, I had an opportunity to run, so I tried that, and went straight into the edge of the stairs. The impact should've knocked me off my feet but I guess I was too worked up for it to register. I absorbed the pain as being irrelevant, tried again, caught my bare foot in something and went sprawling. My head bounced off stone. I pushed myself up with my hands, and under one of them I felt the hatchet handle. Nice hatchet.

Something crashed into me and sent me sprawling. I swung the hatchet and connected; it bounced, and I felt something go wrong with my arm. Not to worry, I had a spare. I switched the hatchet to my left hand and took another swipe, which missed. I plunged forward and slammed into something very hard, dropping the hatchet. I put my arms around whatever it was and pushed against it, like a man trying to push over an oak tree. It pushed back and forced me backwards, until I felt the wall behind me. Oh well, I thought.

There was something digging into my back. If I hadn't

known better, I could've sworn I was being shoved up against a rope. What was a rope doing in a corridor?

Like it mattered. I managed to get my left leg up so that my foot was braced against him, and I pushed as hard as I could. No effect, except to lift my other foot off the ground. Now there's a thought, I said to myself. I let go with my hands, shoved again and scrabbled for something to hold on to. What my hands connected with felt like rock, hard and stone cold: two beams, or arms, horizontal, exactly what I needed. I squeezed myself upwards, like a man climbing a wellshaft, and got my right foot on one of the beams. They shifted as I did so; I toppled backwards, banged my head on the wall, thinking, Why is there a rope in a corridor?

I remembered someone telling me something about a bell-tower.

You can hope faster than you can think, under certain circumstances. A bell-tower, and a rope. Put it another way, a third dimension in a hitherto two-dimensional fight. Me for some of that.

I let go with my hands and flailed about over my head, eventually connecting with the rope. I got my hands around it and pulled, expecting to hear a chime. Nothing – and the rope didn't give. Unimportant. I kicked hard with both legs, then brought my feet together where I desperately hoped the rope was. I found it, third or fourth attempt. I was in business. I started to climb.

When I was fourteen, second year in the order, I was on a roster for whose turn it was to shin up a rope into the bell-tower and unlock the bells for ringing. When not in use, the headstock (the wooden beam from which the bell hangs) was locked solid with a bolt, to keep the bells from swaying about and clanging if a sharp draught happened to come down the tower. I hated that particular job and did my best to swap bell-tower duty for some other chore with my fellow novices, but after a while I got used to it. There was, of course, a perfectly good stair up to the bell-chamber, but it was kept locked in case anyone went up it. Monastic logic.

Hooray for monastic logic, because it saved my life. I felt the rope shake as he grabbed it and tried to pull the rope down, with me still climbing it. Bell-ropes are pretty substantial things, made to the same specifications as ships' hawsers, but it wouldn't last long with him tugging at it. I went up the rest of the rope like a topmast hand on a freighter, and found the headstock with the top of my head.

One last push from the knees; I wrapped my arms round the headstock beam, got my leg over, and fell sideways onto the solid floor of the bell-chamber. At which point, he must have given the rope another almighty tug, because I heard the headstock beam splinter and snap, and then the loudest noise I've ever heard in my life.

Walkers are smart but parochial; we don't have bells or bell-towers in the Mesoge. How was he to know, therefore, that if he pulled hard enough to break the headstock, the bell would come crashing down right on top of him?

I wanted to stay where I was, preferably for the rest of my life. But I knew that time was of the essence.

I found the stairs and scampered down them, arriving at the same time as six guards and a lantern. There was the bell, at an angle and cracked diagonally in two. The leading sharp edge of one of the two pieces was buried in a body, entering it where the shoulder meets the neck. I'm no expert, but at a guess I'd say it was slightly bigger than the biggest bell at the monastery when I was a kid, and that one weighed a ton and a half.

"Keep back," I yelled at the guards. "It's still alive."

Poor bastards, they were paralysed with terror. I grabbed a halberd from one of them, then took a proper look.

His skin was the colour of bruises: swollen, plump-looking, like a ripe berry. He had no hair, fingernails or toenails. At a guess, I'd say he was a whisker under eight feet tall, though it's hard to tell when a body is slumped down. I could see three deep dents in his forehead, presumably where I'd hit him with the hatchet, but the skin was unbroken. There was no blood seeping out where the broken bell had cut into him. As I approached, he turned his head just a little and smiled at me. Long time, no see.

It's not true that you can't cut a walker's skin. It's just very, very difficult. I swung the halberd with everything I'd got, but the shaft snapped and the blade went flying against the wall, bounced off and landed scarily close to my feet. "Give me another," I yelled. Nobody moved, so I took a step back and grabbed one, not daring to break eye contact with those two pale, watery blue eyes. He was grinning. This time, I got smart and aimed for the point where the bell had already cut the skin.

I think I may have mentioned that I'm pretty strong. It was like when you try and split a log but you miss the shake, where the grain runs, and hit crossgrain, and the axe just sinks in a quarter of an inch or so. It was only a little cut, but it was a cut.

"Don't just stand there, for fuck's sake," I howled at the guards. "Help me."

So we set to, like four strikers hammering a bloom of iron on an anvil. It took us a very long time, but we managed it.

Just before the head came off, he looked at me. It was sheer contempt.

I hadn't noticed, but there was now quite a crowd of people jamming up the corridor. That was no good. We had to carry the body, and the head, down the stairs and out into the cloister garden. Then we'd need firewood, lots of it, and a couple of gallons of lamp oil, and buckets and shovels. I found a man who looked like an officer and told him what had to be done. I think he was too stunned to argue. Quickly, I told him, we really don't have much time. How long? I don't know, I said, just not very long, that's all.

It took twelve men to lift the body and three to carry the head. They had to take the lower door off its hinges to get the shoulders through. There were ever so many people around now, getting in the way. I'm afraid I was neither patient nor respectful. I may have raised my voice. In any event, we got the body out onto the grass of the cloister garden, and I think they smashed up some pews and a couple of doors for wood, until I reckoned we'd got enough. Nobody seemed to know where the lamp oil was kept, but someone suggested using brandy instead. There was a barrel of it in the archdeacon's buttery. So we used that, and it worked reasonably well.

We kept feeding the fire with charcoal and brandy, to make sure every last bit of solid matter was turned into grey ash. Then they scooped up the ashes, making sure they got every last crumb, and put them in a barrel, and sealed the lid down good and tight. I explained what had to be done. Would the river do? someone asked. No, I said, it's got to be the sea. Nobody argued, which was just as well.

Someone – I think he was in charge of something, but I

neither knew nor cared – came bustling up demanding an explanation. I was too tired, and everything hurt, so I told him to piss off. The officer who'd been running the show got between him and me and ran interference for me, which was lucky, or I'd probably have thumped somebody. They opened the main gate and brought in a cart and put the barrel on it. I suppose I should've gone with them, seen the barrel loaded on the ship, seen it rowed out into the middle of the bay and the ashes scattered, but by then I'd had enough. I limped away and nobody tried to stop me.

I met her in the cloister. She looked at me. "What the hell happened to you?" she said.

"I won," I told her.

"What do you mean, you—?"

"I killed it. Excuse me, please, I need to go and lie down."

She went with me back to the More Joy. I couldn't make it up the ladder to the hayloft, so she helped me lie down in an empty stall. "I thought you said they couldn't be killed," she said.

"That's right, they can't."

"But you just—"

"Killed it for now. Look, would you please go away? I need to close my eyes for five minutes."

No chance of that. Someone must've recognised me, because it wasn't long before a bunch of men showed up, soldiers and clerks and officials and Vitimer, archbishop of Stachel and de facto chairman of the council following the death of the princess. They wanted to ask me questions, and swearing at them didn't make them go away. So I told them everything they needed to know, except for one pertinent fact, and eventually they ran out of questions and left me in peace, on condition that I presented myself in front of the council at the start of the next session for further questioning. Whatever, I said, and away they went.

When they'd gone, I called her over. She kneeled down beside me. "What?" she said.

"One thing I didn't tell them."

She looked at me. She was scared. "Go on."

"I knew him."

That made no sense to her. I gave her a moment to figure it out. "You mean, the monster? You know who it was?"

"Is," I corrected her. "They don't die."

My voice cracked up as I said it. "You recognised it," she said. "Someone you used to know, in the old country."

I nodded. "My dad," I said.

I'd tried telling myself that I could be wrong, but it was no use. The swelling had distorted his face, and all the years I knew him he'd had a full head of hair and a beard; there was room for scepticism, if you put your shoulder to it and pushed really hard. But that look in his eyes, the scorn, the absolute dismissal – I couldn't mistake that.

I'd seen it so many times, after all, in circumstances that made it hard to forget. I was always a disappointment to my old man.

Svangerd didn't take it well. She didn't say anything. She just stared at me.

"I'm sorry," I said. "I should have told you."

That didn't make it any better. "You mean," she said, "you're one of those things."

"No, of course not." Not yet, at any rate. As I think I may have mentioned, it does tend to run in families. That thought was a particularly shrill voice in the chorus of voices howling at the back of my mind. "I'm me. You know me."

"I thought I did." She was making herself look at me. "But you got rid of it."

"Yes."

"You said they can't die."

"No. But it's been burned to ashes and they're going to throw the ashes in the sea. It'll be a while before he's in any fit state to bother anybody."

"How long?"

"I don't know. Years rather than months. Don't ask me to be more specific than that. There's no way of knowing, because nobody's ever dumped the ashes out to sea before, because there is no sea in the Mesoge. That's why I insisted. He won't know what to do."

"Your father."

"Yes, I know," I said. "I didn't even know he'd died."

I think she wanted to feel sorry for me, but she couldn't. "You're sure it was him."

"Yes."

She doesn't like it when there's nothing she can do. "Was he a bad man, your father?"

"No, not particularly," I said. "He didn't suffer fools gladly and he had a temper, but he wasn't Evil incarnate. It's just something that happens in the Mesoge. It's something you get, like fever. It doesn't mean anything."

She sat down, with her back to the side of the stall. "Why the hell did you want to go and get involved?" she said. "They're going to ask us a lot of questions. If they find out who we are—"

"They won't," I told her. "There's nothing to find out. We're just delegates to the council. Anything else we might have been stopped when the princess died. Relax," I added. "It's over now. We answer their questions, and then we go home."

The last time I saw him was when the cart arrived to take me to Volundardal. We didn't have a cart of our own, so we had to borrow one from our neighbour. My eldest brother drove. I sat in the back, along with a load of wool bales our neighbour wanted dropped off along the way. I saw my father in the long meadow, laying the hedge. He had a billhook in his hand, and he was wrestling a hazel branch, twisting and bending it to make it go exactly where he needed it to be. He must have heard the cart go by but he didn't look up.

Now he was – dead? Well, yes and no. Nobody knows. It's a metaphysical grey area that would have scholars crawling all over it like flies if it happened anywhere other than the Mesoge. Quite possibly it holds the key to a real understanding of the true nature of life and death. But the finest minds of successive generations tended to prefer warmth and sunlight to cold and fog, so nobody ever saw fit to go to the Mesoge and investigate the matter in any depth. Perfectly understandable.

I didn't get any sleep, needless to say.

A dozen soldiers came to take me to the council, just in case it had slipped my mind. When I tried to stand up, I found I couldn't. My knee had swollen up, my ribs ached and I couldn't bend my right arm. There was no skin left on the palm of my left hand, and both my feet were blistered.

That, the soldiers said, wasn't a problem. Two of them held a spear at knee height between them, and I sat on it all the way across town, with people standing in groups to see me as I went by. Nobody cheered and nobody threw stones, suggesting that nobody had yet figured out what to tell them to think.

Every novice who's ever joined a monastic order dreams of the day when he stands up to address a general ecumenical council in full conclave. My turn, and I wished I was a thousand miles away. I tried to stand up, and then somebody brought me a stool to sit on.

I'd been expecting a lot of damnfool questions, but I think they were all too shocked by what had happened. There was no posturing, no spinning the issues to make the other side look bad, no veiled accusations. I guess they reckoned all that could wait, until they had some sort of an idea of what was going on. So I tried to answer clearly and simply. The monster, I told them, was a common phenomenon in the Mesoge, though to the best of my knowledge it didn't occur anywhere else. Yes, I was from the Mesoge, and I'd had personal experience of these creatures. Yes, I recognised the monster's handiwork as soon as I heard the details. I hadn't told anyone because I hadn't expected anyone to listen; besides, there wasn't anything that anyone could do. Yes, I took it on myself to act without reporting my suspicions to the proper authorities, because I knew what had to be done, though I had no reason whatever to believe that I was capable of doing it. The bell-tower and the bell were sheer good luck. If it hadn't been for them, I'd be dead now, and so would an unquantifiable number of other people. Yes, to the best of my knowledge the measures I'd insisted on ought to work; that is, it was highly unlikely that the monster would be able to reassemble itself in the short to medium term. I'd followed the approved procedure used in the Mesoge for time out of mind; my only modification was insisting that the ashes be dumped in the sea. I explained why.

As far as I knew, therefore, the danger was over, unless there were more of the creatures out there – unlikely, I said, because walkers are essentially solitary and have never been known to cooperate with each other. However, I added before anyone could shut me up, since it was unprecedented to find one outside the Mesoge, it would be unwise to assume that any of the previously established facts about walkers still held true. I had no idea, and didn't care to hazard a guess, how it had got here. It would be reasonable to entertain the possibility that someone had deliberately brought it here, though such a thing had never happened before and I couldn't begin to imagine how you'd go about doing it. That said, a walker leaving the Mesoge and coming to Choris of its own accord was even more improbable, in my opinion.

Awkward silence when I'd finished my testimony. I sat still and quiet, and then tried to stand up, but my knees wouldn't take my weight. Nobody seemed to know whether I was supposed to go away or stay there till the end of the session. Unthinkable that there shouldn't be an established procedure for something happening at an ecumenical council. Just one more unthinkable thing to add to the pile.

Vitimer, the new chairman, got to his feet. I looked at him. I felt a bit sorry for him. No doubt he'd dreamed of being chairman, and his dream had come true and he didn't like it one bit, not like this. He had no idea whether I was a true hero or an abomination. I'd mentioned the fact that there was some hereditary element in the occurrence of walkers, though I'd neglected to say that the one I'd killed was my father. But I was from the Mesoge, and everybody knows we're all as interbred as chickens up there; on the other hand, I'd killed it, so presumably it was safe to assume that I was on our side. Maybe.

Under those conditions there was very little Vitimer could say, so he said it. We'd all had a most terrible shock, he said, and surely it was no coincidence that the powers of Evil should choose to strike here, in the heart of all true religion, at this particularly historic moment. Likewise, it should come as no surprise that the victim should have been our dear departed sister, who had done so much to further the cause of the true faith, and who therefore was the most logical target. But, he went on, as usual, Evil had miscalculated. Ever since time began, the true vine has been watered with the blood of martyrs, et cetera, et cetera – he speeded up and relaxed visibly when he got to that bit, because he knew he could do that sort of spiel in his sleep, and probably had on many occasions. Gradually, the mood in the hall relaxed too. They'd been given an explanation, and now they knew what they were supposed to think. Evil did it. Panic over.

At least, they knew what they were going to put in their letters home. Looking round at them while Vitimer was talking, I wasn't quite so sure that they believed it themselves. Indeed, it did occur to me to wonder whether I might not be the only atheist in the building. Saying it was all Evil's fault was all very well, but what if Evil had a few flesh-and-blood accomplices? And as for the political implications . . .

I resolved not to care. As far as I was concerned, I'd done my bit, and the official debriefing in front of the entire council was a good way of drawing a line under my involvement. Besides which, I was genuinely and incontrovertibly wounded in action, therefore excused duty. As soon as I was in a fit state to move, we were going home.

Vitimer's speech got the inevitable standing ovation – I'd have stood and clapped too, if I'd been able – and someone signalled to a couple of clerks to take me away. As they helped me up, someone started to clap, and then everybody joined in, which officially made me a hero, which was nice, or at any rate better than the other thing. I suppose I should've enjoyed the moment, but I didn't. What spoiled it for me was catching sight of the individual who started clapping first. I recognised him. He was a short man.

Being a hero meant that Svangerd and I were moved out of the hayloft and into diplomatic guest quarters at the patriarch's lodgings. Nothing but the very best, needless to say. The patriarch's chamberlain met us at the cloister gate and escorted us up a huge wide stairway to the third floor, then along a gallery, with one side open, overlooking the nave of the basilica, then up another stair and along a corridor, whose walls and ceiling were covered in exquisite, mostly intact, barely faded Archaic-period frescoes – hunting scenes, episodes from Aelian mythology and highly debauched banquets. The chamberlain noticed me gawping and explained; this whole wing had once been part of the imperial governor's palace, a thousand years ago. Amazing. I'd have been in heaven if my knees hadn't hurt quite so much.

The room he showed us to was no larger than the chapter house of the abbey back home, but considerably better decorated. Then it occurred to Svangerd and me simultaneously that the chamberlain was expecting us to share it.

"Oh," he said, when Svangerd gave him a look that should have frozen the marrow in his bones. "I thought you two—"

"No," she said.

"Fine. In that case, I'll see what I can find for the holy sister. This floor is a bit full, but we can probably squeeze you in somewhere in the annexe."

When they'd gone, I lay on the bed and tried to read, but the light was going and there wasn't a lamp, so I spent an hour or so trying not to think about all the things I had to think about, and then the door opened and Svangerd came in, holding a candle in a pottery holder.

"I'm in a sort of undersized hen coop up in the attic," she said, sitting down on the window ledge. "He tried to apologise, but I told him to shut his face."

"You just threatened the Lord Chamberlain," I said. "Swell."

"He's an arsehole."

"Probably."

Something in her voice gave me the impression that she'd forgiven me for whatever it was I was supposed to have done. "Something's been bothering me," she said. "Why did someone try and kill us on the way here?"

"I've been wondering about that too. But it's got pushed to the back of the queue."

"It's something about you," she said. "No, shut up and listen. Someone tries to guzzle us on the way here. Then a monster shows up that only you know about, from a remote and godforsaken place that you come from, and does the job we were supposed to be doing. None of it makes a scrap of sense, but if there's anything like a common theme, it's you."

"Which is crazy," I said. "I'm nobody."

"True." She thought for a moment. I like to watch her thinking. You can see every mental ripple and eddy on her face. "Is there something you haven't told me?"

"As a matter of fact, yes."

It just came spurting out, before I could stop it. She looked at me. "Well?"

"But I didn't say anything, because I was afraid you'd—"

"What?"

"Forget it," I said. "Actually, there's two things."

"Oh for God's sake."

"But you've got to promise," I said. "Look, you know me. We've worked together; you've saved my neck I don't know how many times. I've done the same for you now and again. We've always trusted each other."

"That was before you started keeping secrets."

"Oh, come on."

"No, the hell with it," she said. "I feel like I don't know you any more. Before you came here, yes, I thought I knew you. But all this Mesoge stuff is a bit more than I can take, to be honest with you. I look at you and I'm not sure I know who you are any more. And you said," she added. "It runs in families."

Oh dear. I'm not a brave man. I hate taking risks. You think it'll work and turn out all right, and then you're proved wrong. I hate that. So, obviously I had to tell her, about my father, because it would tend to support her hypothesis: me as somehow the centre of attention, or at least a significant pawn in somebody's game. But the risk was that she'd get up and walk out of the room and never talk to me again. I took the coward's way out. Chickenshit and stupid, that's me.

"Do you want to hear what I've got to say?"

She nodded.

So I told her about the short man. I could almost feel her heart stop. It was like that moment when the smith takes the yellow-hot steel out of the fire and plunges it into the quench. You see the colour and heat drain away into the water, dull grey spreading up the glowing workpiece at a brisk walking pace until the whole thing's turned cold.

I'd said enough; too much. She looked at me and her eyes were terrified.

"Oh, come on," I said. "Pull yourself together, for crying out loud. I talked to him, all right? I talked to a normal, living human being. Not a very nice one, but a man, not the devil."

"He knows all about us. Everything."

"Admirable surveillance work," I said. "He must have a dozen men working for him, at least. Which begs the question—"

"He knows what you're thinking. What's going to happen."

"A sound knowledge of human nature, and a good guesser."

"He knew about the bell."

I shook my head. "Top-notch tactical instinct," he said. "I think what he was trying to do was advise me. He'll have figured out that the only thing in the basilica complex that could stop a walker was the bell. So he guided me to the spot under the bell-tower and hoped I had the common sense—"

"It was dark. You didn't know it was a bell-tower. And how did he know where that thing would attack you?"

I shrugged. "Fine," I said, "maybe I'm wrong about that. Maybe I don't know precisely how he's doing it. But it's all tricks and illusions. He is not the devil incarnate. He's just a man."

She wanted to believe me, but of course it doesn't work like that. Wasn't it Saloninus who said that the three most desirable things – sleep, love and faith – can't be deliberately acquired; you can't reach out and grab them; they have to come over you when you're least expecting it? Something like that. "Why us?" she said. "Why you?"

"I don't know. But we can think about it, based on what we know, and try and figure it out."

She made a valiant effort, and nodded. "Go on, then."

"Things we know," I said. "One: on the way here, somebody tried to kill us. Two: whatever the big idea is, the object of the exercise wasn't to stop us killing the princess, or at least if it was, they must be pretty useless, because the princess is dead. Three—"

"Hang on a moment," she said. "Say that again."

"Three."

"Before that."

"The object of the exercise wasn't to stop us killing the princess—"

She closed her eyes and held up her hand. "What?" I said.

"Maybe the object of the exercise," she said, "was just that. To stop *us* from killing the princess."

You know how it is when it's wet and the ground is squelching mud, and you put your foot in a particularly soft patch and it sinks in, holding it fast and bringing you up short. My instincts told me no, that's not it, but I couldn't get my foot out of the possibility. "Why?" I said.

"I don't know, do I? But then, *I* don't claim to know every damn thing."

"All right," I said. "Let's say for the sake of argument that someone wants to kill the princess himself, as opposed to just wanting her dead. Why?"

"Revenge," she said. "Doesn't just want her dead: wants to see the life drain out of her eyes. Which would tie in with the way it was done. Maximum possible effect. Or he wanted her killed by one of those things, because—" She paused, then said, "Because if one of them kills you, it damages your soul."

"No, it doesn't," I said. "At least, I've never heard that it does. Mind you, we don't think a lot about souls in the Mesoge."

"Maybe it does," she said. "Or maybe he believes it does, or maybe she believed it, so he wanted her last moments to be filled with absolute despair, I don't know. It's the sort of thing you can imagine somebody doing."

"Can you? I can't."

"You wanted explanations," she said. "That's an explanation. Maybe not a very good one, but it's not impossible."

"Three," I said. "There's a small man who wants me to believe he's the devil, and he's put a ridiculous amount of effort into trying to convince me. But I don't think he wanted to stop us killing the princess, because of course he could've done that, easy as pie, just by going to the authorities."

"He's the one who sent the monster. Obviously."

"Nothing obvious about it," he said. "Also, according to your theory, he helped me kill it. Hardly likely, if it was his monster."

"Unless he was finished with it and wanted it got rid of."

Another foot stuck in the mud. "I don't think so," I said, though I wasn't at all sure. "If he could control it enough to get it here from the Mesoge and make it do what he wanted, which is absolutely unheard of and impossible—"

"Why? They're both on the same side."

"No," I said, raising my voice, "they aren't, because there's no such side for them to be on. And if they're on the same side, why would he want to get rid of it?" It. My father. But of course he wasn't really dead. He never would be. Now there's irony, because one of the things you dread most in this lousy, love-infested world is your parents dying. One less thing for me to worry about, I guess. "Absolutely no need," I went on, "to deprive himself of a key asset."

"But he's not," she said. "Like you keep telling me, those

things live for ever. So he's just getting rid of it in the short term. The long game, remember?"

That's the trouble with brainstorming with Svangerd. She always needs to win. And when she gets like that, I need to win too. A lot of valid points get made, but by that point nobody's listening to them. "This isn't helping," I said. "In fact, I don't know why we're bothering with it. We're going home."

"All this shit is about you," she said angrily. "So what makes you think it'll stop if you go home? It'll go wherever you go."

"No, it won't. I'm nobody. I'm the most insignificant man who ever lived."

"Are you sure about that?"

Hell of a question to ask someone like me. "Yes," I said.

6

Next morning I should've gone to prime in the basilica and prayed for the good of my soul, but I didn't. Partly because I haven't got one, partly because Svangerd never misses prime if she can possibly help it.

Instead, I went back to the More Joy in Heaven to collect something I'd hidden in the rafters of the hayloft. I got there and found a small crowd, the sort you tend to get when there's been a fire or a murder.

"What happened?" I asked someone.

"There's been a killing," she said, with her eyes shining; a short, round-faced woman carrying a basket of fish. "It's horrible. Blood and bits of bodies everywhere."

"Let me through," I said loudly, "I'm a priest."

I pushed through the crowd and went inside, where I saw the innkeeper and his son, talking to a watch sergeant. They turned and looked at me. "That's him," the innkeeper said. "That's the man."

Not cheerful words to hear in context, but I was too over-wrought to care. "What happened?" I asked.

"You sure?" said the sergeant. The innkeeper was sure. So was his son.

"Don't even think about it," I told the sergeant. "I've got a cast-iron alibi, not to mention benefit of clergy. What the hell happened here?"

So they arrested me and took me to the watch house, which was annoying. But I had the satisfaction of dragging Vitimer's personal chaplain down there to vouch for me and give the sergeant a talking to he would never forget, after which he was only too pleased to answer my question.

At some point during the night, a person or persons unknown had climbed up on the roof of the hayloft and effected an entrance by ripping off the tiles. Accommodation being scarce in Choris because of the council, the innkeeper had already relet the hayloft, and the new tenant was up there when the intruder intruded.

At which point the sergeant's grasp of Watchspeak lapsed and he started talking like a human being. He'd never seen anything like it before, he told me, and before he got into the watch game he'd been a soldier. Every bone in the poor fucker's body was broken, and his head ripped off and squashed flat, like someone fucking huge had trod on it.

Then he looked at me, and asked me if I was the man who'd killed the monster, up at the basilica. The chaplain had just told him that, but I guess he wanted it confirmed.

"I didn't kill it," I said. "A bell fell on it. I was lucky."

He looked at me. I got the impression he was religious, like Svangerd. Most people are.

"I need to see the body," I said. "And the hayloft."

First the hayloft. There was a huge hole in the roof, and three rafters had been ripped out and flung down into the stable yard. One of them was a rafter I had a particular interest in. I poked about in the straw, then went down to the yard and hunted around there, on my hands and knees in the mud and horseshit. No, nobody had moved or taken anything, so far as the sergeant knew. Why would they?

No trace of the box.

Next the body. The sergeant told me the name the man had given the innkeeper when he paid for his lodgings: Brother Naso. A common enough name-in-religion, in honour of Saint Naso of Perimadeia, one of the first martyrs. Identifying the head wasn't going to be easy, since the face was now three inches wide, but it was bald. I confess it didn't ring any bells, but the body was that of a short man.

Being in way over my head has become something of a way of life for me, ever since I left the Mesoge and took to religion, scholarship and the pursuit of knowledge for its own sake.

My father didn't want me to leave, but he insisted that I should go. I'd have a chance of a better life, he said, make something of myself. Also, I could send money home. I don't think he'd grasped the bit about poverty in the vows, or he didn't believe it. My brothers were glad to see the back of me. There were only so many mouths that our little scrap of land could feed, and I was the least useful and productive member of the household. Usually in the Mesoge infant mortality takes care of problems like that, but all my father's children survived. Just our luck.

On balance, I've always been glad I left and went to the big city and became who I am. On balance, if I had my time over again, I don't think I'd have chosen the church militant, even though that would mean I'd never have met Svangerd. But I didn't really have much of a choice. My talents, such as they were, led me inevitably into the path I've been following ever since, and here I am.

Even so. There was no doubt whatsoever in my mind that the squashed mess I'd seen reassembled on a trestle table in the back parlour of the More Joy was the short man, *soi-disant* representative of the Loyal Opposition. Even in that state, I recognised him the moment I saw him. In which case, I had a horrible feeling that Svangerd was right. All this shit was about me.

Me, for crying out loud. But the evidence was beginning to pile up. The attack on the way to Choris, the box, my father. And now, apparently, a second walker.

Vitimer sent for me. "It can't be the same one," I told him. "It's not physically possible."

He looked at me. "The power of Evil is very strong," he said. "If it can raise the dead, it can reassemble a dead body from ashes and seawater."

"With respect," I said, "no, it can't. We know about these creatures where I come from. Over the years we've learned a great deal about coping with them, and the proof of that is, there are still people living in the Mesoge. I did everything the way you're supposed to, and I added a touch of my own, dumping it in the sea. This can't be the same walker. Therefore, it must be a different one."

"Two monsters." He hadn't wanted to hear that, and he was used to hearing only what he wanted to hear. "Is that normal?"

"No," I said. "It's in these creatures' nature to be solitary. And they don't take revenge when one of them gets taken down, or anything like that. Revenge is a by-product of love, after all. Walkers don't love anyone."

He thought about that for a moment. "In that case," he said, "how do you account for the fact that the monster came looking for you, in the place where you were known to be staying?"

Only of course it wasn't about that. "I don't know," I said.

"You say that these monsters don't take revenge," he said. "But, by your own admission, everything it did, or they have done, is anomalous. You say they're confined to the Mesoge, and here we have one, or two, in Choris. You say they're solitary creatures, but you also say there must be two of them. You say the first one is dead, but—" He shrugged. "Would you at least accept," he went on, "that you were the target of this second attack?"

No. "Yes," I said, "I suppose I must have been. What do we know about Brother Naso?"

"He was the delegate from the exarchate of Galmso in southern Permia," he said. "His credentials are in order. He attended most of the debates, and his voting record is entirely orthodox. Delegates who spoke to him describe him as friendly, well-informed, somewhat garrulous. Other than that—" He made a vague gesture. "He held no elevated rank and had made no significant contribution to the council. It therefore seems overwhelmingly likely that he was not the intended target."

"With respect." There's a limit to how often you can say that, but never mind. "Are you saying that an agency capable of using Mesoge walkers as its tools wouldn't know that I'd moved from the inn to the basilica? I don't think Evil makes that sort of mistake."

Stupid of me to say that. I knew the real reason, but I

couldn't tell anyone. I should have kept my mouth shut and looked blank. "No," he said, "I must confess, I find that rather extraordinary. But so much of these events is beyond rational explanation. I can only assume that the mistake lay with the creature itself, not those controlling it. But that's merely a guess."

He'd run out of things to say, and I'd said everything I was prepared to, so nobody spoke for a while. Then he said, "What do you think we should do?"

"I honestly don't know," I replied. "If you're right and it's me he's after, I should get out of Choris straight away, before anybody else gets hurt. Or I could stay here and fight it, though I really don't see what I can do that someone else couldn't do better. Maybe if it kills me it'll be satisfied and go away. I'm not exactly in prime fighting trim, but even if I was, I don't suppose it'd matter."

Maybe he'd been hoping I had something useful to suggest. "It would be catastrophic if we had to abandon the council," he said. "It would send an appalling message, that Evil is capable of disrupting the exercise of the true faith." He lifted his head and looked at me. "You're a man of learning," he said. "I assume you've heard of Saloninus' razor?"

I nodded.

"The most likely explanation is liable to be the truth. I find that the most likely explanation for these events is that Evil is trying to sabotage the council. Therefore the council must go ahead, at all costs. I confess I can't account for Evil's fixation with you, unless there's something about yourself that you've neglected to tell me." Pause. I did my big stone face. "I can only think that you attract it, or them, like a magnet, because of your Mesoge heritage. That in turn would suggest that Evil's control over it, or them, is not absolute, and that it or they have a degree of self-determination. That I'm prepared to accept. Evil is, as we know, imperfect in all things, by definition. Therefore it follows that it must be imperfect in competence."

A nice bit of reasoning, though garbage. "I hadn't thought of it in those terms," I said.

"I don't suppose you had. So," he went on, "we face a terrible situation. A monster is loose and, if you are to be believed, nothing we do can stop it. We must therefore anticipate further martyrdoms." At which point, I think the implications of what he'd just said hit him, like a branch across the road hitting a galloping horseman. But he went on: "That is as He wills. The history of Holy Mother Church is a record of its martyrs, and there is no greater privilege than to die for the faith. We must accept that and move on."

I think he was talking to himself rather than me, and I felt really bad for keeping so much from him. Also, Svangerd would be livid if she ever found out that I'd effectively lied to a very senior cleric. "I do have one suggestion," I heard myself say; then I scrabbled frantically in my mind to find a suggestion to make.

"Go on."

"If you're right about it targeting me, we can use that. I got lucky the first time, incredibly lucky. There just happened to be a bell, the only thing on the premises that could damage a walker."

"Luck," he said. "I prefer to call it providence."

"Indeed," I said. "In which case, let's learn from providence's example. If it's coming for me, we can set a trap for it."

He looked up. Hope; oh dear. Hope is such an ambivalent thing. I particularly like the old Sashan fairytale, about the box which the gods gave to the inquisitive girl, with strict instructions not to open it. So of course she did, and inside were all the horrors and miseries that afflict us poor mortals; the last winged crawling thing to creep out of the box was Hope, the greatest and most insidious pest of all – because it keeps you going, prepared to endure endless suffering instead of doing the sensible thing and hanging yourself. I'd given Vitimer hope, which was cruel of me, just to tide over an awkward hiatus in the conversation.

"What sort of trap?" he said.

Fatuous, because of course the walker wasn't coming for me. He'd come for the princess, and then the true gospels, or maybe the bureau chief of the Loyal Opposition; definitely not me, because I'm nobody. Therefore I could sit festooned with traps until the sea ran dry and the mountains crumbled into dust and he wouldn't come for me. But never mind. I was showing willing, inspiring hope and clocking up good-conduct points for being a brave soldier.

As I mentioned to Vitimer, over the years we've learned a thing or two about pest control in the Mesoge. We've learned that there's a special sort of greyish sand that you can dig out of the bed of one particular stream; cut open a piece of raw meat and sprinkle a generous pinch of the special sand, then leave it lying about where you know there's a bear, and you've got one less bear to worry about. That approach doesn't work for walkers, because they don't eat, so you have to try something else.

Meanwhile, it occurred to me to wonder what the short man had been doing in the hayloft of the More Joy. He'd made it clear to me that he knew all about the box and what was inside it, and he'd been pretty quick off the mark hiring the loft, when he had perfectly good accommodations already. But, having gone to the hayloft and presumably found the box, he didn't go away again; he stayed there, and got his head stamped flat. Considered objectively, that wasn't the behaviour of a thief. More like he'd gone there to guard the horrible box, until I was fit enough to come and recover it.

Twice that day I nearly told Svangerd about the box, but I couldn't quite make myself do it. She was still right on the edge after hearing about who the short man was, or claimed to be, and I was terrified of losing her completely. And I needed her, more than ever.

"You must be out of your tiny mind," she said.

"It's a well-established procedure in the Mesoge," I said. "And I've got two broken ribs and half a dozen sprains. I can't fight the loathsome thing."

"No."

"Chicken."

That just made her very angry. "If you weren't a pathetic excuse for a man I'd smash your face in for that. I'm not scared of anything. Except Evil."

"There's no such thing as—"

"What if it can kill my soul?" She said it so urgently that I decided to keep my mouth shut. "You don't know, that's the thing. Touching something like that. What could it do to you?"

I took a deep breath. "Listen," I said. "These things are common as mud in the Mesoge. But there's absolutely no reason to suppose—"

"You don't know that." She was controlling herself, barely; trying to explain her fear to me, instead of breaking my jaw and running away. That was amazingly touching. "Suppose it's, what's the word, contagious. You say there's lots of these things. Maybe that's because people who come in contact with them get infected. I don't want to end up like that. It's too horrible."

Sore topic, given that the condition runs in families, as I may have mentioned. "I don't think it works like that," I said. "I've heard all the stories and the legends, and I don't know of a single instance where a foreigner ever turned into a walker. It's strictly a Mesoge thing. I don't know, it's something to do with the soil or the water, something that gets into your bloodstream from what you eat or drink. Or maybe it's purely hereditary, and there are so many cases because we're all hopelessly interbred up there. I really don't believe you can get it from not washing your hands or having someone sneeze in your face."

She gave me a look I don't care to dwell on. "Yes," she said, "but you believe all sorts of stupid, wicked things, so I'm not particularly interested in what you think."

"Based on evidence," I said. "Look, just because it's me saying it, it doesn't necessarily follow that it isn't true. Besides, you're not making any sense. It's not logical. You're a true believer. Nothing can hurt your soul if you have true faith."

"You don't believe that."

"No, but you do."

I felt like I'd been kicking a favourite dog. "What the hell do you need me for anyway?" she said. "Vitimer's got lots of soldiers. Get them to help you."

"I don't trust them," I said. "I want the best."

That got me a sort of lopsided grin. "Piss off," she said.

"Honestly and sincerely," I said. "And anyway, it's not going to happen. The monster won't show up. I'm right and Vitimer's wrong; this isn't about me. It can't be. Either the monster won't come back or it'll come back and kill somebody else, someone who matters. Therefore laying this trap for it is perfectly safe."

"If it's perfectly safe, you don't need me."

"That's assuming I'm right," I said. "Based on what you know of me, are you really prepared to stake my life on my judgement?"

She has a particular expression in which contempt and affection are irrevocably alloyed, like copper and tin in bronze. It's the closest I'm ever likely to get, so I value it highly. "Fuck you," she said. "All right, what sort of trap?"

So I told her about my third cousin Siggeir.

I didn't tell her he was my cousin. But I explained how Siggeir was a particularly annoying specimen. He broke into barns in midwinter, when all the stock was indoors, and slaughtered everything: cows, horses, goats, sheep, pigs, chickens. During the night you'd hear the most appalling racket, and in the morning the yard would be scattered with body parts and the barn was a nightmare. His favourite trick was dumping guts down wells; the water froze over them, so you couldn't climb down and fish them out until the thaw came, by which time they'd rotted and all the water was hopelessly poisoned, so the well had to be drained with buckets before you could draw on it again. That was bad enough, but then he started breaking into houses, at which point the neighbourhood reluctantly agreed that somebody ought to do something.

Define somebody: enter Gisli the Rat. He farmed a large but mostly useless spread on the wind-facing side of Laugardale, so strictly speaking it was none of his concern, but he needed hay for the winter and nobody liked him very much, so he decided to win the love and gratitude of his neighbours by getting rid of Siggeir.

A more unlikely hero you wouldn't hope to meet. By all accounts he was a long, skinny man, somewhere between forty and sixty, bald, with a nose like a beak, practically no chin and an Adam's apple that made him look like he'd tried to swallow an anvil. If you asked him a question he'd look at you as though you'd barked at him like a dog, and he mumbled. His wife had been killed by a bear many years earlier, but he had a son, a smaller version of himself but with bigger ears.

Gisli and his son (I think he was called Eybiorn, but I wouldn't swear to it) took a couple of picks and a shovel and dug into the mound where Siggeir was buried, just deep enough to make a small hole, which they shat into. Then they went home, and sure enough, the next night Siggeir came to call. Gisli had moved all his livestock out of the barn apart from one very fine stallion, the only good and valuable asset he owned; he'd bred it to sell for horse-fighting, which is a really big thing in the Mesoge. Naturally, Siggeir made straight for the barn. He was busily gutting the stallion with his fingers when there was a loud splintering noise and the hayloft roof came down on his head; hardly surprising, since Gisli and the boy had spent the previous week filling it with rocks. All that was holding it up was a couple of hefty tree-trunks, and as soon as Siggeir smashed his way into the barn, Gisli hauled on a rope tied round a padstone on which one of the tree-trunks was resting.

Now under normal circumstances a few tons of rocks falling on his head would only have served to get Siggeir good and mad, once he'd had a chance to dig himself out again. But he didn't get that chance. Outside the barn, Gisli had stacked up his entire winter supply of faggots, plus all the lumber he could lay his hands on, plus twenty twelve-bushel baskets of charcoal he'd made in the autumn to sell at Visby fair. He and the boy worked like madmen, dragged in all the fuel, packed it round the pile of rocks and set it on fire.

The barn burned for a week, with Gisli adding more fuel as fast as he could gather and cart it, and the rocks got so hot they split into gravel; and when the fire was eventually cold, Gisli and the boy dug down and found Siggeir, intact but cooked to a crisp. They smashed him up with hammers until he was basically clinker and cinders, then packed the remains in a couple of barrels and carted them to the big waterfall at Laxarness, where they dumped them into the foaming water. And that was the last anyone heard of Siggeir for over thirty years.

It didn't end well for Gisli, I'm sorry to say. He was left with no barn, no fuel, no lumber, no charcoal and no valuable fighting-horse, so (not unreasonably) he expected his neighbours to chip in and indemnify him for his losses. This, needless to say, they declined to do. Who asked him (they said) to stick his nose into a strictly Gauksdale affair which was nothing to do with him, and if he felt the need to pick a fight with a walker and torch seventy marks' worth of his own property, that was his business and not theirs. Gisli retaliated by taking his cart over to Red River and helping himself to hay from someone's barn there, which led to a bunch of the Gauksdale farmers turning up at Gisli's place shortly before dawn one day, nailing the doors of his house shut and setting fire to it with him and his son inside. That's the Mesoge for you, and you can probably understand why I wasn't entirely heartbroken to leave.

*

Every part of the plan, I decided that night as I sat on a barrel in a room in the Clerestory Tower, was perfect, apart from one thing.

Not that it mattered, of course, because I was in no danger whatsoever, apart from a modest risk of getting pneumonia. I wasn't the target, and the perfect (apart from one thing) trap I'd designed wasn't going to be used, because he wouldn't come for me.

Except, it suddenly occurred to me, my father had come for me under the bell-tower. He hadn't come to kill a dignitary of the Church or recover a copy of the true gospels or murder a short man. It had been me he was after. But my father was now ashes dissolved in seawater, so none of that mattered. Nothing was going to happen, and I was perfectly safe.

The barrel I was sitting on, like the hundred or so barrels in the ground-floor room directly below me, was full of lamp oil; best-quality Blemmyan, shipped to Choris by Sherden traders to fuel the thousand-odd lamps that light the basilica. Blemmyan oil burns clean and with a singularly pure light, and they scent it with some kind of resin that makes it smell of violets. Whale-oil would've done just as well at a quarter of the price, but there wasn't any to hand, and Vitimer didn't seem inclined to argue about the cost.

The plan was pretty simple, which is how a good plan should be. As soon as she heard me yelling, Svangerd, on the floor above, would throw a lever which would dislodge a steel pin which held shut the trapdoor on which were piled three tons of bricks. The bricks fall on the walker; at which point the men in the room below would broach one barrel of lamp-oil and set light to it. The tower would serve as a chimney. By the time the rafters burned through and the bricks and the walker came crashing down, the lamp-oil fire would be good and hot, having spread to the heaped-up mound of charcoal that filled every last bit of space not occupied by barrels. I'd based the design on the set-up they use to smelt iron in Schanz, which produces the hottest fires anywhere since the empire fell and the secret of blast furnaces was lost.

Svangerd would have just enough time to get clear by running down the spiral staircase and out into the cloister garden, to be joined by the oil-lighting detail on the ground floor. Every last detail, in fact, had been carefully thought out and allowed for, apart from the one I mentioned earlier. That detail hadn't exactly escaped my attention; or Vitimer's, for that matter. I think he'd set his mind at rest with the well-known adage about omelettes and eggs. I'd told myself that it didn't matter, because the walker wasn't going to show up, for the reasons stated. Nothing, therefore, for me to worry my pretty little head about.

A barrel is a stupid thing to sit on for any length of time, because the top band cuts into you in a most inconvenient place. I wriggled about a bit, but it didn't help.

Someone or something was in the room with me. Don't ask me how I knew. There was one lamp, which I'd brought with me and placed on the floor. I started to turn my head to look behind me, but a hand pressed down on the top of it to stop me.

"Quiet," said a voice.

"Kotkel?"

Faces change, but voices stay the same. I hadn't seen my brother Kotkel since the day I left home. Of all my brothers he was the one I disliked least. He was spiteful, arrogant and cruel. He stole the food off my plate when Dad wasn't looking, and he broke things and left gates open and said I'd done it, just to get me in trouble. He was the next up from me in the hand-me-down clothes chain, so whenever I was due to inherit a shirt or a pair of trousers, he burned holes in it before giving it to me, then told my father I'd done it, which got me a good hiding.

"Shut your face," he said quietly, "or I'll twist your head off."

Yes, that sounded very much like the Kotkel I used to know. "Kel? What the hell are you doing in Choris?"

Fingers squeezed my skull, reminding me of how very fragile bone is. "I told you to shut your face. Are you deaf as well as stupid?"

"Are you dead, Kel?"

He laughed. "Like you fucking care."

"I care plenty. Are you dead?"

"Like fuck you do. Where's the money you were supposed to send home? All these years and not a fucking penny. I ought to squeeze your head in."

"Why don't you do that, Kel?"

On reflection, I think the reason my brothers didn't like me was that I had a habit of answering back. They hit and kicked me and I retaliated with words, not blows. It was like we were fighting two different wars, and I fought mine with weapons they couldn't use and against which they had no defence. Try as they might, they never could get me to shut up, no matter what they did. "You're an arsehole, you know that? Not one penny. We could've starved for all you cared."

"Fine," I said. "Go ahead and kill me, if that's what you want."

I felt the pressure relax. He couldn't trust himself not to crush me unless he took his hand well away. Good old Kotkel. Never the nicest human being in the whole wide world, but compared to Einar or Kari he was a sweetheart. "What are you doing here, Kel? Who brought you?"

"Nobody brought me."

"Are you dead?"

"Fuck you," he said.

"Why did you come here if nobody brought you?"

Suddenly, I don't know why, it occurred to me that I'd bullied my brothers just as much as they'd bullied me, only in a different way. It must have been intolerable to have my piping little gadfly voice buzzing at them all the time, and nothing would ever make me shut up. Well, that's families for you. See above, under Love.

"Nobody brought me, arsehole. You deaf or what?"

"Then what are you doing here?"

"Shut *up*, will you? Just shut *up*."

"Not till you answer my question."

I didn't see him move, but suddenly he was in front of me. I made myself take a good look.

Kotkel was always tall; now he was easily eight feet, swollen, bloated, like the old monk who had dropsy when I was a novice, his skin rounded and smooth and straining to bursting point, the colour of bilberries just before they ripen. Completely inhuman, unmistakably my brother Kotkel, who I hadn't seen for years. Mostly it was the look on his face, irritation goaded to violence, violence barely restrained by the thought of its consequences. But for a walker, there are no consequences. "What's the matter, Kel? Why don't you kill me?"

"You're a fucking arsehole, you know that?"

"Yes," I said. "Answer the question."

Once, I remember, Kotkel and Gretti and Kari got mad at me – something I said – and held my head underwater. I remember almost drowning. They always seemed to know exactly how far they could go, with a degree of precision which you'd have thought only a scientist could gauge, after a lifetime of research.

This time, however, maybe I'd gone a bit too far. That was the thing, back then, in the Mesoge. I really didn't care how far I goaded them, or what might happen. I only wanted to win.

He looked at me, pure hate. "Fuck you," he said. Then he kicked a hole in the tower wall and stepped through it.

"Vitimer is going to kill you," she said. "All that trouble and expense, and you let it get away."

Valid point, and I wasn't looking forward to my next interview with him, scheduled for immediately after prime. But I can honestly say that that was the least of my worries. "I'm afraid," I said, "that I haven't been entirely honest with you."

We were sitting in the room in the tower, which now had a gaping hole in it. Outside, all the king's horses and all the king's men were scouring the basilica grounds for the monster, while over our heads and under our feet, several dozen lay brothers were dismantling the trap before something gave way or caught fire. I'd told the guard captain that there was no point trying again. Obviously the monster had twigged, which was why it got out in a hurry before the trap could be sprung. Never mind, I told him. I'll just have to think of something else.

"For crying out loud," she said. "Now what?"

So I told her: the true gospels; Kotkel. By the time I finished, I was completely drained and she just sat there. I'd expected rage, hysteria, violence, quite possibly a knife in my heart. Instead – you can see why I've got no use for love. People you love can hurt you so badly.

"Anyway," I said, after the longest silence ever. "That's how it stands, more or less. If you've got any suggestions, I'd be very grateful."

She looked at me. First Kotkel, now her. It was my night for being looked at.

"Fine," I said. "If you want to wash your hands of me, I understand. Go home. I was wrong: this is about me. You don't have to get caught up in it, whatever the hell it is. Go home; tell them what happened; say it was all my fault. Which is true: it is. There's nothing you can do here, and you don't deserve this kind of punishment. Presumably I do, though why, God only knows."

Still not a word. I stood up. "Come on," I said. "It's freezing in here, you'll catch your death."

She stood up and hit me: her signature short right to the solar plexus. It certainly took my mind off my troubles. When the mist cleared, I was on my knees, struggling to draw breath past an apparently insurmountable obstacle. I spared a thought for all the inoffensive guards, jailers, watchmen, goons, innocent bystanders and hired killers I'd seen her drop with that punch over the years. "Get up," she said.

"Not sure I can."

"Get up."

I held out my arm and she hauled me to my feet. I staggered, then sat down on that bloody barrel. "Are you all right?" she said.

"I think so," I said. "Give me a moment."

"You're a complete arsehole," she said. Odd how the people I care about all tend to use that word about me. "You're stupid and thoughtless and you don't give a shit about other people. And really, really stupid."

I managed a small nod. "Sorry," I said.

"You're sorry. Hoo-fucking-ray." Well, at least she was talking to me again. "You're right, I ought to go back home right now. Maybe someone there can figure out a way to clear up this mess you've made of everything. I can't."

"Me neither."

She hesitated, then sat down on the floor next to me. "How about Vitimer?" she said. "You've met him; I haven't. Is he smart?"

I shook my head. "He's an idiot," I said. "No, he's not; he's a politician, which is worse. Smart, but only interested in politics. Can't expect anything from him."

"There's got to be someone we can go to," she said. "For fuck's sake, we've got all the finest minds and purest souls in the world here in this city right now. Somebody's got to know what to do."

"You've been to the debates. Name one."

She couldn't. "It can't be up to us," she said. "It just can't."

"I'd love an alternative," I said. "Can you think of one?"

She lifted her head and gave me a look that broke my heart. "I didn't get your broken rib, did I? Only that could be bad. You can puncture a lung."

"I'm fine," I said.

"We can't go home," she said. "Not till we've sorted this. If it is all about you, it'd be like taking the plague home with us. What's that word? Quarantine. We've got to stay here until we're sure it's over."

"It's about me," I said. "I only wish I knew what it is about me." A thought occurred to me. "If it gets really bad—"

"Oh, shut up," she said. "Yes, if it comes to it, I'll cut your stupid throat with the greatest of pleasure. Right now, though, you're the key to the mystery, so guzzling you would probably be short-sighted. Let me be the judge of that, all right?"

That made me laugh, which hurt. "You're going to have to teach me that right hook," I said.

"Right cross."

"Whatever."

"Your problem is," she said, "you don't bring your shoulder across till it meets your chin. Which means you aren't getting the full advantage of using your body weight. Also, you've got to remember to step into it, instead of just standing there like a fencepost."

"Thank you."

"Another thing you do wrong—"

Ah well. At least we were talking.

Vitimer wasn't pleased with me. It wasn't my fault, he assured me several times. Still, it was a pity, a great pity, an opportunity wasted, and now the monster would be on its guard, suspicious, harder to catch and destroy, and we still knew so little about it, who'd sent it, what it wanted, all useful information that I could have gathered, if only I hadn't let it get away. But there. No use crying over spilled milk, even if it did end up costing who knew how many lives?

He asked me if there was anything I hadn't yet told him that might prove helpful. No, I said. He believed me. Thank you, he said, meaning, Get out of my sight.

People were staring at me as I crossed the cloister garden: that's him, the one who fought the monster; they're saying he's the one it's after; he brought it here . . . All a bit much for someone who likes to be as inconspicuous as possible. In fairytales there's a whole range of handy gadgets for making yourself invisible – hats, cloaks, the juice of herbs, rings, bracelets. I even heard once of a pig's bladder of invisibility, though the storyteller was a bit vague about how you went about using it. Me for some of that, I've always thought. Some people can't live without being seen. It's as though, if people aren't looking at them, they aren't really there. I'm there all right, believe me. I guess it dates back to making myself as hard to find as possible when my brothers were looking for me, and now it's second nature. People knowing where I am bothers me. I can't help it.

Nobody seemed to expect anything of me, so I was able to go to the debate. It was a good one. Friedmund Scholasticus was laying into Trebonian's doctrine of conditional redemption, slowly tearing it into small, neat shreds, with Simboin and Alpbrand of Stachel desperately trying to do damage control whenever he'd let them get a word in edgeways. When he's not attending councils or presiding as judge at heresy hearings, Friedmund lives on a little wooden raft, six feet by six, forty feet up in the branches of a massive oak tree. His disciples bring him food and books, which he hauls up on a rope, and when it rains he gets very, very wet. He may be a trifle eccentric, but he's got the purest classical style of any man living and can do things with the pluperfect subjunctive that you wouldn't believe were possible –

Forgive me. We're all boring about something. With Svangerd it's different ways of hurting people, with me it's fancy wordplay. The point being, for a while there I was enjoying myself, so much so that I almost forgot the depth and plasticity of the shit I was in, and when the debate was over (motion defeated by a whisker; grand exit of Friedmund, stalking out in high dudgeon after placing the whole council under anathema; you really had to be there) I wandered out into the cloister in a sort of happy, rhetoric-fuelled daze and sat perched on a windowsill, relishing the aftertaste.

A man in a grey habit walked past me. He was whistling a tune.

I jumped up so fast that I trod on my own hem and nearly measured my length. Colliding with a passing archdeacon stopped me from falling; he pushed me away and gave me a filthy look, which changed into fear and loathing when he recognised me. I stammered an apology, then looked round for a grey habit. Of course, all the Poor Brothers wear grey, and a quarter of the delegates were Brothers. But then I heard the tune again, right at the far end of the cloister. I set off like a greyhound.

It's a commonplace little tune, simple but cheerful, and there are words that go with it. As follows:

Long years ago, when I was young,
I spent my days a-shovelling dung.
I worked all day and half the night
And my young hands were far from white.

Where Kotkel learned it, I have no idea, because he never went anywhere we didn't go or met anyone we didn't meet. I very much doubt that he made it up for himself, because it's a proper tune and the words both rhyme and scan. Mostly I think he sang it to annoy me, but I guess he liked it too, because he sang, hummed and whistled it incessantly, until one day Dad kicked him clear across the barn because it was getting on his nerves. A high point in my childhood, needless to say.

The point being, I'd never heard anyone else sing it, ever. I hurtled down the cloister just as he turned left through the arch that leads to the little courtyard with the fountain, and then there's another arch that leads to the refectory. No sign of anyone. I tried the refectory door, but it was bolted from the inside.

People don't just vanish into thin air. Like pulling rabbits out of a hat or the existence of a supreme being, it's just not possible. I looked round for a hidden space large enough to hide a man, but there wasn't one. I looked in the fountain, which is six inches deep.

Fine, I thought. Just showing off, that's all. Someone had been to all the trouble of going to the Mesoge, while Kotkel was still alive, and carefully memorising his favourite song. To me that made no sense, but what do I know about anything? Then it occurred to me that it was a bit odd, Kotkel dying so young. Of course, people die young in the Mesoge every day. It's a hard, cruel place, and it uses people up faster than marching on roads wears out army boots. But what if Kotkel would still be alive if someone hadn't wanted him for something; for playing stupid games with me, for example?

You reach a point where you're past caring. I never liked Kotkel much anyway. Revenge and blood feuds have always been the ruin of the Mesoge, more so than the climate or the soil or the landlords; it's something we do to ourselves and it's all our fault. Accordingly, the last thing I needed was an atavistic craving for blood-vengeance. I'm a civilised man, I don't live there any more, I don't do that sort of thing. Really.

Maybe it wasn't just Kotkel. Maybe they'd killed Dad as well.

She hadn't gone to the council session. She thinks Friedmund is a dangerous heretic who ought to be burned on a bonfire of his own books. Instead, she told me, she intended to go and pray for her soul, on her knees in the Mercy Chapel. Fine, I said, whatever floats your boat. That got me a glare that should have shrivelled me like a dead leaf, if I'd had a scrap of decency left in me. But I don't, so it didn't.

The Mercy Chapel isn't far from the courtyard with the fountain. Actually, it's one of the bleaker bits of the basilica, comparatively speaking. Once, according to the books, it was a glorious thing, every square inch of wall and ceiling decorated with post-Mannerist frescoes by the likes of Athelwulf the Elder and Poscinnius. But it was completely gutted during Iconoclasm in the late empire, scraped down to the bare stone; when the iconoclasts were thrown out, it was decided that the redecoration of the chapel should be something really special, to mark the utter discrediting of the iconoclast heresy, and a committee was formed to decide on how to go about it. That was nine hundred years ago, and I understand they're promising an interim report any day now. In the meantime, the walls and ceiling are plain whitewash, with a few icons that someone found in storage hung up to give people something to look at during the drearier parts of the services; these include a Lutbrand Ascension, three Desert Masters and a Revelation by Segipert the Eremite, one of only three still known to exist. Just something someone turned up at the bottom of some old box. That's Choris.

I found her in front of the altar, crouched on her knees and elbows; a bit extreme, even for her. When I spoke to her she didn't look up. "Go away," she said.

"Svangerd? What's the matter?"

"Go *away*."

I knew that tone of voice. The last time I'd heard it, she was telling a visiting archdeacon to leave her alone. I recognised the danger signs and managed to get between them in time, so the archdeacon got away with nothing worse than concussion and a couple of missing teeth; the tricky part came later, covering the whole thing up. In the end I had to swear a deposition that His Holiness had been possessed by a demon, who caused him to make inappropriate advances to a Holy Sister and then threw him down a staircase. Wonderfully useful creatures, demons. They cover a multitude of sins.

Anyway, it was that tone of voice, so I took a long step back. "What's happened? Something bad."

She pulled herself up off the floor onto her knees. "Yes," she said. "Very bad."

"What?"

"Not in here."

Fair enough. We went outside into the cloister. "I saw someone I used to know," she said. "In the old days."

Oh. "Did he see you?"

She nodded.

"I don't see the problem," I said. "Look, your past history isn't exactly a secret. You confessed; you did penance; you were absolved. All over and done with."

She looked at me. "I don't think it works quite like that," she said.

"No, maybe not. But if this character – how did you know him, exactly?"

"Professionally."

"Well, then. He's hardly going to stand up in public and admit to gross fornication, just to get you in trouble. Well, is he?"

She sighed. "It's different for men," she said. "Wicked

women seduce weak but essentially right-minded men; everybody knows that. Come on, you know the score as well as I do."

"But you've been forgiven. You've got a piece of paper to prove it."

She shook her head. "I saw him and he saw me. If I hang around, instead of going straight home immediately, I'll be to blame for reminding him of his going astray, which is bad for his mental and spiritual well-being. They don't exactly spell it out at the reformatory, but it's pretty obvious what you're supposed to do in these circumstances. If I stay here, I'm committing a sin and it casts doubt on the sincerity of my repentance. I've got to leave – I don't have a choice."

I thought about that. "And he just happens to show up, right at this precise moment. Gosh."

She shrugged. "Maybe it's a fix, maybe it's a coincidence. I don't know. But I can't stay here. They could throw me out of the order. I couldn't bear that."

There are times when I reckon she has a much lower opinion of her God than I do. I merely maintain that He doesn't exist. She, by contrast, is prepared to attribute to Him a degree of petty-mindedness that would be deplorable in a human being, let alone the Divine. Svangerd honestly thinks that if they boot her out of the order, her redemption will lapse and she'll go to hell. O, ye of little faith, I said to her once, which led to a very fraught day and a half before she forgave me.

"Fine," I said. "Then you'd better go. It's all right. I can look after myself."

I didn't even try to say it like I meant it. "Yes," she said, "you can. And there's not really anything I can do, is there? I'd only get in the way."

She didn't mean it either. So much for the truth setting you free. Mind you, truth is the most overrated commodity in history, with the possible exception of truffles. "I'll go and see about finding you a ship," I said. "And you'll be able to report back and let them know what's going on. Who knows, they might even have some bright idea we haven't thought of for solving this mess. Anything's possible."

The earliest ship going the right way that the harbourmaster knew about was the day after tomorrow. He said something technical about winds and tides and that sort of garbage; in one ear, out the other. I found the captain and gave him some money. Job done.

"What the hell am I supposed to do in the meanwhile?" she demanded. "I daren't show my face outside of this room. I can't even go to the chapel and pray, in case I run into him."

"So stay here," I said. "It's only for a couple of days."

That, of course, was the most unreasonable thing she'd ever heard in her entire life. I left her to it and went to listen to the evening debate. It was rather a good one – a fairly low-key affair, but none the worse for that after all the high drama we'd been having lately, in one form or another. Nenzimer of Antecyrene was arguing that the time had come to revisit the anathema pronounced on the sixth book of Cartimanduus' *Meditations*. Eight hundred years had passed since the original decision, he pointed out, during which time we'd all had a chance to reflect on the ambiguities surrounding the various issues; furthermore, the last known copy of the work in question had perished when the archduke's library burned down a few years ago, so the point was very likely moot. In practical terms, however, the ban meant that it was extremely difficult to access Odovacar's *Sermons*, since, although they themselves were recognised as flawlessly orthodox, a number of passages from *Meditations* 6 were quoted (for the purposes of vigorous refutation); accordingly, no copies of Odovacar had been made for several hundred years, since it was illegal to copy them out because they contained anathematised material, which meant that anyone wishing to read the *Sermons* had to travel a long way to the remote monasteries who possessed the existing copies, which were in grave danger of falling to pieces through over-use.

Nobody seemed inclined to offer more than token opposition to this proposal, so the acting chairman gave the motion to the floor for further debate. At which point a man I didn't recognise stood up and started to talk.

There was no point, he said, debating Cartimanduus or Odovacar or any of the old authorities, since they had now been superseded and were entirely irrelevant. A new discovery meant that everything we had hitherto regarded as scripture was at best obsolete, at worst useless and positively pernicious. Earlier that day, he went on, he had been handed a copy of the long-lost true gospels, which he had since read, and he was therefore in a position –

That's as far as he managed to get before the shouting started. I froze, naturally enough. I expected the speaker to be torn limb from limb, or at the very least bundled out of the room in a straitjacket. But no, he carried on talking, though nobody could hear a word he was saying. Some of the shouting was outrage and fury, but not all of it, and it suddenly occurred to me that I wasn't the only one who'd heard about the true gospels. Far from it. A lot of the people in the room seemed to know about them, and wanted to find out what they said.

I looked at Vitimer, who was on his feet shouting, but

nobody seemed to be paying him any attention. That was bad, whichever way you looked at it. I felt sorry for him. Holy Mother Church has a long and selective memory, and Vitimer was going to be remembered for all eternity as the president of the council who couldn't get people to shut up while he was talking.

It felt like the yelling went on for a very long time, but it can only have been a couple of minutes. Then someone – I couldn't see who; there were heads and shoulders in the way – grabbed one of the heavy candlesticks off the altar and started banging it on the stone floor. That worked: everybody stopped roaring and howling, and there was a moment of dead silence, really rather spooky in its way. Vitimer snatched the opportunity and announced that the session was adjourned until further notice, then started to walk quickly out of the chamber.

Not quickly enough. If he'd been able to get outside the door, his exit would automatically have closed the session, and nothing said or done after that would have had any sort of official standing, as a proceeding of the council. If I'd been Vitimer, I'd have run, and the hell with the dignity of office. As it was, he was still a couple of yards from the door when the baying and yelling started up again, and as far as I could tell it was coming exclusively from the faction who wanted to hear more about the true gospels.

Procedural footnote – just in case you aren't as obsessively knowledgeable about the minutiae of ecclesiastical protocol as I am. The existence of the true gospels had never been formally conceded; as far as Holy Mother Church was concerned, there was no such thing. Naming them in a council session would at the very least confirm that they existed. Whether they were scripture or anathema was another matter entirely, but ignoring them would no longer be an option. Given their nature, there would inevitably have to be a debate, and by the look of it, that would split the Church as neatly and thoroughly as an axe splits straight-grain ash.

There's a technical name for it: schism, meaning that the Indivisible Body has been divided, a state of affairs so un-natural and terrifying that Holy Mother Church has done everything she possibly could, for two thousand years, to stop it happening. Among the things done and sacrifices made have been any number of martyrdoms and judicial executions, a dozen full-scale wars, the mass excommunication of the Blemmyan church and the reluctant decision to allow the fire-worshipping Sashan to enslave a million of our co-religionists in Olbia, because the Olbians refused to renounce the Donatist heresy. So you'll appreciate that schism is the worst thing that can possibly happen, and here it suddenly was, in the council chamber, on Vitimer's watch; and all because I bought a box in a junk shop in a back street in Mavais. Oops, I thought, or words to that effect.

Even at that late stage, Vitimer might just have saved the day if he'd carried on through the door and shut it firmly behind him. After all, he'd declared the session adjourned. I'm guessing he thought that would do the trick, in which case he was sadly misinformed about council procedure. Even the president can't just adjourn a session unilaterally. He proposes an adjournment motion, which is always carried unanimously without a vote. But he hadn't done that. God only knows why, but he'd chosen the wrong form of words, so it was as though he'd never spoken at all. Now, if he'd got out through the door it wouldn't have mattered, since no council proceedings are valid unless the president is present. But he didn't. Instead, the silly fool turned and tried to make everybody shut up, thereby tacitly admitting that the session was still open. Which meant that anything said (or screamed or yelled) in the chamber by a delegate would be on the record. Which meant schism, sure as the Invincible Sun made little green apples, and left them lying about on a tree to tempt the stupid and the easily led.

I sat there while all this was going on, feeling like I was watching a stone from a siege catapult looping through the sky and heading straight at me. Had there been anything I could have done, would I have done it? Academic question. For a split second, I toyed with the idea of standing up and telling everybody that it was all my fault, I'd found the box and the books and brought them to Choris and negligently hidden them where any passing monster could find them – and then I asked myself what good that would do: answer, none. If it had any effect at all, apart from finishing my career and probably landing me in jail or a remote priory in northern Permia, it'd only make things worse – a provenance (of sorts) for the book and the manuscripts, which might otherwise be dismissed as figments of somebody's imagination. So I kept my face shut and my arse on the bench and did nothing at all while the world as I'd known it began the process of coming to an end.

Someone I recognised – Philo of Lidarend, no less, abbot of the Golden Key and precentor of Brasch – was on his hind legs, pointing a skinny forefinger at Vitimer and howling that the true gospels must be acknowledged and their validity debated in open council. He might as well have stuck Svangerd's pet stiletto into Vitimer's eye-socket; that would have been quicker, cleaner and far more humane. Some people have no consideration for others. Vitimer replied by shaking his head – clearly he'd got way beyond anything that could be fitted into words – and then someone I couldn't see started calling for a vote, which suddenly transformed Philo's demand into a formal motion of the council. Vitimer shook his head again, but gestures don't count. All at once a forest of hands shot up, meaning that a vote was in progress whether the president liked it or not. Lots of hands. I couldn't see properly from where I was, but a moment later I heard the clerk sing out "Carried", and I knew that we were all comprehensively and irrecoverably screwed. Schism. Oh boy.

7

I can't remember how I got out of the council chamber into the cloister, or what happened after the motion was carried. I remember wandering down a corridor that eventually led to a door, which was bolted. I turned round and walked back the way I'd come, and by the time I reached the main cloister it was deserted. I think I ambled around for a while longer and then drifted back to my room.

Mercifully, Svangerd wasn't there. I don't think I could have stood it, her going all to pieces because her beloved Church had just slit its own throat, and presumably blaming me for the whole thing. I'd probably have had to agree with her. If I hadn't bought that stupid box; if I'd told someone about it; if I'd gone back and got it out from among the rafters before Kotkel had a chance to get his huge purple fingers on it. My fault: none of my doing, but all my fault. Technically speaking, that would make it a second-degree sin of omission, punishable by eternal damnation, if you happen to believe in all that stuff. I don't, but Svangerd does. Her faith tells her to forgive evildoers; it also stipulates that you don't have to be alive to be forgiven, since it's the soul that receives the benefit of mercy, not the body. Stab first, forgive afterwards is perfectly all right, if circumstances so demand. Just as well she wasn't there.

But it wasn't my fault, not really. In which case, whose fault was it? The box was hidden in the rafters last time I saw it; therefore, Kotkel must have taken it. Really? No. The short man had known about the box, he'd been at pains to let me know that, and he'd rented our hayloft while the hay was still practically warm. Presumably the incentive hadn't been the fleas or the view over the stable yard. Then Kotkel killed him; but was it robbery with violence or just plain ordinary murder?

That corridor led to a bolted door, so I went back to the start and tried again. Who could I think of who'd want a schism? Who'd go out of their way to achieve that lamentable outcome? Common-sense answers: the Sashan, the Echmen, heathens, enemies foreign rather than domestic. They'd love to see Holy Mother Church collapse in blood and fire. Wouldn't they? Would they hell as like. We're taught to believe that the pagan empires are wolves howling at the gate, waiting in impatient readiness for the slightest opportunity to invade and slaughter us all in our beds. Actually, that's not the case at all. They have their own problems, just like we do, and a major war of aggression against the West would be expensive and dangerous and what would they stand to gain? A load of countries that are poorer and far less sophisticated than the territories they already control; from their perspective, nothing we've got is worth having, except us as slaves – slaves who don't speak their language, which is hugely inefficient, and who'd almost certainly prove to be more trouble than they're worth. The simple fact is, the Sashan haven't invaded and conquered the

West because they don't want to. If they'd wanted to, they'd have done it years ago. But they haven't, so they don't.

Which left enemies domestic. I like to think of myself as a cynic, always ready to prise open people's professed motives to find the pearl of disreputable truth lurking within. Try as I might, though, I couldn't see how anyone in the West would be better off for a schism. Since the empire fell, Holy Mother Church is the only thing we have in common, the way fish have water: mackerel and sharks together, we can't do without it. Destroying the Church would be like fish draining the ocean.

Which left— No, really. I wasn't having that. There is no God, no angels, no devils, no Good, no Evil. Therefore . . .

Yes, I thought, but there's a bunch of lunatics running about, apparently, who *think* they're Evil. I'd met one of them: a short man, who knew about the box and subsequently rented my hayloft. If you sincerely believe that your object in life is to further the cause of a non-existent entity (in this case, the devil), and dumb luck handed you the chance of striking a deadly blow at the heart of the people you believe are the Other Side – I groaned out loud. Because in that case, it really was all my fault, for finding and recognising that stupid box –

Hang on just a moment. I bought the box, from a man who plainly didn't know what it was. Thereafter I kept it a deadly secret. I didn't even tell Svangerd. But the short man knew about it, and that I'd got it. Therefore – Saloninus' razor – he must have known about the box *before it came into my possession*. In which case, why in God's name didn't he go into the shop himself and buy the bloody thing before I showed up on the scene?

A lot of things in this world make no sense, and since this

is the only world that exists, I guess we have to make the best of things or give up and go under. Even so, at that moment, I think I'd have given pretty much everything I had or could've laid my hands on at short notice to find out who knew the tune to my brother's favourite song, and where he'd learned it. If I knew that . . .

But I didn't, and even Saloninus couldn't get very far speculating in the total absence of data. So instead of following a chain of logical premises, like someone following white stones through a bog, I allowed my mind to go off on frolics of its own, like boisterous staghounds in a chicken run, scaring out bizarre hypotheses for the sheer hell of hearing them cluck. You can't do that for very long without drifting off into sleep, so I did.

I was woken by a sustained and ear-splitting racket. Shouting, roaring, boots clattering on floors, doors slamming, heavy objects being moved around. Oh, for crying out loud, I thought. Not again.

I'd fallen asleep in my boots, so I didn't have to put them on again. I had a crick in my neck and my back hurt from dozing in an unsuitable chair. I stood up, looked round for something I could use as a weapon if needs be, realised the utter futility of that, and went out into the corridor.

I emerged just as they brought out the body. A corpse with no intact bones is an awkward thing to handle, particularly when it's fresh and hasn't had time to stiffen. The nearest thing to it would be a very large wineskin. There was no head, needless to say.

"Who is it?" I asked the officer.

"Good question," he replied, in that particular sort of raspy voice you get when you've only recently thrown up. "But the room he was in belongs to a delegate called Ordovic, from out west somewhere. Why, do you know him?"

I shook my head. "Any sign of the—?"

"No. We came running soon as we heard the scream, but it was long gone." He paused, then looked at me. "You're him, aren't you? The one who knows about these things. From the Mesoge."

"That's right," I said.

"You were supposed to know what to do about them."

My fault, in other words. "This one doesn't follow the rules," I said. "Is there anything I can do to help?"

He looked at me. "Apparently not," he said. He moved away, then hesitated. "Actually, there's one thing."

"What?"

"How long is this going to go on for?" he said. "I mean, when does it stop?"

I didn't answer. That bothered him a lot. "That's terrible," he said. "How can people live like that?"

"Welcome to the Mesoge," I said, and went back to my room.

The hell with it. There was once a man called Glam, away out east in Vopnadale, who got rid of a walker by cutting its head off with a billhook. That was well over a hundred years before my time and quite probably there were special circumstances not preserved in the oral tradition, but never mind. Bright and early, I walked down through Coppergate into Poor Town and asked the way to the smiths' quarter. I stopped at the third forge I came to, where a fat man was sitting on an anvil, trying to tease a splinter out of his thumb with a small pair of tongs. Sure, he said, he could forge me a billhook. Good steel? He

looked at me as though I was a keyhole. Sure, he said. He had
a bit of old cart-spring that someone had dug up. That got my
attention. How old? Very old. Show me. He showed me. The
secret of making spring steel died with the empire. That'll do
nicely, I said.

That's the difference between steel and flesh (except in the
Mesoge). You can bury a piece of steel in the wet earth, and
five hundred years later about half of it will be flakes of useless
rust, and the inner half good as new; brush and rasp and grind
off the dead stuff, put it in the fire and get it really hot, and it
comes back to life, ready to be reborn as whatever you need it
to be. I watched him draw out the nose of the hook over the
horn of his anvil, then form the bevel, packing the cutting edge
at dull red; back in the fire to a bright orange, then edge down
in the quench for a second at a time, to let the residual heat
temper the hardness. You want it ground, or just sharpened?
Just sharpened, I told him. I don't care what it looks like. Three
deniers. I gave him five, and he threw in a bit of rag to wrap
it in.

Ridiculous, of course; sympathetic magic. A brought-back-
from-the-dead weapon to kill a brought-back-from-the-dead
monster. Or (I told myself) scientific metallurgy; under the
empire they knew how to make really good steel, capable of
taking and holding a superior edge. In the Mesoge, steel-
making happens more or less by accident. You twist together
a load of stuff at welding heat, and some of it may harden or
it may not. Under the empire, they didn't trust to luck, they
knew. And in Choris, bits of the empire get turned up every
time they plough, including good steel. Science, you see. The
hell with it.

On my way back through Poor Town I found a half-brick.

I sat down on a wall and spent a long time patiently working up a good edge, using spit as a lubricant. I used to sharpen my father's hook for him when he was coppicing; he had high standards, enforced with the back of his hand. The longer it takes to sharpen, the better the steel. The hook was good stuff. I got it to the point where I could shave hairs off my arm with it, then wrapped it up in the rag. I'd get Svangerd to give it the finishing touch. She'd like doing that.

Svangerd was in my room when I got back. She looked as though her father had just died, except (in her case) how would she know?

"That man," she said, "the one who got killed last night."

I nodded.

"It was him."

I took the wrapped billhook out from the fold of my habit and put it down on the bed. "The man you used to know."

"Yes."

Years ago I was walking through the streets of a small town when a slate fell off a roof onto my head. I remember the surprise. Suddenly, no warning, a bewildering, excruciating blow from above, like the wrath of God, only of course He doesn't exist, so it must've been something else. What I remember most about it was the feeling of total and utter stupidity, as if every thought and rational process had been knocked out of my brain. A bit like that.

"Makes no sense," I said.

"Yes, it fucking does," she said. "You idiot, can't you see? It's obvious."

Now she mentioned it, I could see. There was, used to be, a man that Svangerd wanted dead and out of the way, more than anything else in the whole wide world. Next morning he's a decapitated trunk, more of a liquid than a solid. Through the agency of my brother Kotkel. My brother; me feeling the way I do about her. Couldn't be plainer if you wrote it in capitals a foot high.

"I'm doing it," she said. "It's not you, it's me."

"That's nonsense," I said.

"Is it hell as like. I wanted him dead. He's dead. I'm controlling the monster. Can't you see that?"

"Get a grip, for crying out loud," I said. "You are not responsible for my brother's actions. He doesn't even know you."

"I've caught it," she said. "From you. It's a contagion, and you've passed it on to me. I'm unclean, because of—"

"No," I said, painfully aware that I had no arguments to back that up with. Just faith – that old thing. "It doesn't work like that, trust me. It's not your fault."

"This is the worst thing that could possibly happen," she said. "I'm going to go to hell."

"No, you're—"

"Don't try telling me it's a coincidence," she said. "Schism in the Church, and now this. That fucking box you bought."

"Not your fault."

"Yes, it was, it must have been. I was with you. And I wanted the princess dead. I hated her. You didn't hate her."

"No, not really. But I didn't want to have to kill her. So my dad did it for me."

"No," she said. "I *hated* her. Because of what happened when I was a kid."

Sometimes it's just one damn thing after another. "What?"

"When I was a kid," she said. "I never told you about that, did I?"

No, she hadn't; and I, valuing my skin, had never asked. "Tell me," I said.

She sat down next to me on the bed. I could see her go cold, just like the billhook had done when the smith quenched it, as the residual heat bled into the hard edge and was dissipated in the water. "My father was a tenant of the Flawless Diamond in Segwald," she said, "when the princess took over as abbess there. He'd always had trouble raising the money to pay the rent, but the old abbess didn't hold with evicting people so she let things slide. I think we were about four years in arrears. Forty deniers." She reached in her sleeve and pulled out a handful of coins. She held them out on the palm of her hand: four gold bezants, each bezant worth ten deniers. "When Hildigund took over as abbess, she decided the finances were a mess. So she got rid of the old steward and took over the money side of things personally. She brought in a dozen new bailiffs and told them to chase up all the outstanding arrears of rent. My father couldn't find that sort of money, obviously. So they gave him a choice. He had a plough team, six oxen: good stock; his father bred them. And he had a daughter. Me."

She was staring at her hands, as though they were to blame for everything.

"It wasn't really a choice," she said. "Without the oxen he couldn't plough. So they took me. It was supposed to be five years' indentures, but it doesn't work like that in practice. All the time you're indentured, they set off the cost of your board and keep against what you earn, so if they're imaginative with their accounting, after five years you end up owing them money. That's how I came to be what I was, until the day came when I couldn't hack it any more, so I took a skewer out of the kitchen and stuck it in that bastard's ear as far as it would go, and then I ran away and the Sisters took me in, and I was saved—" She stopped, as suddenly as letting go of hot metal. "I hated the princess," she said. "I really wanted to kill her. The only thing was, I couldn't see how I could make her hurt enough before she died. But the monster did that for me. I wasn't strong enough, but it was. That's exactly what I'd have done, if I'd been able to. I'd have broken every bone, and squeezed her head till the brains burst—"

"Yes," I said. "But you didn't."

"Didn't I?" She looked at me. "You don't know that. You say you know all about these monsters, but you don't, do you? You don't know anything at all."

True. "It wasn't you," I said. "You're not from the Mesoge. You didn't buy those stupid books. Don't go taking the blame for things you haven't done. It's presumptuous. It's the sin of pride. You should know better than that."

"The hell with you," she said, which was a bit more like it. "I'm scared," she said. "I feel like I don't know myself any more."

"It'd be nice if we knew what was really going on," I conceded. "Come on, we're supposed to be smart. Why can't we figure it out?"

"I already did," she said. "But you aren't listening. It's me. Can't you see that?"

"No," I said firmly. "Which is why it's up to me to do something about it." I picked up the billhook and unwrapped it. "He's my brother," I said. "So he's my responsibility. Put an edge on that, will you? I need it really sharp."

"What's that meant to be when it's at home?"

"Imperial steel," I said. "A practical solution to a practical problem. I've thought about it, and the only possible explanation for why the old stories say that there used to be certain special weapons that could cut into walkers is that they were made of something else, something we don't have in the Mesoge. Science," I said. "Provable fact. I think those magic swords and elf-made axes were imperial blades brought back by men who'd served as mercenaries in the empire. And if I'm right, I'll get rid of Kotkel and then there won't be a problem. Apart from the schism," I added, "but one thing at a time. At least we'll be doing something."

She gave me a long look. I think I know her, but there are times I can't read her at all.

I went and found the guard captain. He had that look on his face.

"Sure," he said. "Anything you can do would be magic."

He was having a hard time, poor bastard. I don't usually sympathise with law enforcement, since they're my natural enemy and a bunch of predators into the bargain, but I couldn't help feeling sorry for him. By day he had a large building full of schismatic priests to keep a lid on, and by night there was a monster prowling about crushing people's heads. Quite probably he hadn't anticipated anything like that when he accepted the promotion, and he was wondering if it might not have been something of a mixed blessing. "If I were you," I said, "I'd keep my men well clear after sunset. There's nothing they can do, and they could get hurt."

"Love to," he said, "but I've got orders."

"I have reason to believe that I attract this thing like a magnet," I said. "So if I tell you where I plan to be, maybe you could find a way of putting your men somewhere else. Entirely up to you, of course, but I thought I'd mention it."

"Appreciated," he said. "But it's not up to me."

Fine. I left him and went to the council chamber, where the first session of the day was about to start. I arrived at the main gate and found a large crowd of delegates, standing around in small groups, talking in low voices. I got the impression that everybody felt they needed to be there and nobody wanted to go inside.

A man in a grey habit came up behind my left shoulder. I didn't know him. "This is a mess," he said.

"Quite," I said.

"Hard to know what to do for the best," he went on. "Should we be pragmatic and try and fudge some sort of compromise, or would it be better to lance the abscess straight away and let all the pus drain out before it poisons the lot of us? Honestly, I don't know. That's the bitch of it, I just don't know. Uncharted waters."

I decided that I probably wouldn't like him if I got to know him better, which I had no intention of doing. "Indeed," I said, hoping he'd go away.

"You must be feeling it particularly deeply," he went on, "since on one level at least it's all your fault. Now I would maintain that you simply weren't to know. You saw a pretty box in a junk shop, it wasn't a great deal of money, so you bought it. I'd be lying, of course."

That cold feeling again. "Who are you?" I said.

"Sadly," he went on, "my advocacy of your position wouldn't hold up to prolonged scrutiny. You bought a pretty box. But your vows forbid you to own personal property, and by and large you abide by them. Therefore you didn't buy the box because you wanted to keep it. So why did you buy the box? For its contents. But you couldn't read the contents. Why would a man buy a book he couldn't read? Because he knew what it was. Therefore you knew what the box contained, and you bought it and brought it to Choris Anthropou, where you were due to attend a general council. True, your reason for attending was political assassination rather than theological sabotage, but I put it to you, it was in your mind to seek out someone at the council who'd be able to read the books. It may not have turned out exactly as you planned, but I don't think that really matters very much. A crime is made up of two parts, the guilty act and the guilty intention. It would be hard to argue that you didn't perform the one and form the other." He laughed. "Do excuse me," he said. "My speciality is canon law, I tend to think in opening addresses. Not a healthy trait, because you find yourself advocating a position rather than evaluating the facts. Call it an industrial injury, like a stonemason's lumbago."

I really didn't care for him one bit. "Who are you?" I repeated.

"The new man," he said. "Very much everybody's second choice for such a responsible job, including mine. But since my distinguished predecessor was feckless enough to get himself killed at what could easily turn out to be one of the major pressure points in human history, there's not an awful lot I can do about it. Good idea, by the way. Very much along the right lines."

"What are you talking about?"

"Metallurgy," he said. "They knew about that sort of thing under the empire. Eutropius of Carvasa was the first scientist to grasp the true composition of steel; he wrote about it in his *Concerning the Physical World*, which is now regrettably lost. He realised that steel is a mixture of iron and certain key impurities – charcoal dust, would you believe – and that's what makes it possible to harden and temper it. Ratbert the Younger went one step further and noted the growth of crystals in the suddenly quenched fabric, making the link between hardness and brittleness. It's best explained as being the opposite of water. When water freezes it turns to ice. When steel is heated to cherry red and then quickly cooled, it too undergoes a sort of freezing action – I'm sorry," he said, "I do tend to get carried away, and besides, I'm not sure you're allowed to know any of that. Please forget I spoke. Actually it's all magic and nothing to do with science at all."

"All right," I said. "Say for the sake of argument I believe you."

"But you don't."

"Say I do. Why me?"

He looked at me. He had light brown eyes, short, curly black hair and a double chin like a pile of cushions; a handspan shorter than me, so slightly taller than average. He reminded me of a beetle, though I'm not sure why. "You think this is about you. That's interesting."

"Can we go somewhere and talk about this?"

"So you can try and intimidate me with physical violence without everybody seeing? No, I don't think so. Not that I blame you, it goes without saying. It's a perfectly natural reaction, when you feel as impotent as you do right now. Everything is spiralling out of control, and there's nothing at all you can do about it. Believe me, I feel the same way. It's thoroughly wretched, the whole thing."

Vitimer had arrived, and everybody got out of his way as he strode through the main door. One last try. "If you didn't give the books to that idiot," I said, "who did?"

"Ah," he replied. "Long story. Would you excuse me? I do

so want to get a seat at the front so I can hear every word – my ears aren't as sharp as they used to be."

I tried to grab his sleeve but he tugged it out of the way with a slight but perfectly timed twist of the wrist. Then someone shoved me from behind and the crowd of people trying to get into the hall closed round me, and I lost sight of him, and that was that.

The seats at the back were unusually popular, so I ended up in the middle somewhere, wedged in between a very large, very old man in a brown mendicant habit and a thin man in red from somewhere out east who smelled strongly of lavender and took notes on a small wooden tablet coated with beeswax, in which he made tiny wedge-shaped dents with the stub of a whittled reed. Vitimer stood up, and everybody went quiet.

It was impossible, Vitimer said, to ignore what had happened at the previous session. The existence of certain documents (I think everybody in the hall winced when he said that) was now a matter of record, and in his view it would be impossible for the work of the council to proceed until those documents had been discussed and debated and their validity and status put to a vote. We should all remember that the authority of a general ecumenical council was supreme and absolute. Once a decision had been reached, it would be final and binding on everyone present, on pain of instant and irrevocable excommunication. Furthermore, it was not his intention to adjourn this session until such a decision had been reached and such a vote taken. For his part, he felt it was his duty as president to abstain from expressing any opinion on the subject. Only quiet, calm deliberation would serve to untangle this knot. Therefore he urged us to listen carefully, speak thoughtfully and with our minds unclouded by emotion, judge wisely and vote responsibly. Then he sat down; on his chair, presumably, since there wasn't a fence available.

Immediately a man stood up, rocking slightly on his heels to regain his balance after such a precipitate movement. I knew him from earlier sessions, though I hadn't caught his name; he'd always been ultra-orthodox, the straight ticket, but everybody seemed to like him. He'd now had a chance to read the true gospels, he said, and in his view they were exactly that: true and authoritative narratives, of greater authority than anything in orthodox scripture on account of their earlier date and unimpeachable provenance, which was contained in the text itself and therefore not reliant on any external source. True, he had only read them in translation, and since he hadn't yet had an opportunity to learn the original language they were written in, his views must be conditional on the accuracy of the translation being verified. With that proviso, however, he had no hesitation in proposing a motion that the true gospels be officially incorporated into the canon of accepted scripture, and he felt sure –

What he felt sure about was drowned out in a roar of angry voices: the first wave, about half the delegates, angry with him; the second wave, the other half, angry with the first wave. I looked at Vitimer, who'd obviously learned his lesson from yesterday and made no effort to restore order. Quiet, calm deliberation had lasted roughly the time it takes to boil a kettle, and to be honest I was surprised it had made it that far.

A dozen men had jumped up when the yelling started. Ten of them eventually sat down, leaving two on their feet glaring at each other: Taswald of Crasso, and a short, square old man I didn't know. Then someone grabbed Taswald's arm and hauled him back down into his seat. The square man then began to speak, and since he had the loudest voice I've ever heard in my life, eventually everyone shut up and let him.

He too, he said, had read the so-called true gospels. They were, of course, nothing of the sort. Furthermore, it might interest the council to learn where they'd come from. He had it on the very best authority (the square man said) that they had been handed to certain selected delegates, together with an unverified translation into Robur, by no less a person than the current leader of the gang of blasphemers who called themselves the Loyal Opposition. He could prove this, he said (and thanks to his exceptional lung-power, we all heard him, in spite of the yelling) and would be delighted to do so at the earliest opportunity. In fact, he insisted on it, for the simple reason that if he delayed, it was practically certain that he would be murdered by the inhuman and unnatural monster, controlled by the Loyal Opposition, which had already killed three delegates in the most foul and horrible manner imaginable. The prospect of martyrdom (he went on) held no terrors for him; in fact, he welcomed it. But violence as a tool of Evil incarnate could not be tolerated and must not be allowed to succeed. The involvement of the Loyal Opposition meant that anyone who supported the motion was, by implication, making an open declaration of their sympathy and association with that organisation. It was unthinkable that this council should provide its delegates with an opportunity to vote for the devil. Therefore he proposed that a committee be appointed immediately to hear and evaluate his evidence, and he insisted that a vote on his proposal should be taken at once, before anything further was said and the monster had an opportunity to –

You had to be there. It's one of my most painful memories. Come off it; no, seriously. I may not believe in anything, but there are certain things that act as pillars to support my view of the world and stop the sky from falling in; one of them, probably the most important one, is the academic mind. What does that mean? I'm not quite sure, but it includes learning, scholarship, science, the use of intellect rather than muscle and steel to solve problems, the fundamental hope (because that's all it is) that the brain can achieve what the heart and the fist can't – stuff like that. It's why I worship the old empire, strive to preserve old books from being lost for ever, can't believe in the Invincible Sun, get off on theological debate. And the sight of a large hall crammed full of the sort of men I admire the most, philosophers and theologians and men who can argue both hind legs off a donkey and still leave it standing – my heroes, my idols – doing what? Howling and screaming and shaking their knobbly fists in the air, achieving a state where nothing could be said or heard. Well, now. I might as well never have left the Mesoge.

I'd have got up and left if I could, but I was wedged in too tight. It's just as well that I don't believe in hell, because I can tell you exactly what it would be like, for me. Oh dear, or words to that effect.

At some point, someone – I'd like to think it was Vitimer but I doubt it – had a smart idea. He sent out for two dozen handbells, the sort of thing we used to train with when I was a novice, learning to ring complex peals on the abbey bells. In a confined space, those things are loud, and the acoustics in the Chapter House (a masterpiece of late imperial design) are pretty remarkable. Whether by accident or design, the two dozen soldiers wielding them set up a discordant, arrhythmic, irregular pattern that made your eyes water and your teeth ache. Ten minutes of that was more than flesh and blood could stand. The yelling died away, then stopped. Vitimer stood up. For what seemed like a long time he didn't say a word; he just looked round, with infinite contempt. Then he cleared his throat. A proposal had been made, he said, that a committee should be formed to investigate the contents and provenance of the disputed documents. He fully endorsed the formation of such a committee, with the proviso that its report should be voted on by the council. If the committee found in favour of the documents, they would henceforth be included in the canon of true scripture. If it found against them, they would be declared heresy and anathema, all copies of them would be burned, possession of a copy would be a capital offence against canon law, and all reference to them would be forbidden on pain of permanent excommunication. Accordingly the council would now move to an immediate vote, without further debate, on the question of whether or not to appoint a committee. If that motion was passed, it would be followed by a general debate on the composition of the committee. All those in favour –

I don't like Vitimer, but he's not a complete fool. He'd realised that what was needed right then was a proposition – any damn proposition, didn't matter what it was – to which everybody would unanimously agree. And if you want to get the noose off from around your neck, what better way than form a committee? A moment later, every arm in the building was raised, including mine: a moment of dead silence and unity of purpose, marred only by the smell from a thousand armpits.

The motion, Vitimer announced, was carried. The debate on the composition of the committee would take place that evening. In the meantime, he proposed that the council be adjourned.

*

"He's not smart," she said. "He's a coward. There's a difference."

I was too drained to argue. "Fine," I said. "Have it your way. He's an idiot."

The sun had come out, and the courtyard behind the stables was glaringly bright; scriptorium light, an extremely valuable commodity back home. I could have done exceptionally fine work by it, with the right brush and a steady hand.

"I didn't say that," she said. "It wasn't a stupid thing to do, but it was the wrong thing. All he's done is stave off the end of the world for a little while. You can't put a lid on something like this. And the harder you try, the worse you fail."

"Actually," I said, "he's smart. You'll note that he called the big debate for this evening."

"So?"

"So it's going to be a long debate," I said. "I can more or less guarantee it'll last all night. Which is brilliant."

"Is it? Why?"

"Because if all the delegates are cooped up in the Chapter House all night, they can't be in their beds getting murdered by Kotkel. Not unless he plans to smash his way through the entire council, and I don't think that's his style."

She was silent for a moment: high praise. "I don't suppose he intended that."

"Maybe he didn't, but it's still good news," I said. "Another killing really wouldn't help matters. Also, I bet you anything you like it was deliberate. For one thing, Vitimer's got to be the number-one target. Right now, a crowded council chamber's about the only place where he'd be reasonably safe."

"And if you're wrong and the monster does show up in the chamber?"

I shook my head. "I don't think so. Walkers don't like crowds. It's the same with daylight. They're not afraid of them; they just don't like them. Like you and I aren't water-soluble, but we don't go out in the rain."

"You're not going to be there, are you?" she said. "You're going to skip the debate."

"The thought had crossed my mind."

"You're going to hang around here and hope the monster comes after you."

"Am I? That'd be pretty brave of me. Brave meaning stupid."

"Yes," she said. "Brave as two short planks."

"That's me all over," I said. "Besides, I think I'd rather face an eight-foot ravening monster than sit listening to all those intellectuals howling at each other. Not quite so depressing."

"I'll come with you," she said.

My heart stopped. I hadn't expected that – the worst words, proverbially, that a tactician can utter, but I wasn't thinking of it in those terms. "Like hell you will," I said.

"No, shut up," she said. "If you really think there's a chance that a better class of steel will make a difference, you'll need someone who can fight. Don't suppose you've ever noticed, but I'm good at that." She picked up a cloth bundle I hadn't noticed before and unwrapped it.

"Where the hell did you get that from?"

"The abbey treasury," she said. "It's a holy relic. I stole it."

Weapons I can take or leave alone, but that thing was cute. I'd never seen it before but I recognised it from the description in Vespaluus' *Life of Saint Jotapian*. There's a legend, which is presumably bullshit, but what I think really happened is that someone took the blade from a genuine imperial army issue short sword, fitted it with a fancy silver-gilt and ivory hilt, and sold it as the saint's personal sidearm. It's been in the treasury for six hundred years, stone-cold documented fact. Imperial steel, the stuff they don't make any more.

"You put that back right now. If we get caught with it, we'll be in so much trouble—"

She didn't dignify that with an answer. Killing the monster with St Jotapian's own sword was, of course, exactly what orthodoxy needed. It might just possibly be enough to heal the schism, given how gullible most people are, deep down where it matters. "How on earth did you get in there? It's the most secure area in Choris."

She smiled. "Thank you," she said. "Yes, it is."

Grudgingly I allowed my heart to burst into song. I wasn't going to have to do this alone. She'd be with me. She'd be with me because – not a logical conclusion to draw, merely an intuitive one – she liked me and didn't want me to get killed; more to the point, she'd forgiven me, and that mattered a lot. And with her along, who knows, we might even win. The last thing I'd ever do would be underestimate her abilities with weapons. It's the last thing quite a few people ever did, as a matter of fact. Not something to dwell on, but good to have at the back of my mind.

"Fine," I said. "Now put it away, for pity's sake, before someone sees it."

"You," she said, "are a disgrace to your cultural heritage, you know that? I thought you liked fine weapons in the Mesoge."

I rolled my eyes. She was quite right. My grandfather on my mother's side was a terrifying old man who lived in absolute squalor in a turf hut with only two-thirds of a roof. He ate nettles in season, mice and sparrows when he could get them, and

his three acres of land were mostly docks, brambles and withies, but he owned seven magnificent pattern-welded swords, in
exquisite bone and parcel-gilt scabbards, and a halberd worth
a hundred oxen. People used to walk for days across the mountains to see his collection. When I knew him he was so old and
feeble he could barely lift them off their hooks, and when he
died they were buried with him, which everybody thought was
perfectly reasonable. A year later, someone dug into his mound
and stole the lot, which is also a fine old Mesoge tradition, and
none of my family felt any need to do anything about it.

"Put it away," I repeated. "You're making me nervous."

"Six hundred years old and still as sharp as a razor," she said
fondly. "All it needs is a few touches with the water-stone and a
quick brush-up with the steel and it's good to go." She wrapped
it up and laid it down on the ground beside her. "You know,
there might be something in this notion of yours. They don't
make 'em like that any more."

"If I were you," I said severely, "I'd find a nice quiet corner
of a side-chapel somewhere and have a good pray. Calm yourself down, before you get over-excited."

"Actually, that's not a bad idea," she said quietly. "After all,
it might be the last chance I get."

That hurt. If Kotkel came and she was killed – I worry
about her, a lot of the time. She thinks she's indestructible,
and in all the years I've known her she's only got herself badly
cut up twice, which is astounding when you think about it.
The second time, I actually spent the night on my knees in
front of an altar, praying to a god I knew didn't exist, until
someone came and told me she was out of danger. We all do
stupid things sometimes. Luckily, she never found out, or
there'd have been hell to pay. But Kotkel would be a different

matter, and my theory about imperial metallurgy was just that, a theory.

"I'll come with you," I said, on an impulse I only half understood. "I can sit at the back and read a book while you do your mumbling."

"Piss off."

We decided on the Rose Chapel, which was likely to be deserted at that time of day. She went and kneeled in front of the altar (a magnificent Aesthetic-era triptych, flanked by neo-Mannerist frescoes; she didn't even glance at them) and I sat in the window-seat with my feet up and found my place in my pocket-sized copy of Nicephorus' *Commentaries*. The late sun was slanting in through the window, her soft chanting was distinctly soporific and Nicephorus isn't calculated to keep a man awake at the best of times. I was hovering on the edge of a doze when a man and a woman came bustling in.

"Sister Svangerd," the woman sang out. "Is that you?"

Svangerd shot up and spun round. The woman lowered her hood: a thin face, iron-grey hair cropped short. "Sister," Svangerd said. She sounded like she'd been caught in the branches of a tree, stealing apples.

The man stayed where he was. The woman looked at me, scowled, and went over to where Svangerd was standing. She whispered in Svangerd's ear for quite some time. Then Svangerd said, "Of course," or something like that. The woman nodded and walked away, collecting the man on the threshold. I stood up and put my book away.

"What was all that about?"

She looked scared. "Mother Krimhild," she said.

I knew all about Mother Krimhild. When Svangerd left the world and asked to join the order, nobody wanted to have her. She was too far gone, they all said – irredeemably bad, and with violent antisocial tendencies. But Mother Krimhild didn't think so. She ran a small priory in Neidhol, where she wrote commentaries, composed beautiful music and painted illuminated missals so lovely they reduce me to tears. Her *Nine Tears of Grace* is still regarded as the definitive work on the Hermit Fathers, and she's the only woman ever to have been invited to join the Standing Commission on Orthodoxy, though she sensibly refused. I thought she'd died years ago, but apparently not.

"She's here?"

Nod. "She's ill. She's had a stroke. And she wants to see me."

"Go," I said. "Here, give me that. I'll take care of it."

She thrust the cloth bundle at me. "Stay here," she said.

"Sure. Good luck."

It wasn't the smartest thing to say, but it got me a smile. I sat down in front of the altar with the bundle on the floor at my feet, and tried to appreciate the glory of the triptych, but I couldn't really see it. The stroke, presumably, was brought on by horror at the prospect of schism. Some people take things so very seriously. If Svangerd saw Krimhild die, it'd probably be the end of her. Love, you see. It makes a mess of everything.

I don't know how long I sat there, but it was nearly dark when Svangerd came back. She sat down next to me and bowed her head.

"Well?"

"She's really sick," she said. "She could hardly speak."

"I'm sorry."

"She needs me to do something for her."

"Good. Do it."

She took a deep breath. "She's written a speech, to be delivered to the council. She can't do it herself, so she wants me to."

"Good choice," I said. "Is there anything I can do to help?"

She shook her head. "It means I won't be able to come with you."

"Don't worry about it," I said.

She looked up at me. "I'm scared," she said. "She's lying there all alone in the dark. What if the monster comes and gets her?"

Not a bad point. If I were Kotkel and I really wanted to depress everybody, I couldn't ask for a more appropriate victim than Prioress Krimhild. "I'll be there," I said, before I realised I was speaking. "Can you arrange for me to be let in? I can't just go wandering about the nuns' apartments."

"I'll see to it," she said. "Thanks."

Isn't that what every young man longs for, the chance to play knight errant? Have no fear, my lady, et cetera. Instead I felt terrified and guilty, as though I'd just undertaken to play the harp in front of the archduke and his entire court (I can't, of course, play the harp). What if Kotkel turned up and I couldn't stop him? That would be really bad. But that thought didn't seem to have crossed her mind.

"Have you seen the speech?"

"What? No, I haven't. She's dictating it now. With any luck I'll have time to read it through before I have to say it out loud. Come on. I'll take you to her."

My room was on the way. I stopped off to dump the sword and pick up my billhook. She hadn't had an opportunity to put a really fine edge on it for me, but I couldn't actually see that it would matter in the long run. How different, I said to myself, my life would have been if I'd been an only child. Better, quite possibly. Definitely longer.

As I made my way through the corridors and cloisters, I met big mobs of people streaming the other way, going to the debate. They gave off a feeling of excited urgency, as though they were going to an execution, not quite sure whether it was to be someone else's or their own. All in all, I didn't mind not joining them. Confession time: I may not believe in God but I guess I do believe in Holy Mother Church, and the sight of her ripping herself to pieces wasn't one I was eager to witness.

I thought about that as I crossed the inner quadrangle and climbed the long staircase to where I was going. Holy Mother Church is built four square on a lie, rather like the Asecuivo Company in the late empire, which raised millions of bezants to fund the colonisation of a distant country they knew didn't actually exist, because they'd made it up. But they put on such a convincing show that a group of their rivals got together and resolved to find another route to the fabulous Isle of Asecuivo, with a view to poaching on the Company's monopoly, and in the process discovered the genuine and fabulously wealthy Denaura Islands, where spice grows like weeds and the beaches are littered with orange amber. Holy Mother Church may have invented its Asecuivo, but without her we'd never have had Denaura – the books which her libraries preserved when the empire crashed, a handful of seedcorn rescued from the long winter.

For all I know, the Denaura islands are still there, still shaded from the year-round sun by the leafy tops of nutmeg and mace and gum trees, bowed down with priceless fruit and dripping rich orange sap from every trunk; but of course we don't go there any more. One day, maybe, we'll be able to afford to go back, by which time I sincerely trust we'll have learned that there's more to life than nutmeg.

At the top of the stairs I knocked on a door, which opened into a double set of small, cramped rooms. Each room was a semicircle; we were up in a turret, a long way off the ground. The view from the window would have been astonishing, but it was dark.

A man and a woman – the ones I'd seen in the chapel – got up off the floor, where they'd been praying. Svangerd sent me, I told them. They nodded. "She's asleep," the woman said. "Don't wake her." I glanced through the doorway into the other room, where a lamp was flickering. I saw a plain plank bed, and someone very small lying in it.

"Do your best," the man said, which made me feel about three inches tall. I said I would, and they left.

I sat down with my back to the wall, the lamp beside me on one side, the billhook handy on the other, and opened my book. Nicephorus' *Commentaries*. I was given it by my tutor when I was a young novice. He'd copied it himself, using flyleaves and end-papers, offcuts and leftovers from the scriptorium, mostly as an exercise in writing as small as he could while still staying legible. He was good at it, so he managed to cram the whole of Nicephorus into something not much bigger than the palm of my hand. When I accepted the book and thanked him, he smiled and told me I'd failed the test. By agreeing to own property, I had betrayed my vow. I looked properly horrified at what I'd done but he only grinned and told me to keep it, and I have, ever since.

It's not a terribly good book. Nicephorus was a scholar in the middle empire, a lazy-minded man who wasn't nearly as smart as he thought he was; some of his conclusions are plainly false, and some of his theories are more far-fetched than nutmeg from Denaura. Mostly his value lies in the other works he quotes from or summarises, which have of course been lost and now only exist in bits and pieces embedded in his fatuous text – like amber on a beach, or my father's ashes dissolved in the sea. I've carried that book around with me for years, dipped into it every time I was bored and had nothing to do, but there were – are – still bits I've never read, one of which caught my eye as I huddled against the wall, straining to make out the tiny letters by the light of my inadequate lamp.

In the northern waste known as the Mesoge (wrote Nicephorus) we encounter the phenomenon known as afterwalking, which occurs nowhere else and is remarkable. The most comprehensive study of this curious behaviour is, of course, Tractantius' *Concerning Life*, and it would be superfluous to recapitulate his conclusions, since they are widely available and universally known. Tractantius was surely correct in the main thrust of his argument. However, it would be unwise to dismiss out of hand the observations of Thrasamund, in his *Natural History*, and Lactantius, in his *Reflections*; both of which might seem at first glance to contradict Tractantius' hypothesis, but which on closer scrutiny tend to confirm it. Scaphio of Iden's *Universal Geography* contains an exhaustive summary of how the phenomenon originally came about, and Tarsenna in his commentary on Scaphio adds some valuable insights drawn from Permian sources, now lost. By the time Saloninus came to write about afterwalking in the third book of *Beyond Good and Evil*, there was relatively little he could add to our understanding of this remarkable and well-documented syndrome . . .

Tarsenna. Tarsenna, for crying out loud: wasn't there a copy of that listed in the index of the old library at Hauksness? Yes, of course there was; it was about number seven on Simocatta's want list, because there was only one copy in existence, et cetera. In fact, now I came to think of it, I'd been offered the job of going to Hauksness and making a clandestine copy, but I'd turned it down because I hadn't fancied crossing the Hog's Back Pass in winter, so the job was assigned to Brother Polydore, who was killed in action before he could get round to it, so the project lapsed.

Some valuable insights drawn from Permian sources, now lost. Written, no doubt, in Old High Permian, which I can't read; but someone could, and he'd used it to compile a list, with my name on it. A list I wasn't supposed to see.

For some reason I looked up, and saw him. He was sitting opposite me, his back to the wall like mine was, his knees drawn up under his chin and his wrists resting on them. So like my brother. He was watching me. I had no idea how long he'd been there.

I realised I wasn't afraid. "Hello, Kotkel," I said. "Are you going to kill me?"

"Give me one good reason why I shouldn't."

"Oh, I don't know, let me think. Killing is wrong: how about that?"

"Fuck off."

"Not a very compelling argument, I grant you. All right, try this. You're not supposed to kill me. That's not what you were told to do. You aren't allowed to kill me."

He growled, like a wary dog. "I do what I like."

"Of course you do. But you don't like to kill me. Come on, Kel. The other one's got bells on."

Before I could react, he reached across and grabbed the

billhook. He gripped the handle in his left hand, placed his right thumb against the middle of the flat of the blade and curled his fingers round the end. One brisk flexing movement, the billhook bent, then snapped in two. He let the pieces drop on the floor. That's Kotkel for you. He always took great pleasure in breaking my things.

"Happy now?" I said.

"Get out of my way," he said. "I'm going to kill the old woman."

"Why?"

"Because it'll make your girl cry."

I stood up. "Fine, Kel," I said, "but you'll have to kill me first. Oh, I forgot. You don't want to do that."

"I told you to get out of my way."

"That's right, so you did. But I'm not going to."

He was moving his head, peering, looking to see if there was a way to get round me. I could feel his frustration building, buzzing inside his head like angry bees. I took a step back, until I filled the doorway.

"Admit it, Kel," I said, "you're just an old softie. You don't want to hurt me. Why's that, Kel? Afraid Dad'll give you a clip round the ear?"

"You fucking shut up about Dad."

Interesting. "Why, Kel? You forget, I'm out of touch. What happened to Dad, anyway? How did he die?"

There was the time when someone left the henhouse door open, and a fox got in and killed nine chickens. That someone was Kotkel, because it was my job to make sure the turnbuckle was fastened, so I was the one who'd be blamed. And I was, until my father realised that at the precise moment I was supposed to have been negligently not shutting doors, I was with him in the orchard, digging a drain. In fact, the only member of the family whose movements were unaccounted for was Kotkel. Dad hit him so hard he fell over, then gave him a look that was worse than the blow, and the look on Kel's face ... That look, guilt and fury, hatred and pleading for forgiveness; let nobody ever say that my brother wasn't, isn't a complicated individual. "Kel?" I said. "What've you done?"

He moved way too fast for me to do anything about it. I felt his hand round my neck and I remember thinking, Well, this is it. I felt the bones in my neck flex, like the billhook had done. But that was all.

"Shut your face," he said.

No worries on that score; he was crushing my windpipe, so I couldn't speak. He looked me straight in the eyes. I felt sorry for him.

"Fuck you," he said, and let me go. I toppled over backwards, clouting my head on the door-frame. Kotkel turned, I heard the lamp splinter under his foot, and everything went dark.

I lay there for quite a while – no choice in the matter, I felt like I was three parts dead – then I got up on my hands and knees and looked back into the other room. The lamp there was still flickering, and I saw the prioress, just where she'd been when I last saw her. I pulled myself to my feet and staggered into the room. She was still alive, still breathing.

I remember thinking, I hope Kel doesn't get into trouble for not doing as he was told. Weird, the things that cross your mind after you've nearly been strangled.

There was a chair beside the prioress's bed – the only other piece of furniture in the room. I sat down on it. It occurred to me that, judging entirely by outcomes, I'd won, or at least achieved a favourable draw. I'd done what Svangerd asked of me – had she actually asked, in so many words? I couldn't remember. In any case, I'd sort of prevailed, not with imperial steel or heroic strength and dauntless courage; in fact I wasn't entirely sure how I'd managed it, but I had. Curious thought: presumably that put me on a par with Angantyr the Strong and Bothvar Biarki and Gunnlaug of Lithsness and all the other mythical hooligans I'd grown up hearing about – which was patently absurd, of course. It was so stupid it was practically low burlesque (which, if you remember your Polemon's *Aesthetics*, is where a tragic theme is satirised by the introduction of a comic protagonist). Beats cock-fighting, as my dad used to say.

It was so quiet I could hear the prioress breathing. Well, of course: nobody about; they were all at the big debate. Just my luck – a defining moment in the history of Holy Mother Church, therefore the world, and I'm not there to see it. For which, of course, I was profoundly grateful. I wondered how Svangerd was getting on. Had she made her speech yet? Would she have had the chance, or was everybody on their feet yelling?

I mused on the perversity of things – Svangerd the natural-born killer fighting her greatest battle with words; me, couldn't get out of the Mesoge fast enough, doing the ultimate Mesoge thing and facing down a walker – but I decided that these weren't fitting themes for amusing paradox. I still had no idea what was going on, and the world was still very much about to end. Instead, I fell to thinking about that confounded list on Egil's desk. Old High Permian – and how come I'd never seen that passage in Nicephorus before? Probably my head was still spinning from the crack against the doorpost. Maybe I hadn't seen it before because it hadn't been there before; if the devil could bring half my family from the Mesoge to Choris, with being dead not being a problem, presumably he could change the words in some old book . . . Idiot, I told myself. I reached for the book, with some idea of looking at it again, but it wasn't there. Must've dropped it in the fight. Call it a fight; must've dropped it when Kel was throwing me around like a rag doll. Too dark to look for it now. It'll still be there in the morning.

I suppose it's possible that I may have fallen asleep. In any case, she needn't have hit me quite so hard.

"You're supposed to be guarding her, you arsehole," Svangerd said as I opened my eyes.

Well, she was still alive, which was the main thing. "How did it go?" I asked. Difficult to get the words out; my face was swollen and my lips didn't seem to belong to me any more.

"What the hell happened to you?"

"My brother came by."

"You—"

"Yes."

"Is he dead?"

That made me laugh, which hurt. "You know what I mean," she said angrily. "Did you get him?"

"No," I said. "He smacked me around a bit, then stormed off in a huff. Just like old times."

She looked past me, at the prioress, still sleeping. There was a look on her face I don't often get to see. I rather like it. "That's all right," she said. "I'll see to him myself, later."

That was the funniest thing I'd heard in a long time, but I kept a straight, though horribly distended, face. "Sure you will," I said. "How did it go? The debate."

"Oh, that."

"You made the speech?"

She nodded. "Not my speech," she said. "Hers."

"Did they listen?"

"Yes." Suddenly she looked tired, as though she'd just been carrying the entire world. "Doesn't look like there's going to be a schism after all," she said. "Thanks to her."

I forgot about everything else. "You what?"

"It was a good speech," she said. "It went down well. The upshot is, they named a commission of enquiry that everybody was happy with, and they're going to report on your stupid gospels and decide if they're scripture or not."

"And they were all right with that?"

"Thanks to her."

No, I thought; or at least, thanks to her only in part. Now I really wished I could've been there, even if it had meant missing out on quality time with my family. "You did it."

"Oh, shut up," she said. "I really don't want to talk about it."

8

Next morning the world was a very different place: subdued, nervous, like a man in a crowd who realises he's been punched by someone but can't tell who did it. Since I was the only delegate who hadn't been at the session, and Svangerd wouldn't talk to me about it, I tried asking around. Nobody wanted to talk. They looked at me, anxious and hostile, trying to figure out my motive for asking questions to which I obviously knew the answers, so I gave up and tried hanging around in the background, listening. This quickly made me as conspicuous as a hawk in a rookery – counterproductive and exactly what I enjoy least. Then I figured that Vitimer would probably want to hear about my encounter with Kotkel, and I could ask him. But he was far too busy to see me, goes without saying. So I went and sat by the fountain, waiting for the morning session to start. I was leafing through Nicephorus, trying to find the passage I'd seen the previous night, when a shadow fell over me and I looked up.

"Go away," I said.

He sat down beside me on the fountain wall. "This is very bad," he said. "Everything is going to pieces, and we're having to rethink the whole architecture of our medium-term strategy."

"Go away."

"And you," he went on, "aren't helping. The moment we think we've got everything straightened out and we start trying to piece together a coherent narrative, you *do* something and screw it all up. Well, that's got to change."

Light brown eyes, short, curly black hair and a double chin like a pile of cushions; a handspan shorter than me, so slightly taller than average. He still reminded me of a beetle. "What's going to change is your face, if you don't leave me alone. Different shaped nose. Fewer teeth. Go away."

"We need you to do something for us."

"I'm not a violent man," I said, "and I don't believe you're the devil incarnate. But I have a very violent friend who does, and all I have to do is say the word—"

He nodded. "Sister Svangerd," he said. "We'll talk about her in just a minute."

Suddenly I felt scared. "Leave her out of this."

"Alas," he said. "Would that we could. But I'm getting ahead of myself. I suggest you calm yourself, settle down and listen carefully. It's not complicated, but we do need you to do exactly as you're told."

Imagine that very large spider walking across your face, the one we discussed earlier. A bit like that. "Go on."

"We need you," he said, "to stand up in the middle of a debate and confess. You forged the true gospels. You'll have to explain that you're a highly skilled scriptorium monk and that from time to time you've been called on to make absolutely perfect copies of documents, including forgeries. They won't believe you so you'll have to tell them how you did it – how you aged the paper and made the ink and all that technical stuff, which is right up your alley so I know you'll do it very well. You'll say that the princess put you up to it. She promised to make you an abbot, or she was blackmailing you, whatever you feel most comfortable with. You say that your conscience has been torturing you and you can't bear to think of all the damage you've done. Then you sit down, and the rest of the day's your own. Got that?"

I stared at him. "You're mad," he said.

He looked hurt. "You're not going to make difficulties, are you?" he said. "That would be very disappointing. Actually, I don't think you are, not when you've had a chance to stop and think about it. You'll realise that you have no choice in the matter. I don't know about you, but I sometimes think that choice, you know, the opportunity to choose between significantly different alternatives, is responsible for most of the unhappiness in this world. A straight-line trajectory with no bifurcations is so much less stressful, and there's no room for guilt and self-reproach. Don't you think?"

"You're mad," I said. "If I did that, I might as well slash my wrists while I'm at it. That'd be me finished."

"Maybe," he said mildly. "But consider the alternative. Think how bad you'd feel if Sister Svangerd ended up with her head like this."

He moved his fingers to indicate the width of a book, or two roof-tiles on top of each other.

"Which," he went on, "I would genuinely regret having to do, because that girl's got real potential, and I wouldn't mind using her for something really quite important, somewhere further down the line. But you would insist on continually meddling, and now we're in a situation which benefits nobody, and everything's up in the air and hopelessly untidy, which is awful. I'm sorry, but you've only yourself to blame. Just consider yourself fortunate to have me on hand to clean up your messes for you."

"Who are you?" I said.

"Oh please, don't start all that again, you know perfectly well. And your next question is going to be, why are you doing this, and you know that too. In this case, however, I can honestly reassure you that it's all for the best, in the short to medium term as we see it. This schism has to go ahead. It's got to happen because if it doesn't, there'll be another even worse schism in just over a hundred years' time, and that would be disastrous because it'd happen at precisely the worst possible moment, with a rejuvenated Sashan empire poised to seize the Olbian peninsular and carry on across the West like a tidal wave. You really don't want to think about the consequences of that. Neither, frankly, do we. It would mean a whole phase of the plan happening about two centuries too early, before we've had a chance to get certain key assets into optimum position, and that'd be worse for us than no schism at all. So, as far as you're concerned, you and I have the happy privilege of being temporarily on the same side. Actually, that sort of thing happens far more often than you'd imagine, which is hardly surprising if you think about it. Well?"

"This is all fantasy," I said. "I don't know if you believe in it or not and I don't care, but I don't believe, not for a split second. It's all garbage. There is no Evil. It's just a fairytale."

"Oh dear." He pulled a face that I yearned to push through the back of his head: more sorrow than anger; how could you be so *stupid?* "In that case, I'm going to have to resort to threats, which is so demeaning. I honestly thought that you, as an intelligent human being—" He shrugged. "You'll do as you're told, or Svangerd's death will be on your conscience. You've seen what your brother can do. He knows all about her; he's told you so himself. Make your girl cry, isn't that what he said? One word from me—" He winced. "Please don't make me go on," he said. "I find it very upsetting. It's an insult to intelligence and common sense, having to terrify people into doing something that'll benefit everybody."

I felt cold all over. "When do you want me to do it?"

He beamed at me. "That's better," he said. "Tomorrow, afternoon session, you get to your feet as soon as Sulpicius has finished rubbishing Hegedern's doctrine of conditional redemption. Keep it short and to the point, and above all, be convincing. You have no idea how important this is, and we're all relying on you, so please, don't let us down." He smiled and stood up. "You'd better be getting along or you'll miss the start of the session. Eucharistus is going to challenge Porphyrion's defence of the Seventeen Articles; you'll enjoy that. Isn't that precisely the sort of thing you came here to listen to?"

I let him go. No point in stopping him, and I was only too glad to be rid of his company, and the sound of his voice, and the faint smell of lavender from his clothes.

Love, I thought. The moment you start to love someone, you open a split, like the first blow with the axe on a log. I don't have a problem with ordinary friendship. It's one of the pleasures of life. It's nice when someone's glad to see you, when their face lights up because you're there, bringing with you the promise of congenial and welcome company. You help your friends and they help you, which makes life easier; you're not exploiting or oppressing or being exploited or oppressed, because you're glad to help, and so are they. And if you fall out, it's a pity but these things happen; if they die, you're sad but you move on. Friendship is pleasant and useful; it's the honey in life, it's good for you and it tastes nice. Love, on the other hand; love spoils everything. As soon as you find it, you'll never know another tranquil moment, because you can never forget that the bad guys have a hostage, and for two pins they'll cut her throat, and then where the hell will you be?

At least she didn't love me; thank heaven for small mercies. I don't know how people who are loved can bear it, the hideous weight of responsibility. How can you do that to someone, hold their entire happiness in the palm of your hand like that, knowing that if you die (which can always happen, every moment of every day) you'll cause them the worst pain that anyone can ever feel? I couldn't live with myself, carrying that sort of burden. It would crush me flat, like Kotkel's hand around my head.

I didn't go to the council session. Instead, I found a corner of a courtyard (there was a well, I seem to remember, and a stack of oak buckets), sat on a pile of logs and tried to figure out what I'd done, except of course I hadn't.

How did I go about faking the true gospels? Good question. I know everything there is to know about falsifying ancient documents, but I didn't see how it was possible.

Among the delegates, I'd noticed a number of very illustrious men, and one exceptional woman. Let's start with her first: Sister Ululuria, from the Tears of Grace in Ormsfell. She'd spoken briefly in a debate, and I remember looking at her and thinking, So that's her, the woman I've been hearing about all my life. Sister Ulularia is the greatest living expert on parchment. She grew up in a tannery, so she knows every type of skin there is. She left the world and was assigned to a scriptorium when she was twelve years old, so she's been in the business over fifty years. She can tell, just by looking, how old a piece of parchment is, what it was made from, where the skin originated – where on the animal, where in the world – how it was cured, skived and burnished; more to the point, *when* it was made, and if her professional instinct isn't good enough, she'll go through it point by point, like a doctor of logic, explaining how she arrived at her conclusion: colour, texture, smell, degree of translucency, grain direction, as governed by a thousand years of fashions in parchment manufacture. She'd been appointed to the commission of enquiry, so by now she'd undoubtedly seen the true gospels and declared that the parchment they were written on was unimpeachably right, exactly what it should be.

Then there was Father Zosimus, who I already knew by sight: he'd testified in a trial before the canons juridical as an expert witness, pointing out certain fatal errors I'd made in faking a charter. Zosimus is the ink man. He knows as much about ink as Ulularia does about parchment. His oldest and dearest friend is Brother Hunferth – they were novices together at the Holy Mountain – and they often work together. Hunferth's field of expertise is lettering. He was the last man ever to read Callinicus' *Epigraphy* before it was lost in a fire, and they reckon he memorised it, word for word. Someone like me can tell demotic uncials from cursive italics, but Hunferth can tell you exactly when and where a page was written; usually he can identify the scribe, although his name has long since been forgotten, simply by a distinctive hook at the end of a letter or a habit of resting his pen every time he looked up at the text he's copying. Zosimus and Hunferth have been inseparable for sixty-four years, so naturally they were both at the council, and were on the commission. So was Canon Jormunrec of Vaffe, the foremost living authority on ancient languages, and Brother Terving, a man who under other circumstances I'd have fallen down and worshipped like a god, because of his encyclopedic knowledge of ancient imperial prosody. They were all on the commission, they'd all have seen the contents of the little wooden box, and none of them would have had a moment's hesitation in announcing that whether or not the true scriptures were scripture, they most definitely weren't recent fakes, dashed off by a third-rate forger in a remote northern scriptorium with no access to rare or controlled materials –

Their word against mine; oh boy.

Then I pulled myself together just a bit, and thought it through. Why was I being forced to do this dreadful thing? To sabotage the brittle truce that Svangerd's speech had brought about and plunge Holy Mother Church into schism. That was the objective. So what would I need to do in order to achieve it?

Answer: it wouldn't have to be perfect. In fact, perfect would be counterproductive. If I got up on my hind legs and proved beyond a shadow of a doubt that the true gospels were fakes (but they weren't; the truth was, as usual, irrelevant), that would have the effect of knocking the schism on the head for good and all. Precisely what my loathsome new friend didn't want. No: what he was after was an irreconcilable difference of opinion between the experts on the commission, leading to an inconclusive verdict, probably a minority report by the dissenting faction; all of which would be like breaking into a prison and handing out spears to the lifers. If the commission fell apart within days of its formation, that would be the last, best hope for avoiding schism gone up in flames and I'd have done my job, so Svangerd ought to be safe –

Now then, I thought, that's more like it. I only needed to be plausible in one department. All the other experts would pronounce the texts to be genuine, but one expert would stand up and say no, this man could have done what he claims to have done, and therefore there's reasonable doubt. Cue disagreement, dissent, taking of sides, chaos and the violent death of Holy Mother Church, an institution (did I ever mention that?) of which I happen to approve wholeheartedly.

One department. In other words, I had to single out one of the experts and figure out a way of making him (or her) believe that a perfectly genuine document was hooky. That was still impossible, but it was a smaller, more concentrated, more tightly focused impossibility. Things were looking up.

"We should leave," she said. "Go home. This place is starting to get to me."

I'd seen that coming, rather like a soldier in a vastly outnumbered army watching the enemy advancing. "Agreed," I said. "But I don't suppose they'll let me go. They'll need me to give evidence to the commission. You can go, though. In fact, I think you should."

"Balls," she said. "I'm not letting you out of my sight. When I'm not watching you like a hawk, you do really stupid things. Like buying those books."

"One of us needs to report back to the abbot for instructions. In case you've forgotten, we're here as his representatives.

We work for him. And right now, he needs to be told what's going on. I can't go, obviously, so it has to be you."

"Keeping you from making more fuck-ups is more important."

"No," I said. "You can't go making decisions like that off your own hook. Remember your vow of obedience. You used to take stuff like that seriously."

I felt like I'd just kicked a puppy. "Fuck you," she said. "All right, I'll go back. But not until the commission's made its report."

"You can't—"

"Don't be stupid," she said. "So I do as you say and I go back to Simocatta and I tell him, there's a commission which is going to solve the question once and for all, but I decided to come back a day or so before it made its report. Do you think he'll be impressed by that? I don't."

"Fine," I said. "Stay."

"And while I'm here," she added, "I might as well kill the monster."

Oh, for crying out loud. "You what?"

"Well," she said, "you aren't capable of it; that's obvious. You tried and you failed. Not your fault. It just happens not to be your particular field of excellence. But killing stuff is what I'm good at, and nobody else seems inclined to do it, so I guess it'll have to be me. It's all right," she went on, while I was still trying to regain the use of my voice, "you can tell me everything I need to know about these monsters, and then I can figure out a way of guzzling it, and that'll be that."

"You lunatic," I said, "haven't you been listening? They can't be killed."

"So you say," she said, "though what you're actually saying

is, nobody's ever managed to kill one *yet*. And since the only people who've ever tried are a bunch of hick farmers in that godforsaken place you come from, I don't necessarily take that as conclusive proof. But even if you're right, they can be stopped, like you stopped—" She pulled up short, as if she'd just put her foot in a rabbit-hole. "The first one. Well, he hasn't been back, has he?"

"Svangerd, they're *dangerous*."

"Oh, come on."

"They *are*. They're eight feet tall. Weapons won't touch them."

She sighed. "Most of the people I guzzle are taller than me," she said. "You get used to that when you're a girl. And you said that old steel made by the empire—"

"That's just a theory."

"Sounds convincing to me. Look, somebody's got to try. We can't simply let this thing roam around squashing people's heads for ever and ever, that's *not right*. You can't let Evil win just because you're scared it might hurt you."

"Why not?" She'd got me well and truly rattled. "Look, by your own argument, they can only damage the body, not the soul. So what's really happening is, all these good people Kotkel's killing are going to their eternal reward a bit ahead of schedule. Fine. Probably if he didn't kill them before their time, they'd live to commit a mortal sin, and then they'll end up in the Very Bad Place. And it'd all," I added, "be your fault. Did you think of that?"

She gave me that look. "Don't make jokes about it," she said. "I happen to believe that I've been sent here at this precise moment for a purpose. I was here to make that speech when Krimhild was taken ill, and now I'm going to stay here and kill the monster. I'm in the right place at the right time, I can feel it. I can't expect you to understand something like that, but it's true. I know it is."

"For crying out loud, Svangerd. Next you'll be saying the angels are telling you to drive the Sashan out of Rumeli Hesar. Only it's not angels. It's some problem you've got, squirrelled away down deep where you can't get at it, and this is your way of making things right with yourself. I don't know, maybe you want to get yourself killed. Maybe that's what it'd take, to wash away the guilt or whatever it is you feel you have to do. A lot of the time you act like that's what you want, but I generally put that down to you being crazy as a polecat and a homicidal maniac. But trust me on one thing, Svangerd: it may be a lot of things but it ain't angels. Because you know what? There's no such thing."

There was a moment when she was perfectly still. Then she grinned.

"Nice try," she said. "You want me to go home so I'll be safe, so you say a lot of nasty things, to make me mad at you and stomp off in a huff. Actually, that's rather sweet. Just don't ever say them again, or I'll pull out all your teeth."

We looked at each other, a bit sheepishly, as though we'd just fought a long and bloody battle and then realised we were on the same side. "Sorry," I said. "I didn't mean a word of it."

That didn't merit a response, obviously. "It's blindingly obvious what's going on," she said. "The forces of Evil are here – you talked to them – and they brought those monsters here to break up the council and start a schism. And it's equally obvious that I'm here to stop them. I was here to deliver Mother Krimhild's speech, and now I'm here to kill the monster. Simple as that."

Simple as that; naturally I didn't argue, because she wasn't in the mood to listen, and I was on thin enough ice as it was. But it wasn't as simple as that, was it?

The story so far, I said to myself, as I sat on a bench in the shade, watching the delegates go in for the debate. My name is on a list, written in Permian letters. I arrive in Choris, bringing with me the fatal documents, which just happened to be in a junk shop I was drawn to visit. A monster, who turns out to be Dad, kills the princess, who would probably have had the moral authority to stop the schism, had she lived. The *soi-disant* ambassador of the Loyal Opposition retrieves the documents from where I'd hidden them, and next thing you know, they're all over town, and Holy Mother Church is teetering on the brink of disaster. Krimhild and Svangerd save the day, so the new Loyal Opposition rep sidles up to me and blackmails me into trashing the ceasefire. Yes, it all made sense. As simple as that.

But not really. The other story so far. On the way to Choris, before I'd so much as set eyes on that horrible wooden box, someone tries to kill me. Later I dispose of the monster, but only because the Loyal Opposition dropped a massive hint about the bell-tower; if it hadn't been for that, my brains would've been squeezed out through my ears. Then another monster turns up (leaving on one side the fact that it's my brother) and kills the Loyal Opposition agent. Not content with that, he goes on to kill the man who could've discredited Svangerd and made it impossible for her to make the big speech and stop the schism. Later the same monster comes to kill Krimhild – but too late to be useful, since at that very moment, Svangerd was in the council chamber, delivering the speech. So, you see, not simple. Not simple at all.

You could wriggle a way through it by saying there were two opposing forces at work: Pure Evil, trying to bring about the schism and overthrow Holy Mother Church (which would be a perfectly reasonable thing for Pure Evil to want to do); and an opposing faction, trying to stop it. So what name would you give that faction? The angels?

If I was an angel (not that they exist) and I wanted to stop the schism, is that the way I'd go about it? Quite probably not. For a start, if I'm an angel, I'm a servant or agent of the Invincible Sun, who's all-powerful and all-knowing. I wouldn't have to muck about with monsters and counter-monsters. I could stop Dad in his tracks by turning him into a block of stone. I could appear to Svangerd's former john in a dream and tell him to go away somewhere. I could see to it that the true gospels got eaten by mice years before they reached the junk shop. I wouldn't need to resort to violence. I wouldn't need to squeeze anybody's brains out.

Besides, if angels existed (and they don't), they wouldn't behave in this ridiculous, melodramatic fashion. A god who (in person or through his duly authorised subordinates) carried on like that would be a laughing-stock, demonstrating with each feckless and irresponsible move that either He's not omnipotent or else He's too stupid or too perverse to run His universe competently. Bottom line: if Good behaved like that, it wouldn't be Good at all. It'd be good for nothing.

Not that there's any such thing as Good and Evil. Instead, there's a lot of human beings (the vast majority of whom believe in all that nonsense) and a few phenomena, such as the Mesoge walkers, which an ignorant person could easily mistake for acts of God or the devil, but which were perfectly well understood by Tractantius, Thrasamund and Scaphio of Iden, although the books they wrote about it were carelessly mislaid when the empire fell and are no longer available. It's Saloninus' razor: when you have two conflicting explanations, the simplest and most reasonable one is likely to be correct.

True but unhelpful. If Saloninus had been there in the cloister, in my shoes, he'd have used his razor to cut his own throat. Drastic, perhaps, but being the sensible man he was, he'd have decided it was preferable to having to choose between wrecking the ceasefire and being directly responsible for the death of the woman he loved.

The same thought did cross my mind. If I died, I wouldn't be able to tell the big lie, so there'd be no point in harming Svangerd, except pure spite. It was, I realised, the sensible, responsible thing to do. Furthermore, I was in a position to be able to do it, having so thoughtfully arranged my life and my affairs that I could afford to die and not be guilty of causing a single tear to be shed. My sacrifice would save Svangerd and prevent the downfall of Holy Mother Church. In fact, I'd have to be some sort of monster to insist on staying alive, when my death would be so universally beneficial. If I'd wanted to be like that, I'd never have left the Mesoge.

I considered all that, and you know what? I decided to be heartless and selfish. Wrong of me, I know, but nobody's perfect. Least of all me.

In which case – one damned thing after another, as the man said when he saw the policeman chasing the thief – I was going to have to find a way of fooling one of the experts on the authenticity commission.

Question: which one? Answer: consider their various areas

of expertise and decide which one I was best at. Parchment; ink; handwriting; grammar, syntax and dialect.

Not an easy choice. When Assarion faked the Donations of Florian (the document by which the last emperor was supposed to have given the empire to Holy Mother Church), he was only found out because he used a pluperfect subjunctive in a dependent relative clause: spot on for the Golden Age of classical literature, but all wrong for the slipshod language of the late empire. But I didn't actually have access to the texts, so I couldn't go through them looking for an anachronistic verb form or word ending, even assuming there'd be one to find, which there wouldn't be. The same went for handwriting. Without seeing the originals – what was circulating freely around the council were, of course, copies – I couldn't really do much with that. So I was left with ink and parchment. No bad thing. I know a lot – far more than any honest man – about both topics. Besides, I didn't have to find fault with either of them – just as well, since there would be no fault to find. Instead, I had to come up with a plausible way of faking them, and pretend that that was what I'd done.

There was no way of faking parchment and ink of that period. Correction: there was no way *yet*.

Suppose – just suppose – that you were lucky enough to get hold of a genuine copy of an original imperial book, a thousand years old or older. And then try and imagine that you're wicked enough and skilful enough to take a piece of Aelian pumice (itself an irreplaceable antique, since the vein was exhausted seven hundred years ago) and slowly, patiently scrub away at your manuscript until all the writing was ground away. You'd then have a piece of genuine thousand-year-old parchment, minus the surface layer; it'd be the right skin from the right animal, skived with the right tools, cured in the right way. It would be, in essence, the truth – apart from missing the top layer. To restore that, you'd need to grind and burnish it in exactly the same way they did it a thousand years ago, using clerks' tools from the period – very, very difficult, but it could conceivably be done, by a genius-level forger. Do all that, and you've got a surface on which to write what the hell you like, and pass it off as a text from antiquity. Once you'd done that (using what for ink? Don't ask me, not my department, I'm only the parchment expert) you'd have to use a whole battery of tricks to age the finished surface. For example, the putative document would have been written in a hot climate, so you need to warm it just right over a fire, then taken to a cold, damp climate three hundred years later (a bit of damping down with a wet cloth; allow mould to form, then carefully scrub it off) and left on a shelf in a library for over a century (work in some ingrained dust; squash it just right to simulate standing on end; do something or other to fade the outer surface where it would have been exposed to faint but continual sunlight) before being confined in an airtight rosewood box (use sawdust ground off the box itself where it wouldn't show to simulate a very faint but lingering rosewood scent) –

The good news was, I didn't have to do any of this stuff. All I had to do was give the impression that it could have been done, enough to strike a spark of doubt in the lamp-oil store of my audience's mind. If you want to undermine an arch, remove one stone and the rest will come tumbling down. More to the point, I didn't want to convince the whole commission. That would be the worst thing I could possibly do. What I needed was dissent – the parchment expert declaring that there was room for doubt, the other experts swearing blind that the documents were authentic, and the parchment expert must be wrong, or deliberately making trouble. It came as a shock to realise that I couldn't think of anyone other than me who knew enough and had enough imagination to pull this trick off.

I thought about it and decided I was still missing something. I needed to strike that essential spark. There had to be that moment when a faint bell tinkled in the back of the parchment lady's mind, edging her over from scepticism to subconscious belief (which would then do my work for me, because she'd be on my side without realising it) So, let's think. If I was the parchment lady, what would tilt the balance for me?

I scrabbled about in my mind for a bit, like someone trying to climb up a wellshaft, and then I got a toehold. Books – rare books – yes, that'll do nicely. Seven years ago or thereabouts, back when I used to work for the archduke, he sent me to the monastery at Kreuz to copy the last surviving manuscript of Svartbald's *Types of Ethical Theory*. But it wasn't there. Being young and naive I made a hell of a fuss about it, until someone took me aside and patiently explained that the abbot had sold the book (which he had no right to do) to a wealthy collector, and if I insisted on calling attention to the gap on the dusty shelves, something awful would almost certainly happen to me on my way home, and that would be a great shame but probably, in the grand scheme of things, no big deal.

When I say a hell of a fuss, I'm not exaggerating. I'd actually got as far as registering a formal complaint with the patriarchal legate; which means three copies, sealed and notarised, and the legate's office takes everything that crosses its desk so very, very seriously. There was a good chance, therefore, that people right across the scribal community would have heard about it, including, pray God, the parchment lady.

The last copy of Svartbald would have been about the right age, written on the right parchment. Stealing it and cutting it up into four strips – cutting it lengthways, that would've been my masterstroke; because in the relevant period, they did that all the time. Parchment was expensive, even then, so if you wanted to copy something, it was cheaper to buy a second-hand book, cut it into strips and grind off the writing than to lash out good money on virgin material. So I would confess that it was me who stole the copy of Svartbald, and that's what I used to make the true gospels. Clever old me.

I stopped and thought it all through from the beginning, just to make sure I wasn't being too clever by half. I was reaching that point you often get to in this sort of scam where the truth and your lies get so hopelessly intertwined and alloyed with each other that you can't tell them apart. That's a good thing, in context, usually, but you can trip yourself up if you're not careful. Now then. Take it step by step, and do try and remember which bits are true and which bits aren't.

It's a bit like the coinage. In theory, a denier is pure silver: silver and nothing else. But if you add a cupful of copper to a ton of silver, nobody's ever going to know the difference and you're in profit by the difference in value between a cupful of silver and a cupful of copper – say ninety deniers, roughly what a master mason makes in a year. Governments realised this about two thousand years ago and turned it into an instrument of fiscal policy, so that by the time the empire fell, the coinage was 99.95 per cent pure copper with a tiny sprinkling of silver added to the melt like a flux, or the dab of holy water on your forehead that's supposed to wash away all your sins. Once you start alloying truth and lies, you end up with a currency that's patently debased but which passes everywhere as legal tender, mostly because it's got the emperor's head stamped on it, so it must be all right. When the empire fell, of course, there weren't any more emperors, so for five hundred years we've been minting deniers in the name of Florian VIII – except that the people cutting the dies and hammering out the coins couldn't read or write, so the letters became weird and garbled, and Florian's portrait gradually sort of slipped, melted like he'd been left out in the sun, and these days he looks rather more like a hedgehog than the Emperor of the Robur, Defender of the Faith.

Moral: presumably there is such a thing as the truth, in abstract, in Saloninus' Ideal Republic or somewhere like that. But the currency, the circulating medium we all use every day, is an alloy. The emperor Callimachus the Drunkard, so I read somewhere, took to drink to help himself forget about the catastrophic state of the imperial economy, which led (among other things) to an unprecedented level of base metal in the coins. It got so bad that, after a month or so, all the silver rubbed off the raised portions of his portrait, revealing the red copper beneath (the silver in the alloy migrates to the surface as the molten metal cools) – which is why Callimachus the Drunkard came to be known as Old Coppernose, a very good joke which didn't amuse him in the slightest.

Naturally, the art of skilfully diluting silver was lost when the empire fell. Like so many things. We aren't nearly such good liars as they were. Oh, we lie, all the time, but our lies are so much harder to believe. But a really good old-fashioned imperial lie, like imperial silver or imperial steel: they don't make 'em like that any more. Except for me. If I was lucky.

Armed with her magic sword, swathed in an old habit she'd pinched from Mother Krimhild's trunk (for added sanctity) and doused from head to toe in water that had been used to wash up the Holy Chalice after Communion, Svangerd got into the guest wing by climbing onto the roof and prising open a skylight. She spent the night in a corridor waiting for Kotkel, who didn't show, so she gave up and went back to bed.

While she was huddled in the shadows with her teeth chattering, Kotkel smashed his way into the guardhouse and killed four sentries who'd just come off watch. A fifth sentry, who'd gone outside for a piss, saw the whole thing through a crack in a shutter.

"It's my fault," she said. "I should've guessed what it would do next, but I didn't. I suppose I underestimated its tactical abilities. I won't do that again."

"Oh come on," I said, a bit desperately. "Of course it's not your fault. If it's anyone's, it's mine, because he's my brother. But it's not my fault, and it definitely isn't yours."

She gave me a sour look. "What you mean is," she said, "you're really glad I screwed up, because you think I don't stand a chance against it. Silly of me, but I really thought you had a better opinion of me than that."

A fool would've pointed out that Kotkel had slaughtered four armed and armoured men without any apparent difficulty. Fortunately, this fool wasn't that stupid. "I don't think fighting Kotkel is the answer," I said. "I think there's a better way of solving this."

"Really? What?"

"Find out who's controlling him. Find out what they want."

That got me a cold, hard stare. "I believe I can tell you that right now."

"In general terms, maybe. I want names and faces. I mean, it's got to be somebody here on the spot, at the council. If we can figure out who it is, identify him, talk to him——"

"Cut his throat."

"Yes, that might do it; it all depends. Think about it. If you do manage to get rid of Kotkel, what's to stop whoever it is getting hold of another one of my horrible relatives and carrying on, business as usual? Wouldn't it be better to find out who's controlling the operation? We need the archer, not the arrows. Otherwise, we're just putting ourselves in harm's way for the fun of it."

She frowned. "Fair enough," she said. "Just one thing."

"What?"

"You reckoned that short man who got killed was the man in charge."

"That's what he told me."

"But he got killed. Therefore, he must've been lying."

I could feel it all slipping through my hands, like when you're droving sheep, and one of them drifts off, and while you're rounding it up another one wanders off a different way, and then another —

"Forget about him," I said. "Maybe he was executed by his own side for failing to do something, or because he warned me, I don't know—"

"Yes," she said. "Why did he do that?"

"Doesn't matter," I said firmly. "Not now, at any rate. What we need to do is find out who's in charge *now*. Find him, talk to him—"

"Guzzle him."

"If that's the best course of action, guzzle him by all means. "At the very least," I added temptingly, "if he sees us trying to out him, he'll probably send Kotkel after us, and then at least we won't have to find my brother: my brother will find us. Either way, we get our chance. Smart, or what?"

She scowled. "Kind of smart. Yes, all right, we'll try it your way. How do we go about it, exactly?"

To which, of course, I had no answer, since I hadn't expected her to agree. "Simple, straightforward intelligence work," I said confidently. "We circulate, ask questions, find out what we can: process of elimination. Isn't that supposed to be our job?"

"Speak for yourself. Mine is taking out the bad people." She shrugged, then nodded. "It's got to be better than camping out in draughty corridors," she said. "All right, we'll try it. It's not like we've got anything better to do."

It occurred to me, as I left her in the main courtyard and headed over to the council chamber, that I'd unintentionally said something rather perceptive. Asking questions might well prompt the double-chinned man to do something nasty, though I was pretty sure he'd stop short of killing Svangerd. If he did that, he'd have no way of forcing me to confess to forging the true gospels. But there were plenty of other people he could kill. My guess was that the four sentries died to let me know that Kotkel was still very much a force to be reckoned with. I hate it when people show off just to impress me. Fortunately, it doesn't happen all that often.

Talk, or think, of the devil. I wasn't aware of him until he tapped me on the shoulder. I spun round and there he was: brown eyes, curly hair, plethora of chins. "How's it going?" he said.

"Get lost."

He took hold of my arm. He had a weak grip, like an old lady you're helping across the street. "Come and sit down for a minute," he said. "Over here, in the shade."

Well, I thought. "What do you want?"

"To tell you things," he said. "Actually, I have a confession to make. I may have given you the wrong impression about myself. Deliberately," he added, with a sort of twinkling grin. "Sorry about that."

I sat down. "Let me guess," I said. "You're misunderstood. You had an unhappy childhood."

"No, actually. In fact I didn't really have a childhood at all, not the way you understand it. But let's not go there right now. Later, maybe. Who do you think I am?"

"You're an arsehole."

"That's what, not who. Answer the question."

I took a moment to rally my thoughts. "I think," I said, "that you somehow believe that you're a duly appointed agent of the Powers of Darkness. Which is dogshit," I added, "because there's no such thing, but I think you believe it. Which makes you a dangerous lunatic, especially when you drag my family into it."

"Interesting," he said. "You very seldom swear, but you've just used two obscenities, practically in consecutive sentences. So you think I'm Loyal Opposition."

"That's what you good as told me."

"I may have been bending the truth," he said. "A little. Actually, rather a lot. Maybe a hundred and eighty degrees, something like that."

One time when I was a kid, I was having fun with Kotkel: taunting him, running verbal rings round him, hurting him just because I could; and I was in full flow and mid-sentence, and he suddenly lashed out and caught me on the point of the chin. I remember to this day the sudden feeling of utter bewilderment. I had no idea who I was, or what was going on, or what had just happened to me. "You what?"

"Oh, don't look at me like that. You're not stupid. I'm not the Loyal Opposition. I pretended I was, in order to get you to do as you were told, but I was fibbing."

"What's that supposed to mean?"

He sighed. "You know perfectly well. Let's just say, I'm on the side of the angels." He laughed. "You know, I really wish I had a mirror to show you. I thought you didn't believe in any of this stuff."

"I don't."

"Are you absolutely sure about that?" He was beaming at me. "Because if that's true, how come you're so desperately shocked and horrified? You are, you know. I've just turned your entire world upside down. I couldn't have done that if you don't believe just a teeny bit. Now then," he added quickly, "there's no call to get violent. You're better than that. You're an intellectual."

I took a long, deep breath. It didn't help one bit. "So all that stuff about forcing a schism," I said. "What was all that about? Were you testing me? Temptation? To see where my true loyalties—?"

He shook his head. "No," he said, "we need you to do that; it's really important. That's got to happen, and you're the only one who can do it. There's got to be a schism. It's essential."

Why me? I thought. I'm not important. "I don't understand."

"Of course you don't," he practically cooed, "but that's all right, you're not supposed to. It'd be a miracle if you'd been able to figure it all out for yourself, from first principles. You'd have to be Saloninus to do that. It's all about the long game, you see. Which is so long, and so indescribably vast, that you couldn't possibly fit understanding it into one mortal lifetime. If you tried to step back far enough to see the whole thing, you'd almost certainly fall off the edge."

"This is all bullshit."

"Three times in five minutes. Obviously you're feeling a bit overwrought, and I don't blame you." He paused. "You do know about the long game, don't you?"

"Yes. No. What about it?"

He smiled and folded his hands in his lap. "It's the name we give to the eternal battle between Good and Evil," he replied. "It's been going on since the moment of Creation, and it won't finish until the world does. World without end," he added, tweaking his face into a grin, "which adds a different dimension to it, don't you think?"

I looked away so I wouldn't have to see his face, which I'd decided I didn't like. "Oh," I said. "That."

"Yes, that." He was enjoying himself, as though he'd made the speech ever so many times before, and was just getting to his favourite part. "Now you may ask, why doesn't Good just stamp on Evil once and for all? And if you ask that, you're missing the point completely, because 99.9 per cent of the things Evil does to further the grand design aren't evil at all. A child is born: what's evil about that? It's only when he's grown-up and recruiting soldiers for his crusade that he counts as evil per se and Good's entitled to step in and squash him. A man stands at a crossroads. If he goes west, he'll get a job as a clerk in a sawmill, marry a nice girl and end up a respected member of the community and a churchwarden. If he goes east, he'll start a heresy that leads to a whole nation being excommunicated and a thousand blasphemers being burned at the stake. Evil nudges him into going east, but choosing which road to follow at a crossroads isn't an evil act; people do it every day. Good can't step in and make a commandment, 'Thou shalt not go east'. And if it did, Evil would simply make a few adjustments and be right back in business. It's the long game," he said, with a happy smile on his face. "It's huge and all-pervasive and because it's been going on for such a very long time, every single thing that happens, every single man and woman and dog and tree-stump and drop of rain is caught up in it somehow or other. And tell you what, Eternity would be a real drag to get through without it. But you're not supposed to think of it like that, so forget I said it."

I stared at him. It was all I could do.

"You, of course," he went on, "don't believe in any of this. You think that there's no plan or grand design, therefore no planners and designers, so everything happens by random chance, good luck, bad luck, whatever. That's perfectly all right," he said; "in fact it's rather sweet, and people like you give us hours of innocent amusement as we watch you trying to make sense of life. How you manage to get past the blindingly obvious nature of Saloninus' clock I have no idea, but somehow you manage it, and good luck to you."

"Saloninus' what?"

"Clock. Oh, sorry, I forgot, that book was lost in a fire. Or at least it wasn't. There's still one copy lurking on a dusty shelf somewhere, but it hasn't been rediscovered yet. Fine, here goes. Imagine there's an island a thousand miles out in the middle of the sea. The people who live there don't know there are any other countries: they think they're the only people in the world. And they're primitive. They don't have wheeled vehicles or metal tools or spinning or pottery. Anyhow, an islander is walking on the beach and he finds something he's never seen before. He picks it up and stares at it. It's a Mezentine mechanical clock, and it fell off a ship a thousand miles away, and it washed up on the island. Now, what does the islander make of it? Does he assume it's a rock that's been battered about and eroded and partially dissolved by the seawater until, purely by chance, it's developed into an object that just happens to move a pointer through exactly three hundred and sixty degrees in precisely twenty-four hours? Or does he say to himself, someone must have made this, and therefore there must be another island?" He beamed at me. "I like that one. Old but gold, as they say. When that book turns up again, it's going to make a lot of people sit up and think. Saloninus' *Mechanics*. I'd keep your eyes open for it, if I were you."

My head was swimming. "Thanks," I said, "but I've gone off collecting old books; it makes too much trouble for people. And I don't believe a word of any of it."

"You don't believe there ever was such a book, or you don't believe it's got the story about the clock in it? Not that it matters. You've got to believe there's a story, because you've just heard me tell it, therefore it exists, in your memory, like maggots in a wound."

"I don't believe in your long game," I said. "And if a Mezentine clock was in the water that long, it'd have rusted up solid."

He laughed. "I like you," he said; "you're cute. You're also the man who's going to make the schism happen, because we're all relying on you. Because if you don't, and this split doesn't happen, all the underlying problems in Holy Mother Church are going to stay buried for another hundred years and then burst out in a really bad schism that'll split the West in two just when the Sashan are strong enough to invade, and the result will be very, very bad indeed. But we can't let that happen, can we? No, of course not. So we have a little schism now, get it all over and done with and then shake hands and make friends, so that when the Sashan come we'll be ready for them and we'll drive them back into the sea. Also," he added, looking me in the eyes, "if you don't do it, Kotkel really will kill your darling Svangerd. On that you can rely."

I opened my mouth but I couldn't speak.

"Because," he went on, "who knows, Svangerd may turn out to be the next arch-heretic, or she may have a son who's the next Etzel the Butcher. But that wouldn't be allowed to happen, and you know what they say about omelettes and eggs. Sometimes you've got to be ruthless, when you've been entrusted with the welfare of the human race."

"I'm on it," I said. "I've got it figured out."

"Good boy. I knew we could rely on you." He stood up. "Quite possibly," he went on, "all your life you've been trained and guided and beaten into shape to do this one job, and you never even knew it. Or maybe not, and it's all just serendipity, and you're a pebble that just happens to tell the time. I know the answer, of course, but I'm not supposed to tell you, and of course you wouldn't believe me if I did. Go carefully. Don't take any wooden deniers."

I watched him walk away. If I ever wanted to commit murder – as opposed to assassinating princesses or strangling sentries to stop them raising the alarm, or crushing my father with a bell, not homicide so much as pesticide, it was that moment. I'm not a violent man, but everybody's got their limit.

Blessed, someone once told me, are those who have seen and yet have not believed.

What are friends for? Answer, or one answer that makes a sort of sense: friends are so that you can have someone to talk to when it all gets too much, someone you can tell, so you don't have to keep the whole swarm of maggots kettled up inside your own head. Also, friends don't lie to each other, or keep secrets. Svangerd was my friend, but I couldn't tell her. It'd kill her.

Angels, for crying out loud. No, thank you.

I like to be prepared. If you have your bags packed and your ducks in a row before the killing starts, you have a slight edge. Usually the advantage gets lost in the whirlwind, but it's worth making the effort, for those few occasions when it does make a difference.

I was prepared. I'd figured out a way of casting doubt on the authenticity of the true gospels. I knew what I was going to say. The debate I was supposed to make my confession in wasn't until the next day. That gave me one night in which to try and be clever. If it didn't work out, I'd make my confession as I'd been told to do, or I'd be dead. If it worked out, I'd probably have done the wrong thing, but what the hell. What do people expect from me? I'm nobody.

Kotkel had snapped my billhook like a carrot, but that didn't actually prove anything. So I stole the sword of St Jotapian from Svangerd's room – she'd only hidden it under the bed, wrapped in a pillowcase; I despair of her sometimes – and went to find the captain of the guard.

"You again."

"Yes," I said. "Look, I need to have the run of the guest wing tonight. That's not a problem, is it?"

He gazed at me. "I can't let you do that."

"I'll be armed," I went on, "but nothing you need to worry about. Just keep your sentries off the second and third levels. I wouldn't want them getting hurt. And if they hear anything – yelling, screams, sounds of a struggle – tell them to stay put and not interfere. I can go and get it in writing from Vitimer if you like, but I'd rather not bother him right now. He's got a lot on his plate, poor devil."

"I ought to arrest you."

"On what charge? Conspiracy to help? Besides, if you do that, I'll tell Vitimer I could've stopped the monster only you wouldn't let me, and then you'll be really popular. Look, it's not like your men could do anything except get themselves killed, so why don't you just give them the night off and leave everything to me?"

I realised what I was doing. I was bullying him, the way I used to bully Kotkel. I guess that wherever I go, even now, I take a tiny bit of the Mesoge with me. "Sure," he said, giving me a look I deserved. "I'll make a note in the log: you're assuming full responsibility."

"Thank you," I said, too little and too late. "I know it's hard to believe, but I do actually know what I'm doing. This is all about the Mesoge. There's no reason you and your men should have to suffer for it."

He gave me a doubtful look – fair enough, because I was lying – and walked away. Fine, I thought. I needn't have done any of that: I just wanted to. Old habits, among other things, die hard.

But what else could I do, I asked myself as I wandered along the corridor, looking for anything that might give me the faintest scrap of tactical advantage. If Kotkel was got rid of, or if I was dead, that would take care of the threat to Svangerd, which was the main thing. And if Kotkel didn't show up, or both of us survived the night, I'd just have to do as I'd been told and trash the ceasefire, unleashing schism on Holy Mother Church and reserving myself a nice prison cell for the rest of my life, or the gallows, which on balance would be preferable. Of course, following that line of argument to its logical conclusion, what I really should have done was slash my wrists straight away and have done with it – no me, no threat to Svangerd, no schism. But that logic was just a bit too icily perfect for my taste. To the dickens with logic, or words to that effect.

I scrounged a small lamp from an alcove, sat down on the floor outside a room chosen at random with my back to the wall, put the sword where I could grab it in a hurry, opened Nicephorus at random and started to read.

Dualism (said the bit of Nicephorus that caught my eye) is a fertile breeding-ground of heresy. The Miletian anathema, for example, would have us believe that Good and Evil are equal and opposite forces, allowing for the possibility that Evil may one day prevail. At the other extreme, the Bomite heresy of dualistic unity regards Evil as nothing more than a subsection of the Good principle; a subordinate department in the celestial bureaucracy, but answering to the same hierarchy and the same officers as the Blessed Angels. The Invincible Sun, so the Bomites argue, created everything, therefore He must have created Evil. Therefore, Evil has a purpose. Its function is to be the dark background against which the light shines: without darkness, there can be no light. In more practical terms, the celestial agents assigned to Evil are tasked with the job of weeding out the weak and the malignant, those who are unfit to partake in the kingdom of heaven. This is necessary, not to say holy work, and the angels who carry it out are no less servants of the divine plan than their more iridescent colleagues, and for this reason they have come to be known as His Celestial Majesty's Loyal –

I looked up. He scowled at me and trod on my lamp.

"Clumsy idiot," I said. "You never did learn to look where you're going."

My fingers closed around the hilt of the sword. It wouldn't move. He was standing on it.

"What the fuck do you think you're doing here?" he said.

"I'm here to stop you, Kel," I said. "You can't just charge around the place killing people, not here in Choris. This isn't home. You can't just do what you like."

"Says who?"

"Me," I said. "This isn't the Mesoge. This is civilisation, what's left of it. And I won't have you spoiling it, like you spoil everything else."

"You going to stop me, then?"

At which moment, I guess the moon must have come out, because a shaft of moonlight slanted in through a window I hadn't realised was there, and lit up the corridor a sort of cobwebby grey. It was, in fact, a typical Mesoge moment, because in all the old stories there's always a bit where the moon comes out and the hero gazes into the walker's cold, dead eyes. "Yes," I said. "If you want to carry on playing your games, you're going to have to kill me first. And there's something stopping you doing that. Isn't there?"

"Fuck you."

I needed him to move his feet: not far, just enough so I could free the sword. After that, I'd be on my own, except that I knew the stories by heart. Sighvat the Peacock overcame his walker by goading it into rushing at him, then holding out his magic sword so that the walker impaled himself on the point; Sighvat wasn't strong enough to drive a sword through the monster's hide, but the monster was. Same as boar-hunting, where you use the enemy's own strength and impetus to destroy him, or so I read in a book somewhere.

"I wonder what it can be," I went on. "It's not because I'm your brother, and it's not because you like me, because you don't. You always did hate me, Kel, and you know why? Because I'm smart and you're not."

Nothing. He didn't move. He should've lunged forward to smash me, or at the very least sworn at me, but he just stood there, looking at me.

"I'm smart," I repeated, "and you're just plain stupid. You always were stupid, Kel, thick as a brick, thick as two short planks. Dad used to say, what did I do to deserve a moron for a son?"

"He never said that."

"Yes he did. How can any son of mine be so stupid, he used to say. He's so stupid, I wish he'd never been born, or he'd died when he was a baby. He used to say that all the time."

"You're lying."

"It's funny, he used to say, I don't remember him ever being dropped on his head when he was a little kid. But he must've been, or how come he turned out such an idiot? He used to say that to Mom, and it always made her laugh."

"Liar."

"No, I'm not. Oh, we all used to laugh at you, the moment your back was turned. Dad, Mom, Einar, Gisli, the neighbours, we all thought you were a great joke, because you're so dumb. Didn't you know that, Kel? You'd have to be pretty dumb not to realise we were all laughing at you, all the time. But there you go. Proves my point."

"I'll get you for that."

"Go on, then."

"I'll kill your girl."

Talking of stupidity. A trait that runs in the family, apparently. And the truth of the matter was, Kotkel wasn't stupid. Not the sharpest arrow in the quiver, maybe, but in some ways he was really quite smart. Like, for instance, the moment you betrayed some slight vulnerability, he'd be on it like a snake. I suddenly realised I couldn't think what to say.

But I also knew I had to say something, because silence would be an admission that he'd hit the mark in the gold. "That's just the sort of chickenshit I'd expect from you, Kel," I said. "You don't dare kill me, so you beat up on a girl instead. Why don't you dare kill me, Kel? Somebody's got you well trained, I can see that. Good dog. Sit. Beg. And if you're really good, you can have a bit of chicken skin."

He moved. Not forward to attack, but back. I didn't analyse it at the time, being preoccupied with other things, but I think he was putting distance between us; to keep himself from lashing out, or simply because I was making myself too loathsome to be close to. No matter. I dragged the sword out from under his foot and rose to my feet, sliding my back up against the wall. Great tactics. He'd rush me, but he couldn't push the wall out of the way. I'd probably break both my wrists, holding on to the sword hilt while he impaled himself on it, but his onset and the wall between them would get the job done –

He was looking at me. Pure contempt.

Of course, he knew the story of Sighvat the Peacock too. Maybe he wasn't as dumb as all that, and maybe I wasn't so smart. "You're a real piece of shit," he said to me. "You know that?"

"I'd kind of gathered," I said. The sword was too heavy to

keep outstretched for very long. I lowered it. "Go home, Kel,"
I said. "You don't belong here."

"Fuck you."

"I belong here," I said; "you don't. How are they making you
do this? Come on, you can tell me. I'm your brother."

I didn't know he could be so quick. He darted forward and
slapped the sword out of my hand. I heard it clatter on the
stone floor, and he was blocking out all the moonlight from the
window. I felt his fingers, all five of them, close round my head.

"Nobody's making me do anything," he said.

"Liar."

"Was it true? Dad and Mom laughing at me?"

"No, of course not. I made it up."

I wasn't sure he believed me. "Fuck you," he said. "Why'd
you want to say a thing like that?"

"To piss you off, Kel. You always were so easy to get a rise
out of."

He was holding my life in his hand, between the tips of his
fingers. "I ought to kill you for that."

"Then why don't you?"

I couldn't see his eyes, because he was between me and the
light. "You're pathetic," he said. "You're a real piece of shit."

More than an element of truth in that. "Who's making you
do this?" I said. "Tell me. I can help."

With a flick of his wrist he sent me flying. I hit a wall. I realised I was lying on top of the sword. Small world. "You can't
help me," he said. "You're nobody."

"What happened to you, Kel? How did you die?"

"Fuck off."

"Who killed you?"

He didn't know what to do with his hands. He waved them

in the air, like a man trying to restrain two large dogs. "What do you care? You never gave a shit about any of us."

"Was it Dad?"

"No." He was shouting.

"He killed you, didn't he? His own son."

He punched a hole in the wall. Solid stone, imperial masonry. A direct hit from a trebuchet couldn't do that. "Shut up, will you? Just shut the fuck up."

"Sorry, Kel, but I need you to tell me. Who's doing all this? How are they doing it? It shouldn't be possible. If you tell me, I can fix it. You don't want to be here, I can see that. You don't want to be doing this. I can help you."

He lunged at me, amazingly fast. By the time I'd grabbed the hilt of the sword, he had his hand round my head and was holding me up, so my feet were off the ground. "I don't want your fucking help," he roared in my face, and I noticed the lack of breath. Kel's breath always smelled bad when I was a kid. When he breathed in my face it made me want to wash it off with ashes and water. But no smell, because no breath. "You never helped anybody in your whole life."

I could feel my skull flex under his fingers. Now that's a weird sensation. "Go on," I said, "do it. Maybe it'll make you feel better."

He dropped me. I landed badly, folded my ankle over and flopped in a heap at his feet, like a shirt he'd just taken off and dumped on the floor. I had the sword in my hand. I didn't know if he'd noticed it or not.

"You're an arsehole," he said, "you know that? Why can't you just leave me alone?"

He was standing with his weight on his left leg, which was what, two feet away from me. In the books I've read, there's this thing called the centre of percussion, which is the place on a sword blade that delivers the maximum force; Svangerd calls it the sweet spot, which is much the same thing. If I took a swing at his knee from where I was kneeling, the sweet spot would catch him just above the kneecap. I'd be able to put my whole body behind the cut, and as I think I may have mentioned, I'm no weakling, not physically at least. It was what Sighvat would've done, and Angantyr the Strong and Bothvar Biarki. The hell with it, I thought, and put the sword down on the ground. I guess I couldn't bear the look on his face, when I swung at him and it bounced off.

"I'm sorry," I said. "Look, I don't like you and you don't like me. But we're brothers, and someone's playing stupid games with our family. That's not right. Is it?"

"Fuck all you can do about it."

"That's where you're wrong," I said. "I can fix it. I can make it stop. All you have to do is tell me. Who's doing it? How are they doing it? That's all I need to know."

He roared and kicked me. I think he must have mostly missed, because if he'd connected fair and square, you wouldn't be reading this. I went spinning, hit the wall with my shoulder and fell in a heap. I looked up and he was standing over me, one foot raised. One stamp. The last thing I'd ever see.

I heard another roar, but not from Kotkel. He turned his head. I couldn't see, because he was in my light. He swung round, away from me, and past him I saw a huge shape, swollen, familiar: another walker.

They slammed into each other. The noise was unbelievable, and not like anything I've ever heard before or since. You wouldn't believe so much force could be expended in a confined space without bringing the walls and the ceiling down.

Each of them had his hands clamped round the other's head, squeezing. You couldn't call it a fight. It was a race, to see who could crush the other one first.

The newcomer took his hands off Kotkel's head and brought them up inside his arms to break his grip. Then he shoved him against the wall. It was a trick Dad used to show us, when he taught us to wrestle.

I saw Kotkel look down and grab something. I couldn't see, but I guessed I knew what it was. I yelled, "Dad, look out," but I was too late.

The grip of the sword was too small for Kotkel's hand, so he threw it, like a knife. It hit Dad in the eye socket, either pure fluke or the sweetest throw you ever saw. Dad staggered back, and Kel sprang forward, grabbed the sword with both hands and pushed, a massive thrust, with all his strength and weight behind it. I heard that unmistakeable sound, more a click than anything else, that you only get when a hardened and tempered blade snaps. So much for that theory, I remember thinking; I'm ashamed of myself for that.

The sword breaking took Kel by surprise. He staggered forward, and Dad punched him in the face, his trademark short right cross. It made Kel stagger two steps back but it didn't floor him. Then they were grappling again, Dad squeezing Kel's head, Kel pushing on the broken sword-blade, trying to force it out through the back of Dad's skull with the heels of his hands.

I don't know how long it would've gone on if Dad hadn't caught his foot on something and stumbled. Kotkel pulled quickly away, and Dad fell on one knee. As he tried to get up Kel lashed out a kick at him, but Dad caught his foot in both hands and twisted it. I expected to hear a bone snap, but I didn't. They charged each other and came together with a crash like a falling tree, but Kel hadn't got his balance quite right. He toppled backwards, grabbing at Dad to break his fall, and they both went down together. They were next to the window. It was solid enough: massive granite jambs and mullions. It crumpled under their combined mass like a spider's web, and they fell out.

For a moment I thought they'd brought the whole building down, but hooray for imperial architecture. Instead, they'd left a huge hole in the wall.

It was a long way down from the third floor, but not nearly far enough. I forced myself to peer out through the hole in the wall, and I saw them, in the courtyard below, crashing into each other like two stags in the rut.

I was scared stiff that people would come running when they heard the noise and get themselves killed, but I needn't have worried. Nobody, not even clerics or the guard, was stupid enough to go anywhere near them, or put themselves in a place where they might be seen – except for me, of course, staring out at them framed by the hole they'd made, but I didn't care. Not that they were the slightest bit interested in anything but each other.

If you forced me to venture an opinion, I'd have to say that Kotkel was a tiny bit stronger, but Dad made up for it in skill and experience; after all, he taught Kotkel everything he knew about fighting, but either he'd neglected to teach him all his best moves or Kotkel's attention had wandered at some point. Since neither of them could hurt or harm the other it really didn't matter terribly much. They kept on at each other, with no slackening of pace or intensity, no fatigue or diminution of will. Neither of them could win, neither could lose, and there was no reason at all why they shouldn't keep it up indefinitely.

And then they stopped. I couldn't understand why. But Dad suddenly took his hands off Kotkel's head, and Kotkel stopped trying to push the broken sword-blade through Dad's skull. They both took a long step back, looked at each other for maybe two heartbeats, then turned and strode off in opposite directions, walking fast, like they were late for dinner.

9

"I don't think anybody's going to make a fuss about me stealing the sword," she said, as we sat together on the refectory steps the next morning. "Obviously they found the hilt and recognised it, and someone's bound to wonder what it was doing there when it ought to have been in the treasury. But they'll figure that one of the monsters must've stolen it, and besides, nobody's going to want to highlight the fact that an agent of Evil was able to steal, use and break a holy relic, because that'd be very bad for morale. My guess is, at some point soon a new blade is going to appear in the old hilt, and it'll be so like the old one that nobody will be able to tell the difference, and that part of it won't have happened."

Indeed. A job for a skilled faker of historical artefacts. Talking of which ... Only I couldn't bring myself to. She'd find out soon enough, but too late to stop me and then with any luck she'd be safe.

"You were wrong about the steel thing," she said.

"Not entirely," I said. "It penetrated his eye, didn't it? I reckon, if it'd been a newly made sword, it'd have snapped."

"It did snap."

"Only when Kotkel put his full weight on it. I still think that if he'd used it to cut with, instead of throwing it, he'd have been able to break the skin at the very least. But like I said, the grip was too small, and it's got one of those ditzy half-moon pommels that bite into your wrist when you take a swing, so he didn't have that option."

She gave me her what-the-hell-are-you-talking-about look, and I shut up. I really wasn't interested in the steel thing, and neither was she. What we both wanted to ask was, why? Why had two of the monsters suddenly decided to fight each other? But since we had no answers, we didn't ask the question. Too depressing.

But not nearly as depressing as the answer I could have provided, if I'd been truly cruel or thoughtless. Even after seeing it (blessed are those who have seen and yet . . .) I couldn't quite bring myself to choke it down and swallow it. Had I really watched a bout in the never-ending battle between Good and Evil? My friend with the chins would have me believe that that was precisely what I'd seen. In which case, which monster was Good and which was the bad guy? My pal had as good as claimed Kotkel for his own; in which case Dad was Evil. But in that case, why had he turned up like that, presumably saving my neck, and how come he'd been able to fight a duly authorised representative of the angels to a standstill?

"Another thing you were wrong about," she was saying. "Flushing the ashes out to sea. Obviously that didn't work either."

"Obviously."

"It should've worked, though. It was a good idea. So you really can't blame yourself for that."

For *that*, as opposed to —

"No," I said. "And I don't, so there."

She turned her head and looked at me. "You don't suppose—"

"What?"

"Your dad turned up when he did to rescue you. Because if he hadn't, you'd have been killed, right?"

"I don't know," I said. "Kotkel had plenty of chances, God only knows. And I said some pretty stupid things, trying to rile him. And Kel always hated me, and he always did have a vicious temper. I'm surprised he didn't kill me, to be honest with you. It's not like there'd have been consequences, and Kel never did worry about things like that."

"Well, there you are, then."

I shook my head. "But he didn't do it," I said. "There were at least three times last night when I said to myself, This is it, I'm going to die. But he didn't do it. And I was pushing him really hard, just like when we were kids."

She gave me a look of wisdom and compassion, expertly blended. "You must've been a real fuck-up when you were a boy."

I nodded. "Last night," I said, "I think I was pushing him to see how far he'd go. I needed him to admit he couldn't kill me. And I think I was almost there, only Dad showed up. And that," I added, "would make a certain amount of sense."

"Would it?"

I was in danger of going too far. "Thinking aloud. Ignore me."

"So what are you thinking?"

"Just my usual drivel. Forget it." I made a show of yawning. "I don't know about you, but I'm pooped. Didn't get much sleep last night, what with one thing and another. I think I might just crawl away under a rock and close my eyes for ten minutes."

She knows me too well. "What is it?" she said. "What haven't you told me?"

"Oh, loads of stuff," I said, manufacturing another yawn. "None of it relevant. If I were to tell you *everything*, you'd be so bored you'd strangle me just to make me shut up. For instance, did you know that in the second edition of Theophrastus' *Elements of Botany*, the chapter on the shapes of tree-trunks is very slightly different? It's almost the same, except—"

"What haven't you told me?"

I'd done exactly what I didn't want to do. That's not like me. "Nothing," I said. "Trust me. I'm just having a bit of a crisis of faith, that's all. Please don't go on about it."

I know her quite well. I know that it bothers the life out of her that I'm not a believer; partly because that makes me a form of anathema, and she really shouldn't associate with me; partly because she's worried that I'll go to hell when I die. A crisis of faith would suggest that maybe I was on the verge of seeing the light and being saved. Well; maybe she'd think that, and get off my back.

"Sure," she said. "None of my business." She stood up. "You were right," she said. "We ought to leave. We're not doing any good here."

Where had that come from? "I'm not so certain about that any more," I said.

"Really? Why?"

"Last night," I said. "I stopped Kotkel from hurting anyone. Well, I did. Nobody got killed, did they?"

She thought about that for a moment. "I don't know," she said. "Maybe he came for you. Maybe he wasn't after anyone else. Maybe if you weren't here, he'd go away."

You can't expect help if you lie to people. "Maybe," I said. "The bitch of it is, I think I could've made him tell me who's controlling him, if Dad hadn't shown up. Or he'd have killed me, one or the other. I think I still could, if I faced him again."

She gave me a long, hard look. "I think we both know who's controlling the monsters," she said. "Only you won't admit it."

"Then why did Dad—?"

She shrugged. "I think he came to save you. Because he was human once, and even Evil can't scrub the last bit of goodness out of someone. I think your father came back because he loves you."

Oh dear, I thought, or something to that effect. But I let her go without saying anything. More often than not, I've come to believe, the last word simply isn't worth having.

I was in the main quadrangle, waiting for the next council session to begin, when someone called out my name. I didn't recognise him: a stocky man, in an army coat and a big felt hat. "That's me," I said.

He took a small brass tube from his sleeve. "Letter for you."

He didn't seem inclined to hang about, so I thanked him and found a quiet spot in the corner of the quad. The letter was addressed to Svangerd and me, from Secretary Hildegern back home. You remember, the young smart-arse who made me go to Choris in the first place.

Hildegern to Desiderius and Svangerd, greetings.
    We have heard – not from you, which we find disturbing – about the deplorable events at the council.

We would remind you that you work for us. We trust that you do not need to be reminded where your loyalties lie.

Clearly your original mission has been superseded by the turn of events. We consider it essential that we are fully represented at the council for its full duration, and we rely on you to remain in attendance, with a view to making a full report on your return. Furthermore, you are instructed to take all necessary action, verbally and physically, to protect and maintain the interests of this abbey, Abbot Simocatta and the true faith, including but not limited to casting your votes in favour of the election of Vitimer as permanent head of the council.

In other words: stay put, do what you have to do, but everything you do will be your fault, not mine. Exactly what I'd have expected from him, worse luck.

I skipped the opening session and took the letter for Svangerd to see. She was sitting with Mother Krimhild, watching her lying motionless in bed, neither dead nor alive. There seemed to be a lot of that about at this council, one way or another.

"Any change?"

"No." She wasn't looking at me. "What are you doing here? And keep your voice down; she needs to rest."

"Letter from home."

"Give it here." She read it and handed it back. "Wonderful," she said. "We're stuck here."

"Looks like it."

"Of course, they don't know all the facts. For a start, they can't have heard about the heresy or the schism yet, or they'd have sent instructions."

"Presumably," I said. "But I guess that's covered by protecting and maintaining the interests. Good phrase, that. I must remember it. What were you doing in the castle strongroom at midnight, with a sack and a ten-inch knife wedged in the top of your boot? Well, your honour, I was protecting and maintaining the interests of the true faith. Case dismissed." I sighed. "Do you remember the days when we were just thieves? Everything was so simple then."

She turned her head to scowl at me; not in front of the holy mother, even though she can't hear a word of it. "You'd better go to the council," she said.

"You?"

"I'll stay here and pray a bit longer."

Pray for what? I asked myself, as I picked my way down that horrible spiral staircase. Krimhild was never going to get better; nor did she seem to be in any hurry to die. If there really was an Invincible Sun, He'd been very badly brought up, and never learned to take proper care of His toys. You wouldn't let a dog linger like that, not one you were fond of. And on the other hand, there was Kotkel, and my dad –

I realised, as I reached the bottom of the staircase and emerged into the comparatively blinding sunlight, that I wasn't going to stand up in the next session and pretend I'd forged the true gospels. All along I'd been kidding myself, but it was time to face facts, if I was serious about putting together a Plan B. I wasn't going to do it because – well, for a start it'd be the end of me; the letter had reminded me that there was a world outside Choris and this appalling mess, and I wanted to go home. Also, I'd reached the point where I didn't believe *anything*. Good, Evil, angels, the Loyal Opposition, the Invincible Sun – everybody was trying to sell me something, even though they knew perfectly well I had no money. So it was time to think about it rationally, something which, as a good atheist, I ought to be able to do. As it happened, I couldn't; I'd tried, but no dice. Even so –

The *Institutions* of Florian the Great, setting out in unambiguous detail the entire law code of the empire, was lost hundreds of years ago, and only a few fragments remain. All the laws comprised in it, however, remain in force (because they were never repealed) and are still binding on every one of us, even though nobody knows what they are. This has allowed judges and law enforcement a substantial degree of scope over the centuries, mostly in the direction of holding that the prisoner at the bar must be guilty of *something*, but that's not the point. One of the few scraps that survived is Florian's double standard of the burden of proof. In criminal and ecclesiastical cases, guilt is established if the prosecution can prove its case beyond reasonable doubt. In civil cases, liability is established if the case is proved on the balance of probabilities. Big difference.

Fuck – I rarely swear to myself, but sometimes you simply have to – fuck beyond reasonable doubt. Doubt was everywhere, reasonable, unreasonable and purely intuitive, and trying to get rid of it was like trying to get rid of the last rat under a chicken coop. The balance of probabilities, on the other hand: that was more like it. On the balance of probabilities, everyone who'd been trying to influence me lately was lying to me and more full of shit than the East River, so the logical thing to do was not believe a word of it and do the best I could with the few facts I could verify by personal observation. Which were as follows.

Two walkers – my father and Kotkel – had come to Choris

from the Mesoge. They'd killed the princess and the fat man
and Svangerd's ex-john and some soldiers. Dad had tried to
kill me, but Kotkel ... Face it, he'd gone out of his way not
to hurt me, even though I'd done my best to provoke him.
Someone was controlling him, he'd as good as admitted it,
but he wouldn't say who. Why was that? Fear, maybe, except
what on earth would a walker be scared of? And if it wasn't
fear, how could you control one of those things? You can't bribe
them with gold or sweeties, because there's nothing they want,
except to hurt people, and they could do that just as well in
the Mesoge. Implication, therefore, that there's some power at
work capable of controlling the uncontrollable, which in turn
would tend to suggest a supernatural agency –

I didn't like that, but I caught sight of Saloninus, leering at
me and brandishing his razor, so I stuck with it. A supernatural agency. Talking of Saloninus, his third law states that any
sufficiently advanced technology is indistinguishable from
magic, and that what we poor fools take to be the supernatural
is in fact science that nobody's invented yet or, more likely,
that used to be known to every schoolboy under the empire
but which has since been lost and forgotten. But just because it
isn't magic doesn't mean it isn't real. In practice, the advanced
technology and the magic achieve the same result, and a kick
in the head from either of them hurts just as much. In other
words, magic or science, it doesn't matter a toss.

Which in turn, therefore, suggests a very powerful agency,
supernatural or scientific; at any rate, much bigger and stronger
and nastier than me, which was all that mattered. Fine. Now
then; did I honestly and sincerely believe that the man with the
chins was the duly authorised representative of such an agency?

Think about it. If I was incredibly powerful, would I choose a tosser like that to be my agent? And would I need someone like me to get what I wanted done; and would I want the sort of thing the man with the chins apparently wanted?

Good question, and one I've put to theologians before now, usually when I and the theologian are both very drunk. What, I've asked, does the Invincible Sun want us *for*? What function could we possibly serve? Why should He give a damn whether we're naughty or nice; what does He get out of it that He couldn't get elsewhere or in another fashion, given that He's omnipotent and infinitely wise? Does He keep us as pets – which is the only possible explanation, if you look at it rationally? And if so, what does God need with a dog or a cat or a hamster? If He needs one, he can't be God, by any meaningful definition. God, after all, doesn't *need* anything – just like a Mesoge walker.

If you ask me, that's an argument so cogent that it's hardly surprising I remember it the morning after, when my head's splitting and my mouth tastes like the floor of a pigsty. (And, while we're on the subject of the balance of probabilities, with that in Pan A, you can stuff whatever you like into Pan B and it won't make the slightest difference, world without end, amen.)

Well, then. I brought the force of that to bear on the big question, which was: did I believe the man with the chins when he told me he'd set Kotkel on Svangerd if I didn't do as I was told, or not?

Answer: yes and no. Balance of probabilities? No, I didn't. Beyond reasonable doubt?

Ay, there's the rub. If I guessed wrong, and anything happened to Svangerd –

Just a moment, I thought. I know that man.

Panic. That's the bitch about cities. You bump into someone, you take your eye off them for two seconds and they're gone, lost, swallowed up in the crowd. A certain degree of thought is therefore called for. Now then. If I was a messenger who'd just come a long way very fast, what would I do, as soon as I'd accomplished my mission? Actually, that was misleading. What would *he* do?

Answer: have a drink. For which he'd go to an inn, or a beer-shop, or a tavern. Or a brothel; no, probably too tired for that, because we're none of us quite as young as we were. I ran back to the place where I'd been handed the letter, and looked around. The nearest watering-hole would be the place under the arches, where the clerks and students went, but my man was a stranger in town and it was the sort of place you had to know about to find. The nearest obvious watering-hole: just look around, the way he'd have done, and let your eyes do it all for you.

It was called the Poverty and Persistence, and sure enough, he was there. I didn't recognise him, but I recognised the hat, which he'd taken off and put down on the bench next to him; likewise the army coat, revealing the clothes he wore under it, which were dead shabby and a shade of homespun butternut linen that was painfully familiar.

Flax does grow in the Mesoge – reluctantly, like it's doing you a favour and it knows it'll get in trouble for it if it gets caught. Linen means status; only the big farmers can be bothered with it, to show off, because it's far less warm and practical than wool. Therefore, if you wear linen, it means you aren't out in all weathers, implying that you have hired men to do all that stuff for you. And, when it starts to wear out and fray at the seams, you intensify your grandeur by giving it to your grateful retainers. Thus, in the Mesoge, linen is worn exclusively by the top five per cent and the bottom five per cent of society: the cream and the scum. This man, if I'd identified him correctly, was not the cream.

Big if. I hadn't seen the man I took him to be since I was ten years old, though I had reason to remember him. Don't you go anywhere near him, my mother had told me. Stay away from him, my father said, and if he follows you, run and holler and make as much noise as you can. What it was that Rotlaug did to children nobody was inclined to tell me; he ate them, I assumed, in the absence of further and better particulars, and so I kept the hell away from him, having taken pains to commit his face, shape and way of walking to indelible memory.

I bought a jug of beer and took it over to the corner where he was sitting. "Hello, Rotlaug," I said. "I didn't recognise you under that hat."

He grinned at me. "You haven't changed," he said.

"Nor you." That was overstating it a bit. His face was quite different. At some point, someone had broken both his nose and his chin, and they hadn't set quite right. Also, the scar was new. Someone or something had gouged or sliced a chunk the size of the palm of your hand off his left cheek, and the hair didn't grow there any more. But it was his expression and the look in his eyes that you remembered about Rotlaug, and that hadn't changed one bit.

"What are you doing in these parts?" I said. "You're a long way from Unnsvik."

He laughed. "So are you," he said. "Maybe I did what you did. Left to better myself."

Plenty of scope for that. "Maybe," I said. "But I don't think so. How can you improve on perfection?"

"Or maybe," he said, "I'm here on a job. What do you think?"

"Give me a letter, you mean."

"That and something else." He drank half the beer straight from the jug. "Fucking horrible," he said.

"I think the water's too hard for successful brewing," I told him. "What sort of job?"

He turned his head and smiled at me. "I guess I'm what you might call a specialist," he said.

"Good for you. Doing what?"

He drank the other half. "Pest control," he said. "Same as in the old country."

Ah, I thought. And that made sense, too. All through my childhood I wondered why nobody had strung him up or cut his head off, seeing what a nuisance he was, what with eating children and so on. I'd assumed it was because if he was killed he'd only come back as a walker and be even more tiresome. But if he was – well, a specialist – that would explain why he was tolerated. "Old country pests?" I said.

He nodded. "Good money," he said. "Stupid money. And I felt like a change anyhow. My face don't fit back home any more, for some reason. Time to move on, see a bit of the world. Can't say I care for it very much, but what the hell."

"Pest control," I repeated. "Are you any good?"

"Yup."

"It's true, they have got a problem here at the moment. Who sent for you?"

"Dunno," he said. "Three arseholes showed up looking for me, offcomers. Priests. They gave me a shitload of money just for listening to them, and said they'd give me a real shitload more if I did them a job. Piss-easy job. So I said yes, and here I am."

I nodded to the sutler for more beer. "Maybe not as piss-easy as all that," I said.

"Piss-easy," he repeated. "I know that. I done it before. I can do it again."

"Maybe," I said, "but not these particular walkers."

He looked at me and grinned. "These same walkers," he said.

Oh, I thought. "Kotkel."

"Yup. And your dad."

"Back home."

He nodded. "Piece of piss," he said. "I done them before, so I can do them again." He looked at me, like a surveyor or a mason considering an angle, or a forester assessing which way a tree will fall. "Actually, it'll be the third time."

"Really."

"Yup. I killed 'em both once, and then I killed 'em again."

His hand had dropped to his waist. I glanced down and saw a handle. I knew what it was. Back home we call them hog knives, or Mesoge toothpicks. Blade a foot long, two inches wide, heavy, with a clipped back edge. Plain, effective, absolutely no sophistication whatsoever. "No doubt you had your reasons," I said. "Don't worry, I'm not going to make a fuss about it. I left home a long time ago, and I'm never going back."

That seemed to satisfy him, and he put his hand back on the bench. "The first time you killed them," I said. "Were they alive?"

He laughed. "Yup," he said.

"Just out of interest—"

"They tried to push me around," he said. "I don't take kindly to that. They tried to stomp me, so I stomped them back. So they came out one night when I was asleep and tried to burn me in my house. Nailed the door and the shutters up, set fire to the thatch. But I busted out through the hayloft hatch, and then I did them, with my little toothpick. You don't blame me for that, do you?"

I shrugged. "Clearly the best man won," I said. "Natural justice."

"Yeah, well. About six months after that, they started to walk. Did a lot of damage, killed a lot of sheep and a couple of women. Folks blamed me, can't say why. They said to me, you made this mess; you clear it up. So I did."

I looked at him. "How?"

That grin again. "Brute force," he said.

The way he said it made my teeth ache. "You're good at that, I bet."

"Yup, me and my little toothpick. Helps if you've got the knack, of course. I've been doing walkers since I was nineteen years old."

"Which is why they let you stick around."

He nodded. "Till recently," he said. "So it came at a good time, this trip. I got to tell you, I've done a lot of walkers, like I said, and your brother and your old man, they're nothing special."

"Is that right?"

"You bet. Not like some. There was one fucker at Holmgard, gave me this." He pointed at his face with his index finger. "Real sweetheart, he was. Another one, out Jormundale, a woman, stuck a fencepost clean through my leg. Thought I'd had it that time but no, I tickled her up with my little toothpick and down she went, and everything was just fine. Bet you never knew women can do it too. Not many people know that, but they can." He smiled. "I guess the thing is, they know I'm not scared of them. They know it's only going to end one way when they see me." He tapped his head. "Up here, that's where the real fighting's done. They can't beat me there."

"Clearly you have a special gift," I said. "And what a blessing that you were available. Are you sure you don't know who sent you here?"

"Just three arsehole priests with a shitload of money," he said. "Get there fast as you can, they told me, there's a bonus if you get it done before the Calends. What the fuck's a Calends, I said. They told me, first new moon after autumn sowing. No problem, I said. They even gave me a horse, a real beauty. And a coat and a hat, and new boots. Didn't reckon much to sailing on boats, though. Made me chuck my guts."

"I've got a friend who's like that," I said. "Doesn't bother me, for some reason." The beer arrived. I paid for it and stood up. "Well, it's been wonderful to see you again, Rotlaug. The very best of luck, and I hope you succeed. You'll be doing us all a favour. Me especially."

He nodded. "That's me," he said. "All heart."

"Sure you don't know who sent you? It wasn't the abbot, was it? The man who gave you the letter?"

He shook his head. "This arsehole came up to me in a bar," he said. "Heard I was going this way, and did I know you? Yes, I said. Then give him this letter, he said, and here's ten deniers. I thought, for ten deniers, why the fuck not?"

"Indeed."

"I mean, I could've used the letter for arsewipe and kept the ten deniers, but I thought, fuck it, I'm going that way anyhow. Also it tickled me, seeing a face from the old country, wondering if you'd shit yourself when you saw me again. You always were chickenshit when you were a kid."

"Still am," I said, "and proud of it. So long, Rotlaug. And God speed your little toothpick."

That made him laugh. I left him to his beer.

I found Svangerd on her knees in some side-chapel. "Guess what," I said.

"Shh."

"Sorry." I lowered my voice. "Guess who's just turned up. A hero."

She looked at me. "You what?"

"A genuine hero," I said. "The stuff of legends. Right now he's in the Poverty and Persistence drinking himself into a stupor, but in due course I have complete confidence he'll knuckle down to business and that'll be that. We're off the hook."

"Pull yourself together," she said, not unkindly, "and try making some sense. Who's in where and how does it help us?"

I told her. She shook her head. "Nah," she said. "He doesn't stand a chance."

I felt as though I'd given her a rose and she'd stuffed it in my ear. "You don't understand," I said. "What we've got here is an expert. A professional. There *are* people like that, I know. I heard about them all the time when I was growing up. There are exceptional people who can subdue walkers, and this Rotlaug is one of them."

"According to him."

"Yes, but it makes sense. If he didn't have the knack, he'd have been strung up years ago. But he's got the knack, so he was too valuable to lynch and people learned to put up with him. He's the genuine article. And like he said, he's killed them once – well, twice – so he can do it again."

Her eyes were scepticism in a sapphire setting. "I doubt it," she said. "Back in the sticks, maybe. But not here. You still don't get it, do you? Those monsters have been brought here by the Evil One, to do his bidding. They're not just wildlife any more; they're soldiers. It's about, what's the word, context. Sorry, but your homeboy is dead meat."

I sighed. "I don't suppose you can understand," I said. "After all, it's a Mesoge thing. It's a bit like, oh, I don't know, composing music. Most of us can't do it to save our lives; a few people can. They look just the same as normal people, but they've got the *knack*. He's one of them. It's a known phenomenon, back home."

No dice. She frowned. "While we're on the subject," she said, "you're really weird, you know that? Here's a man who's just confessed to slaughtering your father and your brother, and you're actually pleased to see him. How in God's name did you ever turn out that way?"

Valid point. The truth was, I hadn't really given it any thought. "I guess that's what makes these people so special. Their gift is so rare and so precious, you tend to forgive them their peccadillos."

"Like murdering your family."

"The way he told it, it was self-defence. And burning a man in his house does sound rather like my dad's style, I have to admit. And Kotkel's."

"You're amazing," she said. I'd always wanted to hear her say that. To quote her, it's all about context. "Well, it just goes to show. You can take the boy out of the Mesoge, but you can't take the Mesoge—"

"Yes, all right. I only told you because I thought you'd be pleased."

She was thinking. "You need to find out who paid him to come here."

"I tried. He doesn't know."

"If we knew that—"

"But we don't. Besides, it doesn't matter. Some philanthropist. I couldn't care less, so long as he solves the problem and we can all go home. I'm not really interested in the whys and wherefores any more. I just want it to be over."

"Wishful thinking. Try not to be too disappointed."

The hell with it, I thought. I'd done my duty and told her. If she was determined not to believe, that was her lookout.

Blessed are those. I did say that, didn't I?

I went to the session where I'd been instructed to stand up and make trouble. I went early so I could get a seat near the front. I felt like it was market day, and I was waiting to find out if I was the pig or the butcher.

The session was important because the authenticity commission was due to give an interim report before the scheduled debate got under way. Just as well I arrived early, though it was noticeable that it was the seats at the back, close to the doors, that people wanted to sit in. Plenty of room at the front until the last moment. In fact, the seat next to me was empty until the doors closed, at which point the man with the chins bustled in and plonked himself down next to me, so hard that the bench flexed under him.

"All set?" he whispered to me.

I smiled instead of speaking.

"Break a leg."

Yours for choice, I didn't say. On the rostrum, Vitimer stood up and cleared his throat, looking like a brand-new target face in the archery butts: not a mark on him, but that was liable to change. The commission, he said, had now had an opportunity to examine the disputed documents. Without further ado, therefore, he called on Sister Ululari to present her findings.

I watched her stand up. I could see she was terrified.

She'd examined the documents, she said, with particular regard to the age and nature of the parchment on which they were written. She gave us a brief precis of her qualifications – her years in various scriptoria, the work she'd done, the monographs she's written; she took a long time over that, as if she wasn't keen to get on with the next part of her speech.

The parchment, she said, was definitely old, quite possibly old enough to be what it purportedly was. The fact that it had been ground down and erased, more than once, was not in itself a barrier to authenticity, since reusing parchment was common practice at that time in that place. However –

(It was the way she said it, and the scared look in her eyes, like some hunted animal.)

However, she went on, there was the question of the burnishing. After a piece of parchment is scraped and sanded for reuse, it has to be burnished, to close up the pores and fibres and present a smooth surface to write on. If this step is neglected, the ink tends to seep into the fibres. The manuscripts she'd been given to examine had indeed been burnished, to the standard she'd come to expect in documents of that age. But she had reason to believe that the burnisher used was made of bone, or possibly walrus ivory. For an imperial-era document of that age, she would expect to have seen the marks of a glass burnisher – a shinier, closer-packed surface, more even, as you might expect from a harder, more uniform instrument. The secret of making glass burnishers was, of course, lost when the empire fell, and no example was known to have survived; modern burnishers were all made of bone, wood or steel. There were, she quickly went on, instances of bone burnishers being used under the empire, but only in the frontier provinces and in satellite kingdoms not under direct imperial control; given the purported provenance of these documents, it was unlikely that they would have been copied in any such place. By contrast, the use of a bone instrument would be entirely consistent with a modern scribe recycling an ancient document – in other words, a forgery. While not conclusive, this evidence would seem to cast a certain degree of doubt –

Something hit me in the ribs. It was the many-chinned man's elbow. He was staring at me. "You *arsehole*," he whispered in my ear. "It was a bloody fake all along, and you *knew*—"

He stopped. Everybody was staring at him. That's what you get when you whisper in a room with excellent acoustics, when everybody else is keeping dead quiet.

A certain degree of doubt, continued Sister Ululalaria, on the authenticity of the documents. For further corroboration, she would now call on her colleague, Father Zosimus.

She sat down. Zosimus stood up. The ink, he said, was wrong. Very, very nearly right, but all wrong. It had been made to an authentic imperial recipe fortuitously preserved in Theophilus' *On Sundry Arts*, but the verdigris in the mix had been derived from Permian copper (which tarnishes to a slightly redder brown), and Permian copper only began to be imported into the empire after the loss of Sirupat to the Sashan empire, two hundred years later than the purported date of the documents. There was of course the remote chance that the scribe had somehow got hold of Permian copper two centuries before it was commonly available in the South, but Saloninus'

razor would tend to indicate that the ink was a modern for-
mulation, closely following the ancient recipe – precisely the
behaviour, in fact, that one would expect from an expert forger.

"You shit," murmured the many-chinned man. "Why
didn't you tell me?"

I ignored him. I was concentrating on Brother Hunferth,
who was saying that the handwriting was perfect for that
place and time; in fact, it was too perfect. The documents
were written in demotic cursive script, and the handwriting
was distinctive enough to be identifiable. It was the writing of
a scribe, known from over a dozen surviving manuscripts and
referred to in scholarly circles as the Stachelburg Master – and
that was interesting, because the Stachelburg Master worked
exclusively in one northern monastery, where he copied works
of unimpeachable orthodoxy over a period of forty years. It was
conceivable that at some point he left the north, came south
and embraced heresy. Conceivable, but rather unlikely. More
likely was the explanation that a very clever forger, searching
for a model, had lighted on a Stachelburg manuscript and
copied the handwriting style impeccably, without realising that
in doing so he was giving himself away –

You could've heard a pin, or a jaw, drop. Mine was on my
chest, and none of the muscles that were supposed to control
it seemed to be working. Then Jormunrec got up and said that
the texts were written in flawless, pitch-perfect Antecyrenaean,
a language so dead that (as far as he was aware) only he and
about a dozen other scholars now living could read it; he could
name the other twelve; he named them. He knew them all and
none of them, he ventured to suggest, were the sort of man or
woman who'd assist in perpetrating such a heinous forgery,
not to mention the blasphemy or the heresy. It was conceivable

(he said, with a sideways glance at Hunferth) that there was someone else who knew the language well enough to write it like a native, but where and how such a person could have learned it, he couldn't begin to imagine. Whereupon Brother Terving jumped up, without waiting to be called by the chair, and said that the metrical forms used in the versification of ancient Antecyrenaean poetry were so complex and so little understood that he couldn't think of anyone who'd be capable of faking them convincingly, and that as far as he was concerned, he neither knew nor cared about the parchment or the ink, but the words themselves were unmistakeably genuine.

The man with the chins had gone white as a sheet and was clutching his left arm as though in pain. I think I was the only person in the room who noticed, or who'd have given a damn if they had. For a very long time nobody moved or spoke. Then a very old woman in the white habit of the Poor Sisters got up. "So what you're saying is," she said, "we're right back where we started."

Zosimus stood up and nodded. "The conclusion of this commission," he said, "is that the manuscripts are a modern copy, probably intended to deceive, of ancient texts written at the time of or shortly after the Passion of Our Lord, in the region where the events described took place."

Someone yelled, "Then the true gospels are true."

"Not necessarily," someone else called out. "Just because they're old doesn't mean they're not a pack of lies. Just a pack of very old lies, that's all."

At which point everybody started yelling at once, and I decided to leave while I still could.

10

There was a fountain in the courtyard. I went and stuck my head in it. It didn't help.

All right, then, I said to myself. The story so far. For some reason, somebody saw fit to plant on me a fake copy of the true true gospels, which the short man got hold of a short time before Dad flattened his head; the Loyal Opposition, meanwhile, didn't want a schism, but the angels did. No, it still didn't make any sense. But Rotlaug of Unnsvik was in town (he'd killed my father, but nobody's perfect) so pretty soon we wouldn't have the walkers to worry about, just the collapse of Holy Mother Church and the very real prospect of a slew of civil and religious wars –

"Why are you all wet?" she asked.

I hadn't seen her. "I stuck my head in the fountain," I said.

"Ah. Like that, was it?"

"You betcha. Worse. The copies are fake but the gospels themselves are probably true. Or true lies, depending on your point of view. Oh, and I think the devil was having a heart attack as I was leaving. I didn't think devils could do that."

She sat down beside me. "Say that again," she said. "Slowly."

So I told her. Her frown got deeper and deeper as I talked. "So," she said, "that doesn't really change anything."

"No," I said. "Well, yes and no. It means it all comes down to a question of faith. Do you believe the true gospels are true gospels, or don't you?"

"That's bad."

"The worst," I said. "The way that lot were yelling and carrying on—" I stopped. A thought had just struck me. "What?" she said.

I took a deep breath. "There's something I didn't tell you."

"Oh for crying out loud. Not another one."

"Afraid so. Look, the man who says he's the Loyal Opposition told me to get up during that session and tell everyone that I'd faked the gospels. Otherwise, he'd set Kotkel on you, and you'd die."

All traces of expression drained out of her face. To those who know her, a bad sign.

"I didn't do it, obviously. I don't know if I would or not if Rotlaug hadn't shown up, but I didn't do it."

Not a word. Very bad.

"So what I'm wondering now is," I blundered on, "did whoever put that stupid box there for me to find do it on purpose, with a view to blackmailing me into pretending I'd forged them? No, wait a second, I'll try and explain. Because if the texts are fake and you want people to accept them, one good way to do that is to have someone stand up and say, I faked them, when he didn't. Because then you can prove that he's lying, because he is, and it'll look like you've won." I stopped for a moment. "I think what's what I was trying to say. It's all getting a bit too complicated, to be honest with you."

She rolled her eyes. "You're an idiot," she said.

"Probably."

"Though," she went on, "you might have something there. Sort of pre-emptive defence. No, let me think about this. If you say you faked them, and then they prove you can't have done, because you never had the opportunity, or access to the resources you'd have needed—"

"Which I didn't."

"Shut up. In that case, proving you didn't fake them would look like proving the horrible things were true. Or at least it'd be enough to stir up a lot of trouble, which is what these bastards want to do." She looked me straight in the eye. "Why did we get picked for this job? Do you know?"

I tried to think. "Someone else wasn't available," I said. "Something like that."

"Oh, that'd be easy enough to arrange, if you were in charge of the assignment roster. Actually, that's quite a good point. It sort of answers the question, why you? Because everybody knows you're a red-hot forger."

"Everybody does *not* know that," I pointed out. "It's supposed to be a secret. If it wasn't, I'd never be able to work again. I'd be useless."

"Enough people know," she said airily. "Makes you the perfect man for the job. Though it doesn't explain why those men tried to kill us on the road. Because if I'm right, that could only have been the angels, and they wouldn't have failed. They'd have succeeded."

"Bullshit," I said. "God doesn't rely on *assassins*. He just waves a magic wand or something. Or He would if He existed, which He—" I stopped talking. A broken jaw wouldn't help matters. "I don't think it works like that," I said. "And maybe you're right. It does make a sort of sense, me being involved."

"Too damn right it does," she said. Clearly she'd forgotten it was my idea to begin with. "But it turns out they didn't need you after all. Except to collect the stupid box and bring it to Choris."

I wasn't sure if that made me feel better or worse. Both, probably. "If they're who you think they are, surely they'd have known—"

"What?"

I paused for a moment. What would they have known? "That the books were fake. It came as a real shock to that man in there, believe me."

She shook her head. "No," she said. "We're saying they knew they were fakes, and they planted them on you so they could discredit you when you confessed—"

She stopped. She was looking at something. I turned my head and saw a small procession coming out of the council chamber. Four men were carrying what looked like a door, on which was something that could easily have been a dead body, dressed in a monk's habit, with the cowl drawn up over the face.

"Like I said," I muttered. "It came as a bit of a shock to him."

She looked mildly stunned. "Tell you what," she said. "Nobody lasts very long in that job. Looks like you were right: he wasn't expecting that. In which case—"

"I give up," I said. "Oh, while I think of it, there was something else."

She knows me too well: every pathetic attempt to bury bad news, every unintended tremor in my voice. "What?"

"That man who just had the heart attack," I said. "He told me he wasn't Loyal Opposition; he was an angel. Or on the side of the angels, something like that. But clearly he was lying, because angels don't die. Presumably demons do, or else he wasn't really a demon either. Personally," I added, with feeling, "I think he was a nutcase, but that's just my opinion. Or what I believe, if you prefer it in those terms. And you've said it yourself a million times: you can't argue with faith."

"Piss off." She frowned thoughtfully. "Really? He said that?"

"Yes."

"It can't have been true. He must've been lying."

"Really?"

She looked at me. "Go away," she said. "I need to think."

"Sure," I said, standing up. "I think I'll take a stroll down the hill and find out about ships going north. After all, a man can dream."

I got as far as the main gate, then turned back. Ships going north were all very well, but what I needed was the best library in the world. Which, fortuitously, just happened to be about a minute's walk away, across a quadrangle and turn right.

I wasn't allowed in it, of course. It's a closed library, meaning you need a pass to get in. Originally it belonged to the Poor Sisters of Ap' Escatoy, and in the middle to late empire it became the custom for a copy of every newly written book to be deposited there, along with every new scholarly edition of every old one. When Ap' Escatoy was besieged by the Aram no Vei, the Sisters smuggled out the entire library – about six thousand books, can you believe it? – in wicker baskets, which they loaded on barges and punted through the vast underground sewers, emerging eight miles away under the waterfall at Lake Timo. The Aram saw them doing it, put two and two together, found the outflow and used it to break into the city and slaughter every living thing inside the walls, but by that time the Sisters were well along on their way to Beloisa with their precious cargo. There the library was split into two halves. One half was sent to Olbia – I guess it seemed like a good idea at the time; the other half ended up in Choris, and what's left of it is still there, to this day. There was a fire, and quite a few of the rarer books were quietly stolen and sold, and about five hundred were declared anathema during the Purge and burned by the public hangman, and of what was left, about a quarter simply fell to bits before they could be recopied; even so, it's the biggest and best library in the world, so naturally nobody gets in there without a ticket and a very good reason.

I had neither. What I did have was a piece of parchment, which I'd picked up off the floor of the council chamber when some fool carelessly dropped it (or maybe it was on the point of falling out of his sleeve and I sort of eased its fall, I can't remember) and somehow I hadn't got around to handing it back. What made this piece of parchment rather special was the seal; a big chunk of lead about the size of my thumbnail, stamped with the matrix of the Precentor in Ordinary – a busy man; as well as hiring all the head office clerks and auditing all the finances of Holy Mother Church and presiding over the probate and shipping divisions of the ecclesiastical court, he's responsible for granting access to controlled areas, such as the library.

The document I'd picked up was nothing to do with all that. It was a requisition on the Treasury for two hundred deniers; as good as cash money in your hand, you could take it anywhere, the paymaster's office or the Merchant Venturers, and they'd give you good silver for it, no questions asked. Or you could find a quiet corner with good light, such as the top end of the ostlers' yard behind the mounting block, and you could have at it with the edge of a sharp knife, a palmful of brick dust, a stag-horn burnisher, a bottle of ink you'd absent-mindedly picked up off some clerk's desk and a goose-quill, fresh from the goose's reluctant wing. By the time I'd finished with it, Sister Ululuaria and Father Zosimus would've signed off on it without a qualm. I'm that good.

The librarian barely glanced at it, after all that work. Now that's praise indeed. "What're you after?" he asked me.

"This is a bit of a long shot," I said, "but if you haven't got it, nobody has. Tractantius, *Concerning Life*."

He frowned, then shook his head. "Sorry," he said. "Never heard of it."

"What about Scaphio of Iden?"

"You what?"

"Thrasamund's *Natural History*? Lactantius' *Reflections*?"

He thought for a moment. "I haven't got either of those, sorry," he said. "But I have an idea that there's large chunks of Lactantius quoted in Ratpert of Schanz's *Institutions of Oratory*. I've got that, if it's any help."

"Oh, go on then. Why not?"

I'd heard of Ratpert's *Institutions*, though I'd never seen a copy. It's basically a collection of ready-made speeches for the lazy or incompetent public speaker: whole speeches, and bits you can incorporate, all drawn from the lesser-known works of the best authors, so you can steal them with very little risk of being found out. It was written in the middle empire, and later editions took out the material that had been used too much and was starting to sound familiar to audiences, and replaced it with new stuff. The Sisters' edition was very late, a sixth- or seventh-generation copy, made by a semi-literate scribe with a penchant for drawing sea-serpents in the margins. I found a desk in the corner, under a window, and sat down to read.

The librarian was clearly a very learned man, because sure enough, there were four lengthy extracts from Lactantius in the second appendix, labelled *for sundry occasions*, whatever that was supposed to mean. One of them was a description of a sea-battle. One was a virulent attack on someone or other's fiscal policy. One was a best man's speech at a wedding. The fourth –

In this regard, Scribonian may be held to resemble the so-called ghost-masters of that remote and barbarous region known as the Mesoge, whose peculiar skill, so men say, is to summon from the grave the dead bodies of murderers, blasphemers and other outcasts, instilling in them new life and compelling them to do their bidding. Just as these uncouth necromancers pluck the unwilling dead from their moorland tombs, Scribonian seeks to resurrect the long-dead heresies of Mercullus and Diapason, dragging them back from the very pit of hell to torment the credulous and the unwary. But, whereas the unquiet revenants of that savage country may easily be disposed of by means of a diapygon's dagger and the remorseless element of fire, Scribonian's afterwalking lies and delusions, his false premises, his unsustainable conclusions, his specious arguments irredeemably tainted with anathema and condemned doctrine –

Whoever the hell Scribonian was. Not, I'm afraid, that I cared terribly much. I closed the book and went back to the desk.

"You wouldn't happen to have such a thing," I asked, "as a dictionary?"

"Four," he said, with monumental smugness. "What're you after?"

I looked in all four. None of them could tell me anything about the word diapygon. Ain't that the way.

The librarian gave me an amused smile. "No dice?"

"Apparently not."

"What's the word you're after?"

I told him. He laughed. "Well," he said, "*that* wouldn't be in a dictionary. It's naughty."

"It's what?"

"Naughty. Rude. You know." He grinned. "Well, depends on when. By the late empire it wasn't something you said, but earlier I think it was all right. Funny how words change like that. For instance, *piss* is quite acceptable in Orosius, but—"

"What does it mean?"

He frowned. "Actually," he said, "I'm not sure. It's just something you call someone if you don't like them very much."

"Fine," I said. "Can you think of anywhere I can find out what it originally meant, before that? It's actually quite important."

He shrugged. "There's Polemon's *Philology*," he said. "Back wall, two shelves down, seventy-six from the left."

My heart flooded with lust. "You've got a copy of Polemon?"

"The only one east of Auxentia," he said. "Be careful with it, for God's sake. The binding's not what it was."

Dear God, I thought; Polemon of Sirupat, the greatest

lexicographer the world's ever seen, whose book was lost in the Great Fire – apparently not, because here was a copy, a great big thick thing, codex-bound between two massive elm boards, which at some stage would appear to have been used as a butcher's block, to judge by the knife-cuts and the lingering traces of dried blood. At any other time I'd have been transfixed with joy and wonder. A bit like the hermit in the story, who was hoeing his beans when a stranger came along and asked the way to somewhere or other. "Straight down the road," the hermit answered, not looking up, "Just follow your nose, you can't miss it"; and then, an hour or so later, the penny dropped and he realised that the man he'd been talking to was the Risen Lord, made manifest as a result of a lifetime of his solitary prayers. But at that moment, all I wanted was to know what a certain word meant.

Polemon wrote in the early empire, about two hundred years before Ediulf of Cledda invented alphabetical order. To find a word in Polemon, you start at the top of the first page and work your way down to the bottom. If it's not there, you start at the top of the next page, and so on. The *Philology* isn't a dictionary; it's a concordance: it tells you the books each word is used in, quoting scraps of sentences by way of context, with a definition tacked on at the end if he feels it's necessary. I'd scanned about seventy pages when the light suddenly went out. I looked up. Someone was standing between me and the window.

"That was pretty low, wasn't it?" he said.

An old man, quite tall, thin, with a tiny line of white hair on his upper lip, clipped perfectly straight. "Excuse me?" I said.

"Leaving him to die like that. You knew perfectly well what was happening. You could have helped him."

"I'm sorry," I said. "I don't know what you're talking about."

"A man dying of a heart attack sitting right next to you," he said. "There was a little glass bottle in his left sleeve. Foxglove essence. Two drops on his tongue might have saved him. But no, you just sat there. People like you make me sick."

"Who are you?"

"As of a couple of hours ago, his replacement. A promotion, I might add, that I could very well have done without. He wasn't just my superior officer, he was my friend. I don't suppose it crossed your mind that he might have had friends, or a family."

Oh for crying out loud. "Would you mind standing a bit to your left? You're in my light."

He reached down and closed the book, losing my place. He was tall but old and frail looking; I could've smashed him as easily as Kotkel could've smashed me. "There's no time for that," he said. "You've got to put right the mess you've made."

I looked round for the librarian. No talking in the library; I could perfectly legitimately have him thrown out. The librarian wasn't there. "Get lost," I said. "I've had enough. I don't want to play any more."

"So it's all a game to you," he said. "That doesn't surprise me in the least. Everything's a game to you: science, learning, religion, even lying and stealing and killing. You don't seem to appreciate, some things *matter*. Some things have consequences."

"You wouldn't happen to know what diapygon means, would you?"

"Typical," he said. "I point out your abominable lack of common decency and you reply with vulgar abuse." He put his hand on the cover of the book, to stop me opening it. "Now listen to me. The situation is clearly disastrous, but it can still be retrieved. You need to kill Vitimer."

You think you've heard it all. "Say that again."

"You should find it simple enough. Vitimer trusts you. If you ask him for a private audience, there shouldn't be a problem. I imagine you can find a way to escape afterwards. You seem to be quite resourceful when it comes to saving your own skin."

"Why," I said, "would I want to do a thing like that?"

"Because if you don't," he said, "your father's reanimated corpse will crush Sister Svangerd's head like an eggshell. We both know that you won't let that happen. You have until this time tomorrow. I suggest you don't leave it too long. If it's to do any good at all, it has to be done quickly, the sooner the better."

I shook my head, to give myself time to recover. "I'm afraid you're a bit behind the times," I said. "I'm not scared of walkers any more. There's a hero in town, from the Mesoge. The genuine article. This time tomorrow, there won't be any walkers in Choris."

He gave me a thin smile. "I suppose it's possible you're stupid enough to believe that," he said. "In which case, let me give you a word of advice. Prepare to be disappointed. But," he went on, before I could say anything, "that still gives you time. Tomorrow morning, after your hero's been found with his head crushed. I suggest you speak to Vitimer's clerks straight away about an appointment. If you leave it too late he might get booked up."

"Like hell I will," I said, lifting his hand off the cover of the book. "And now, if you don't mind, I've got work to do."

He flipped the book open, ripped out a page, screwed it into a ball, put it in his mouth, chewed a couple of times and swallowed. "No," he said. "If you carry on looking you'll be wasting your time. Feel free to do that if you wish, but it won't be work; it'll be foolishness."

He walked away. I was too horrified by what he'd just done to stop him.

After a while, I pulled myself together enough to close the book and put it back on the shelf. The mutilated book ... That's me, right? I can look at dead bodies and heads squashed flat and think nothing of it, but somebody hurting a book ... Yes, but not just any book. Polemon's *Philology*. And it takes a day to copy just one page of something like that, whereas a human life can be created in a couple of minutes, by two drunk kids in a haystack.

"This is no good," she told me. "We're pulling in opposite directions, you doing your stuff, me doing mine. We need to pull together."

"Agreed."

"What we need to do is sit down and figure out a plan of action."

"Absolutely," I said, looking past her out of the refectory window. In an hour it would be dark. A few hours after that, Rotlaug the hero would kill, or at least dispose of, the two walkers and that would be that. I wouldn't have to assassinate the head of Holy Mother Church, and we could go home. True, there was going to be a schism; but maybe it wouldn't be so bad away up north, where we're mostly out of it anyway.

I tried to think what it would mean, in real terms. Probably what we'd notice most would be not being able to get things. Schism would mean closed borders, disruption of trade, all the stuff that comes in on ships or pack-mules. Big deal. We're too poor and too remote to be major importers and exporters, so mostly we make what we need and only need what we can make. And stuff is just stuff, after all. We'd survive.

There'd be wars, of course. There always are, when Holy Mother Church isn't there to stop the children quarrelling and breaking each other's toys, and for some reason people dearly love to kill each other over questions and interpretations of faith. Thou shalt not suffer a heretic to live, so soldiers would be recruited from the villages, would march away and not come back, then when harvest came round there'd only be women and old men to do the work, so half the crop would spoil before it could be cut and stacked, and half of the other half would go for taxes, to pay for the war effort. The hedging and ditching wouldn't get done over winter, so there'd be flooding and escaped livestock, and too little grain in winter would mean having to slaughter the plough oxen (either they eat or we do), so spring ploughing would be drastically curtailed. Coppicing and winter logging wouldn't happen, so come next winter it'd be pretty cold with no faggots or firewood; also no charcoal for the forge, so tools would break and not get mended or replaced; no share for the plough or hooks for cutting back brambles and withies, so gradually the wilderness would spread and the useful land would be lost, like the books in the Sisters' library. Then more soldiers would be needed, to replace the ones who'd been killed or died of dysentery. More villages would be looking to buy food rather than sell it, and before long there wouldn't be enough, so people would starve or leave, heading for the towns and cities under the mistaken impression that things might be better there, rather than worse. Life would go on, of course, but diminished, downsized, pared and withered away. Sulpicius calculated that as a result of the Third Social

War, the population of the empire declined by just under forty per cent; that was a thousand years ago, when there was still an emperor, and things were properly organised, and most of the knowledge hadn't been lost. How long the starving and shrivelling process would take I couldn't begin to guess – five years? Twenty? A hundred? There was no Sulpicius around to do the maths when the empire fell, but at a rough guess I'd say that there were easily ten times as many people alive then as there are now, quite probably more. They didn't all die at once, of course; there wasn't a terrible year with bodies stacked like cordwood. It was a trend more than a cataclysm. Eventually it bottomed out, and now here we all were, suffering no major collapses and making no progress; until, that is, some fool comes along and drives a wedge into the head of Holy Mother Church, and the whole world breaks up in splinters.

That fool would be me, yes? Well, yes and no. I'd had no idea what I was doing, just as the crew of the ship who brought the Great Plague to Perimadeia had no idea that the swollen glands in their armpits were going to wipe out two thirds of the human race. It wasn't done on purpose. Was it?

Was it?

"I said," she repeated, "what are we actually going to *do*?"

Done on purpose; actually, yes, by a bunch of lunatics who believed they were serving the devil. What's done can be undone, sometimes, if you're quick, if you know what you're doing. I had no idea what needed to be done, but then, I wasn't a student of the long game. I wasn't – but I knew someone who was.

I turned and looked at her. "These people who think they're the Loyal Opposition," I said. "Do you believe they know what they're doing?"

"They're evil," she said.

"Yes," I said, "I know that. But are they competent?"

"You what?"

It seemed such a simple, obvious question. "Are they any good?" I asked. "Do they understand politics and economics and the ebb and flow of cause and effect? Are they capable of figuring out complicated long-term plans? If they say doing this will have that result, are they likely to be right or are they just guessing, or talking drivel? Come on, it's important. What do you think?"

"I don't know," she said. "I assume they are. After all, Evil is very powerful."

"Really? It always loses. Well, does it or doesn't it?"

"In the long term, of course it does. But in the short term—"

I closed my eyes and opened them again. "I guess we're going to have to trust them," I said. "Put our faith in them and hope they know what they're doing. It's ghastly, I know, but I really can't see any other way."

"What in fuck's name are you talking about?"

Deep breath. "Something happened earlier today that I may have neglected to mention," I said.

She took it better than I'd expected. She swore at me, called me names, almost hit me but didn't, and that was it. "He said he'd kill you if I didn't do it," I explained. "Well, my dad would. Same difference."

"Your *dad*? What about Kotkel?"

A valid point, which I'd entirely missed. "Doesn't matter," I said. "I think he was right. This new man wants to stop the schism, same as we do. Apparently he has reason to believe that murdering Vitimer will do the trick. I have absolutely no idea what those reasons might be, but that doesn't mean he's wrong. So I think that's what we've got to do. We've got to kill Vitimer."

"You're out of your tiny—"

"We came here," I said, "to murder the princess. Why? Because someone who knows much more about these things than we do reckoned it'd be a good idea. And now someone who knows a lot more about these things says we should kill Vitimer. Think about it. Can you see a difference, because I can't."

"But they're *evil*—"

"We've got to kill Vitimer," I said. "It's the only way."

I'd hoped I'd get a good night's sleep after all the excitements of the past few days, but no such luck. About an hour before matins, I was woken up by yelling and crashing about and booted feet running in corridors and cloisters. No rest for the wicked.

I blundered my way down the horrible spiral stairs into the courtyard, which was crowded with people and bright as day with lanterns and torches. In the middle of the yard was Rotlaug, sitting on the decapitated trunk of a walker. In his right hand he held a Mesoge hog knife. With his left, he was hugging a severed head, like a mother nursing a baby.

I walked over to him. He saw me and told the high official who'd been talking to him to go away. "Told you so," he sang out as I reached him. "Piece of piss."

The head was Kotkel's. "Nice job," I said. "Thanks."

"It's what I do," he said. "I'm good at it. Fucking good at it."

Poor Kotkel, I thought. He never stood a chance. "So," I said, "what's the drill?"

"Big bonfire," said Rotlaug. "Then wait till the ashes get

cold and mix them with piss. Don't ask me why piss, but it works. Then flush it away in running water. Job done."

I nodded. "I dumped the ashes in the sea," I said. "Didn't seem to make much difference. Dad still came back."

He frowned. "Fine," he said. "Let him come back, I'll do him again. I don't mind getting paid twice, specially for a piece of piss job like this. That priest I was talking to, he says they'll give me a thousand gold besants." His brows narrowed. "How much is that in silver money?"

I told him. He looked like he'd been struck by lightning.

"I can't help noticing," I said, "there's only one of them. What about my father? I take it he didn't show up."

"No. But what the fuck. Here, do you reckon they'll pay me the same for doing him when he does show?"

I smiled. "If I were you," I said, "I'd haggle. Say you're not going to kill any more walkers for a denier under twelve hundred besants."

I'd shocked him, something I really wouldn't have thought was possible. "You reckon they'd stand for that?"

"I think it's probably a seller's market," I said. "Definitely go for twelve hundred. And fifteen hundred if Kotkel comes back."

He looked like an eyewitness to the Transfiguration. "Thanks," he said. "I might just do that."

"I would," I said. "If I were you."

He looked at me. "You know what," he said, lowering his voice, "I think maybe you ought to come in for a slice of the action. After all, they're your folks. Say five per cent. I feel like I owe you, somehow."

I was touched. "That's really sweet," I said, "but no thanks. I've got my vow to think of. Besides, you've earned it. I haven't."

"True," he said. "Bollocks to it, then. You know what, I might just settle down and live here. It's a damn sight better than home."

"I think so."

"I think you're right. I mean, what's the point having all that scratch in the Mesoge, with nothing to spend it on?"

"With twelve hundred gold besants," I said, "you could buy the Mesoge."

That made him laugh – not a sight for the faint-hearted. "I might just do that," he said. "That'd show the fuckers, right? When I chuck them all out and tell them to get off my land. That'd be a sight to see, you fucking bet."

Quite, I thought, and left him alone with his glory.

11

"You're quite right, of course," she said.

Stunned is putting it mildly. "You what?"

"We've got to do it." She'd spent the night on her knees beside Mother Krimhild's bed, imploring the non-existent Invincible Sun for a miracle. "We've got to stop the schism. We can't let that happen, can we?"

"No," I said. "Look, have you thought this through? Really thought about it, I mean."

"Spent all night doing just that," she said. "And you're right. It's got to be done. I don't know why," she added, with one of those savage bursts of anger you get when you're trying to explain something, but you've got a splitting headache and you just can't *think*. "I just know, that's all. I was praying, and I suddenly realised."

Oh dear, I thought. "There weren't voices, were there?"

"Piss off. I realised," she went on, "that that's how the long game works. It shouldn't, but it does. I mean, look at that man who died of a heart attack. He really didn't expect that. So he must've been telling the truth."

When I was a young novice, they tried very hard to teach me mathematics. It was a lost cause, as it happens, but I learned a few very useful things. Such as: there was this kid who always got the right answer, invariably. He was infallible. But when the tutor asked him to show his working, he couldn't, because he hadn't done any. He'd just looked at the problem and known the answer. Needless to say he got no marks, and he was always being whipped for wilfully refusing to do as he was told – he must have done the calculations, they said, in order to get the sum right, so pretending he hadn't was just wickedness. Svangerd's a bit like that kid (who ended up as a minor canon in some cathedral in the north-east, which probably served him right); she has this knack of going straight to the right answer without bothering with the steps in between, like a knight on a chessboard jumping over the enemy's heads. I could probably retrace her steps, like a man on the ground following a buzzard to a mountaintop, but why bother?

"So," she went on, "we're going to have to take it on trust, just like you said. They *do* want to stop the schism. So do we. So, if they reckon guzzling Vitimer's the only way, I guess they're probably right."

"I've been thinking about it," I said. "And now I'm not so sure. You've heard, haven't you? Rotlaug killed Kotkel."

"Who the hell is Rotlaug?"

"The hero," I said, "from the Mesoge. He fought him last night and cut his head off."

"Killed *Kotkel*."

"That's right."

"Not your dad?"

"Not yet, no. But what's that got to do with anything? We

can forget about the walkers now. And if they can't use them to blackmail us, we don't have to do anything."

"Unless we want to."

"You don't get it, do you?" I said, and I'm afraid I may have raised my voice a little. "You're safe. You're out of it. We can go home."

She looked at me. "No we can't," she said. "Oh, come on. Last night, just for once in your life, you said something that was actually sensible and right and the right thing to do. Don't spoil it now by being pathetic."

Well, I thought. She's right, of course. She always is. "Fine," I said. "I'll do it. Before this afternoon's session, he said, or it'll be too late."

Her eyes were on me. "No," she said. "You're not doing anything. I'll do it."

"No."

"Yes. It's got to be done properly; we can't afford to fuck it up. I'll have to do it. You're useless at this kind of thing."

That was so unfair; moderately unfair. "But I'm the one with access to him," I said. "I can walk straight in and ask to see him and they'll let me."

She shook her head. "Not so sure about that," she said, "not any more. You were important when you were the only one in town who knew anything about the walkers. But you screwed up, and now there's this Rat person. If I was Vitimer, I wouldn't be bothered with you any more. But I can go and say I need to speak to him with a vitally important message from Mother Krimhild which could heal the schism, and I'd be in through the door so fast you wouldn't know I was there. It's got to be me. It's as simple as that."

"But the man in the library told me to do it."

She frowned. "I can't see how that matters."

"Maybe not," I said, "but it could. Maybe it's vitally important that I do it. Don't ask me why, I have no idea, but I have no idea why Vitimer's got to die, either. Look, we do exactly as we're told or we leave well alone. Otherwise—"

"Point taken," she said. "Though personally I think he told you to do it because he reckoned he could blackmail you by threatening me, on account of you being soft in the head. We'll do it together. How does that sound?"

Like a recipe for disaster. "Fine," I said. "Let's do it."

But we didn't. We were on our way to Vitimer's chambers, which meant going past the council chamber. The doors were shut, and there were soldiers guarding them. What goes on, I asked someone. Hadn't you heard? The monster came back last night. Yes, I said, and the hero from the Mesoge got him. Yes, but not before he smashed his way into the council chamber through the roof and defiled it. Defiled? Sheep's guts, mostly, and chicken feathers, and the body of some old woman off the streets dumped down on the patriarchal throne, with her head pulled off and a pig's head substituted. So the whole room's got to be thoroughly cleaned and reconsecrated, which'll take all today and half tomorrow, so all debates are on hold and they're going to reschedule.

We walked on till we reached the west cloister. "Now what?" I said.

"What?"

"Don't you see? This probably changes things."

She frowned. "Really?"

"Almost certainly. It screws up the timings. Look, the man in the library said it's got to be done before this afternoon's debate.

But the debate schedule's gone all to blazes. So, maybe the reason Vitimer's got to die is something that should happen or be said in a debate, only now that debate isn't happening. Or something like that; the point is, we don't *know*. We need instructions."

"Just a moment." She had her headache face. "*Kotkel* did all that."

"Before Rotlaug killed him."

"Kotkel," she repeated, "not your father. You know, I can't help thinking there's some significance in that."

"Maybe there is. The point is, we don't know. And Rule One clearly states, don't go doing anything drastic unless you have a pretty clear idea of what's going on. Which," I added forcefully, "is no longer the case. We need to talk to that man, before we do *anything*."

The look in her eyes said, that's twice you've been right; just don't go making a habit of it. "Probably," she said. "All right, where do we find him?"

"I don't know, do I? I've only met him once."

She sat down on a stone bench. "Why would Kotkel desecrate the council chamber? Is that the sort of thing your walkers do?"

"Yes," I said, "pretty much. Well, they seem to get a kick out of ripping up sheep and draping the bits off trees and things. Mischievous behaviour generally."

"But this was the first time he'd done it."

"Yes. Does it matter?"

"No idea. I'm just thinking out loud. The point being, did someone tell him to do it, or was it just something he felt like doing?"

"We need to talk to that man," I said. "Otherwise we're just going round in circles."

"Fine," she said. "What does he look like?"

"I told you."

"Tell me again."

Not as easy as it sounded. "Tall man," I said, "frail-looking, white hair, he's got this little tiny white moustache, like he's just been sipping beer." Come to think of it, I was having trouble picturing him in my mind. "Unmistakeable," I said. "I'll know him when I see him."

With the debates cancelled and the miasma of schism heavy in the air, of course, there was nobody about; nobody in the quadrangles, courtyards or cloisters, no clusters of buzzing conversationalists lingering in the refectory or sunning themselves like seals on the portico steps. The delegates to the ecumenical council had gone to ground. I could picture them holed up in their rooms and cells, scribbling long letters home – pleas for instructions, frantic attempts to sound out opinions, rally support, call in favours, apply pressure to the recalcitrant: all the things you do when you know there's going to be a war ... Or they'd be on their knees, in side-chapels or in front of a foldaway travelling triptych, imploring Someone who wasn't actually there to save them from the time of trial. Politics and religion, always to the fore when everything's about to go all to hell; why is it, do you think, that humanity's first instinct, when there's a fire, is to try and put it out by dousing it in lamp oil?

Which meant there was no point in just cruising around the precincts hoping to bump into the man I needed to see. So I went back to the library (not there), tried the basilica and all the chapels (no luck), the refectory and the gatehouse and the Gardens of Sulpicius; waste of time. I even tried asking random strangers: have you seen an old man, yay high, little white tache like an eyebrow? That got me nowhere, especially as I was starting to be recognised – the man from the Mesoge who fought the monster (no, not that one, the one who tried and failed); the man who just happened to find the box in a shop, and if you believe that, I have a wide selection of quality bridges you might be interested in buying . . . I got the feeling that even if they knew, they weren't about to tell me, of all people. If I'd gone round with UP TO SOMETHING written on my back in two-inch-high illuminated capitals, I couldn't have made more of an exhibition of myself. Counterproductive; stupid.

I came back to my room expecting to find her there, but she wasn't, so I went looking for her in the other place she was likely to be, at Mother Krimhild's bedside. But when I got there, I found the big oak door closed, and when I banged on it, nobody came. Now what, I asked myself.

I headed back out into the fresh air and ran into a crowd in the east cloister garden. Lots of people standing around, not saying anything, all looking very depressed. I edged my way through and saw an open space in the middle of the crowd, where four sextons were digging a hole in the manicured grass. Oh, I thought, and then I called to mind the closed door I'd just been hammering on.

Vitimer was there, gorgeous in a purple chasuble, embroidered dalmatic, stole, rochet and tasselled maniple; he was mumbling the funeral service, dust to dust, ashes to ashes, the sure and certain hope of the Resurrection. It occurred to me that we usually cut that last bit in the Mesoge, probably because there are some things that are sure and certain, but which don't really constitute hope . . .

Svangerd was at the back of a clump of nuns, who were

charitably pretending she wasn't there. I felt angry with them, and with the stupid old woman for dying and breaking Svangerd's heart – people can be so inconsiderate. And then it occurred to me that maybe it wasn't all bad, because here we had a great many delegates, all gathered together in one place and not yelling bloody murder at each other; it had been Mother Krimhild's big speech that calmed things down and made the commission possible, though that had turned out to be a bust. In fact, I thought, this would be the perfect moment for Vitimer to make an impassioned plea for unity, invoking the memory of our dear departed sister, et cetera; here were all these scared, desperate people, no doubt longing to be let off the hook if only some way could be found to extract them from the political and ethical corners they'd backed themselves into. He wouldn't need to be particularly eloquent, provided he said the right things in roughly the right order. Here was the perfect opportunity – I could feel it, like thunder in the air. I scanned the crowd, and I got a strong feeling that that was what they'd come for. An excuse, a note from their mothers to say they had a chill and couldn't go to war today. A heaven-sent opportunity –

It occurred to me to glance up at the side wall of the Old Library, on which there was a rather beautiful and ornate sundial. It was a bit overcast, so the shadow was a bit blurry; even so, I could make it out well enough to know that if Kotkel hadn't trashed the council chamber, the afternoon debate would be just about to start; the debate before which I'd been duty bound to kill Vitimer if we were to have any chance at all of preventing a schism.

Nuts, or words to that effect.

"I need to speak to you," said a voice in my ear. "Now."

I followed him back through the crowd, out of the garden into the cloister. "I was looking for you," I said. "I wanted to ask—"

He was furiously angry. "One small thing," he said. "One simple thing, and you couldn't be bothered to do it. You make me sick."

"Yes, but then the debates got cancelled," I said. "I didn't know if that meant the plans had changed."

"So you took it upon yourself to decide. How could you have been so stupid?"

"Just a moment," I said. "I need to think about this."

"No," he said. "You don't need that. What you need is to go out there, right now, and kill Vitimer. You have just under three minutes before he starts making his speech. I don't suppose you've got a knife with you, so I suggest you strangle him. You do know how to do that, don't you?"

"I need to think about this," I repeated. "Vitimer's going to make a speech."

"Obviously."

"And everybody's going to listen, because they'll know this is the perfect opportunity for wriggling out of having to have a schism and a war and bringing the roof down on everything. So it'll work. And there won't be a schism, or a war." I looked at him. "Isn't that what we want?"

He gave me a look of pure distilled contempt. "You don't know anything about it," he said. "You're an idiot and a blunderer and you don't obey orders. Now get out there and do as you're told."

"It doesn't make sense," I said. "If I kill him right now, in front of everybody, when he's just about to make his speech, how's that going to stop the schism? Surely—"

"You don't understand." He was losing what little patience he had. "It's far more complex and involved than you can possibly begin to appreciate, and I simply don't have the time to explain it to you." He was trying to burn holes in me with his eyes, but for some reason it wasn't working. "You now have one minute to go out there and do it. Otherwise you will be directly responsible for the deaths of millions."

"I don't believe you," I said.

"What you believe or don't believe is supremely unimportant." He fought hard and managed to get a grip on his fury. "I know I can't rely on you to do it because it's the right thing, so I've made sure I have other levers to move you with. Go and kill Vitimer, or by this time tomorrow Svangerd will be dead. Your father will crush her skull like an egg. Do you understand me?"

"No," I said. "If you want it done, do it yourself. I think you're full of shit."

He opened his mouth, then stopped. I could hear Vitimer's voice. He'd begun his speech.

"This is your last chance," the old man said. "Your very last chance. Do you understand me?"

"Perfectly," I said. "And you're still full of shit."

He'd have made his fortune as an actor, back in the empire. He could register furious anger, blind terror and grim resolution without actually moving a muscle, and he did. Then he took a short knife from his sleeve and turned to walk away.

"Oops," I said. "Sorry."

I'd tripped him up, and he'd gone sprawling on his nose. I moved to help him up, inadvertently standing on the knife as I did so. "Out of interest," I said, "I thought you people weren't allowed to take direct action. The puppet-masters, not the puppets, and all that."

He gave me a glare that should've shrivelled me up like a leaf in a furnace. "You lunatic," he said.

"Really?"

All the force had gone out of him. He looked so weary, he was having trouble standing up. "A million deaths," he said. "A dark age lasting a thousand years. The end of civilisation as we know it."

"Balls," I said. "There isn't going to be a schism. So there won't be a war."

"Not *now*," he said. "But in five hundred years' time, when the Great Schism rips the West apart and leaves it defenceless against the Sashan hordes—"

"Oh, I see. That schism." I grinned at him. "I wouldn't worry about it, if I were you. Sufficient until the day. Besides, something's bound to turn up. It generally does."

He registered contempt at me so intensely that I couldn't help giggling, and stalked away.

"What do you mean, you missed it?" she said.

"I was talking to that man," I said. "Why, was it good?"

"Only the best, most beautiful speech ever made," she said. "God knows I don't go for that sort of thing, but I'm not ashamed to admit it, I was in tears."

"I was stopping the Loyal Opposition rep from assassinating Vitimer," I said. "So, what did he say?"

She shook her head. "You had to be there. Really, it was the most amazing—"

"Yes, all right."

"It's funny," she said. "You were so mad keen to come to this bash because you particularly wanted to hear the speeches. But—"

"Yes," I said. "Thank you."

We were sitting in a side-chapel. Sunlight slanted in through one of the six (that's right, six) remaining examples of imperial stained glass to have survived Time, a dozen sieges and the iconoclast movement. It bathed the altar in a wild jumble of seething, dancing colour, like a funeral pyre for an angel. This chapel had been on my must-*must*-see list when I left home, and I'd completely forgotten about it until then.

"Really," she was saying, "it was all Mother Krimhild. She stopped everything going to shit with that speech, and then she did it again by dying. You know, thinking of it like that, I can't feel sad that she's gone. Just amazingly proud that I was allowed to know her."

"That's nice," I said.

"Nice," she repeated. "You really do have the soul of a slug."

"Probably. But it doesn't matter. There isn't going to be a schism, which is all that matters, I was at the session this morning, and you wouldn't believe how polite everybody was being. Open-mindedness, the importance of rational discussion, freedom of conscience and respecting the other man's point of view. It takes all the fun out of it, but I reckon it's probably better than the end of the world."

She nodded. "I think we should go home," she said. "Go and find out about ships."

So I did that. There was a lumber freighter sailing in two days' time, and the captain said we could go for free. He liked having holy men on board, he said. It was good luck.

I went to the afternoon session, but there was so much sweetness and light everywhere that I fell asleep, and when I woke up the chamber was empty. So I went looking for a pastry shop and embezzled half a denier from our travelling fund and blew it on honeycakes and spice buns. If ever you're in Choris, people had been telling me all my life, for crying out loud make sure you try the honeycakes and the spice buns. So I did, and they weren't bad, at that.

I sat eating them on the steps of the Four Winds bridge (also on my must-*must*-see list), and I took a moment to think about things without Svangerd buzzing in my ear. Quite probably, I thought, the old man had been right. By not acting, and then by interfering, I'd most likely doomed generations yet unborn to unspeakable misery. But that's the long game for you – if you believe in it, which I didn't, though it was beginning to make an eerie sort of sense. And the whole point about the long game (if you believe in it) is its fluidity. Something *would* turn up, or someone would turn it up with a big wrench, because the fated inevitable never does happen. The fated inevitable, according to the rules of the game, is the triumph of virtue, justice and goodness – because it's His chessboard and His pieces – but in a world without end (amen), the inevitable outcome is eternally, indefinitely postponed . . . On those terms, I decided, I could almost bring myself to believe in God.

Almost, but not quite. Suppose you were an ignorant savage and you were walking along a beach and you found a Mezentine mechanical clock; and its works were rusted solid after being in the salt water for a hundred years, so it wasn't working and would never work again. You'd pick it up and you'd say, Oh, just another useless chunk of corroded minerals, and you'd be right.

The spice buns were particularly fine, so I went back and got another half dozen. Eating them under the arches of the gateway to the Gardens of Sulpicius (number seven on my list), I tried to figure out where we were, godawful-mess-wise.

There wasn't going to be a schism, so the dreadful thing I'd done, buying a box in a junk shop in Mavais, was effectively cancelled out. We hadn't murdered the princess; we hadn't murdered anybody, which was unusual for us when we're out and about for any length of time. The weird alchemy of circumstance had apparently transformed Vitimer from a self-serving placeholder into some kind of holy prophet; well, stranger things had happened, see above, and Holy Mother Church was now being guided by someone that everybody seemed to approve of, in itself a miracle of no small magnitude. As for the walkers, I reckoned I could safely leave them, or him, to Rotlaug of Unnsvik, certified hero and soon to be the richest man ever to come out of the Mesoge, the ultimate local boy made good. The buzzing swarm of unanswered questions didn't really bother me any more, so long as I could safely afford to ignore them. They involved Home, which is a sore topic with me at the best of times, and for all my scholarly curiosity, I could honestly say that I didn't want to know. Somehow, with precious little valuable input from me, the mess I'd started had smoothed itself out, I was free to go, and the rest of the day was my own.

For Svangerd – No, I thought, things have turned out pretty well for her, too. She'd be able to see it in good old-fashioned dualistic terms, which is how she likes things to be. Evil reared its ugly head, but Mother Krimhild gave her life to save us all, and being Mother Krimhild's particular pet made her something special – blessed, I believe, is the technical term. I didn't begrudge her that, not in a million years. Life will never be easy for Svangerd, or pleasant, or anything less than a painful, gruelling struggle, in which you fight and never count the cost or heed the wounds; all that matters is winning, and I reckoned she'd be entitled to go home claiming a victory. The unanswered questions wouldn't bother her too much, because you don't worry about that sort of thing when you've won.

One of the pamphlet stalls at the south gate of the gardens was selling a Life of Mother Krimhild, written on scraps of triple-skived goatskin in tiny letters with the ink barely dry, a bargain at half a denier. I bought a copy, to give to Svangerd, and sat reading it as the sun started to go down. Born to humble parents in a remote village, heard the call when she was twelve years old, novitiate at Adlersfell, meteoric rise to be prioress of Stikeslad before she was thirty; all good stuff, and probably a certain amount of it was true, though I recognised some elements from books written a thousand years ago: the miracle at the washing-pool, for example, and the feeding of the forty pilgrims. Still, it was possible that history had repeated itself, or that Krimhild had done these things in conscious imitation of sacred exemplars, or maybe it was just coincidence, or some formula or gambit in the long game. None of my business, that was for sure, and I definitely wouldn't spoil things by pointing any of that stuff out to Svangerd.

I went back to my room and lit a lamp to finish reading the pamphlet. I knew how the story ended, of course, but I wanted to see what sort of take the pamphleteer had on it; had he turned the speech to the council and the graveside reconciliation into full-blown miracles, or was that a step too far for the present? I was just getting to the good bit when I heard the most appalling racket. Appalling because familiar.

Oh, come on, I thought. But no, it's no bad thing, because Dad would've been a loose end, but now Rotlaug will deal with him and that'll be that. Good old Rotlaug, and how lucky we all are that he's here to protect us.

Then the door of my room flew open, and something huge was in there with me. My lamp had gone out. "Dad?" I said.

Something grabbed me. I remember being ground against a wall, and all the air being forced out of me. Then something landed on my head. I felt oversized fingertips on the left side of my skull, and a giant thumb on the right. Nuts, I remember thinking, or words to that effect.

Then a roaring noise, and the fingers let go. Then a colossal thump, as two massive, enormous creatures crashed into each other. They were between me and the door. Then they were fighting, like two stags in the rut, hammering into each other; no attempt at skill, just what Rotlaug called brute force. If one of them were to be pushed back and step on me or stumble against me, I'd be crushed, all my thin, fragile little bones, like a bird in a child's ignorant fist. There was nowhere I could go and nothing I could do, and the outcome would be pure chance.

One of the monsters was winning. It slammed the other one against a wall, which cracked, and the air was full of dust. The other one fought back – I heard the thump of its fist, and the air in the room was compressed by the violence of the blow – but it wasn't enough. The winner gave it another slam against the wall, which gave way, letting moonlight into the room.

I saw two walkers. One of them was my father. He was losing. He launched a terrific punch at the other one's head. It landed, but the head didn't even move. Then the other one – its back was to me – put its hand on my father's head and squeezed. For a moment nothing happened, and then his skull gave way. The winner's thumb disappeared inside the fractured bone, and his face folded up like a towel and all his features were lost, ironed out, gone. I don't know how I knew it, but I knew it. That was that. My father was dead. Really dead.

The other monster lifted him off the ground and peered up at him at arm's length, as if saying, what have I got here, I wonder? The moonlight showed me a little gap between my father's uplifted body and the wall, with the doorway beyond. That'll do me, I remember saying to myself, and I darted at it like a startled rabbit. A hand swished past me as I went, brushed against me but didn't close in time. I was in the corridor. I ran.

It was following me; I could feel its footsteps through the stone floor. It was gaining on me. But there was a stairwell leading off the corridor – I couldn't see it in the dark, but I knew it was there. One of those horrible, terrifying corkscrew spiral stairs, only just wide enough to get your shoulders through, if you're a big man like me. And not wide enough for a walker.

Two steps and I lost my footing, tripped and went cascading down. I hit my head against the wall twice, maybe three times, and I came out head first at the bottom of the stairs, landing on my neck and doing a sort of backwards somersault that should've broken my spine. But it didn't, and I could hear and feel the walker's footsteps through the ceiling. I stood up. No bones broken; I was mobile. Time to go.

Something stamped on the ceiling overhead, twice, three times. Then the ceiling gave way and it fell through, landing in a heap of tumbled stone and mortar. Oh, for crying out loud, I remember thinking, and I ran.

It followed me out into the courtyard. There were people and lights. I saw Rotlaug, stark naked apart from a pair of boots and his hog knife in his hand. Thank God, I thought, forgetting for the moment that He didn't exist. "It's after me," I yelled at him, and ran straight at him.

He wasn't looking at me. I turned my head and followed his gaze.

It was a walker, no doubt about that. It was Mother Krimhild.

The sure and certain hope of the Resurrection. I remember wondering, in some compartment of my addled mind, if the remote village where she'd been born to humble parents had been anywhere in the Mesoge. I decided I wouldn't be the least bit surprised if that turned out to be the case.

If Rotlaug was fazed, it was only for a moment. He sprang forward, hog knife at the ready. She dodged him, nimble as a dancer, and grabbed his head as he passed her. She closed her hand and there was a crunching noise. I heard the hog knife clatter on the paving slabs.

She looked up. She was looking for someone in the crowd. She was looking for me.

Everybody started running at once, and I guess that's what saved me. I've seen the same thing happen with a bear, when a pack of dogs tries to pull it down. What does for the bear is, it can't decide which dog to swat first. It just stands there, a helpless victim of indecision, and by the time it's made up its mind, there's a dozen pairs of jaws locked in its flesh and the question has become academic. I think it's the multiple patterns of movement, or something like that, not that it matters particularly.

Anyway, people were running in every direction, so maybe she lost sight of me, and that was what gave me time to get clear. I don't know. I remember running and running, through doorways, under arches, through a gatehouse, down streets, then alleyways. I slipped and fell over a dozen times, then scrambled up and carried on running. The thirteenth time I fell and couldn't get up, because I'd done something very bad to my ankle, so instead of running I crawled. I wasn't going to stop moving, not for anything. Then I guess my strength failed me, and I remember dragging myself into a doorway and thinking, Oh well, she'll just have to gore me; and the next thing I remember is waking up, in sunlight, and still being alive.

"And you a priest," said the woman standing over me. "You make me sick, you know that?"

Yes, but the sun was shining and I was alive, so it really didn't matter. "I wasn't drunk," I said. "I was being chased by a monster, and—"

She rolled her eyes and walked away. No matter. I stood up, winced as the cramp in my legs asserted itself, followed by aches in every joint and muscle, quite possibly something to do with falling down a flight of stone stairs and being hammered against a wall by –

Nuts, I thought, or words to that effect. Svangerd must know by now. It might easily kill her.

No, I told myself, people don't die of stuff like that. People can die of most things – a cough, a mushroom, a cut finger – but not grief or heartache or their world suddenly dissolving in doubt and misery. Would that it were that simple. But it might easily break her, like Krimhild had broken my father's head, and that was something I really didn't want to contemplate.

I limped slowly back uptown, and gradually the sharp pains subsided into dull aches, and I could put my foot down on a paved surface without wanting to burst into tears. Just inside the main gate, I met the elderly man.

"I want a word with you," I said.

He didn't speak, but maybe that was because I had my hands round his throat. I eased off, just a bit. "What have you done?" I said.

"Let me go."

"I've had about enough of you," I said. A couple of respectable-looking clerics in grey habits walked past, staring at us. "You and your colleagues. Look, I don't care if you want to play your stupid games with me, but you leave her out of it, understood? Or so help me, I'll—"

The Mesoge way, I realised. We collect all those valuable weapons but when we're mad, we use our bare hands. Could I crush his skull between my fingers and my thumb? Probably not, but I was itching to find out. Not now, I decided, but very possibly later, one day, when it's my turn.

"It wasn't me," he said, and I felt his Adam's apple move against the web of my hand. "It wasn't us. We didn't do it."

"Like hell. You aren't going to tell me Mother Krimhild decided to go walking of her own accord."

"She was born in the Mesoge," he said. "Hauksfell, the other side of the lake from you. Her father was Einar Egilson, your third cousin on your mother's side. Her grandfather was a walker, and one of her uncles."

I relaxed my grip a little more, but only because I was starting to get cramp. "If it wasn't you," I said, "who was it?"

"Them," he said. "The Loyal Opposition."

"Why? What's in it for them?"

"They're trying to cause a schism."

I felt like I was the one being choked. "But that's what you want."

He tried to shake his head. "The plan's changed," he said.

"Well, of course it has, because of you. Because you wouldn't do as you were told. So, naturally, we had to go back to the drawing-board and reroute. Now all our strategies are posited on there not being a schism. So, naturally, the enemy wants one. And that—" he tried to nod at the courtyard behind me "—is the outcome. I trust you're pleased with yourself, because it's all your fault."

It was then I realised what Kotkel must've gone through, when we were kids. Words can be so much more effective than mere brute force. I felt like he must have felt when I taunted him and wouldn't shut up. It spoke volumes for Kel's self-control that he hadn't killed me. In his place, I'd have done it, I'm pretty sure. "Shut your face," I said. "It's nothing to do with me. You're the one who's playing stupid games."

"Is that right? So I bought the box in the shop in Mavais. I decided to keep it, rather than immediately throw it on the fire. I came here intent on murdering the princess. And I'm the one who's prepared to unleash schism and war and a new Dark Age because I'm in love with a whore. A whore who likes murdering people."

Decision time: crush his windpipe or let him go. I had to do one or the other before I drew another breath. I knew which one I wanted to do. I did the other. "Fine," I said. "Can you stop it?"

He was crouching against the wall, sucking in deep breaths. "Can you? Answer me."

"No."

"The hell with no. You're the angels, you're supposed to be able to do anything."

He looked up at me. "Hardly," he said. "I couldn't even make you obey a simple instruction, and you're supposed to be a *monk*. You swore *vows*. Clearly your definition of obedience isn't the same as mine."

"So you can't stop Krimhild."

"No."

"But they can?"

He shrugged. "How should I know?"

I'm sorry to say I kicked him, rather hard, on the shoulder. "You could control Kotkel," I said, "and my dad. Tell me how it's done, or I'll kick your head in."

"I don't know," he said. "That information is restricted. It's not my job to handle assets directly."

"But you can find out."

He shook his head. "It's not something I need to know. If I ask, they won't tell me."

"You need to know it, trust me," I said. "In order to stay alive."

"I don't think that would constitute a good reason, as far as my superiors are concerned."

The more he spoke, the more I wanted to hurt him. "Fine," I said. "So take me to whoever controls the walkers, and I can beat it out of him. Come on. Now."

He made an enormous effort and stood up. "I can't do that," he said. "You'll just have to kill me. I'm prepared for that. We all are."

Kotkel, I recalled, had punched a hole in a wall. But my hands weren't as robust as his, and I had work I needed them to do. "I can't do any good if I'm in a prison cell on a murder charge," I said. "That's the only reason you're still alive. Later, when I'm free of my obligations, I'm going to find you and rip you apart. Got that?"

He shrugged. "You must do as you see fit," he said. "It's the sort of thing I'd expect from someone like you, a savage, from the Mesoge."

"You think this is me being savage? Trust me, you ain't seen nothing yet."

That made him grin – painfully, as though he didn't want to but couldn't help it. "What?" I shouted at him. "What's the joke?"

The grin spread, like plague. "You'll see."

That made me turn cold inside. "The hell with you," I said. "You're not the angels, or the devil. You can't do magic and you can't see into the future. Either you're a fraud or you're really, really gullible. At any rate, it's all dogshit and I don't believe in any of it."

"No," he said, with a hint of mild surprise in his voice, "I don't think you do, which is really quite remarkable, in context. Actually, you're just as much a true believer as the rest of us, except in a negative rather than a positive sense. Anyway, it's something we've got in common: the blessed integrity of the closed mind. I suppose it's like courage or determination, one of those things that can just as easily be vices as virtues, all depending on which side you're on. Which means, I guess, that sides are the only things that matter, and everything else is just spin. Also," he added, gently removing my hands from his neck, "you're a bloody fool. Whether that makes it better or worse I really couldn't say. Nor do I care." He stood up. "I suggest you think about what's happened – really think – and then perhaps you'll realise what a truly stupid thing you've done. By then it'll be far too late, of course, but I should like to think of you suffering."

He started to walk away, then turned back. "The librarian," he said, "has a friend who knows classical Aelian. I'd ask him, if I were you."

"Ask him what?" I said, but he'd disappeared round the corner into the lodge.

"Go away," she said.

"We need to talk about this," I said. "Look, I can understand how you feel, but the implications—"

She threw a chair at me. I got my head out of the way, but it caught me on the shoulder and hurt like hell. "Get out," she said. "This is all your fault. I ought to kill you."

Fine. No use trying to point out that she was in my room, so properly speaking she was the one who should leave. I backed out into the corridor and shut the door behind me.

All my fault. All your fault: a favourite phrase of my mother's. She used to alternate it with, It's all *my* fault, for bringing you up so badly. As far as Svangerd was concerned, I could see where she was coming from. I had, after all, bought a box in a shop in Mavais. And I'd brought the Mesoge into all our lives, or at the very least I'd woken it up from its tomb-confined slumber and provoked it into walking. In consequence, Mother Krimhild wouldn't be resting easily in her grave (apart from the few odds and ends they'd trimmed off to keep as holy relics in gold-and-enamel reliquaries); instead, she'd be a full-on exemplar of the Resurrection and the life everlasting, world without end, right here in Choris Anthropou, the most horrible thing anyone could imagine happening to anybody.

And I did that; or it wouldn't have happened except for me, which is more or less the same thing, isn't it?

Think about it, the old man had urged me; really think. Unfortunately I wasn't really up to it at that precise moment. My head was full of wasps, swarming, buzzing, billowing up in my face, and I couldn't get in there with Saloninus' razor and clear them out for fear of getting stung. The implications: who was controlling who, who was on which side, who was under control and who was out of control, and what all that meant for the future of humanity and civilisation as we know it. One of my few gifts is a better-than-average capacity for concentration, but I can't concentrate with my head full of buzzing, stinging things. It's times like that when you discover that *I can't hear myself think* is a strikingly precise and accurate description of a particular state of mind, rather than just a cliché.

If I didn't think things through, however, who else would? Vitimer didn't have the facts and wouldn't listen to me if I went and told him. Svangerd was dissolving in grief, and would probably damage me quite badly if I tried to talk to her about it. The enemy – it's surprising how often talking to the enemy can improve things, but I'd tried it and been stonewalled, so that was no good. Rotlaug had failed and was dead – at least for now; it didn't bear thinking about – and there wasn't anyone else. Beautiful irony: here we had the most brilliant minds, the highest concentration of scholarship and learning in the known world in our generation, all cooped up in one place, and whose job is it to sort things out? Mine. It was enough to make a pig laugh.

Talking to the enemy . . . He'd stomped off in a huff (because it was all my fault), but at the last moment he'd relented and thrown me some sort of crust. Why? To mislead me? I didn't think so. Maybe, in spite of everything, on some level he felt sorry for me. Sympathy from the devil. Or maybe he'd grown as sick of it all as I had, and just wanted it cleared up, by someone, even if that someone was the other side.

The librarian was in his office. He looked awful. "Isn't it

dreadful?" he said. "Mother Krimhild, of all people. Who would have thought Evil could do a thing like that?"

"She's my third cousin, once removed," I said. "From the Mesoge."

His eyes grew wide. "Really?"

I nodded. "I can see why she never mentioned it to anybody," I said. "It's not something you'd want people to know about you. Still," I added, with a grin, "life must go on. No pun intended."

That, he didn't say, was in rather poor taste. "Is there something I can do for you?"

"As a matter of fact," I said, "yes, there is. And it's really, really important. Would you happen to know anybody who's fluent in classical Aelian?"

"Yes. What does—?"

"I need to talk to him. Right now."

He looked at me as though I'd put a knife to his throat. "That's not a problem," he said. "He works in the muniment room, in the next building. I can take you to see him, if you like."

"I like."

"Fine. We'll go and see him tonight, after the library closes."

I shook my head. "Now."

"But I can't—"

"Yes, you can."

He looked at me, and I could read his mind. From the Mesoge; they're all dangerous lunatics up there, cut your throat soon as look at you. "All right," he said. "We'll go there and I'll introduce you. It won't take a moment."

It was raining as we crossed the yard. It hadn't rained for

weeks, not since before we got there. There was that delicious smell of freshly watered stone, which I particularly enjoy, and then we were back inside, climbing flight after flight of horrible screw thread stairs. Not so horrible as all that, I found myself thinking. If it wasn't for stairs like these, I'd be dead.

Brother Unctuarius was sitting at a lectern, under a tall, narrow window, copying a book. He looked up, smiled at his friend, then saw me.

"This man," the librarian said, "needs to know something about classical Aelian. Excuse me, I've got to get back to the library."

He darted off, leaving me with the good brother. "Classical Aelian," said Brother Unctuarius. "Not a lot of interest in it these days, I'm afraid, but it's a beautiful language."

"Quite," I said. "What does diapygon mean?"

He raised both eyebrows. "I beg your pardon?"

"I know it's a swear word and rude and all that, but what does it actually *mean*? If it means anything."

He pursed his lips. "Well," he said, "it's a compound, as you've probably already gathered. Dia, meaning in or through. Pyge, meaning buttocks. Thus a diapygon is one who enters, or is entered, in through the buttocks; by extension, one who experiments with unorthodox sexual practices, subsequently a male or female prostitute, and thereafter a mere term of vulgar abuse."

"Male or female."

He nodded. "The feminine form should, properly speaking, be diapygaena, but in late classical Aelian, where the extended meaning is more common, we have the tendency to dispense with feminine and neuter forms of compound words, and so the masculine form is also used for the feminine and neuter.

Also, in this instance, you have societal and ethical shift, with the change in attitudes towards same-sex relationships that came with the rise of fundamentalist religion in the latter stages of the late empire. Essentially, people could no longer envisage such a thing as a male prostitute, so the term came to refer to females exclusively, despite the masculine form."

"But that was later."

"Oh yes."

"So when, say, Lactantius was writing—"

He smiled at the thought of Lactantius. "Late classical Aelian," he said, "but archaising, therefore deliberately using words in their earlier, uncorrupted meaning. Thus, if Lactantius uses the word, he intends it to be understood with its earlier definition and connotations."

"One who enters or is entered."

He frowned slightly. "In Lactantius, yes. If, say, Varro or Athanaric were to use the word it would carry its later meaning, even though they were Lactantius' contemporaries. But Lactantius and the Archaic movement as a whole sought a return to a purer, more authentic Aelian, by which they hoped to regenerate a society they saw as increasingly decadent and corrupt—"

"Thanks," I said.

"Was that helpful?"

I nodded. "You may just have saved civilisation as we know it," I said, and left quickly.

12

Rotlaug, I thought; and I heard my mother saying, Don't you go near that man, and if he follows you, shout and holler. And Svangerd; diapygaena, one who takes it in the arse, therefore by extension (allowing for societal and ethical shift) a female prostitute. The diapygon's dagger.

Lactantius, of course, was a great one for assonance; hence dagger, instead of plain old knife. A plain old knife such as Rotlaug's little toothpick. Societal factors, too, as Unctuarius would say. In the Mesoge we don't have prostitutes as such, just as we don't have tailors or pastry chefs or teachers of elocution. But we do have men like Rotlaug, only the word we use for them is hero, because they're the only ones who can stop a walker.

Why, I thought. Why, for crying out loud? I shrugged as I walked. Presumably there was a reason, and presumably someone knew it once, back before the empire fell and there was so much more knowledge and understanding. Too late to do anything about that now. For a moment I felt an almost physical pain, because once we knew so much and then it was all lost, burned, rotted, used for arsewipe or wrapping cheese – But that, I decided, was a stupid thing to get upset about, when there were people hurting and dying, and ever so many more who'd hurt and die if I didn't get things precisely right in my mind –

It's all fashion, I remember thinking, and in spite of my cherished cynicism it came as a shock to me to find I'd been right all along. Fashions in heroism and buggery and Good and Evil; in the early to middle empire it was perfectly all right and nobody thought anything of it, but by the late empire it was a term of vulgar abuse, and then it got stamped on so hard, we forgot what it originally meant. Fashions in morality, in Good and Evil – that's all it is. Fashion: is there an inherently true and perfect hemline, established by God at the moment of Creation, and from which all other hemlines are heresy and abomination? Is there an ideal sleeve, or a shoe-buckle that we hold to be self-evident, that's exactly right because it just *is*, has been and ever shall be, world without end, amen?

But that wasn't what I was supposed to be thinking about; regarding which, see Saloninus' second law, which states that a person is capable of doing an infinite amount of work, just so long as it's not the work he's supposed to be doing. No; I was meant to be thinking about knives, and what could be done to stave off the end of the world. So I did that, and went back to my room.

She looked up as I came in. "I'm sorry I threw a chair at you," she said.

"That's all right."

"I was upset."

"I'd sort of gathered." I closed the door. "I've discovered something."

"Oh yes?"

"Something important. But I want you to promise not to attack me if I tell you."

She heard me out, I'll say that for her. Then she looked at me in dead silence.

"Say something," I said. "Please?"

"There's a flaw in your reasoning."

"Is there?"

She nodded. "According to you, your Mesoge pal was a, what you said. And he killed one walker, but then another walker killed him. So it doesn't make sense."

"I don't think it works like that," I said. "I think it means that a special type of person *can* beat a walker. I don't think it means they necessarily will."

"Ah."

I took a cloth-wrapped bundle out of the front of my habit. "I stopped by the Mercy Chapel and stole this," I said. "That's where they've laid him out, poor bastard. They're going to bury him in the crypt, along with all the saints and bishops."

She frowned. "Is that wise?"

"Possibly not. But he died a martyr, so it's more or less obligatory, so I gather. Anyway, you might find it useful," I went on, putting the bundle in her hands. "It worked on Kotkel, at any rate. I don't know if that means anything any more or not."

She unwrapped it and played with it in her best professional manner. "Not bad," she said grudgingly. "A fair degree of distal taper, putting the weight back in the hand where you need it, and the edge geometry's all right. Centre of percussion's nicely on the climax of the curve. Ugly piece of shit, but I guess you can't have everything. It's probably more suitable than anything else I've got with me at the moment. Thanks," she added.

"You're welcome," I said.

She stood up. "I suppose I've got to do this," she said.

"I think you probably do."

"Me too. I'd have thought you'd have tried to stop me. You were the one they were able to blackmail: do this and do that or the girl gets it."

"Funny, that," I agreed. "Maybe you could've stopped all this at the start."

"Or maybe not, and the next time you see me, my head'll be yay thick." She held her fingertips two inches apart. "I can't say I like that idea very much."

"No," I said, "nor me."

She did her thoughtful frown. "When she was about to guzzle you, and your dad showed up."

"Yes," I said. "I thought about that too."

"Did he come to save his little boy from the monster? Or was it just a case of two monsters scrapping over territory?"

"Or just because they like to fight," I said. "I don't know. I think it's one of those cases where you have to choose to believe something. I believe it was just two monsters who liked to fight."

"Your choice."

"Yes."

"Well, you always were a miserable bastard. I think I'll go and pray in the Rose Chapel for a bit." She paused, then added, "She was the closest thing I ever had to a mother, and he was your dad."

"The Mesoge way," I told her. "Basically we're all monsters, where I come from."

"Now you're just being glib," she said. She was right, of course.

Except – I didn't point this out to her, of course – it hadn't been Vitimer or one of the extra-holy holy men or even Svangerd that she'd come for. It had been me.

Sometimes, hedging your bets just means you get to be wrong twice, simultaneously. I'd told her about Lactantius because she deserved to know. I'd stolen the hog knife for her because if anyone in Choris might have a use for it, that'd be her. But the painfully obvious thing – I was under no obligation to draw her attention to it, so I didn't. My mess, after all. My fault.

Mother Krimhild had come for *me*. Therefore there was the possibility, which I was duty bound to explore, that I was the object of the exercise, the point at issue, the centre of percussion, whatever. Put it bluntly (something I was reluctant to do, but what the hell): maybe I was the problem, and Mother Krimhild was the solution.

Why her? Because she was on the spot, and from the Mesoge. Because my father and my brother had tried, or been tried, and had failed. Get rid of the problem, and maybe everything would be fine. Any other explanation necessarily referred to, or dragged in, concepts and issues of destiny, predestination, by extension the supernatural, God and all that rubbish. I was *meant* to recognise that stupid box for what it was. I was *sent* to Mavais, or the box was *put there for me to find* – all those lines of speculation had a horrible tendency to look like periphrases for the divine plan, the long game: something I couldn't quite bring myself to bear to think about. But if I was the problem, and having my skull flattened would solve it . . . The trouble was, I wouldn't be around to see if it did the trick or not, but that was a risk I was just going to have to take.

My room no longer had a door, and parts of the walls and floor were distinctly sketchy, but I'd turned down the offer of alternative accommodation. No point, I thought, in any more of the irreplaceable architectural heritage of Choris getting trashed. I hadn't said anything to her, but I was pretty certain that Svangerd would be making her stand outside Vitimer's chamber door, or in the basilica – somewhere to do with Good and Evil, bless her. Somewhere a good long way away from where I was; somewhere safe. But if I was right, the real action –

A gust of wind blew the lamp out. Something large was in the room, moving about, squeezing out the air.

"Just one thing," I said.

Pitch dark. No moonlight tonight. She made no sound, but I knew she was getting close.

"Once you've killed me," I said, "will it be over?"

She laughed. I'd said something funny. "Well?" I asked. "Will it?"

A hand closed over my head. Her thumb was in my ear; her fingers were spread out over my left temple. "What do you think?" she said.

"No," I said. "It won't be, will it?"

"No."

Nuts, I thought, or words to that effect. She began to squeeze.

"Get off him," someone said. A woman's voice. "Please."

Krimhild roared, like a bull or a bear, and let me go. I could see her now, a huge silhouette defined by pale lamplight behind her. Then I heard the lamp smash, and it was dark again.

Something hit the wall, hard enough to make the whole room shake. Then I heard boot-heels on the floor, and another roar – anger, frustration, a tantrum because someone wasn't getting her own way. Another thump; something brushed against me; which of them it was I have no idea. My hand touched something hot enough to burn – my lamp, which had blown out. I had a tinder-box in my sleeve. I groped for it, got it out, felt for the groove in the lid. Another thump, and a cracking noise overhead. Then a sound I remembered from my childhood, from when my father used to kill the pigs: a cleaving noise, steel on bone.

My fingers were burning. I'd lit the tinder-box without knowing it.

Light. Not very much of it, but enough, welling up uncontrollably like blood from a wound. I saw Svangerd, from the waist up; there was something big at floor level between me and her. She was holding the hog knife in one hand, and something that looked like a sack in the other.

"Are you all right?" I said.

She looked at me as though it was the most stupid question ever asked. Quite possibly it was.

"Now what do I do?" she said.

The walls, I couldn't help noticing, were cracked. I looked up. That splitting noise must've been the rafters.

"We need to get out of here," I said. "Bring the head. Now."

"We can't just leave—" She couldn't bring herself to be more specific. "What if it wakes up?"

"Not without the head. Bring it. Come on, move."

I was on my feet, pushing past her, grabbing her elbow.

She'd probably have hit me for that, but her hands were full. "Is it safe to—?"

I pulled her out into the corridor. The nearest way down was the spiral staircase. I started towards it, then stopped. There was a huge crack in the plaster just above the lintel that hadn't been there before. "Other way," I said. Then I realised there wasn't one.

The groaning noise was woodwork under intolerable strain. She looked at me, then darted down the spiral stair. I followed; a dozen steps and then I slipped, pitched forward. Here we go again. I cannoned into her and knocked her off her feet. I hate spiral staircases.

I think I landed awkwardly at the bottom of the stairs, because she had to pull me to my feet, and then I fell over again. "Come *on*," I remember her yelling, as she tugged on my arm. She got me up and we tumbled into the courtyard, just as the staircase began to give way.

First the staircase, then the building. It slumped and slid rather than fell down, almost like a very slow-moving liquid, and there was surprisingly little noise, just a soft grinding, and ever so much dust. The courtyard was full of people – they'd cleared out of their rooms in a hurry when the fight started – and they kept well back from us once they realised what the sack-like thing was. When the building collapsed, they ran, and then it was just me, Svangerd, and the head of Mother Krimhild.

She was still holding it, by one ear. I don't know what had happened to the knife; buried, probably, in the rubble. The building appeared to have stopped collapsing, at least for the moment. There was a big gap where a section of it had been but wasn't any more, like the gap left by a pulled tooth, and a big sprawl of stone blocks, brick, tiles, shattered mortar, cracked and splintered beams and rafters, all gushed out onto the courtyard cobbles like vomit.

"Put it down," I said. "You don't have to keep holding on to it. It's not going anywhere."

It was too dark for me to see the look on her face, which was probably just as well.

Someone must've gone and fetched Vitimer, because he showed up quite quickly, with lanterns and soldiers. She showed him the head. He looked at it, then threw up all over his shoes.

Clerks appeared, and then more clerks. One of them said the whole complex should be evacuated, until the master mason had had a chance to assess the full extent of the damage. So, shortly afterwards, there we all were in Foregate Street, on the other side of the main gates, a lot of us in bare feet and without hats or hoods, just as it began to rain. Vitimer, who'd been busy with the clerks and the soldiers, came over to talk to me.

"I want to see you first thing in the morning," he said. He didn't sound like he was pleased with me. He made a point of not looking at the head. "Can't you put a bag over it or something?" he said, and I pointed out that we hadn't got a bag. So someone was sent to fetch one. "What about the rest of it?" he asked me. "Is it safe?"

"Yes," I said. "For the time being."

He really hated me for that, and I can't say I blamed him. But as he scowled at me, a tiny idea fluttered leaf-like through the branches of my mind. I caught it, considered it, and thought, Why not?

"What we need," I told him, "is a goldsmith."

*

The master mason made his inspection as soon as it was light enough to see. It was no good, he said. The damage was too great. To shore it up, you'd have to prop it with iron girders, not timber, and take down the side walls, then put in columns to take the weight. Whoever originally built it would've known how to do that, but he didn't. The whole block was going to have to come down, and he just hoped the rest of the wing wouldn't come down with it. Maybe it wouldn't but maybe it would. A great shame, but there was nothing anyone could do.

"I think it might work," I told Vitimer. "It's never been tried, of course."

If anything, he hated me more for saying that than he had the previous night. "Fine," he said. "We'll do it."

My idea was basically quite simple. Where we'd been going wrong all these years, I told him, back in the Mesoge, was burning the decapitated bodies. When you burn something, it turns to smoke and ashes. The smoke drifts away, the ashes crumble into dust; in other words, they disappear, and you have no idea where they go. At some point, some power or influence draws them back together, they reform or condense or crystallise or whatever the hell it is they do, and pretty soon you're back to square one, which is the last place you want to be. An approach, I told him, with a proven track record of failure. So instead, let's try something else.

The head, I argued, was the key. I knew all the Mesoge walker stories, and in none of them was there any mention of a headless walker. So, if you kept the head separate from the body, it stood to reason it couldn't get itself back together again. But that was where we'd gone wrong, from generation unto generation. We'd buried the head under a cairn of stones, or dropped it down a well, or pitched it into a bog; in other words, we'd taken our eyes off it for five minutes, or even longer, and as a result we had no idea where it ended up or how it got there; not until we came across it again, back on the walker's shoulders and itching to do mischief.

So, I said, how about this? Get a really good goldsmith to make a reliquary shrine. You know the sort of thing I mean, I said to him (he knew): big and gaudy and encrusted with pearls and gemstones, the triumph of piety and conspicuous display over good taste. Put the head in the shrine, fixed in real good so it won't fall out, then put the shrine in the Rose Chapel and have teams of monks in there with it, twenty-four hours every day of the year, singing masses for Mother Krimhild's soul and never taking their eyes off the head for one second. Before you know what's hit you, I added, you'll be getting pilgrims and miracles and more pilgrims; very much a secondary consideration, obviously, but relics are really good business; just think for a moment about the Hand of St Vespaluus at Stennvik – ten thousand pilgrims a year, minimum; each pilgrim bringing in ten deniers, conservative estimate, that's a hundred thousand deniers a year for doing practically nothing, not to mention the miracles and the prestige and the political leverage –

He looked at me. He hated me so much he could hardly breathe, but maybe I'd got something there.

Later that day, he addressed the council. He'd had a vision, he said. Mother Krimhild had come to him in his vision and told him to build a shrine to house her horribly abused remains. The shrine, she'd told him, would be a perpetual symbol of forgiveness, purification, redemption, reconciliation and the unlimited power of faithful prayer, and of the unshakeable and fundamental unity of Holy Mother Church. For as long as it stood, he said, Saint Krimhild's shrine would be a fortress of light against the power of darkness, an imperishable reminder of the eternal covenant, the resurrection of the flesh and the life everlasting.

Proposed, seconded, passed unanimously. Lots of cheering. Job done.

There was still, of course, another walker to get rid of: my father.

They'd put his body in a coach-house, covered over with old oilskins, and his head in a vinegar barrel in the charcoal cellar under the porter's lodge. There were terrified soldiers watching both locations, night and day. Some halfwit lawyer told Vitimer that it was up to me to get rid of him, as legal next of kin. No problem, I said, but my suggestion as to how to go about it wasn't well received.

"Simple logic," I told Vitimer. "If it works, it works. So why not my dad as well?"

"Yes," he growled in pain, "but there's a limit to the blasphemies I'm prepared to commit in the name of convenience. Mother Krimhild was a saint. She was one of us. This other monster—"

"Will probably be back again in a week or so," I told him, "unless you do what needs to be done. If you can live with that, fine. If not—"

He groaned, out loud. "An abomination," he said. "Conjured and controlled by Evil."

There are times in a negotiation when it's best to shut up and let the other guy do it all for you. I wiped my face neutral and sat still and quiet, while he thought about it. "I can't see how we'd get away with it," he said. "Everybody here knows what happened."

"Everybody *here*," I said, "that's the point. But Permia's a very long way away."

"I can't tell a deliberate lie."

"Of course not," I said. "But you can repeat what I tell you. And I'm telling you that the Blessed Krimhild came to me in a vision—"

He gave me a really nasty look.

"Came to me in a vision, which is absolutely sort of true because she definitely did come to me, and she told me to send the head of the monster to Eichestamm and house it in a shrine, with a college of monks to pray for it, and in due course there'd be good luck and miracles, and it'd be a beacon and a lighthouse for the entire North. And there you go," I added. "Problem solved. Everyone's a winner. Eichestamm's much too far away to interfere with your action, sorry, the flow of pilgrims to St Krimhild, and the abbot of Eichestamm will love you to bits and pieces once the money starts flooding in, which will be good since you need him on your side for the diocesan audit this autumn, and best of all, there'll be a minimum of thirty monks at any given time to make sure the head doesn't go anywhere. You'll be disposing of a horrible threat and getting a valuable ally in the process, not to mention bums on pews in Permia, which strengthens Holy Mother Church and the Kingdom on Earth generally. And in twenty years' time, the story will have changed out of all recognition, and nobody will know any different. What's not to like?"

He looked at me. "Do you honestly and sincerely swear that you had a vision?"

"I swear by the Invincible Sun," I said, "the True Faith and my hope of salvation. Will that do?"

He gave me a miserable look. "I suppose it'll have to," he said.

I hadn't seen Svangerd since it happened. She'd been in the Rose Chapel, while the goldsmiths were taking measurements and bickering with the clerk of the works about drilling holes in his plasterwork, praying for the soul of Mother Krimhild. I had an idea (or the Blessed Saint came to me in a vision and told me; same difference) that I was the last person she'd want to see at that particular moment, so I left her alone. I can be sensitive sometimes, and I didn't want a broken nose to go with all my other aches and pains.

I think people had noticed the way Vitimer had taken to looking at me; in any event, I didn't seem to be popular, so I took a packed lunch and my copy of Nicephorus into the Gardens of Sulpicius and found a shady corner of the arboretum, next to the compost heap. I opened the book at random, the way I usually do, and read:

... Aspect of the Orovincian heresy was the insistence on actual bodily resurrection, rather than the sublime reconstitution of the soul in new and imperishable fabric. To which the blessed Maroboduus objected that there would be many who died in the faith whose flesh would be unavailable or unsuitable for eternal habitation; for example, those who had been eaten by wild animals, or fish, or ants; those who perished in fire; those who passed away in extreme old age or as a result of wasting diseases or leprosy. Was it conceivable, Maroboduus argued, that the Invincible Sun would countenance the streets of the Eternal City littered with the broken and deformed bodies of cripples, the one-legged hopping eternally on crutches, the blessed martyrs scorched and shrivelled by the flames of the fires in which they had so gloriously perished? Or consider the monstrous forms of the Mesoge revenants, swollen and purple, lurching obscenely through the gates of the City of God, their sins finally washed away but their bodies still proclaiming the power of the Evil One, who by his servants and agents summoned them from the grave and compelled them to do his bidding. Was there to be no rest for them, unwilling tools of the Armies of Night?

I closed the book, swallowed my last mouthful of honeycake, and went looking for someone to be nasty to.

"Me again," I said.

He didn't reply, mostly because, if he had, he'd have cut his own throat on the blade I was holding under his chin. It wasn't a hog knife, because they don't sell them in Choris and I hadn't had time to get one made, but it was close enough for country dancing.

"This time," I said, "I want the truth. Actually," I added, "no, that's not what I want. I want you to be all noble and say you'd rather die a martyr's death, because then I can kill you and dump your body down the disused well out back of the kitchens. But the truth will do, at a pinch."

I took my fingers out of his mouth and relaxed the pressure I'd been applying with the knife. "Very well," he said. "It doesn't matter now. The harm's been done."

I let him go, on the off-chance that he'd try and make a run for it, and I could kill him for that. But he didn't. He turned and looked at me; more in sorrow than in anger, which I really hate. "Not here," he said.

"Why not? It's private."

"I need to sit down."

Fair enough. He was getting on in years. There was a little side-chapel not far away where nobody ever went. We sat down on a wooden bench in front of a diptych of the Resurrection. I put the knife away. I didn't want to kill him any more. "Well?" I said.

He slumped forward, knees on elbows, head in cupped hands. "The worst part of it is," he said, "I told a deliberate lie. Oh, I had clearance, from my superiors. But it's been on my conscience, let me tell you. I've hardly slept."

I stared at him. "Which lie would that be?" I asked.

He ignored me. "Our primary obligation is to the truth," he went on, "the truth as we see it. To tell a deliberate lie under-cuts everything we stand for and fight for. It goes against the very essence of the true gospels. From time to time, yes, we lie because it's expedient," he said bitterly, "but every time we do it, something irreplaceable is lost. You can understand that, I imagine, as a scholar."

"This would be very interesting," I said, "if I was interested, which I'm not. Tell me the truth. What's going on?"

He sighed. "You need to know," he said, "that the Loyal Opposition is no longer a united entity. For some time now there's been a deep and far-reaching schism within the or-ganisation. For convenience we refer to the two parties as the orthodox and the provisional wings, though needless to say, that's a gross simplification of a complex doctrinal—"

"I get you," I said. "Two wings, like an angel. Which lot are you?"

"We don't differ on objectives," he went on. "Both wings sincerely and passionately believe in the same cause, the same values, the same fundamental core beliefs. Where we part company is methodology. The orthodox maintain that the long-term plan should follow a certain specific course. The provisionals would prefer to adopt a different strategy. We respect each other, God knows we do; that's the tragic thing about it. Each wing knows that the other is entirely devoted to bringing about the same end we all yearn for. But we're divided, and the division would appear to be irreconcilable."

A tiny light flickered in the back of my mind. "So when you were rattling on at me about schism, it wasn't Holy Mother Church you were talking about, it was—"

He nodded. "We had an opportunity to reunite the Loyal Opposition," he said. "An opportunity now lost for ever. Thanks, in no small part, to you."

He'd taken my breath away, temporarily. When I got it back, I said, "That plinking noise you can hear is my heart breaking. Now get on with it."

There were, he told me, these two factions. The original grounds for division were classified and technical and I couldn't hope to understand them; suffice to say, there were two ways of playing the long game, both equally valid, and the orthodox supported one way and the provisionals supported the other.

The orthodox engineered the convening of a general ecumenical council, with a view to using it to bring about a complete and irreversible schism in Holy Mother Church. To achieve this, they planned to use the last remaining copies of the true gospels (which were, in case I cared, an accurate and utterly reliable account of the Invincible Sun's ministry on earth). Needless to say, the provisionals were determined to prevent the schism, at any cost. The choice of who was to bring the gospels to the council devolved on a senior Loyal Opposition manager –

"Egil," I said. "My friend Egil, back home."

He nodded. "The list you saw on his desk was a schedule of possible candidates for the mission. Unfortunately, Egil isn't the loyal orthodox he made himself out to be. We now know that he'd been secretly working for the provisionals for some time."

Ouch. "So that means you're—"

He nodded. "I represent the orthodox wing, naturally. Egil chose you because he knows you well. In particular, he knows that you're an atheist, therefore not liable to be swayed by considerations of doctrine, faith or morality. At least, that was the rationale he gave us, and it seemed perfectly reasonable, so we were happy to endorse his choice."

"But?"

He sighed. "As a spy for the provisional tendency, he had another reason for choosing you. He knew that we intended to use a Mesoge walker to dispose of the princess, who we saw as a major threat to our plan for schism. In fact, I seem to recall—"

"Why a walker?"

"The most formidable creature on earth," he said (stupid question, implied). "An unstoppable force that would do exactly what it was told. I seem to recall," he went on, "that it was Brother Egil who suggested using that particular walker, though I'm not entirely sure. In any event, acting for the provisionals, he made sure we chose you, because you were from the Mesoge, and the chosen walker's son."

You get punch-drunk after a while. "Egil did that?"

"Yes. Clearly he believed that you would have some influence over the walker, though that proved not to be the case. He was a very treacherous man, but not as intelligent as he believed himself to be."

"Past tense," I noted.

"Yes. Egil died three days ago. A seizure of some sort."

Ah, I thought. Well, they'd saved me a job. "So who tried to kill Svangerd and me on the road?"

"The provisionals," he said. "But it was a rather half-hearted attempt, also arranged by Egil, in accordance with a direct order he'd been given by his superiors but had no faith in. We gather that he was pinning his hopes on using you to kill or neutralise our walker, so he deliberately chose inept assassins, who you easily defeated." He shrugged. "And then, of course, you arrived in Mavais and acquired the true gospels, as we knew you would. That was another point in your favour, according to Egil. He knew you to be a bibliophile, and you'd told him about finding some bargain or other in that particular shop. It was, therefore, inevitable that you'd go there again, and he knew you could be relied on to recognise that particular box, since you were familiar with the one in the late archduke's collection."

Good old Egil. "Go on," I said.

"The walker killed the princess shortly after your arrival in Choris. It was at this point that we became aware of the relationship between you and the walker, a point Egil had neglected to mention to us, for reasons which I'm sure are now obvious. Our representative in Choris immediately saw the danger. You would feel it incumbent upon you, as a son of the Mesoge, to try to stop the walker. This would lead to your death. But we needed you—"

"Why? I'd already brought the box to Choris."

He gave me a look of profound loathing. "You don't need to know what we need you for. Suffice it to say, the reason has nothing to do with these events. Our representative, realising that you were in imminent danger of being killed—"

"Hang on," I said. "What do you need me for?"

He scowled at me. "Something else."

"*What?*"

"Realising," he went on, "that you were in imminent danger, he took it upon himself to warn you, making it possible for you to survive your encounter with the walker and, indeed, dispose of him. I should point out that in doing so, our representative greatly exceeded his authority; his excuse, had he lived to make it, would presumably have been that he had to act quickly and had no opportunity to consult with his superiors or take instructions. Bear in mind that we hadn't yet had a chance to adjust our plans to take account of the fact that you were the walker's son."

"Fuck you," I said.

He took no notice. "Our representative immediately took steps to secure the text of the gospels, which you had hidden in the rafters of a hayloft. He found them and made sure they fell into the hands of those best equipped to disseminate them. Shortly afterwards, of course, he was killed."

"I meant to ask you about that," I said.

He gave me a look. "None of our doing, it goes without saying. The provisionals had enlisted a walker of their own, your brother Kotkel. I imagine their original intention was to try and use him to stop or impede our walker – relying on the family relationship, I imagine, in which case it speaks volumes about the diligence of their research – but the loss of your father made that unnecessary. Therefore the provisionals found themselves in the position of having a monopoly of that particular brand of force, together with the added benefit of being able to blame the monster's actions on us." He sighed. "My superiors believe that that was part of your friend Egil's treachery, but I don't think so myself. I think it was an unhappy accident, to which the provisionals adapted with great shrewdness. A case of fortune favouring the bold, if you like. In any event," he went on, "they were too late to prevent the dissemination of the gospels. That had already taken place."

He paused, to gather his strength and to give me a singularly filthy look. "There's a tendency to refer to the work we do as the long game," he said. "It's an expression I dislike intensely. It is *not* a game. We serve a vital function in the operation of the Divine plan. We are, quite literally, doing His work on earth." He stopped, briefly overcome by emotion. "I suppose that's why our two rival wings strive so intensely against each other," he went on. "If our work wasn't so important, so holy, these differences of approach wouldn't matter. We'd find a way to compromise, for the sake of unity and good fellowship. But we can't help thinking they're *wrong*, and it *matters*. If we follow the path endorsed by the provisionals, we'll *fail*. And that, quite simply, is unacceptable."

"And they think the same way about your scheme."

He nodded. "There has to be an opposition," he said. "Light presupposes darkness. Joy is posited on sorrow. Good is meaningless without Evil. It's all there, in Saloninus' fifth law."

"*Fifth* law?"

"To every action," he said, "there is an equal and opposite reaction." He looked at me, and the denier dropped. "From the *Mechanics*," he said. "His greatest work, a summary of everything he ever achieved. Lost now. There used to be a copy in the library of the Great King of the Sashan, but it was burned in a religious purge thirty years ago. I was probably the last person to read it, now I come to think of it. In any event, the principle is fundamental. There has to be an opposition. We carry out that function. Without us, there could be no light, no heaven, no salvation, no Kingdom of God. They'd all be meaningless."

"Cheer up," I said. "Obviously you're on the right lines. You've got an opposition within your Opposition. According to you, that's a good thing."

He refused to dignify that with a reaction. "With the text of the true gospels circulating freely among the delegates," he went on, "the provisionals turned their attention to your companion, Sister Svangerd. They recalled the relationship between her and Mother Krimhild, one of the most respected and revered figures in Holy Mother Church. Their sources inside our organisation had informed them of our intention to poison Krimhild, to prevent her from stopping the schism—"

"But she had a—"

He gave me a pitying smile. "Yes," he said. "Brought on by six drops of tincture of white hellebore root. It was one of the few manoeuvres in this whole sorry debacle that proceeded according to plan. Svangerd, the provisionals realised, would be Krimhild's choice to deliver the speech she herself couldn't give. Naturally they were aware that we were aware of that—"

"Naturally."

"Please don't interrupt. When we made the decision to debilitate Krimhild, needless to say we took steps to ensure that she would have no one to do her work for her. Accordingly, we arranged for one of Svangerd's former clients to be present at the council. When Svangerd rose to deliver Krimhild's speech, this man would get up and denounce her. The speech would not be delivered, or if it was, nobody would listen."

"So Kotkel killed him."

He nodded. "At that point, your brother was still under the control of the provisionals."

"At that point?"

That gave him some degree of grim satisfaction. "Therein lies the difference between the provisionals and the orthodox, if I may say so. We take time to lay our plans. We research; we find out all relevant and necessary information. Until we've done that, we forbear to act, even if it means passing up on an opportunity. We are naturally cautious. We act *responsibly*." He shook his head. "The same, I'm sorry to say, can't be said of the provisionals. When they found out that we were intending to deploy walkers, they decided to deploy them too. But they hadn't done the research. They thought, or assumed, that they knew what they were doing, but sadly that was not the case. From the very beginning their control over Kotkel was shaky at best. Your brother had acquired a taste for killing. Also, I think, something had made him angry."

"That," I said, "would be me."

He looked at me. Enough said. "At this juncture," he went on, "you encountered the provisional agent in Choris. He claimed to be the official representative of the Loyal Opposition – not a lie, from his perspective."

"Curly hair and a double chin."

He nodded. "Brother Aviragus. A notable scholar and a fine administrator. Under other circumstances, I would have been proud to call him my friend. He came up with the idea of using you to prevent the schism. He was aware of your criminal tendencies—"

"Steady on."

"Forging documents," he said. "Stealing books, falsifying evidence. I have to say, his idea was quite brilliant. He would compel you to assert that you had forged the gospels. When your claim was refuted, it would naturally raise a strong presumption that the gospels were genuine. Once the authenticity of the gospels was generally accepted, the doctrinal debate over their contents would quickly cool down into harmless scholarly discussion, and outright schism would be avoided."

"I guessed that was what he was up to."

"Indeed? Well, you failed to let that insight influence your actions. In any event, your hands were tied. You were forced to agree to do as he asked, for fear of harm coming to the woman you love." He didn't make that sound like a good thing. "You tried to circumvent the threat by confronting your brother, but the encounter was inconclusive. In fact, though you weren't to know it, there was no threat. By this point, Aviragus had no control at all over your brother. When Kotkel threatened to kill Svangerd because it would make you cry, he was being entirely honest. That would have been his sole motivation, had he taken that step."

The thought made me shiver. Me and my big mouth.

"We had, by this time, reassembled your late father," he went on. "We had realised that Kotkel was out of control and presented a clear and present danger. We felt responsible, since it was our deployment of a walker that prompted the provisionals to follow suit. We sent your father to stop Kotkel, in which he was partially successful. We also recruited a specialist hunter from the Mesoge and arranged for him to come to Choris, as quickly as possible. Allied to our feeling of responsibility was the hope that, if Kotkel was destroyed or removed, Aviragus would lose his hold over you, and you would not proceed to obstruct the road to schism. In that, broadly speaking, we were successful. You did not disrupt the council meeting. One sad consequence of that was Aviragus's death, from a heart attack, brought on by rage and frustration." He paused for a moment. "He was my opponent, but I respected and honoured him. I had no idea his health was so poor, or I would have taken steps to save him. Too late now, of course."

"My sympathies for your fucking loss. He was an arsehole. So are you."

He rose above me, like the rising sun over a bog. "The rest," he went on, "should be self-evident. We still had a chance of bringing about a schism in Holy Mother Church, and healing the schism within our own ranks. That happy end could have been achieved by Vitimer's assassination. I blame myself. I chose you as my instrument, based on my assessment of your character. I thought you to be weak, cowardly, primarily motivated by your love or lust for the woman Svangerd. I believed that you would find some way to justify your act in terms of your own abstruse and woolly-minded philosophy – frankly, I believed that as an atheist you had no principles, only physical urges masked by a veneer of sophisticated decadent rationalisation. In short, I overestimated your intelligence. It never occurred to me that you'd turn out to be *stupid*. My mistake, and I accept full responsibility for my choice."

"Just a minute," I said. "What about Krimhild? Turning her into a walker. Whose brilliant idea was that?"

"Nobody's." He gave me a haven't-you-been-listening-to-a-word-I-said look. "It just happened. Or, to be exact, she succumbed to her inherently malignant Mesoge nature. I believe," he added, "she's some sort of relative of yours, third cousin once removed or something like that? No, it wasn't part of any plan. Sometimes, things just happen. And of course she was under nobody's control but her own, so it's just as well that your lady friend was able to deal with her so quickly."

"But that's—" I stared at him. "But it made *sense*."

He raised an eyebrow. "To you, maybe."

"It was pure Evil," I said. "Taking the body of a particularly holy saint and turning it into an abomination. It was the ultimate desecration."

He shrugged. "I suppose you can view it in that light if you want to. But if so, it was sheer random chance. We had nothing to do with it, and I happen to know from my sources inside their organisation that the provisionals were as surprised and shocked as we were." He made a sort of tongue-clicking noise. "Doubtless at some point in the future, the provisionals will claim it as a masterstroke on their part, because of the part it played in putting a stop to the schism once and for all, but if they do, they'll be lying. And they'll know it. No, the simple fact is, it was something that nobody intended and nobody predicted. Things like that happen all the time."

For some reason, I had a strong mental image of a Mezentine mechanical clock, washed up on a beach. Things, I wanted to tell him, don't just happen, not in your entirely fictional mechanical universe, in which I don't believe. But I couldn't see any point in making a fool of myself, so I kept my mouth shut.

"Meanwhile," he went on, "Vitimer has prevented the schism. Doing so means he'll enjoy unprecedented honour and prestige, which is another unintended consequence that nobody foresaw. We all had him down for a nonentity, but now he's acquired genuine stature. Which," he added, "is a good thing, as it turns out. We've been back to the drawing-board, and we've reshaped our entire plan based on him. In point of fact, it's a much better plan than the one we were compelled to abandon, and since the outcome will be exactly the same, I can honestly say that this whole process has turned out to be positive, and the Cause as a whole has benefited from it. There's even a possibility of a window of opportunity for a reconciliation of the two wings of our movement. They were always opposed to a schism. We, for the reasons I've just stated, are now entirely content that no schism should take place at this time. This gives us common ground, something we might just possibly be able to build on. No thanks," he added quickly, "to you. Thanks rather to the exceptional recuperative and regenerative powers of the orthodox movement, which enabled us to—"

Enough is enough, I thought. So I hit him.

She was still in the chapel. Here goes, I said to myself.

"What happened to your hand?" she said.

I unwrapped the bit of cloth I'd bound round my knuckles. "Cut myself," I said.

"What on?"

"Someone's teeth."

She clicked her tongue. "You want to put some plantain on that," she said. "Or it'll turn nasty."

Everything does, I didn't tell her, sooner or later. "I've been talking to someone."

"Who?"

I told her, most of it. She sat there in solemn silence, then shook her head. "That's not how it happened," she said.

"No?"

"No. The Enemy tried to wreck the council with schism and monsters, but Mother Krimhild stopped them. She gave her life for Holy Mother Church. Then they tried to spoil it all by stealing her dead body, but I prayed to her and I was given grace, and I drove the devil out of her body, and now it's going to be a shrine." She looked at me. "Isn't that what happened?"

"Of course it is," I said. "Didn't I just say that?"

There was, of course, a ceremony. At that point in the consolidation of his power, Vitimer needed all the ceremonies he could get. So there was a formal consecration of the shrine of Saint Krimhild, attended by the entire council. The Order of St Krimhild was graciously bestowed on Svangerd by Vitimer himself. On closer inspection, it turned out to be a little badge, enamel on gold-plated brass. Couldn't you at least have managed real gold, I asked him later. He gave me a foul look and pointed out that all the available gold had been used up making the shrine; and besides, Svangerd had sworn a vow of poverty, and it was the thought that counted. He also said that, in light of my rather clever idea of building the shrine, which had got a lot of people off a lot of hooks, he'd decided not to press charges against me and I was free to go back home, as soon as I liked, or maybe even sooner.

"Charges of what?" I asked.

"Theft," he said. "Breaking and entering. Assault on two delegates. Multiple counts of criminal damage. Conspiracy to murder my predecessor. Conspiracy to propagate heresy. Conspiracy to—"

"Ah," I said. "Those charges. In that case, thank you for being so broad-minded."

He looked at me. "If ever you breathe a word about what we—"

I drew my fingertip across my lips. "Sealed," I said. "Cross my heart and hope to die in a cellarful of rats."

"Be careful what you wish for," he said. "It could be arranged. Now please, go away."

We managed to get two berths on a freighter carrying dried bat manure to Scona. Two days there, just long enough for Svangerd to recover from an amazingly productive bout of seasickness, and we caught a lumber barge headed up the west coast of the Friendly Sea to Sirupat. On the fifth day we were boarded by pirates, but Svangerd was too ill to join in, and by the time she'd dragged herself up on deck they were all dead. It had been, I told her, that sort of a mission.

"The hell with it," she said. "I just want to go home."

I'd wanted to avoid Mavais, so it was practically inevitable that the ship we boarded in Sirupat, bound for the Pillars with a cargo of salt cod and copper ore, should be blown off course by a singularly unpleasant squall, and end up in the Mavais roads. By this point it had lost one of its masts and both rudders, so there wasn't much point in my making out a case for soldiering on to the Pillars. I tried, but I knew it was a losing battle.

We landed in Mavais, me and what was left of Svangerd after three days and nights as the plaything of the wind and rain. I counted our remaining money, which was going to have to get us home, unless we wanted to beg, which I personally didn't. Fortuitously, I knew a cheap inn just across the road from a tannery. Technically, Svangerd was barred for life for rowdy behaviour on a previous visit, but the old landlord had died and been succeeded by his daughter, which I maintained constituted a sort of general amnesty. The daughter didn't recognise us, so that was fine.

"Will you be all right for a bit?" I asked her. "There's someone in the town I want to see."

She groaned. It could have been a yes groan or a no groan. I put a blanket over her and went out.

When I got there, the shop was closed, on account of having burned to the ground. There was a man sitting on a folding stool among the ashes and bits of blackened rafter. He wore a monk's habit and a big straw hat, and when I approached he looked up from his book and smiled.

"Pity," he said. "There were all manner of rare and fascinating treasures, but they were all destroyed in the fire. Still, omelettes and eggs."

He was about my age, a bit taller and broader than me, and when my shadow fell on him he produced a length of chain from his sleeve and started wrapping it round his right fist. "Just a precaution," he assured me. "My boss made a great point of telling me how dangerous you are, and at the first sign of trouble I'm to hit first and rationalise afterwards. He's a bit of an old woman, my boss."

"I mean you no harm," I said. "What happened to the man who ran the shop?"

"Inside when the fire started," he replied. "Nothing anyone could do. It turns out that some fool had nailed the doors and windows shut, from the outside." He shook his head. "Health and safety nightmare, these old timber-frames. They ought to tear them all down and rebuild."

I sat down next to him, in the ashes. "Who are you?" I said.

"Nice try." He smiled indulgently. "I imagine what you

mean is, which am I, provo or doxy? To which the answer would have to be, 'Yes'." He unwrapped the chain and put it away. "Speaking purely for myself, I think all these divisions are purely arbitrary, and it's high time we put them behind us and started acting like grown-ups."

"Purely arbitrary," I said.

That made him grin. "Let me guess," he said, "I took the words right out of your mouth. Thought so; they're all warm and spitty. Yes, purely arbitrary, the whole nine yards. The way I see it, we all work for the Man; our lot, the other lot, the two warring halves of our lot, the numerous conflicting factions of the other lot, and the dumb thing is, we all basically want the same thing. The Kingdom. The promised end. But unfortunately, there's Saloninus' stupid old fifth law. You know about that?"

I nodded.

"Course you do, a smart man like you. There's got to be an opposition, or none of it actually works." He frowned. "My boss says you're an atheist. Is that true?"

"Yes."

"Good heavens. How on earth did you arrive at that conclusion?"

I thought before answering. It was a good question, worth taking a bit of trouble over. "Intuition, mostly, I guess," I said. "I just know there's nothing there."

"You believe."

I nodded. "But just lately," I went on, "I've been able to back it up with a bit of hard evidence."

"Good for you. Such as?"

I took a deep breath. "Let's suppose," I said. "Let's suppose there's such a thing as the long game."

He frowned. "Go on," he said.

"Because of the complexity and adaptability of the long game," I said, "actions contributing to the benefit of Evil can be Good, and vice versa. Therefore Good and Evil are essentially interchangeable. A Good act can further Evil's ends. An Evil act may be necessary for Good. And since the plan's constantly changing and evolving, there's no way of knowing whether any given act is Good or Evil, since no act is Good or Evil per se. Since the plan keeps changing, what was Good yesterday may easily be Evil tomorrow, and so on. Since the plan is going to keep on changing for ever and ever, world without end, nothing can ever be intrinsically Good or Evil. How am I doing?"

"I like the word intrinsically," he said. "Or you could use inherently. Same difference."

"So," I went on, "there is no Good or Evil. There's only sides: the side I'm on; the side you're on. The side of the side you're on. Each of us wants his side to win. Good and Evil are just the stones we throw. In fact, they're meaningless. As meaningless as a random chunk of rock—"

"Washed up on a beach on a far-away country of which we know little. Yup, let's drag that in too, while we're at it." He was grinning again. "I think I like you," he said. "Now I bet you that's not something you hear very often."

"Let's suppose," I said, "that there is no Good. There's just two factions of Evil perennially at each other's throats under the misapprehension that there is a Good God, and through their ignorance, mutual antipathy, inefficiency and plain stupidity, Good prevails as often as not. Saloninus' razor," I added. He shook his head.

"No, actually," he said. "It's more Saloninus' sixth law."

"*Sixth*—"

"Yup. Saloninus' sixth law: never attribute to malice anything that can be explained by incompetence. Probably my favourite out of the whole nineteen."

I felt my jaw drop. Just when you think you've heard it all.

"You're wrong, of course," he went on. "There is an Invincible Sun – there He is, look," he added, pointing up at the sky, which happened to be cloudy. "And He is the Good principle, and He will inevitably prevail, which is exactly how it should be. But in the meantime we've got the long game. And you're right, a lot of it's about sides. Actually, let's make that sub-sides, since we're all on the same side really, except for the Public. You know, the man in the street, the little people, the ones whose hearts and minds we do all this shit for." He paused. "Are you going to hit me now?"

"No," I said. "I probably ought to, but you're bigger than me."

"Sensible," he replied gravely. "And yes, you're right, a certain degree of arrogance and contempt goes with the territory. But you can despise someone and love them at the same time. You should know that, better than anyone."

"Excuse me?"

He rolled his eyes. "Monks," he said. "No more idea than my old mother's cat. All right, I'll say it again, and you can make of it what you will. You can despise someone and love them at the same time. Now, think of someone who despises you."

"No, thank you."

He shrugged. "Suit yourself," he said. "It was supposed to be your going-home present, but it's no skin off my nose if you don't choose to accept it. So," he said, standing up, "you might as well have this instead." He threw the book he'd been reading at me. It hit me in the mouth. I overbalanced and fell over. "So long," he said. "See you around."

"Oh, I hope not."

He grinned enormously. "Tough," he said. "I've been assigned to you. We're going to be seeing a lot of each other in future. I'm Sigurthus, by the way. Actually, I'm your second cousin twice removed, from Jarlsness, in the Mesoge. Small world, isn't it?"

My lip was starting to swell where the book had hit me. "Too small," I said, "for the both of us."

"Ah well. It was a pleasure making your acquaintance." He held out his hand. "You're all right."

I didn't take his hand. He withdrew it. "Now go away," he said. "Go and buy your girl dinner or something."

I went back to the inn. She was asleep and I didn't want to wake her, so I looked at the book Sigurthus had thrown at me. Saloninus' *Mechanics*.

extras

orbit-books.co.uk

extras

about the author

K. J. Parker is a pseudonym for Tom Holt. He was born in London in 1961. At Oxford he studied bar billiards, ancient Greek agriculture and the care and feeding of small, temperamental Japanese motorcycle engines. These interests led him, perhaps inevitably, to qualify as a solicitor and emigrate to Somerset, where he specialised in death and taxes for seven years before going straight in 1995. He lives in Chard, Somerset, with his wife and daughter.

Find out more about K. J. Parker and other Orbit authors by registering for the free monthly newsletter at orbit-books.co.uk.

if you enjoyed

SISTER SVANGERD AND THE NOT QUITE DEAD

look out for

HOW TO BECOME THE DARK LORD AND DIE TRYING

by

Django Wexler

Davi has done this all before. She's tried to be the hero and take down the all-powerful Dark Lord. A hundred times she's rallied humanity and made the final charge. But the time loop always gets her in the end. Sometimes she's killed quickly. Sometimes it takes a while. But she's been defeated every time.

This time? She's done being the hero and done being stuck in this endless time loop. If the Dark Lord always wins, then maybe that's who she needs to be. It's Davi's turn to play on the winning side.

Prologue

Life #237

It takes me two weeks to die, locked in my own dungeon.

Not for lack of trying on my part, mind, but orders have come down from the Dark Lord that the Princess isn't allowed to pop off early. I found a bit of chicken bone in my soup once, but the spoilsports got to me before I could choke on it.

On the plus side, to the extent that there is a plus side to being tortured to death, I don't have to see what's happening out in the city. I assume it's bad. It's usually bad. If I got into therapy and unloaded half the shit I've seen, Dr. Freud would take a running leap out the nearest window. So not having to actually watch is kind of a relief.

I hear Artaxes coming, the *clank clank clank* of his rusty iron shitkickers. When he opens the door, I give him a little wave with my fingers. This is all I can manage, since I'm manacled to a wooden contraption that raises my arms like I'm in the middle of a cheer routine.

"Morning, chief!" I sing out. "What's the haps?"

I keep hoping being cheerful will annoy him, possibly

enough to rip my throat out, but so far no joy. It's hard to tell how anything lands with Artaxes, since he wears his iron armor like a second skin.[1]

"How do you poop?" I ask him. "Just between us. I won't tell anybody."

He gives a grunt and steps aside. There's someone else in the doorway. Tall and gaunt, black robe hanging limp from her bony shoulders, mouth full of long curving teeth. Sibarae. She looks me over and raises her scaly eyebrow bumps.

I'm naked at this point, modesty provided only by a crust of dried blood and matted hair. For all that matters to Artaxes, I might be a side of beef on a hook. I mean, maybe he has a raging hard-on inside his rusty codpiece, but I doubt it. I've seen Artaxes serve as the right hand of the Dark Lord more times than I can count, and he always goes about his business with the dumb brute efficiency of a buzz saw. You get exactly what you expect with him. It's comforting, in a way, although obviously not when he's tearing my fingernails out.

Sibarae is a whole other kettle of snakes. She's practically drooling at the sight of my gory tits. Her tongue comes out, long and forked, to taste the air. I briefly contemplate what it would be like to get head from a snake-wilder,[2] but I have let's say a premonition that this is not on the agenda.

"Look, clanky," I tell Artaxes, "I realize you're worried about not . . . you know, getting the job done anymore, but you can't just introduce a third wheel into our relationship without talking to me about it. We have something special together, I don't want to spoil it."

"My master worries that you may become accustomed to the

---

1 He seriously never takes it off. How does he poop? *I have to know how he poops.*

2 The tongue would be fucking weird, right? Dunno. Maybe I'm into it.

conditions of your imprisonment," he says. His voice is as cold and dead as his armor.

"And I *begged* him to be allowed a turn," Sibarae says. "I've always wondered what a princess tastes like."

This is *not* a sex thing, trust me.

"Sorry, scaly. I only date girls with tits."[3]

"Those bulbous mammalian things?" She glides forward. "So soft and ... vulnerable. Like the rest of you. *Skin*." She pronounces the word with a contemptuous flick of the tongue.

"Remember our lord's instructions," Artaxes admonishes.

"Oh yes," Sibarae hisses. "I'll be sure to show ... restraint."

He clanks out, shutting the door behind him. She gets on with the business at hand. Which, let's not put too fine a point on it, fucking sucks. You think you'd get used to this shit after a while, but nooooo, when someone bites your finger off, your body's gotta be all like, oh no, someone bit my finger off, pain pain pain! I know, okay? I was fucking there, you don't have to remind me.

So I scream a lot and piss myself, which is breaking character a little. Cut me some slack. Artaxes at least doesn't *bite*. In between screams, I amuse myself planning how I'm going to kill her next time we meet. Rusty, jagged metal will be involved. There may be, like, a little corkscrew bit on the end, possibly some kind of barbed flanges. I'll use my imagination.

Eventually I pass out, thank God. When I wake up, there's a teenage girl in the uniform of the palace healers, the glow of green thaumite leaking between the clenched fingers of her shaking hand. A small pool of vomit by the door marks where she lost her lunch at the sight of me. I wonder what the wilders have threatened her with.

---

3 This isn't really true. I'm just trying to piss her off. No offense to my flat-chested sisters!

She grows back most of my missing bits, but leaves me with a few open wounds just for shits and giggles. Dark Lord's orders, presumably. Fucker likes to twist the knife, figuratively and distressingly literally. At least when he killed Johann, my poor beautiful himbo boyfriend, he didn't have time for any of this sadistic bullshit.

Now that I can think without being *completely* submerged in white-hot agony, I'm getting pissed off. I know you're thinking, Davi, *just now* you're getting pissed off? And it's true, this anger has been building for a while. It's taken some time to bubble to the surface, but it's been stewing down there in the acid swamps of my subconscious.

To put it bluntly: I am about done with this shit. The whole being-tortured-to-death thing, *obviously*, but also the rest. Finished. Kaput. No more. Fuck every last little bit of it. I have a new plan and it's time to get started.

Fun fact: Did you know that snakes lose their teeth and constantly grow more, like sharks? Actually I have no idea if snakes do that, what the fuck do I know about snakes, but snake-wilders do. I know this, as of today, because I have one of Sibarae's fangs embedded in my palm.

The healer has grown the skin back over it, but it's merely the work of an excruciatingly painful eternity to dig it out with my fingernails. The fang has a nice curved shape and a vicious point, and I grip it between two fingers and press it against my wrist, right on the artery. I don't have much leverage, so the best I can do is work the point back and forth, sawing through the skin. Hurts like a motherfucker, but sometimes a girl's just gotta die, you know?

When the artery finally pops, the spatter of blood hitting the floor is like music to my ears. I keep tearing at the cut, opening it wider, willing my stupid heart to pump harder and get my whole blood supply out before someone notices. The fang slips through my fingers about the time my vision starts to go gray, but by then I can taste victory. Also blood.

I slip into the sweet embrace of death with a contented sigh. So long, #237. Go fuck a porcupine.

Life #238

"Well now." The voice is frustratingly familiar. "That won't do at all."

Chapter One

I sit up out of the cold water of the pool, gasping for breath. Again.

Twelve seconds.

Done done *done* with this shit, for real. No more.

Still naked, of course. Death, birth, nudity, very mythic. Frankly if it has to be that way, I'd rather die in bed during an epic fuck[1] than bleeding out after weeks of torture in my own fucking dungeon, but beggars, choosers, you know.

Ten seconds.

Anyway. Naked in a rancid pool of chilly water at the top of a hill. Edge of the Kingdom, right up against a wilder-haunted forest. I'm healthy and hale of limb once again, and also about three years younger, with a lot less muscle tone and a ghastly sort of pixie cut. Same as always. I figure it's what I looked like when all of this kicked off, when whatever happened happened and I got here from Earth some-fucking-how.

Six seconds.

I focus on breathing. Calm and centered, that's me.

---

1 Managed it once!

Four seconds. Sound of someone scrambling up the rocks.

Take a deep breath. Hold it. Let it out.

Two. One.

"My lady!" Tserigern says. I mouth the lines with him. My timing is perfect. "So it's true, then. Gods preserve us. We have a chance."

I look over at him with my best expression of doe-eyed innocence. He climbs the last few feet, dusts off his motley robe, and approaches reverently.

Tserigern is a wizard, a very old and famous one. Everyone says he's the most powerful wizard in the Kingdom, but *frankly* I've never seen him do magic for shit. Light the way in caves and get cryptic messages, that's about it. You could replace him with a flashlight and a walkie-talkie. But he at least looks the part: He's a bony old motherfucker with a beard you could lose a sheep in, like Santa Claus after a debilitating illness. He has kind, crinkly eyes and a sly grin, a weathered, avuncular voice perfect for laying out the mysteries of the universe for an awestruck young naïf. Just the guy you want on your side when you wake up all nudie in a weird fantasy universe with no idea what the fuck is going on.

He bends to one knee and offers me his gnarled hand.

"My lady," he says as I wrap my fingers around his, "I—"

He doesn't get to finish, because I grab the back of his head with my other hand and slam his face into the fucking rocks. I hear his nose break with a *crunch*, and my heart sings, it's so goddamn cathartic. He lies out flat and I swing astride his back, both hands in his hair, and start pounding his stupid fucking face into mush against the stone edge of the pool.

Seeing as how he's a little occupied, I say his lines for him.

"I know you must be frightened"—*crunch*—"but I swear to you, I mean you no harm"—*crunch*, you fucking liar—"I have hoped against hope for your coming, and I thank the gods my reading of the texts was true"—*crunch*, they didn't predict this, did they, motherfucker?—"you must come with me, the fate of the Kingdom is balanced on the blade of a knife"—*ca-crunch*.

Holy fuck, it's better than sex. I don't stop until long after his legs have quit kicking and bits of blood and brains are floating in the water.

"I'm done," I tell the body, leaning back and breathing hard. "Hear me? Done. I'm not some holy savior here to protect your fucking kingdom." I've been doing that for, hold on, let me check my watch, *fucking ten centuries*, and where the fuck has it gotten me? A fucking snake-woman eating my goddamn fingers, that's where.

I strip off his nasty-ass robe and wrap myself in it. He's wearing trousers, too, but I'm not touching them without a hazmat suit.

"What am I going to do instead?" I say in response to an inaudible question. "I will tell you what I am going to fucking do. We have an expression back home concerning what course of action to take if you find yourself under no circumstances able to beat 'em. I intend to follow its advice."

I tie the corners of the robe under my chin, plant my hands on my hips, and let it flap behind me like the cape of an extremely inappropriate superhero.

"I," I announce to the world, "am going to become the *fucking Dark Lord*."

* * *

Okay. I've been going full speed ahead in the interest of keeping my *res* fucking *in medias*, but it's possible you have some questions, such as:

1. How could you beat a friendly old man to death like that? and
2. Didn't you die, like, two pages ago? What's the deal?

To which I answer:

1. The key is getting a good grip on the wispy bits of hair on the back of his bald-ass head. Once your fingers are really dug in there, then it's pretty simple.
2. It's a long fucking story.

To keep confusion to a minimum, though, here's the airline safety video version: Hi! I'm Davi. I'm in my early twenties, dark hair, light brown skin, freckles like someone flicked a paintbrush at my nose, body you'd probably swipe right on but maybe not brag to your friends about afterward.

For the last thousand years,[2] I've been trapped in a time loop, like in that movie or that other movie. When I die—and I always die, for reasons I'm about to explain—I wake up here, now, naked in the pool. Tserigern turns up to give me his spiel. What he would have told me, had I not enmushified his head, is that the Kingdom is in dire peril from the impending rise of the Dark Lord, and *only I* can save humanity from the monstrous armies of the Wilds. Chosen by the fucking gods, promised by prophecy, generally just absolutely lousy with momentous portent. Get your ass in gear, Davi, there's heroing to do.

There was a time when I bought this horseshit. I mean, it's not like he's completely off base here. Try to maintain appropriate humility all you want, it's hard to believe the world doesn't revolve around you when it rewinds the tape every time you fall

---

2 Give or take a few hundred. I try to count but it's not like I can keep a fucking diary.

on your head. And whatever prophet wrote the one about the Dark Lord destroying the Kingdom makes Nostradamus look like a stock-picking hamster, because that shit happens *Every. Fucking. Time.*

It's not always the *same* Dark Lord, and sometimes it takes a little longer, but they always turn up. And as of a few minutes ago, I have fed 237 quarters into this fucking game and I *cannot* get past the last boss. I have tried *everything*, and it always ends with me getting sliced into sashimi. I am becoming *a little peeved* about this, hence my admittedly emotional outburst slash face-smashing.

So! Yeah. Davi. Freckles. Time loop. That's me.[3]

* * *

Anyway. Dark Lord! Plenty of other people have managed it, why not me?

There's actually a whole itemized list of reasons. The two big ones are (a) I'm a human, not a wilder, and (b) my total current resources consist of a ratty cape and whatever Tserigern has in his pockets. I may have a bit of a hole card in re (a), but (b) is definitely going to be a significant obstacle. I don't know exactly how they pick the Dark Lord, but a major factor is personal charisma as measured in armed henchpersons; most candidates turn up with armies, and I don't even have *pants*.

---

3 Where was I before the time loop? Honestly, I don't fucking remember. Somewhere on Earth, obviously. I speak English. I think I was an American because I'm kind of an aggressive asshole. I know stuff: Superman is Clark Kent, Darth Vader is Luke's father.* That really fucking awful guy is president. Not that one, the other one. At this point, I've been here in the Kingdom five hundred times longer; how much do *you* remember from the first month of your life?

* Is Superman Darth Vader's father? This shit all kind of blurs together.

When I go with Tserigern, as I usually do, he helps me manage this transition. He's not the *most* popular guy in the Kingdom, but he can provide me with an entrée to high society and also pants, probably not in that order. Having tenderized his face region, I am more or less on my own in the pants department and also all other departments. I will have to be extremely lucky to get this enterprise off the ground.

Fortunately, in this *very specific* time and place, I can manufacture my own luck.

I tear some strips from Tserigern's grody robe and tie them around my feet, because fuck if I'm putting his boots on. I also help myself to the contents of his pocketses, which are distinctly subpar. Dude is supposed to be a badass wizard and he only carries around enough thaumite to stock a village rectory.

Then it's down the hill and into the forest. The spot where I wake up is on the shifting border between the Kingdom[4] and the Wilds. Every year, the Guild pushes its patrols a little farther out, and the Guildblades kill a few more gangs of wilders, with axe-wielding peasants following behind to turn the forest into farms.

Ordinarily I'm all for this, of course. It's hard to shed many tears about people who kill you over and over, right? But if I'm going to be Dark Lord, I need to flip my perspective. *Screw* those humans and their jerk-ass Guild, coming into our forests to kill us for our pretty stones! What a bunch of total dicks!

Honestly, you can see why they're pissed at us.

Anyway, once I get to the bottom of the hill, it's pretty easy going. This is old forest, and the big craggy trees drink in so much light there isn't much left for pricker bushes. I walk on a soft carpet of decaying leaves. Another strip from Tserigern's

---

4 No, it doesn't have a name. It's just *the* Kingdom, definite article, because there's only one of it.

robe becomes a makeshift pouch, and I gather a few handfuls of maidensrest vine for purposes that will eventually become apparent.

So far, so good. There's a crunch of footsteps ahead of me, and I freeze and try to memorize exactly where I am. Half a second later, a couple of orcs emerge from behind a tree.

I mean, *I* call them orcs, because I've had the benefit of a classical education. What they call themselves means something like "the tusked ones." They have greeny-gray skin and curling tusks at the corners of their mouths, which to me says orcs. They're pretty common among wilder bands on the border, especially north of the Kingdom. I have personally slain enough orcs to fill a soccer stadium.[5]

These two orcs are a bit ragged-looking even by raider standards. One has a sword, the other a spear, and their dress sense might euphemistically be called "rugged."

The way they're gaping at me isn't promising, but you have to start somewhere. I put my hands on my hips, push my cape back over my shoulders, and tell them, "Hello, my friends! I am the next Dark Lord! Will you join me?"

The one with the spear stabs me right in the tit. Fucking orcs.

* * *

So, about what I expected. But here's the thing about being so close to my starting point—it doesn't bother me much.

I mean, don't get me wrong, being stabbed fucking hurts. Other than that, though, I haven't lost anything. Another quick walk through the forest and I'm in a position to try again. And again, and again, and again, if necessary. I can't help but

---

5 Although in fairness, a lot of those were the *same* orcs, multiple times. Is that better or worse?

think of this as "save-scumming," after the old gaming practice of loading your save over and over to try to get a good result on some RNG.[6] I don't even count these mayfly existences against my total roster of lives. Keeping track is hard enough as it is.

Point is this is not an unexpected result. Next time I go into the forest, I know where my orc friends are going to be patrolling. They catch me one more time (sword to the back of the head, instant death, 5/5 stars), and then I've got an idea of their route, which makes it easy to get past them. I'm tempted to murder them, if only for their boots, but given my ultimate objective, it seems counterproductive. I guess that they're walking a circuit around a raider camp, and lo, so it comes to pass. There's a whole bunch of tents pitched around a big clearing with a bonfire. I can see a gang of wilders, maybe thirty, mostly orcs with a few wolves and lizards for variety.

I know these guys. In fact, I've killed them many times. A more typical start to a life might go like this:

1. Follow Tserigern after his stupid fucking speech.
2. Meet up with a party of Guildblades in the area. Offer to guide them to their prey to prove my worth.
3. Find the closest raider gang (this one) and get to hack-'n'-slash.

It's a nice trick because it gets me in with the Guild from the very start, which helps propel me into the thick of the

---

6 A question that might occur to you: Davi, are you in some kind of video game world? Believe me, I've thought about it. I know a surprising amount about that stuff; I think past-me was kind of a nerd. Anyway, apart from me starting over after getting snuffed, nothing about my situation screams that I'm in the Matrix. And if it *is* a game so perfect that I can't tell the difference, then isn't that just reality? What if, like, *I'm* real and *you're* in the game, man? Pass me a bong and let's talk about the simulation hypothesis.

Kingdom's affairs without too much "Who's this scruffy girl who says she's here to save us?" style bullshit. Since I'm now reversing the polarity on everything, though, it behooves me to get to know these people as something other than a red mess on the other end of a battle-axe.

The trick is living long enough to do this, since as far as they're concerned, I'm just some human wandering into their camp, and for wilders pretty much the only good human is a dead human. Some fast-talking is called for.

"Hello, friends—*gark*!"

"Can I speak to you before—*blarg*!"

"Please listen for a minute before you stab—*whatever noise being stabbed in the eye makes*!"[7]

It takes a few tries.[8] I vary up my approach, trying different angles. The direct route brings me up against a big deep-green orc with a sideways mohawk who barely seems to notice what I say before he slaughters me. Taking the long way around means the first wilder I encounter is a woman stitching leather who seems less inclined to immediate violence.

At this you might say, Davi, why bother? I get that you don't want to fight the orcs, for altruistic and/or emotional reasons relating to your mindset on this particular life, but you could at least go around them. Just dodge the scouts and get on with the plan!

So, first of all, where the fuck do you get off giving me advice, imaginary person? Have you been horribly killed an unknown but four-digit number of times? I suspect not, and I invite you to (a) respect my expertise, and (b) fuck off into the sun.

---

7 *Pop? Squish? Psquish?*

8 You may be asking, Does this mean you have to kill Tserigern over and over again? To which I say yes, yes, it does. I can feel my stress just melting away.

Second, if I *must* elaborate, talking to the orcs *is* the plan. See, Dark Lord isn't a thing you just stroll into. You have to work your way up. For obvious reasons, I don't know very much about the actual process, but the Dark Lord gets crowned[9] at a big wilder shindig called the Convocation, way up past the mountains at the other end of the Hedsine River. As noted, it's a bring-your-own-minions sort of occasion.

In other words, just turning up isn't going to do me any good. Ideally I'd be at the head of a vast horde, but even a little horde[10] is better than none.

Thus: orcs. Small-time and close enough to my starting point that I can fuck around.

"Hey," I tell the leather-stitching orc, who startles and jabs herself in the palm with a needle. "S'up."

She looks at me wide-eyed but doesn't immediately disembowel me. Progress!

"Please don't scream," I tell her.

She screams. A whole gang of orcs arrives and does unpleasant things with edged weapons until I stop moving.

I reconsider. Maybe a more layered approach is needed. Next time I stay out of sight around a tent and call out, "Hello? Lady with the sewing?"

There's an intake of breath, and then, "Barlav? Is that you?"

Actual conversation![11] "Um, sure?"

---

9 They don't wear a crown, usually just a helmet with spikes on. Helmeted? Behelmed?

10 Hordette? Hordella?

11 Let's get this out of the way. Language here doesn't make any fucking sense. The humans have one language, which I of course think of as Common, though like the Kingdom, it doesn't really have a name. The wilders all speak a single language, too, even though there are, like, zillions of them spread out across probably a whole planet. While the structural linguists are trying to get a handle on that, you can add the fact that as far

"What?"

Footsteps. She looks around the corner and I give her a reassuring grin.[12] She screams. *Chop chop chop ow ow splat.*

Try again.

"Madam, I am forced to admit that I am not, in fact, Barlav."

"What?" A rustle. "Who's there?"

"Before you turn the corner," I say, "let me put my cards on the table and further admit that the sight of me will probably alarm you somewhat. I assure you that I have no intention and indeed no ability to harm you or your companions, and my sole desire is to establish peaceful relations and amicable dialogue."

"What the *fuck*—" She turns the corner, screams. *Choppy choppy.*

Again. Maybe adjust the verbiage to be a little more immediately approachable.

"Please don't scream. I just want to talk. I don't have any weapons."

She turns the corner, sees me, sucks in a breath. Pauses. Lets it out slowly.

"You—" Her eyes flick to me, then back toward the center of camp, where the choppers are waiting. "You're *human.*" A deeper shade of green colors her cheeks. "And naked. Why are you naked?"

"As to the first, I'm not, I swear." Better to start laying the

---

back as I can remember, I've been able to speak Common—it sounds like English to me unless I really concentrate on the sounds. (Wilder I learned the hard way, but I've had a thousand years to practice.) Makes no sense; it has to be magic. I gave up trying to figure out how it works a hundred lifetimes ago; the thing about a fantasy world is that "A wizard did it" is a perfectly valid explanation.

12 I have occasionally been told, after a thousand years and God knows how many violent deaths, that my grins are no longer reassuring.

groundwork early. "I'm guilty on the second count, though. It has been a rough"— thousand years—"couple of weeks."

"You speak properly." She straightens up a little, coming out of a defensive crouch. "I've never met a human who can do that."

"As I said, I'm not a human." I cough. "May I ask your name?"

"Maeve," she says.

"It's good to meet you, Maeve. I'm Davi."

"What are you doing here?" Her eyes flick over her shoulder again. "They'll kill you if they find you."

"Believe me, I am aware of that," I say with a certain amount of well-earned gravitas. "I need to speak to your leader about something important. Is it at all possible we could arrange that without too much bleeding on my part?"

"You . . ." She shakes her head. "You must be mad."

"As a March hare," I answer automatically.

"A what?"

"Never mind. Can you just . . . go and find the person in charge and tell them I would deeply like to have a word? They're free to kill me afterward."

"Maeve?" a deeper voice says from around the corner.

"Over here, Barlav," Maeve says, backing away from me. "There's something you should see."

The sideways-mohawk orc comes into view. He sees me and his eyes go wide. But, crucially, Maeve is between him and me, so he has to pause a moment to push her out of the way.

"Wait!" I shout at him. "Please. I know I look human, but I'm a wilder and I can prove it. Please just let me show you."

I reach into my makeshift pouch and pull out the thaumite I got from Tserigern. There's not very much, two green stones, one orange, one purple, none of them larger than my pinky nail. They're polished into smooth spheres, like marbles that glow very slightly from the inside.

The sight of the little gems at least gets Barlav's attention. I grab one of the green ones, put it on my tongue, and swallow. It makes a hard lump in my throat as it goes down.

Maeve and Barlav stare at me. I stare back at them, waiting.

* * *

So, thaumite.[13] Thaumite is pure arcane power crystallized into glowing gems, which come in every color of the rainbow. Back in the Kingdom, it's considered the ultimate bling, and for good reason—with the right training, humans can use thaumite to do magic. What exactly they can do and how much of it depends on how big a chunk you have and in what color, among other factors; if you ever see someone coming at you with a chunk of red stuff the size of a fist and an angry expression, for example, *all* your shit is about to get blown up and/ or combusted. On the flip side: I am, of course, probably the best magic-slinger the world has ever seen, but with the junk Tserigern had on him, I can probably manage to cast "Heat to the Point of Mild Discomfort" or "Cure Hangnail."

That's what *humans* do with thaumite. Wilders have a much more basic, primal relationship with the stuff, which is a fancy way of saying that they eat it. The magic runs through them and lets them do things, not as flashy as human sorcery but more reliable. But the salient point at this *specific* juncture is that if a human is stupid enough to eat thaumite, that human is going to have a bad time, somewhere along the axis from "painful and immediate death" to "actually exploding like a decomposing whale."

So, Davi, you say, are you about to explode? Because that

---

13 That's my name for it, incidentally. The Common word just means "magic rock," and saying it over and over sounds dumb.

seems like kind of an elaborate prank, talking your way up close to these orcs only to shower them in your mangled guts.

And you would think so! Because I am, as best I've been able to determine,[14] human. Like I don't have fangs or cat ears or a snake tongue or the other shit that wilders usually have. And yet, as I determined by experiment long ago, I can eat thaumite with no ill effects and even use it the way wilders do. *And* I can use human-style magic! Kind of a cheat-level skill set, right? Not that it's done me much good, since in the Kingdom if they find out you can eat thaumite, they burn you at the stake and not as a figure of fucking speech.

Now, however, I'm hoping I can take advantage of the opposite. By popping a chunk of thaumite like a happy pill and then conspicuously not exploding, I can demonstrate my bona fucking fides to Maeve and Barlav. Wilders can look like all kinds of things; the idea that one could pass for human isn't *too* implausible.

Worth trying, anyway. What's the worst that can happen, I get brutally murdered?

* * *

Somewhat to my surprise, I do not get brutally murdered. At least not *immediately.*

Barlav grabs me, not gently, and twists my arms behind my back. He frog-marches me through the ring of tents to the central fire, with Maeve making vaguely distressed noises as she follows behind. The rest of the raiders quickly gather round, two dozen or so variously armed orcs, wolves, and lizards versus little naked me. I've stared down worse odds.[15]

Up until this point, I've been too busy dying to pay much

---

14 And bearing in mind that I have *literally* been dissected.

15 And then, admittedly, I've mostly died horribly.

attention to the details of the camp. The gear is your basic raider mishmash: half wilder-made stuff—lots of leather, bone, bits of shell and carapaces from beasts—and half looted human junk, not particularly well cared for. I have to admit that it doesn't get my hopes up. But this riffraff somehow manages to squash the civilized Kingdom, with its knights and castles and flush toilets, every single time. Which is why I'm here, right? Get on the winning team for once.

There are a few family-sized tents and a lot of smaller ones, some little more than a ratty hide on a couple of sticks. Out of one of the nice ones comes an orc woman who has the unmistakable air of someone In Charge and with no patience for your shenanigans. She's big, a head taller than my admittedly below-average height, with her hair shorn down to a thin stubble and curling tusks carved with elaborate abstract patterns. She stares at me and scowls, and I stare back and try to look like a harmless little bunny.

I *kind* of want her to step on me and make me lick her toes, if we're being honest. What can I say? Something about a girl who can wrap her fingers all the way around my neck does it for me. Her biceps are as big as my thighs.

"What the fuck is going on?" she says. "Who's this?"

"Looks like a human," one of the other orcs says.

"Might be a spy for the Guild," a wolf mutters.

"I caught her sneaking into camp," Barlav says.

"She said she wanted to talk," Maeve puts in, raising her stock with me about a million percent.

"Nivo and Myr are supposed to be on patrol," the leader snaps. "They're in for a kicking when they get back."

Sorry, Nivo and Myr. You did a fine job killing me the first few times.

"She says she's a wilder," Barlav goes on. "Took a piece of thaumite right in front of us."

"Wilder?" The leader's eyes narrow. "Seems human to me. Must be a trick."

"She speaks properly," Maeve says. "Not that human gibberish."

"I do," I say, judging this to be the time to put my verbal foot in the door. "And I am. A wilder, I mean. I know how I look, and I thank you for not leaping to judgment"—*this* time—"and giving me a chance to speak."

"No one said you could speak," Barlav says, shaking me. I ignore him.

"To be perfectly honest about my intentions," I tell them, "I am on something of a quest, and I'm looking for companions. I can promise excitement and plunder and such. Hear me out?"

"What the *fuck*?" the leader says, staring at me as though she's discovered a talking cockroach.

"What kind of quest?" Maeve says.

"I'm going to become the Dark Lord," I say. "And you can get in on the ground floor."

There's a long pause, then a round of laughter.

"Just another fucking madling," the leader says, waving her hand as she turns away. "Get rid of her, Barlav."

I try to say something else, but a knife is already sliding across my throat. Barlav holds me by the hair as blood sprays, then lets me flop face-first into the dirt.

At least, I have time to think, he keeps the fucking thing sharp.

* * *

Well. Crap. I thought we were making progress there.

Still, better than last time. I've got a chink into which I can insert a lever. I just need to figure out which lever is going to be most effective. And I have at least an idea.

See, in the Kingdom there's so much talk of wilder bands raiding the frontier you'd think that was their primary occupation. But the wilders would much rather stay as far from humans as possible—we're aggressive and unpredictable and probably smell bad. The dreaded raider bands that the Guild is always clashing with are the lowest of the low, wilder-wise, forced to live next to a bunch of genocidal lunatics because they're not tough enough to carve out a place anywhere else.

Consequently, it's a safe assumption that things are not going great for sexy bald orc lady and her merry band. I figure if I can credibly promise to deliver better times, they might be willing to get aboard the train to Dark Lord Central. The trick there is *credibly*, of course, since my current state doesn't do much to instill confidence. But I have my stupid little magic trick, and maybe that'll get me somewhere.

Thus my next few forays aren't so much serious attempts as fishing expeditions. I get their attention and ask leading questions until somebody's patience runs out and they gut me with a meat hook. Back again, different questions, scribble in the mental notebook until Barlav twists my head all the way around with a crunch like a bite of breakfast cereal. Back again, so what do you guys like for breakfast, ow ow ow. You get the idea.

Eventually, after a great deal of pain and suffering:

"What the fuck is this?" says sexy bald lady. Her name is Tsav, as it turns out.

"Looks like a human," says Strak. Strak is an asshole.

"Might be a spy for the Guild," mutters Fezginorix. He's a wolf-wilder and basically a softie. I want to pet his adorable ears.

"I caught her sneaking into camp," Barlav says. I have negative feelings toward Barlav, thanks to him being the one who keeps killing me.

"She said she wanted to talk," Maeve says. She's the best.

"Nivo and Myr are supposed to be on patrol—" Tsav begins.

"Nivo and Myr have good eyes," I interrupt, "but not good enough to spot me. I know what I look like"—frankly I've stopped paying any attention to my bedraggled nudity at this stage—"but I've come here to offer you a spectacular prize. Anyone who joins me will have more thaumite than they can eat, I swear here and now."

A little bombastic, yes, but it feels like the right tone for the situation. Everyone glares at me.

"Who in the name of the Old Ones are you supposed to be, then?" Tsav says, brow furrowed.

"My name is Davi," I tell her. "And I'm going to be the next Dark Lord."

No grins this time. I fix Tsav with my best intense stare, trying to make my eyes go all swirly. Some of the others laugh but she doesn't.

"Madling," Barlav says into the silence that follows.

"When was the last time any of you had your bellies full?" I say before Tsav can speak. "When was the last time you had more than a chip of thaumite?" And, finally, the trump card. "When was the last child born to this band?"

Wilders don't need thaumite just to throw fireballs at one another like humans. It's part of their basic life cycle. Every wilder needs a certain amount of thaumite just to exist, and so wilder children can't be born unless the mother has enough to spare. A wilder can *live* for a long time without thaumite, but any wilder band lacking a supply is doomed to eventual extinction.

"What exactly would you know about it?" growls Fezginorix, whom I am hereinafter dubbing Rix because wolf-wilder names are too long.

"I know a great deal," I tell them, channeling the late Tserigern's mysterious-old-wizard act. "I know your last raid over by Bentpenny Lake netted only a sackful of chickens before the Guildblades chased you off." Barlav had blurted that one out two lives ago, right before sticking a knife in my ear.

"What if she's Guild?" Strak growls, and for a second, I think this round is a bust too. But Tsav comes to my rescue.

"Guild wouldn't fuck around being clever for the likes of us," she says. "They'd just ride in here and start hacking." She glares at me, but there's an element of curiosity in it now. "How do you know all this?"

"The same way I know I'm going to be the next Dark Lord."

"Spidershit," she says. "There's been three Convocations in my lifetime, and none of 'em raised up a Dark Lord.[16] There's no one with the stones for the job, not anymore."

If only that were true. I wiggle my eyebrows mysteriously. "This time there *will* be a Dark Lord. I have seen it, and I'm never wrong."

"And you say it'll be *you*?" Barlav says with an explosive snort. "Even if you *are* a wilder, you look about as tough as a day-old pup. I could squash you under the heel of my boot."

Finally, what I've been hoping-slash-dying for. I favor him with a mad grin.

"Is that a challenge, then?"

Everybody goes quiet. Challenges are no laughing matter.

Barlav's lip curls. "Are you serious?"

"As serious as you are."

"Fine." He hawks up a mighty loogie and spits it at my feet. It looks like green scrambled eggs. "I challenge you, 'Dark Lord.' Just because I'm tired of listening to your prattle."

I look around at the others, especially Tsav. "If I win, I get

---

16 *Dark Lord* is the Common term that the Kingdom uses, of course. The wilder word means something closer to "High Chief" or "Great King," although it has the same connotation of being a scary motherfucker. Wilders are honest about their leaders, I guess.

some food, clothing, and a chance to explain my offer to everyone in peace."

Tsav raises one eyebrow at Barlav, who gives a theatrical sigh and nods.

"Then it's a challenge," Tsav says.

* * *

The rules for a challenge vary from band to band, but usually at least the basics are similar. One against one, a knife each. This is a big step forward for me! Instead of fighting a whole camp full of orcs with no weapon at all, I get to fight *one* orc with a knife. Progress!

Unfortunately, he's a pretty fucking big orc. It would have been nice to goad Strak into making the challenge, he's a little closer to my weight class, but he's too chickenshit. No, it has to be Barlav, with his hair like a Roman centurion's helmet and pecs like watermelon halves. They're on display now because he's stripped to the waist, grinning at me around his tusks. I don't have anything to take off except my ratty cape, so I do that. Maeve hands me a short triangular dagger, made for brutal thrusts. Barlav has a longer curved blade, which I know from the feel of it across my throat.

"I'm sorry you have to die this way," Maeve tells me.

"The feeling's mutual," I mutter, then decide that's lacking in bravado. "I hope you won't miss Barlav."

"Nobody'll miss Barlav," Maeve says, almost too low to hear.

The rest of the band gathers around, a lot of orcs I don't know, a couple more wolves, and a tongue-flicking lizard-wilder with madly swiveling eyes. They make a rough circle, ready to shove back anyone who tries to run. Inside it's just Tsav, Barlav, and me.

"Old Ones favor whoever's cause is just," Tsav intones, then shrugs. "Though fuck if I know what that means this time. You two ready?"

"Ready," I say, licking my lips. Barlav nods.

"Fight!"

He comes straight at me, shoulder first, like he's breaking down a door. Not a subtle approach, and I try to fade to one side, but my legs feel like rubbery noodles. I jam the blade into his ribs, or try to, but the noodle thing has happened to my arms as well. I only manage to give him a long scratch. Then he hits me dead-on and I feel my breastbone crack. I stagger back, get shoved sideways by unsympathetic hands, and Barlav catches my wrist as I totter helplessly. He pulls me close enough that I can smell his stinking breath. I feel cold steel lodged in my guts down below my belly button.

"Fucking madling," he spits, and rips the knife upward till it catches on my ribs. All my organs *blorp* right out into the dirt, a big nasty pile of torn intestines and other important shit, along with just an astonishing amount of blood. It's not long before I'm back in the pool waiting for Tserigern.

More or less what I expected. The problem—I contemplate, as I once again murderize everyone's favorite wise-arse—is muscle memory, or the lack thereof. Or just muscles in general, really.

See, I know how to fight. I ought to, I've had enough fucking practice. I'm good with a sword, I can handle a knife, and if you give me a bow, I will clip the feathers from Robin Hood's fucking cap. Or at least I *could* do those things back before Artaxes and his psychotic snake-lady went to town on me, and I *will* be able to do them again if I manage to survive for longer than it takes to burn a roast. *Right now* I'm stuck with the body I arrived from Earth with, and past-me was evidently on a strict training regimen of Netflix and Reddit.

The chances of me beating Barlav in a fair fight are roughly zero point zilch. But the whole seeing-the-future thing isn't just useful for conversations.

Back through the woods, gather maidensrest, dodge the patrol, sweet-talk Maeve, swallow thaumite, give my spiel, piss off Barlav, here we go again. Barlav does his shoulder-charge right on schedule and this time I know which way to dodge. I step in behind him, knife raised for an overhand strike. I'm not fast enough. He kicks my noodle legs out from under me and shanks me in the ribs before I can catch my breath.

Cue the training montage. Save me, "Eye of the Tiger." Except I'm not actually getting any stronger or quicker, because my dumb body is the same each time. Just a little more knowledgeable about how Barlav fights, what specifically he's likely to do when I do *this*, and then if I respond with *this*, then will he—ow, fuck, no that didn't work.

It fucking sucks, let me tell you. He's *mostly* the same each time, but not *exactly* the same, because I can't do everything *exactly* the same way. So sometimes there's a promising route and I try to push on a little further and then *wham* he decides no, consistency is for losers. I'm getting real sick of it before long. The worst part is making sure he kills me fast, which sometimes means trying to keep fighting on a broken leg or some shit. It's only a flesh wound! The naked crazy girl is never defeated!

When I fuck up, it's because I'm finally getting somewhere. I feel like I've got him if I can just move fast enough, I've gotten past his knife hand, and then *wham* I get his knee in my stomach and *crunch* his elbow in the back of the head and the world goes all cartoon Tweety Birds and then black. But not black *enough*.

Time Loop Survival (ha!) Rule Number One: Never get captured. Because dying sucks, but at least it's over quickly.

Getting captured is how you end up in the torture dungeon with Snaky de Sade.

This time I wake up with a splitting headache and my hands tied together, lying on a pile of stinking rags in a shabby excuse for a tent. I'm still naked, of course. Since the orcs haven't been particularly concerned with taking prisoners to this point, I'll give you three guesses what they want me for, first two don't count. My suspicions are confirmed when I get a look out the tent flap and see Strak outside taking off his belt. Of course it's Strak that has to get rapey. Fucking Strak.

Fortunately, I'm prepared for this. Maidensrest! There's a handful tied to my arm with a strip of Tserigern's robe. Even with my hands bound, I can work it loose. It falls on the floor and I squirm around like a caterpillar to gather the leaves with my lips and start chewing.

Maidensrest gets its name from a Kingdom play called *The Maidens*, sort of their version of *Romeo and Juliet*. Two teenage girls fall in love,[17] but their families are at war. After many trials and tribulations, they take maidensrest together and sink gracefully to the earth in each other's arms. The families find the still, sad lovers, too good for this world, and are shamed into making peace forevermore and blah blah blah.

It works faster and less painfully if you concentrate it, but chewing the raw leaves will do the trick in a pinch. You don't actually sink gracefully to the earth, though—there's a lot more thrashing and foaming at the mouth involved. But by the time Strak comes in with his pants off, I'm down to a few last twitches. Kinda wish I could see the look on his face.

---

17 In spite of being literally medieval in many respects, the Kingdom is refreshingly free of our nasty Earth package of patriarchy-misogyny-homophobia toxic awfulness. Instead they have their own *unique* brands of toxic awfulness!

Fuck, though. That could have been much worse. I need—hi, Tserigern, *cronch cronch cronch*—a fucking break.

* * *

Interlude:

I know the area around the wake-up pool, on this particular day at this particular hour, about as well as anyone has ever known any specific time and place in the history of the universe. If there's a spot within about a day's walk that has anything useful to a would-be savior, I've been there, probably many times. I know every sheep in the shepherd's flock and every plant in the farmer's field. (The one gap in my info has been on the wilder side of things, but I'm rectifying that now.)

Anyway, there are some places that while not strictly helpful on the saving-the-Kingdom path are interesting on their own merits. To wit: Gerald.

Gerald is a peasant. That's not pejorative, that's just what he is. He lives in a hut at the edge of the woods, tending a patch he took over from his mother when she died. It's lonely, a long day's walk from the nearest village, and Gerald is a shy lad of twenty or so summers who keeps himself to himself. He has not, much to his frustration, known the touch of woman, although he has known plenty of the touch of himself. This is a shame, because Gerald is fit, halfway handsome if you gave him a wash and a shave, and endowed like an Ivy League university.

What I have learned from experience is that if I—a naked and not-unattractive young woman obviously in dire straits—stumble into Gerald's doorway, he will wrap me in a smelly but warm blanket and take me inside for a warming bowl of soup and a rest. And if I then indicate my desire in some hard-to-miss way, such as grabbing his cock and kissing him, he will not require much persuasion to put his physical gifts to good use.

It's not all about equipment, of course. Gerald is sweet, naïve, attentive, and appreciative, a tender and virginal soul eager to be corrupted. He's also a remarkably quick study, and I can get him from the first coy brush of the lips to the noisome depths of the dark web in the course of an afternoon. The fact that he's dumb as a box of rocks isn't a drawback; every time he starts to talk, I just shove something in his face to suck on.[18]

Anyway, after the run-in with Strak, I take a day for me-time and avail myself of Gerald's services. In the evening I leave him satisfied and exhausted, lying face down in a pile of straw. I grab his rusty sickle and slash my throat, feeling much better.

* * *

Back to the challenge. I've just about got it right, I think I hope I pray.[19] I square off against Barlav with, if not total confidence, then at least a cocky grin. Always act like you know what you're doing—if you win, you look awesome, and if you lose, then you're dead and who cares if they think you're a poseur?

Barlav lowers his shoulder and charges. That fucking charge. It seems so dumb, so *obvious*, I went through a dozen loops trying to find a way to take advantage of it. But he's (a little) smarter than he looks, Barlav. And credit where it's due, he's not afraid of taking a cut to get this over with. Makes him

---

18 Is it ethical to use someone like this? Dunno. I feel like I left Planet Ethics behind a thousand years ago and accelerated out into the dark void of Who Gives a Fuck. He seems to enjoy it, and given that after our carnal carnival he'll reset along with the rest of the world, I can't be bothered.

19 Figure of speech. In the Kingdom, they pray to the Founders, eight mythical heroes who are supposed to have established the first human settlements. I've seen a lot of desperate prayers, though, and it's never seemed to do anybody any good. And if *my* prayers accomplished anything, I would not still be in this mess, let me tell you.

look tough in front of his buddies. Best to stay out of his way, so I roll sideways and pop back to my feet across the circle, now coated in even *more* dirt. He turns with a snarl and comes at me again.

Keep the distance open, that's the key. He's impatient. He's not going to edge across the circle and back me into a corner slow—that looks weak. But he has to commit to the charge too far out, and I can see him coming. Dodge, roll, jump aside, back off.

Muttering from the peanut gallery. Barlav's lip curls further.

"I thought you said you wanted to *fight*," he growls. "Quit fucking around."

"*I* thought you were supposed to be good at this," I tell him, still smiling. "You can't handle a little game of tag?"

"Fucking *vrinsh!*"[20] he shouts, and comes at me again.

But not, crucially, as he did before. That was calculation, accepting the possibility of a slash on the arm or shoulder to bowl me over and get to close quarters. Now he *expects* the dodge. He thinks all I can do is run, so his stance is open, his arms wide, looking to slice or grab me as I evade. Oldest trick in the book—give 'em one thing till they think they've got your number, and then—

I hesitate, looking one way, then the other. Then when he's too close to stop, I drop to one knee and raise my stubby knife in both hands *just so*. My pathetic noodle arms may not be able to get the blade deep enough, but his momentum does a fine job of it, especially when I'm braced like a linebacker.

My bare feet slide back a few inches and my fingers are almost forced from the hilt. Then Barlav stops, looking down at me, his brows furrowed as though he's trying to figure

---

20 Mostly untranslatable, lit. "one who ruts with squirrels," implying both sexually indiscriminate and anatomically improbable.

something out. He coughs, and a drizzle of blood drips along his tusks and patters onto my upturned face. For a moment we're balanced there, me crouching, him leaning forward, arms hanging limp, all his weight on the little blade wedged between his ribs. Finally his knees buckle and he slides off, taking the knife with him. He flops into the dirt.

Silence. Total silence.

If they kill me *now*, I swear to fucking God—

"Davi is the winner," Tsav pronounces.

Muttering from the other orcs. Maeve steps forward and indelicately prods Barlav onto his back, checks his breathing. She sighs and gestures to another couple of orcs. They grab him by his limp arms and haul him away.

"You asked for food, clothing, and a chance to explain," Tsav says. "I can offer—"

"Yeah, actually, maybe a rain check on those," I say. "How about somewhere to just lie down for a bit?"

Tsav looks a little mystified, but nods and gestures to a large tent. "Use my furs, if you like."

I stagger in the indicated direction. Adrenaline is fading, vital force draining out of my body like coffee from a cup with no bottom. I barely have the energy to check out Tsav's tent, noting with some disappointment it's not full of handcuffs and bondage gear. There's a big pile of ratty fur jumbled up into a nest, and I just belly flop into it.

Lights out instantly. Davi signing off for a while.